EVERY
HUNT
ENDS
IN A
KILL...

NO ESCAPE

Trying to catch her breath, Erin focused on the phone in her hand. For the second time in a week, she dialed 9-1-1. She was about to press the SEND button when something flew over the top of the stall.

Startled, Erin recoiled. The small lightweight object bounced off her shoulder, then landed on the tiled floor.

Erin saw what it was, and all at once she couldn't breathe or move. Paralyzed, she stared down at the pair of glasses with square tortoiseshell frames.

One of the lenses of Molly's new glasses was cracked.

"*Oh my God . . .*" Erin whispered. With a shaky hand, she punched the Send button on her cell phone.

Suddenly, she felt something sting her just above the ankle. Crying out, Erin looked down and saw a rubber-gloved hand reaching beneath the stall partition. She saw the glint of a knife. It slashed at her ankle again.

Erin screamed and tried to back away. But like a snake, the gloved hand darted under the partition and grabbed her by the ankle. All at once, the cell phone flew out of Erin's hand and she struggled to keep her balance, but it was impossible. She slammed against the partition wall and then tumbled to the floor. She screamed and kicked, but the hand wouldn't let go . . .

Books by Kevin O'Brien

ONLY SON

THE NEXT TO DIE

MAKE THEM CRY

WATCH THEM DIE

LEFT FOR DEAD

THE LAST VICTIM

KILLING SPREE

ONE LAST SCREAM

FINAL BREATH

Published by Kensington Publishing Corporation

FINAL BREATH

KEVIN O'BRIEN

PINNACLE BOOKS
Kensington Publishing Corp.
www.kensingtonbooks.com

PINNACLE BOOKS are published by

Kensington Publishing Corp.
850 Third Avenue
New York, NY 10022

ISBN-13: 978-0-7860-1777-5
ISBN-10: 0-7860-1777-5

First printing: January 2009

10 9 8 7 6 5 4 3 2 1

Printed in the United States of America

This book is for my brother-in-law, Denny Kinsella,
one of the nicest guys I know.

ACKNOWLEDGMENTS

I couldn't have written this book without my friend John Scognamiglio, who also happens to be my editor. Thank you, John! I also need to thank the wonderful and talented Doug Mendini. Thanks to everyone else at Kensington Books for their hard work.

I'm also grateful to my terrific agents, the marvelous Meg Ruley and the charismatic Christina Hogrebe, and the rest of the gang at Jane Rotrosen Agency. They rule!

Thanks also to my talented writer friends for their encouragement and for suffering through early drafts of this book and coming up with great suggestions to improve it. I couldn't ask for a better Writers Group: Cate Goethals, Soyon Im, David Massengill, and Garth Stein.

A special thank-you goes to my friend Thomas Dreiling. Tommy, you're terrific!

I'd also like to thank the following friends for their support and for pushing my books to their other friends: Lloyd Adalist, Dan Annear & Chuck Rank, Marlys Bourm, Terry & Judine Brooks, Amanda Brooks, Kyle Bryan & Dan Monda, George Camper & Shane White, Jim & Barbara Church, Anna Cottle & Mary Alice Kier, Paul Dworskin & the gang at Broadway Video, Tom Goodwin, Dennis and Debbie Gotlieb, Cathy Johnson, Ed & Sue Kelly, David Korabik, the cool people at Levy Home Entertainment, Jim Munchel, Eva Marie Saint, John Saul & Mike Sack; Bill, JB, Tammy and Fran at the Seattle Mystery Bookshop; Dan Stutesman, Doug & Ann Stutesman, George & Sheila Stydahar, Marc Von Borstel (who always makes me look good), Michael Wells & the gang at Bailey/Coy Books; and my nice neighbors at The Bellemoral.

A great big thank-you goes to my family, especially my sister, Mary Louise Kinsella, who gave me the idea for this book. Adele, Mary Lou, Cathy, Bill, and Joan—you guys are the best.

Finally thanks to two great writers and teachers who helped me become an author: Anne Powers Schwartz (at Marquette University) and Zola Helen Ross (1912–1989) in Seattle.

CHAPTER ONE

Seattle—December 2005

"I swear to God, I'm going to kill her," he whispered.

Erin Travino didn't pay attention to the man seated in the row behind her. She switched on her cell phone, activating the little blue display light. It glowed in the darkened movie theater. Erin punched in the code to check her messages again.

Up on the big screen in front of her, Judi Dench was reprimanding Keira Knightley for something. Erin hadn't paid much attention to *Pride and Prejudice*. Maybe she should have been. She had a book report due next week, and hadn't even chosen the stupid book yet. If she'd been following the movie more closely, she could have pretended to have read *Pride and Prejudice*. Her English Lit teacher was a sucker for Jane Austen.

Then again, she really didn't have to try too hard at school lately. Most of her teachers were cutting her some slack. Erin simply had to say she was still traumatized over what had happened last week, and her teachers would grant her an extension or raise her C to a B minus.

Erin intended to milk the situation for as long as she could. Along with Molly Gerrard, and that nut job, Warren Tunny, she was prominently featured in all the newspaper articles. The *Seattle Post-Intelligencer* even ran a photo of her, the halfway-decent snapshot from her high school ID. At least her wavy, shoulder-length, auburn hair was freshly washed, and the dimpled smile looked natural. Plus she appeared really thin in the picture.

Erin was constantly dieting, even though her friends insisted it was the last thing in the world she needed to do. Tonight, for example, her best friend, Kim, had bought a soda and a large buttered popcorn for the movie. Kim asked if she wanted some popcorn, but Erin just shook her head and sipped her medium Diet Coke. Didn't Kim know that stuff had the fat equivalent of three Big Macs? At least that was what Erin had heard.

She squinted at the illuminated display on her cell phone: NO NEW MESSAGES.

Someone tapped her on the shoulder, startling her. Erin almost dropped the phone. She glanced over her shoulder.

"Would you mind putting your phone away?" growled the man behind her. He was in his late thirties—as was the lean, Asian guy with him. "The light is very distracting."

Erin shifted in her cushioned seat. "Well, I wasn't *talking* on it," she whispered, rolling her eyes.

The man glared at her. The light from the movie screen flickered across his handsome, narrow face. "That's the fifth time you've pulled out your phone and switched it on since the movie started. Do you have ADD or something? How about showing a little courtesy for the people around you, huh?"

Her mouth open, Erin let out a stunned little laugh.

Suddenly her phone chimed out this ancient tune, "I Just Called to Say I Love You," in ring tones. She'd programmed it by accident last week and couldn't undo the damn thing.

"Shit," she muttered. A few people in nearby seats shushed

her. The man and his buddy were frowning and shaking their heads.

Flustered, Erin grabbed her purse and retreated up the aisle toward the lobby. Ignoring the filthy looks from several people seated along the aisle, she pressed the Talk button on her phone. "Hello?" she whispered, pushing at the door with her shoulder. She stepped into the narrow, dimly lit foyer. The door swung shut behind her.

"Hello?" Erin repeated, louder this time.

She heard a click. Frowning, she checked the caller ID: NUMBER NOT LISTED.

With a sigh, Erin headed into the Harvard Exit Theater's lobby. They showed mostly foreign and independent films. Erin got a waft of popcorn smell as she wandered through the large lobby. It had a fireplace, a grand piano, and worn, antique parlor furnishings that were true to the building's 1920s architecture. The concessions stand was in the far corner, and beyond that, a stairway to the restrooms and another theater on the third floor.

Erin paused at the foot of the stairs. She dialed Molly's number and got her machine again. Erin clicked off. She'd already left three messages. They'd arranged to meet in front of the movie theater tonight. But Molly had never shown.

Molly was one of the most popular girls in Erin's class. She was thin and pretty with gorgeous, long, black hair that was right out of a shampoo commercial. Molly wore designer glasses, and somehow managed to look chic—even in just a sweater and jeans. Molly's stock only went up after what had happened last week. Erin's stock soared, too. Suddenly, she mattered.

The day before yesterday, Molly had asked if she wanted to hang out after school. They went to pick up a new pair of glasses for Molly at this store on Capitol Hill. The glasses had square lenses with tortoiseshell frames, slightly nerdy, very funky. Only someone as popular and pretty as Molly could have worn them without looking like a total dork. While in the optical shop with her new friend, Erin wished she had weak eyes so she could get glasses like Molly Gerrard. Afterward, they had Diet Cokes and shared a plate of cheese fries at the Broadway Grill. Erin ate only seven fries and was still hungry, but it didn't matter. She felt so cool, hanging out with Molly.

Kim was an okay friend. But Molly was queen of the "A" crowd, and being friends with her put Erin in the "A" crowd, too. She was devastated Molly hadn't shown up for the movie tonight. Erin wondered if she'd done something wrong. Maybe Molly didn't want to hang out with her *and Kim*. Kim wasn't "A" list. But no, that wasn't like Molly; she was nice to everyone.

Erin was still trying to figure out what must have happened when she glanced over toward the lobby and spotted one of the older guys who had been sitting behind her. It was the man's friend, the slim Asian guy. He seemed to be headed for the concessions stand, but his eyes suddenly locked with hers. He passed by the concessions counter and came toward her.

Erin automatically turned and started up the stairs. She wasn't afraid of him; she just didn't feel like hearing another lecture about movie theater etiquette. Halfway up the stairs, Erin figured she could duck into the women's room and avoid him altogether. But the cell phone slipped out of her hand and skipped down a few steps.

The man paused on the landing—in front of a huge old poster for *An American in Paris*. He retrieved her cell phone, climbed the stairs, and plopped the phone in her hand. "Well, I know you couldn't live without this now, could you?" he muttered.

Her mouth open, Erin didn't reply.

Brushing past her, the man started up the next flight of

stairs—probably to the men's restroom on the third floor. But he paused and glanced back down at her. "A *thank you* might have been nice," he said. "You know, you're very rude." Shaking his head, he continued up the stairs.

Erin wanted to say, *"Well, screw you!"* But instead, she just retreated into the women's room. It was dimly lit and slightly creepy. The partition housing the two stalls was painted dark green, and the floor was old, chipped black-and-white tile—little hexagons. The old sink had separate faucets for the hot and cold water, and there were rust stains on the porcelain.

Erin could hear people laughing in the smaller theater upstairs. Some comedy from Italy was showing.

She caught herself frowning in the bathroom mirror. She flicked back her auburn hair. That guy who had just called her rude would have been asking for her goddamn autograph if he knew who she was. Obviously, he hadn't seen the newspaper last week. They called her a hero for what she did. *A hero*.

It had happened last Tuesday in Mr. Gunther's fifth period study hall. Only about half of the students actually studied or did their homework in study hall; the rest napped, doodled, or tried to pass notes to each other. Gunther, a short, wiry, balding, forty-something wannabe-jock, wouldn't let anyone talk while he lorded over the classroom. He was a real hard-ass. He sat at the front of class with his nose buried in the *Seattle Times* sports section.

Erin was at her desk by the windows in the last row, listlessly paging through her *Us Weekly*. Gunther was such a Nazi, he'd assigned seats and wouldn't let anyone switch. Erin was stuck with a view of the faculty parking lot on one side and squirrelly Warren Tunny on the other.

Warren sat hunched over his sketchpad. He was always drawing these weird cartoon monsters that looked like a cross between SpongeBob SquarePants and Godzilla. Erin never admitted it, but she found his drawings fascinating—

gory, graphic, and oddly funny. No one else appreciated Warren's artwork—except maybe his geek buddies, if he even had any buddies. Erin couldn't see what he was drawing at that moment. His arm and shoulder blocked her view. He was probably protecting his sketch pad. It was new. The previous week, while Warren had been at his locker, one of the guys had grabbed his old sketch pad out of his hands and torn it up in front of him. Erin hadn't seen it happen, but she heard Warren had cried.

The guys were constantly picking on him and the girls made fun of him. Warren was skinny, with a pale, splotchy complexion and ugly, kinky, rust-colored hair that he parted on the side. Some of the guys called him "Pubes" because of that awful hair. Erin felt sorry for him, but the guy was definitely weird. Warren wore the same green army jacket to school every day—even in warm weather. And he kept it on all day long.

Bored, Erin tried to peek at what Warren was drawing. She still couldn't see the sketch pad. But she noticed something shiny inside Warren's fatigue jacket. It looked like a gun.

Erin gasped.

Warren stopped drawing and stared at her.

Quickly, she turned away and did her best to look bored. With a shaky hand, she flipped through a few pages of her magazine. After a minute, she swallowed hard and stole a glance over at Warren again. He seemed focused on his artwork once more. She could clearly see it now, the gun handle sticking out of his inside coat pocket.

How the hell had he smuggled a gun past the metal detectors?

Biting her lip, she helplessly glanced around the classroom—at the other students and at Gunther up in front. None of them had a clue.

She was the only one who knew Warren Tunny had a gun.

Squirming in her chair, Erin wondered if maybe—just maybe—the gun was a fake. She tried to catch another glimpse of it. Just then, Warren leaned back, and Erin saw his sketch-pad—and what he'd been drawing.

It was a very creepy, detailed rendition of a smiling skull, with a caption underneath it: *THEY WILL BE SORRY*. Then, below that, he'd drawn a circle with a strange, tilted "V" inside that circle. Below this cryptic image, he'd written in even bigger letters than before, embellished with vines winding around each consonant and vowel: *PREPARE TO DIE*.

Warren sighed, glanced up at the clock for a moment, and then went back to his drawing.

Erin looked up at the clock, too: 1:05.

She suddenly realized, the tilted "V" inside the circle was supposed to be the hands of a clock. Her mouth open, she watched Warren draw the clock digits around the inside parameter of that circle—1:10 was the time on the clock in his picture. Just five minutes from now.

Was that when he planned to start shooting?

She could be wrong. Still, she wasn't about to wait until he pulled his gun out to know for sure. Her heart pounded furiously, and she could hardly breathe. She had to do *something*. Her cell phone was in her purse. Gunther didn't allow people to use them during his study hall, and she couldn't pass anyone a note. Warren was her only neighbor.

Biting her lip, Erin glanced around the classroom again—at all her classmates, looking so bored, so unaware that within minutes there could be screams and blood and chaos. Erin glanced at the clock on the wall again: 1:07. Hunched forward, she took her spiral notebook out of her purse, opened it, and jotted down a few words. She glanced over her shoulder to make sure Warren couldn't see what she was writing. Then she tore the piece of paper from the notebook and folded it.

Warren put his pencil down and flipped over the sketch pad. Erin wasn't sure why he'd done that. Maybe his work was finished. He probably didn't want anyone in the class to see it—not just yet. Perhaps it was for later, for the police to discover. Erin felt a chill race through her.

Warren's eyes met hers for a moment. Erin tried to smile, but it was forced, and she quickly looked away. He could probably see her shaking.

Warren sat back at his desk and studied the clock by the classroom door. He seemed to be breathing hard. His hand—black ink and pencil lead on the fingers—slowly reached inside his fatigue jacket.

Grabbing her purse, Erin unsteadily got to her feet. "Mr. Gunther?" she said, hardly able to get the words out. Any minute now, she expected Warren to shoot her in the back. Making her way to the front of the classroom, she approached Gunther's desk. She tightly clutched her purse against her stomach. "Mr. Gunther?" she repeated.

He barely looked over the top of his newspaper. "Go back to your seat," he muttered.

Erin cleared her throat. "Mr. Gunther, I need to use the restroom. I have a—a problem." She handed him the note she'd just written, then started for the door.

"I said, back to your seat!" he barked. His chair made a scraping noise on the floor as he pushed himself back from the teacher's desk. Everyone was looking at them.

Erin headed for the door. She wasn't sure she would make it. Her hand fumbled for the knob, then she swung open the door and ducked out to the hallway. She could hear people murmuring, and Gunther's voice: *"All right, enough! I want quiet!"*

Erin shut the door behind her. But she still couldn't get her breath. This wasn't over yet. It hadn't even begun.

There was a window in the door—with thin, crisscrossed wire in it. Erin could see Gunther standing at his desk with her note in his hand. But he hadn't looked at it yet. He scowled at everyone in the classroom. "I want quiet!" he repeated. She could hear his muffled voice through the closed door.

Pulling her cell phone out of her purse, Erin switched it on and dialed 9-1-1. It rang twice. Through the window in the door, she watched Mr. Gunther finally glance down at her note.

She hadn't had much time to write anything. All it said was: *"Warren Tunny has a gun in his jacket. I'll call 9-1-1."*

A click interrupted the third ring tone: "Seattle Police Emergency," the woman said. "9-1-1 operator."

For a moment, Erin was speechless. She was watching Gunther's reaction. Frowning, he set her note on the desk, then glanced in Warren's direction. *"Tunny, stand up!"* she heard him bark.

Oh, no, no, no, you stupid son of a bitch, she wanted to scream.

Erin became aware of the 9-1-1 operator on the other end of the line: "Police Emergency. Can I help you?"

"Yes, I—I'm not absolutely sure if this is a real emergency," Erin said under her breath. "But—but I think maybe—"

"Could you please speak up?" the operator interrupted. "What's the nature of your emergency?"

While the operator talked, Erin could hear Gunther's voice, raised in anger. Suddenly a girl in the classroom screamed: *"Oh, God, no!"* Then there were more screams, and it sounded like someone knocked over a chair.

"Oh, Jesus," Erin said, louder this time, her voice cracking. "I'm at—at—James Madison High School, outside room 207, and this guy's got a gun . . ."

Through the window in the door, she could see Gunther shaking his head and raising his hands. He looked terrified. Any minute now, she expected to hear the first shot.

The 9-1-1 operator was telling her to remain calm. The woman wanted to know if anyone had been hurt and how many gunmen there were.

"It's just one guy, a student, Warren Tunny. I'm outside the classroom right now, but I can still see them in there. I—" Erin fell silent as she caught a glimpse of Warren and Mr. Gunther in the window. Warren pressed the gun barrel to Gunther's head. The wiry little hard-ass teacher was cringing and trembling.

"Everyone, just shut up and sit down!" Warren screamed. He shook even worse than Gunther. Warren's face was so flushed it was almost matched the color of his frizzy red hair. "I mean it, shut the hell up, all of you . . ."

"Oh, my God," Erin whispered into the phone, backing away from the door. "I think he's going to shoot somebody. For Christ's sakes, please, do something! Send the police here . . ."

"All right, stay calm and tell me your name," the operator said.

"Erin—Erin Travino."

"Erin, I want you to confirm for me that you're calling from James Madison High School on Ridgeway Drive, and right now in room 207, one of the students has a gun and he's threatening people. Is that correct?"

Erin couldn't answer her. She couldn't move or speak, because at that very moment, the door to room 207 was opening. Warren Tunny stood at the threshold, gazing at her—with the gun aimed at her heart.

"Come on back inside, Erin," he whispered.

She gaped at him. Tears welled in Warren's eyes. He looked scared but determined.

Erin could hear some girls quietly sobbing in the room. She didn't know where Gunther had gone, but he wasn't in the doorway with Warren.

"Put away the phone, and come here," he whispered.

"Erin? Can you answer me?" the 9-1-1 operator was asking.

With her eyes fixed on the gun in Warren's trembling hand,

Erin obediently clicked off the phone and slipped it into her purse. She shook her head. "Please, Warren, don't shoot," she whispered. "Can't we just talk? You—you don't have to do this . . ."

"Inside," he said, nodding toward the classroom.

Terrified, Erin edged past him and into the room.

Warren stepped in after her and shut the door. There was something so final about the sound of that door closing and the catch clicking. It made Erin flinch.

She saw Gunther in the far corner of the room, facing the blackboard with his hands behind his head. Shaking, he warily glanced over his shoulder at her and Warren.

Someone had thrown up, and the horrid smell filled the room. Erin noticed several classmates crying helplessly—and not just the girls. Some students had their heads down and hands clasped in prayer. Others seemed in a state of shock. It was as if they were all paralyzed in their seats. No one would dare move. No one wanted to take the first bullet.

That seemed reserved for her at the moment. Warren still had the gun pointed at her.

From her desk in the middle of the room, one girl cried so hard she started convulsing. The whole desk shook as the mousey, thin, long-haired girl sobbed uncontrollably.

Her neighbor, Molly Gerrard, stood up, grabbed the girl's hand and steadied her. "Warren, you need to put that gun away," she said, with a slight tremor in her voice. Most of the guys in the junior class were hot for Molly; Warren was almost certainly among them. "You're scaring everyone," Molly said to him. She nervously touched her glasses. "I know you've suffered, but you're better than this—"

"Shut up!" he cried.

Erin felt the barrel of the gun poke the back of her head. She gasped.

"No, Warren," Molly continued, her voice still shaky, but even louder than before. "You need to hear this. You're so much better than the assholes who have picked on you. You're not a bully, Warren. You have all the power right now. But you also—you also have an opportunity to show everyone that you're—better than the people who have been mean to you. You're better than them, Warren. You know you are . . ."

Grabbing Erin's auburn hair, Warren snapped her head back. She recoiled and cried out again. Yet at the same time, she realized he was now pointing the gun at Molly. His breathing was even heavier than before, more agitated.

"Listen to her, Warren," she managed to say. "Molly's right. You don't have to do this. You—you're a nice guy, and a good artist. Your cartoons, they're—brilliant—"

His grip loosened on her hair. "I don't want to hurt anybody," he muttered.

"I know you don't," Molly said. "You're a good person, Warren. So, please, put the gun down . . ."

"You're only making things worse for yourself, Tunny!" Mr. Gunther called out from his corner. With his hands still raised, he glanced over his shoulder toward Warren. "You're already in a heap of trouble, mister, and I can guarantee—"

"Why don't you just shut up?" Molly retorted. "You're not helping!"

Someone in the classroom gasped at her remark. Erin glanced back at Warren for a moment. A smile flickered across his splotchy face, and he lowered the gun.

"Warren, don't listen to him," Molly continued. "Listen to your heart. You haven't hurt anyone yet, and I don't think you will. Everyone in this room—right now—realizes that you've gotten a raw deal. And I for one am very sorry. I hope you'll accept my apology . . ."

Warren said nothing. But Erin felt him let go of her hair. For a moment, no one said anything. Then Erin heard a click. Panicked, she swiveled around and saw it was merely Warren setting the gun down on Mr. Gunther's desk.

He started to cry.

At that same time, she heard the sirens shrieking in the distance. Warren must have noticed them, too. Tears streaming down his face, he turned toward the window.

All at once, someone in the front row yelled out: *"Grab him!"*

It happened so quickly, Erin barely saw the two guys charging toward her and Warren. One of them shoved her out of the way, and she slammed into the teacher's desk. It knocked the wind out of her. Screams filled the classroom—competing with the sirens' wail outside. One guy savagely pummeled Warren, who cried out and fell to the floor. The other student started kicking him. It was utter chaos—with everyone suddenly jumping out of their seats and heading for the door. Desks and chairs were knocked over. All the while, Gunther kept screaming, "Hold him down! Hold the son of a bitch down!" He sprung from his corner and grabbed the gun off his desk.

"Stop it!" Molly yelled. "Stop! You're hurting him!" She ran up the aisle and tried to pull one of the guys off Warren, but he shoved her away. Molly's glasses flew off her face and she tumbled into the front row of desks. "My glasses!" Molly cried, just as someone inadvertently stepped on them.

Dazed, and curled up on the floor by Gunther's desk, Erin tried to catch her breath. The sirens outside were getting louder and louder, almost deafening.

When it was all over, Warren Tunny had two cracked ribs, a fractured arm, a broken nose, a black eye, and several cuts and bruises. The police took him to Harborview Hospital. In the ambulance, Warren had insisted that he hadn't intended to kill anyone—just himself. He'd planned to shoot himself in front of his classmates. He'd figured, maybe then, they'd be sorry for treating him so badly.

Of course, no one believed him. By the end of the day, the same people who made fun of Warren were making jokes about what had *almost* happened, and they were still referring to him as Pubes.

Warren's two study hall classmates, after beating him so severely, had figured they would be portrayed as heroes of the day by the local press. But Molly and Erin garnered all the attention and accolades. They'd been the ones who had defused a potential bloodbath. They'd been the ones who had pleaded and reasoned with the gunman. They'd gotten him to surrender, and the media linked them together as heroes.

Maybe that was the only reason Molly had asked Erin to hang out with her after school the day before yesterday. While picking up those cool new glasses with the square tortoise-shell frames, they'd talked about Warren and the creeps who had been mean to him. Molly had wanted to visit Warren in the hospital, where doctors and police kept him under surveillance. She'd asked Erin to come along with her and show Warren she had no hard feelings. "You don't have to say yes right now," Molly had told her. "Think about it, and tell me later. I just figure it would mean a lot to Warren if he knew you'd forgiven him, you know?"

Erin hadn't yet committed to making the hospital visit. The notion of seeing Warren Tunny again and being *nice* to him—so soon after he'd held a gun to her head—kind of freaked her out. At the same time, she didn't want Molly to think she was a jerk. They'd agreed to talk about it later. It had seemed as if they were becoming very good friends.

So Erin couldn't understand why Molly blew off their movie date tonight. Hell, *Pride and Prejudice* had been Molly's idea.

With a sigh, Erin frowned at her reflection in the wash-room mirror again. The audience watching the Italian comedy upstairs let out another round of laughter.

Erin's cell phone rang once more—that same, stupid "I Just Called to Say I Love You" tune. She quickly retrieved the phone from her purse and switched it on. "Yes, hello?"

"Erin?" the woman said edgily. "Is this Erin?" The voice wasn't familiar.

"Yes. Who's this?"

"Erin, I'm Hannah Gerrard, Molly's mother. Is Molly with you—by any chance? Have you heard from her?"

"No, she's not, Mrs. Gerrard," Erin murmured. "She was supposed to meet me and my friend here at the Harvard Exit for a movie about an hour ago, but she didn't show."

An older woman with short-cropped silver hair stepped into the restroom. She frowned at Erin, then brushed past her and ducked into one of the two stalls. Erin ignored her.

"Listen, Erin," Molly's mother said, a tremor in her voice. "The police found Molly's car an hour ago—on that little road behind Lakeview Cemetery. The car had a flat. The driver's door was open, and the hazard lights were blinking. It—it just doesn't make sense. Molly's got a cell phone, for God's sake. Why didn't she call us for help? We're only five blocks away . . ."

Erin knew the road: a narrow strip of pavement that ran a few blocks alongside the sprawling cemetery's high chain-link fence. There was a park on the other side of the road—with a smaller, unfenced, old cemetery for Veterans of Foreign Wars. Only a block away, quaint, charming houses bordered the park, but there was still something remote and slightly foreboding about that little back road—especially at night. Surrounded by so many graves, it was an awfully scary spot to have car problems.

But Erin figured Molly had kept a cool head, the same way she had with Warren last week. Molly was a lot braver than her. Still, Mrs. Gerrard was right. It made no sense. Molly's car was found only five blocks from her home—and less than a mile from this very movie theater. Why hadn't she called anyone for help? What had happened to her?

"Young lady?"

Erin swiveled around and gaped at the woman with the

close-cropped silver hair. She still had that same haughty look on her wrinkled face as she emerged from the stall. "The use of cell phones is prohibited in public restrooms," she announced.

Erin curled her lip at her. "What?"

"You're not supposed to use cell phones in here!" the woman said loudly. "Why are *you* an exception? There are cameras on cell phones. It's prohibited to be using—"

Erin started to wave her away.

"I don't appreciate having my privacy invaded!" the woman declared. "I'd like to take a pee without having it broadcast coast to coast on your stupid cell phone! Why don't you go talk in the lobby, for God's sakes? Why do you have to talk in here?"

Erin held the phone against her breast for a moment as she ducked into the other stall. "Christ, lady, get off my case!" She shut the stall door and locked it.

"Rude!" the woman exclaimed, over the sound of the water running in the sink. Then Erin heard the roar of the hand dryer.

"I'm sorry, Mrs. Gerrard," she whispered. Standing in front of the toilet, Erin had her back pressed against the divider between the two stalls. "There's this crazy woman here . . ."

"The police are combing the neighborhood right now," Mrs. Gerrard explained. "When she left, Molly told me she had to run an errand before the movie. That was at five o'clock, over three hours ago. I keep thinking—if Molly was meeting someone, maybe this person has an idea where she wandered off to. Does she have a new boyfriend she didn't tell me about?"

"I—I don't think so."

"Erin, please, if—if you know what she planned on doing before the movie, and Molly asked you to keep it a secret—"

"I swear, Molly didn't say anything to me," Erin cut in.

She didn't know Molly well enough yet that they'd share secrets. She wondered if perhaps Molly might have gone to the hospital to visit Warren without her. But hell, if Molly's car was found five blocks from her house, then she must not have even reached the hospital.

The hand dryer shut itself off, and all Erin heard was the sound of the faucet dripping in the restroom sink. She figured the silver-haired woman had left.

"Will you call me if you hear from Molly?" Mrs. Gerrard asked on the other end of the line.

A shadow suddenly swept across the tiled floor, distracting Erin for a moment. She couldn't see anyone's feet in the gap beneath the stall door, but obviously somebody else was there. Was that crazy lady still in the bathroom?

"Erin?" Molly's mother said.

"Um, of course, I'll call you the minute I hear from Molly, Mrs. Gerrard," she said, at last. "I—I'm sure Molly's all right. Could you have her call me when she gets in?"

"I will," Mrs. Gerrard said with a tremor in her voice. "I hope that's soon. Thank you, honey."

Erin heard a click on the other end. Someone passed by the stall again. She spotted a shadowy figure—so briefly—through the crack in the stall door, where it was hinged. Whoever it was, they hadn't gone into the other stall or used the sink. So why were they sneaking around in there? She could still hear the faucet dripping, but no footsteps.

Maybe it was the disconcerting news about Molly that unnerved her, or the fact that two people had just chewed her out for using her cell phone. But she had a feeling something was horribly wrong. She'd had that same awful sensation in her gut last week when she'd been sitting next to Warren Tunny in fifth period study hall.

With the phone tightly clutched in her hand, Erin leaned toward the hinged side of the stall door. Something darted past the door again, and Erin gasped.

It was a man. She saw him this time, but she didn't get a look at his face. He moved too fast—toward the stall behind her. It looked like he was wearing one of those clear, thin, plastic rain jackets over his dark clothes.

"Who's there?" she called out, her voice quivering.

No response—just the sound of that faucet dripping steadily.

"I know someone's there!" Erin said loudly. "I'm gonna scream in a minute, I mean it!" She turned and glanced down at the gap under the stall partition and the floor. It didn't look like he'd ducked in to the next cubicle. If someone was playing a perverse joke on her, he certainly would have given himself up by now.

But this was no joke.

Trying to catch her breath, Erin focused on the phone in her hand. For the second time in a week, she dialed 9-1-1. She was about to press the SEND button when something flew over the top of the stall.

Startled, Erin recoiled. The small lightweight object bounced off her shoulder, then landed on the tiled floor—right by the base of the toilet.

Erin saw what it was, and all at once she couldn't breathe or move. Paralyzed, she stared down at the pair of glasses with square tortoiseshell frames.

One of the lenses to Molly's new glasses was cracked.

"Oh, my God . . ." Erin whispered. With a shaky hand, she punched the SEND button on her cell phone.

Suddenly, she felt something sting her just above the ankle. Crying out, Erin looked down and saw a rubber-gloved hand reaching beneath the stall partition. She saw the glint of a knife. It slashed at her ankle again. She felt the blade scrape against her bone this time. Blood sprayed across the black-and-white tiled floor.

Erin screamed. She tried to back away. But like a snake, the gloved hand darted under the partition and grabbed her by the ankle. All at once, the cell phone flew out of Erin's hand and fell into the toilet. Water splashed out of the bowl. Erin struggled to keep her balance, but it was impossible. She slammed against the partition wall and then tumbled to the wet, tiled floor. She screamed and kicked. The more she kicked, the more blood spurted from the wounds across her ankle.

But he wouldn't let go. He was pulling her through the gap under the stall divider and dragging her across the floor. He still had the knife in his other hand. Terrified, Erin struggled and cried out for help.

But her shrieks were muted by a thunderous wave of laughter from the audience in the theater upstairs.

No one else heard her screams.

Only him.

Lisa Briscoe noticed the two police cars parked in front of the Gerrards' white stucco—three lots down from her own house. She was walking Toby, the family's miniature schnauzer. That was what she got for working late tonight. Her husband had taken the kids out to the Olympia Pizza and Spaghetti House. He'd called from the restaurant five minutes ago, saying none of the kids had walked Toby yet, and he'd bring her back an order of cannelloni.

With one hand clutching the collar of her winter coat and the other holding Toby's extendable leash, Lisa passed the Gerrards' house. She'd heard the Gerrards had been hounded by snoops and people driving by the house at all hours. Some of them even snuck across the lawn and tried to peek into the windows. They wanted to look at Molly, the pretty—and now famous—seventeen-year-old who had been on the TV news and in the papers for thwarting a possible massacre at James Madison High School last week. Lisa had heard the Gerrards had phoned the police twice last week because of those obnoxious people skulking around outside their house. Lisa couldn't believe it was still going on.

The residents of this quiet, upscale neighborhood in northeast Capital Hill weren't used to a lot of activity, much less police activity. The houses, ranging from charmingly quaint to old-world impressive, were close together and not far from the street. While walking Toby, Lisa could see the bell tower of nearby St. Joseph's Catholic Church looming over the tops of the bare trees. She could also see her breath. Shivering, she buttoned up her coat.

Lisa approached her usual stopping point: Interlaken Drive, a dark, winding road through dense woods—with the occasional secluded, ridiculously expensive home. Lisa took Toby only to the edge of Interlaken because those woods were full of possums and raccoons, and she didn't want Toby chasing after one. He was no match for such creatures. Ages ago, when she was a kid, her dad had told her how he'd once seen a German shepherd try to tussle with a raccoon—only to be torn apart in seconds. Lisa had steered clear of raccoons ever since.

There was something else about the dark, lonely, snakelike road that scared her. "Sometimes when I'm on this road, I half-expect to find some guy standing there around the next curve," her husband had said, steering down Interlaken late one night after a party. "I can see the headlights suddenly illuminating this dude in a hockey mask, carrying a meat cleaver. And then, farther up the road, there's this car with a hacked-up body in it . . ."

"Well, gee, thanks for that image, hon," Lisa had said, squirming in the passenger seat. As a joke, she and her husband often referred to Interlaken as "Hockey Mask Lane."

So, raccoons and possums weren't the only reason she rarely took Toby beyond the edge of Interlaken Drive.

But on this December night, Toby still hadn't pooped. Plus it was early, and the cops were parked in front of the

Gerrards' house—only two blocks away. So Lisa started down Interlaken with Toby. She pulled a small flashlight out of her purse and switched it on. She would give Toby until the first curve in the road, and if he still hadn't done his business by then, she'd turn around. "C'mon, Toby, this is your last half block," she muttered, glancing at the darkened woods around her. "Time to shit or get off the pot."

There was no sidewalk on the road, and the thicket came right up to the curb. A chilly wind rattled the tree limbs. Bushes swayed slightly and dead leaves scattered across the pavement. Toby strained on the leash. He eagerly sniffed at the base of practically every tree and shrub they passed. Suddenly he stopped, raised a paw, and looked deeper into the woods as if he saw something moving in there. He strained at the leash again.

Lisa gazed over in the same direction. Through the trees, she noticed an eerie red glow in the distance—perhaps around the next curve in the road, or maybe even farther. Was it a car with its parking lights on?

Toby was still staring in that direction. His ears moved, and his little body seemed to stiffen.

Lisa shined the flashlight into the woods. The beam cast strange, flickering shadows as Lisa directed it across the trees and shrubs. She couldn't see anything. "Okay, kiddo," she said, in a shaky voice. "Here's where we do a U-turn . . ." She tugged at the leash, but Toby wouldn't budge. "C'mon now, there's nothing out there . . ."

But there was.

A few yards away, deeper into the woods, her flashlight's beam caught a shrub moving—as if someone might have just ducked behind it. She heard twigs snapping.

Lisa tugged at the leash again. But Toby was immobile, still staring in that direction. He let out a yelp. Again, Lisa saw something move amid the shadowy trees. She directed the flashlight's beam past the base of a tree. Close to the forest floor, she saw two eyes staring back at her. They glinted in the light.

"Oh, my God," Lisa gasped.

The raccoon didn't seem startled or riled. He merely glanced up from his meal for a moment. Then he went back to gnawing at the bloody slash across the dead girl's throat. The pale cadaver was clad in just a bra and panties.

Lisa couldn't move. She watched in horror as the raccoon half-stood on its hind legs, hovering over his feast. Tresses of the girl's long black hair were caught in the creature's claws, and her head turned a little when he moved again.

In the flashlight's beam, Lisa could see her face now.

She recognized the dead girl—even though Molly Gerrard wasn't wearing her glasses.

"The person you are calling is not available," said the recording on the other end of the line. *"This call is being forwarded to an automated voice system. Please leave a message for . . ."* Erin's voice chimed in for two words: "Erin Travino." Then the recorded generic voice took over again: *". . . after the tone."*

Standing on the stairway landing of the movie theater's lobby, Kim held the cell phone to her ear and waited for the beep. On the wall behind her was a huge old poster of Gene Kelly dancing with Leslie Caron in *An American in Paris*.

She only reached the automated voice system when Erin switched off her cell phone or her battery was dead, and Erin practically *never* switched off her phone. Erin's regular message had her own voice with rock music in the background: *"Hey, this is Erin, and you know what to do!"*

But right now, Kim didn't know what to do.

She'd been sitting in the theater for the last fifteen minutes with an empty seat beside her and Erin's coat draped over the armrest. One of the guys behind her had stepped out and come back in the duration, but that had been at least ten minutes ago. Finally, Kim had gotten up and hurried to the lobby, but she hadn't seen Erin anywhere. So Kim had pulled out her cell phone, dialed Erin's number, and started up the stairs to the women's restroom.

Beep.

"Hello, Erin?" she said, holding the phone to her ear as she continued up the stairs. "Where are you? Did you ditch me or something? I can't believe this. You've totally ruined a really good movie for me. You're not in the lobby, so I'm about to check the restroom. I'm hoping you're there." She let out an exasperated sigh. "If not, for God's sakes, call me, okay?"

Kim clicked off the line as she approached the women's restroom on the second floor. Pushing open the door, she stopped suddenly. The light was off. As far as she could tell, no one was in there. Past some muffled rapid Italian dialogue from the film showing upstairs, Kim only heard the rhythmic drip of a leaky faucet. She felt along the wall for the light switch.

Her hand brushed against something wet on the wall. Shuddering, she stepped back and gazed at her fingertips. Blood.

He paid for his latte, and then politely asked the barista for the bathroom key.

No one in the Joe Bar Café paid much attention to him. As far as he could tell, none of the other customers in the bistro had seen him emerge from the old, three-story brick building that housed the movie theater across the street.

He found a small table by the window, with a view of the theater entrance and the lighted marquee. Leaving his latte on the table, he asked the bearded twenty-something man with a laptop notebook at the next table to make sure no one took his spot while he was in the washroom.

"Sure, no sweat," the guy said, barely looking up from his notebook.

He thanked the man, then carried his Nordstrom bag into the bathroom at one side of the barista counter. It was tiny, with a narrow door and barely enough room for the sink and toilet. The walls were painted burnt orange, and the management had posted a reminder above the sink that all employees had to wash their hands after using the facilities. Above that little sign hung a mirror.

He studied his reflection for a moment. His face was clean, and his hair appeared slightly damp. With a sigh, he lowered the toilet seat lid and set down his bag. Then he turned to the mirror again. With his hand, he pressed down on the top of his head, mashing the hair against his scalp. Drops of blood slithered down his forehead.

He quickly grabbed a paper towel from the dispenser above the toilet and dabbed up the blood. Then he ran the paper towel over his head, and glanced at the crimson streaks soaked into the fiber sheet.

He should have worn a shower cap when he'd killed her.

Earlier, in the women's lavatory at the movie theater, he'd quickly rinsed off his face. He'd shucked off the blood-spattered, plastic rain jacket and gloves. They were now in a dark plastic bag stuffed inside the Nordstrom tote. He hadn't much time to clean up in that theater washroom, and the job on Erin had been messy.

Molly Gerrard had been much easier—and neater—three hours earlier.

She had been his first kill—ever. He'd tried to kill before, years ago, but it hadn't worked out. That failure was still the source of a lot of bitterness and frustration in him.

So he was surprised to have pulled off Molly's murder

without a hitch. He'd been following her around for days now. He knew her car and had overheard several of her cell phone conversations. So he often knew what Molly was going to do before she did it.

Late this afternoon, he'd skulked up the Gerrards' driveway, crouched down behind Molly's Honda, and set a small board with four nails driven through it under the left rear tire. Less than an hour later, she stepped out of the house and hurried into the car. It only took four blocks for the tire to deflate—and in a perfect, remote spot, too.

He pretended he'd just happened by. And Molly looked so glad to see him—right up until the moment he punched her in the face. With one blow, he bloodied her nose, broke her glasses, and knocked her unconscious.

He drove her eight blocks to the ravinelike drive, where she started to regain consciousness. She was dazed and almost docile as he hauled her into the dark, wooded area. But then Molly seemed to realize what was happening. She pleaded with him—employing, no doubt, the same kind of reasoning and logic she'd used in school last week to save the lives of her classmates. Only it didn't work this time. It was hard for Molly to rely on those powers of verbal persuasion once he slashed her throat. Instead of words, a strange gurgling sound came from her mouth during the last few moments of her life.

He'd gotten only a few drops of blood on his glove and on the sleeve of his clear rain jacket. He wiped it clean with two Kleenex.

Along with Molly's broken glasses, he took her cell phone. There were three messages from Erin Travino about the movie: first, saying she'd meet Molly in front of the theater; next, asking Molly what had happened to her; and, finally, saying where she and Kim were sitting if Molly was still interested in meeting them.

As if Erin hadn't already made it easy enough for him to

find her, she was the one who kept switching on her cell phone and checking her messages during the movie. That little blue light had stood out in the darkened theater. He'd followed her—and that blue light—out to the lobby, then up to the women's restroom.

He wondered if someone had discovered her body yet. Standing over the small sink in the coffeehouse washroom, he rinsed Erin's blood out of his hair. He watched the pink water swirl against the white porcelain. With some paper towels, he pat-dried his scalp, then checked for more blood on his jeans and shoes. He'd lucked out, just a few drops on his black sneakers.

After cleaning off the sink, he was about to toss away the used paper towels, but hesitated. They were smeared with blood. He didn't want anyone in the café later linking him to the murder across the street.

He stuffed the bloodied paper towels into the plastic bag, which was tucked inside his Nordstrom tote. Then he stepped out of the bathroom, returned the key to the barista, and headed back to his table. He set the Nordstrom bag down by his chair.

Sipping his latte, he stared at the theater across the street. He couldn't help feeling a bit disappointed. Perhaps that was why he took a chance coming here. He would have been better off getting as far away from the theater as quickly as possible. But he needed to see people's reactions to what he'd done. From this front-row seat, he could see their shock and panic. Maybe then it would feel complete.

He heard sirens in the distance.

Across the street, the theater door flung open. He spotted the woman who had taken his ticket earlier. With a look of alarm, she paused at the threshold, a hand over her heart. She anxiously gazed up and down the sidewalk. The pale, stocky, baby-faced guy who worked the concessions stand trotted around from the other side of the building. Like his friend, he, too, was looking in every direction. "Shit, I didn't see anybody!" the guy screamed to the ticket taker. "Jesus, maybe he's still in the theater . . ."

The girl shook her head and started sobbing. She said something, but her words were drowned out by the sirens. The piercing wail grew even louder. Swirling beams of white and red lights from the approaching patrol cars already illuminated the street.

He noticed other people in the café. They'd stopped talking to their friends or typing on their laptops, and now they were looking toward the window.

He had to contain a smile.

He couldn't stay here much longer. If the police did their job right, within five minutes, they'd hold everyone in this café and question them about who they saw coming out of the theater. He didn't want to stick around for that. Slowly, he got to his feet.

Three police cars and an ambulance raced up the street and came to a halt in front of the theater. But he wasn't watching them. His eyes were on a middle-aged woman with a peacoat, purple scarf, and a shopping bag. She headed down the sidewalk in the opposite direction. Grabbing his Nordstrom bag and his latte, he hurried out the door, and caught up with the woman—so they were walking almost side by side.

"What do you suppose happened over there?" he asked her as they passed the ambulance and police cars.

She shrugged and shook her head. "Drugs, probably. It's always something around here. This neighborhood has gone to hell in a handbasket—if you'll pardon my French." She picked up her pace—almost as if to avoid him, then she turned down a side street.

His first instinct was to follow her home, maybe even kill her.

Perhaps that would have made him feel better, but he doubted it. He'd been elated for only a few moments tonight, a rush of excitement as he watched them die by his hand. He'd felt so powerful. But the elation hadn't lasted long.

Those girls—as much as they deserved to die—were just substitutes for someone else. He was thinking of that certain someone when he'd killed Molly and Erin tonight. He wondered if their deaths would affect her at all.

It would be a lot harder to get to her. It would take more planning. But he vowed he would make her suffer. He would wage a campaign of terror against her, inflicting so much pain and anguish that she would almost welcome her own execution.

He paused on the corner and watched the woman with the purple scarf disappear in the night's distance. He smiled.

He was thinking about the next time and how it would be better.

CHAPTER TWO

Portland, Oregon—Two years later

"So, sweetheart, I'm thinking of Tom, Bernie, and Pat for my groomsmen," Jared said to Leah as they walked from his car toward one of their favorite haunts, Thai Paradise on Hawthorne. It was 8:40 on a cold Tuesday night in early December. Holiday lights and decorations adorned the storefronts, but right now the street was nearly deserted.

Jared had his arm around Leah's shoulder. They were an attractive couple. Jared, tall and lean with wavy blond hair, blue eyes, and perpetually pink cheeks, looked like a thirty-year-old version of Prince William. Leah was thin and pretty, with short chestnut hair. "Waiflike" was how Jared's mother described her, and Leah wasn't entirely sure if that was meant to be flattering or not.

"You mentioned your cousin, Lonnie, as a candidate if I wanted someone from your side of the family as a groomsman," Jared went on. "But you guys aren't really that close. Maybe Lonnie could do a reading or something . . ."

Leah didn't say a word. She eyed the restaurant's red awning with green Christmas lights wrapped around the poles. She felt the knots in her stomach tightening.

"Are you pissed off?" Jared asked. "If having Lonnie in the wedding party is really that important to you—"

"No, it—it's fine," she said. But it wasn't fine at all. Everything was so screwed up. Jared didn't know it yet, but she couldn't go through with this wedding.

She needed to break up with him—tonight. That was why she still couldn't settle on a wedding date. Poor Jared—in a role usually reserved for the bride—became preoccupied with wedding plans, and she—like an apathetic groom—merely shrugged and said, "That's fine," every time he told her about some terrific caterer or a really cool place to hold the reception. Last week her mother came over and started talking about the wedding. Then Jared chimed in, and Leah had nuptial talk in stereo. It was all she could do to keep from running out of the room, screaming.

It wasn't fair to Jared, stringing him along like this. He was a terrific guy, who did very well at his accounting firm. Leah repeatedly told herself she was lucky to be his fiancée. Everybody else—her family, his family and all their friends—told her the same thing

But she didn't love Jared. Her infatuation with him had petered out two months ago. If she'd had any guts, she would have told him "no" on Thanksgiving night when he'd surprised her with the seventeen-thousand-dollar engagement ring. Thank God he didn't have it engraved or anything. He could still get his money back.

She couldn't marry him. It was that simple.

Leah planned to tell him tonight over dinner in Thai Paradise. She figured he couldn't yell at her or cause a big scene in one of their favorite restaurants.

Jared held the door open for her. "You feeling okay?" he asked. "You're awfully quiet tonight."

She shrugged. "I—think maybe I'm just hungry."

The restaurant felt almost steamy after the cold night outside. A blend of sweet and spicy aromas filled the place. The busboy who met them at the door wasn't much bigger than Leah. He was in his mid twenties, with long black bangs that fell over one eye. He had a sweet, handsome face, and he smiled a lot—perhaps to compensate for the fact that his English was horrible. That never stopped Jared from trying to strike up a conversation with him.

Tonight was no different. While the busboy led them past the empty counter area and around the huge tank full of tropical fish, Jared asked how he was, and how business was, and gosh, it sure didn't seem too busy tonight.

The busboy just nodded and smiled—until he sat them in a secluded booth against the wall in the windowless, dimly lit eating area. Leah used to think it was charming the way Jared was so friendly with waitpersons and salespeople. Now it just got on her nerves. It seemed phony and oversolicitous.

Slipping into the booth, Leah shed her coat and thanked the busboy as he handed her a menu.

"Looks like we're just about the only ones in here," Jared said to their busboy. "Hope we aren't screwing up your chances for an early quit tonight."

He doesn't have a fucking clue what you're saying, stupid, Leah wanted to tell her dear, well-meaning fiancé. But she just kept a pleasant smile frozen on her face, and took a quick inventory. Jared was right. There were only two other customers in the restaurant—in a booth across from them. They were finished with their dinner and donning their coats. Leah's hopes that Jared wouldn't pitch a fit in a restaurant full of people vanished as she watched the other couple head for the door. She and Jared were now the only customers in the place.

The busboy filled their water glasses. Leah waited until he left their table, then she cleared her throat. "I need to talk with you about something, Jared," she said, squirming a bit in the booth's cushioned seat. "This has been really heavy on my mind lately . . ."

He looked up from his menu. "What is it, sweetheart?"

The busboy returned with their tea in a medium-size stainless-steel pot. "Tea very, very hot," he said, filling their cups. He set the pot on a trivet on their table.

Leah's stomach was still in knots. She watched the busboy retreat toward the front of the restaurant. He hung the CLOSED sign on the door. It occurred to Leah that after tonight, she wouldn't want to come back here again. It would always be *that place where she broke up with Jared.* This was probably her last time in here, and it was too bad, because she loved their garlic chicken with wide noodles.

"What is it?" Jared repeated.

Leah couldn't answer him.

The waitress approached their table. Delicate and pretty, she had a round face and a shy manner. Her black hair was swept back in a barrette, and she smiled a lot—like the busboy. In fact, they were brother and sister. Her English was better than his. After Jared subjected her to his requisite chitchat, she took their drink orders.

Once the waitress withdrew, Leah sighed and nervously drummed her fingers on the table top. "Listen, Jared, if I've seemed distracted and on edge lately, well, there's a reason . . ."

Staring at her, he put down his menu.

"This just isn't working out," she said finally.

"What isn't working out, babe? This booth? You want one on the other side of the room?"

She quickly shook her head and then looked down at her engagement ring. "No, that's not it. I'm sorry, Jared, but it wouldn't be fair to you if I—"

"No, we closing, we closing!"

Leah glanced up—just past the fish tank, toward the front of the restaurant. The busboy was shaking his head and half-bowing to two men who must have ignored the sign on the door. "We closing now!" he repeated.

But the two men were already in the restaurant, and they

didn't look as if they were ready to leave. One was tall and skinny, with long, greasy, wavy black hair and a goatee. He wore jeans and a black leather jacket, and had a tattoo on the side of his neck. He muttered something to the busboy. Leah was too far away to see what the tattooed image was, and she couldn't hear what he'd just said. But she had a terrible feeling about this. The meek little busboy was still shaking his head at him and his friend.

"What's wrong?" the man asked loudly. "Answer me in English, asshole. What? Are you all out of food? Did the kennel stop delivering the dog meat?"

Jared half-turned in the booth and looked over his shoulder. "What the hell?" he murmured.

The tall, creepy man's friend laughed—a high-pitched cackle. Shorter and stockier than his buddy, he had a marine buzz cut and muscular arms covered with tattoos. Despite the frigid weather, he wore only a T-shirt and jeans. He was all twitchy and seemed hopped up on something. Still laughing, he reached over and slapped the busboy on his shoulder.

"You go, please, we closing!" the busboy repeated. He pointed at the sign on the door.

A hand over her heart, Leah watched as the cook emerged from behind the counter. A thin, older man, he had a red apron over his short-sleeve shirt and baggy black slacks. He, too, was shaking his head at the intruders and pointing to the door. Between his hushed tone and the broken English, Leah wasn't sure what he was saying. The young waitress hovered behind him.

"Fuck you, old man," the skinny goon said, laughing.

"Who do these scumbags think they are?" Jared muttered. He started to climb out of the booth, but Leah grabbed his hand to stop him.

"Please, Jared, no—don't," she whispered urgently. The *scumbags* obviously hadn't yet noticed two customers were still in the restaurant. Part of Leah wanted to stay inconspicuous, just lay low until all of this was over. It seemed like the safest option right now: avoid a confrontation at any cost.

Then the stocky man suddenly pulled a revolver from the waistband of his jeans. His T-shirt had been camouflaging it. All at once, he slammed the butt end of the revolver over the older man's forehead. The waitress let out a scream as the cook collapsed on the floor. "No, no, no!" she cried, rushing to his aid.

But the stocky man grabbed her. His friend pushed the busboy against the counter and sent him crashing into two tall counter chairs. They tipped over and fell to the floor with a loud clatter while the busboy clung to the counter for balance. The chubby guy thought this was hysterically funny.

Paralyzed, Leah watched in horror. "Oh my God," she whispered. "Call 9-1-1. . . ."

Jared quickly dug into his pants pocket for his cell phone.

The two assailants still hadn't spotted them on the other side of the large fish tank.

The skinny one grabbed the busboy by his hair, and then hit him in the face. The waitress screamed out again as her brother tripped over the fallen counter chairs and tumbled to the floor. The thug kicked him in the ribs.

"Who else is back there?" he asked, nodding toward the kitchen area behind the counter. He glanced at the waitress. "You got somebody washing dishes back there?"

Tears streaming down her face, the waitress shook her head and said something. Leah couldn't hear it. All the while, the hulky creep pawed at her and cackled.

"Do you have a safe in this dump? A safe?" the tall one asked her.

Once again, Leah couldn't hear her reply. But the man must have heard it. "Fuck!" he hissed. "Okay, so where do you keep the money?"

With the phone to his ear, Jared peered over the top of their booth. His earlier fortitude had disappeared. Leah could tell he didn't want to be a hero right now any more than she did. This was something for the police—if they ever picked up.

"Yes," Jared whispered into the phone—finally. "I'm reporting a—a—a robbery in progress at—um, at Thai Paradise on Hawthorne . . . No, I'm sorry. I can't speak up. I'm here in the restaurant. It's happening right in front of me . . ."

The busboy let out a frail cry as the tall, skinny creep savagely kicked him again. It broke Leah's heart—and enraged her—to see that sweet, quiet young man brutalized. His sister sobbed uncontrollably in the other thug's clutches. "I'm getting some of this yellow tail before the night is over," he announced, groping her.

"Take her into the can," the one with the goatee said. "Let's move them *all* in there and get away from this front window. I'll clean out the register. Then we'll cap them all. I don't want any fucking witnesses . . ."

"Oh, my God," Leah murmured. She'd heard that term *cap* in a movie about street gangs. It meant shooting somebody in the head.

Jared was still whispering into the phone, explaining he couldn't talk any louder. "These guys have guns!" he said under his breath. He peered over the top of the booth. "They're going to shoot everyone in the place, for God's sake. Please, send help . . ."

"Where's the restroom?" the skinny one asked the waitress.

She timidly pointed toward the dining area—past the fish tank. The man's gaze followed, and suddenly, he locked eyes with Leah.

She gasped and tried to duck. Jared shrank back in his seat as well. But they were too late. They'd been spotted.

"Shit, we got company," the skinny creep muttered. "Let's round them up."

"My God, they've seen us," Jared whispered into the phone. "Tell the police to hurry. Did you hear me?"

Leah flinched at a loud, tinny clattering sound. Peeking around the edge of the booth, she saw the taller one kicking the fallen counter chairs aside. He grabbed the dazed, beaten busboy by the arm, and pulled him up from the floor. Blood streamed from the young man's nose. He could hardly walk. The tall guy seemed to hold him up as they moved toward the dining area. The stocky thug followed them, his tattooed arms still around the waitress. Both assailants had their guns ready.

"Come out of there, you two," the skinny one called.

"Yeah, come out, come out, wherever you are!" his friend chimed in, laughing.

The two hoods stepped into the dining room area with their terrified hostages.

Leah recoiled in the corner of the booth. Sitting up straight, Jared switched off his cell phone and nervously stared back at them.

"Get up," the skinny guy whispered. With one hand, he had the trembling busboy in a choke hold. With the other, he pointed a gun at Leah and Jared. "Get the hell up," he repeated. "We're gonna stick all of you in the restroom for safekeeping."

But neither Jared nor Leah moved. Her heart was racing.

The tall, ugly gunman violently shoved the busboy to one side. The young man collided into a table, knocking it over. Glasses, plates, and silverware flew in every direction. He hit his head on the top of a chair, then fell to the floor, unconscious.

The stocky one cackled. Following his friend's lead, he hurled the poor waitress toward another table. The petite girl slammed into a chair, but somehow managed to keep from falling. Wincing in pain, she clung to the chair and caught her breath.

Horrified, Leah sat frozen in the booth, watching it all.

"Yahoo!" the hulky guy yelled. He swiveled around and fired his gun three times—at the large fish tank. There was an explosion of glass and water. He must have hit some electrical wiring, because sparks shot out from the top of the tank. There was a loud bang, and the lights in the restaurant flickered. Water gushed from the broken receptacle, and suddenly the restaurant floor was a quarter-inch deep in water and flopping, floundering exotic fish.

The stupid thug seemed to think this was hysterical, but his skinny friend was visibly annoyed with him. He glanced down at all the water and the fish twitching at his feet. Still chuckling, his buddy went to step on one of them.

Leah gazed at them. Then she turned and glanced at the stainless-steel teapot on their table. Something kicked in—maybe anger, maybe a survival instinct. Whatever it was, she suddenly grabbed that teapot by the handle and flung it at the tall man's face.

She was close enough to hit her stationary target dead-on. The lid flew off just as the pot struck his cheek. He let out a startled howl. Scalding tea splashed his face. It must have burned his eyes, because he dropped the gun and immediately covered his eye sockets. Staggering back, he spewed a stream of obscenities—between loud, high-pitched, agonizing shrieks.

Before the stocky guy seemed to realize what was happening, Jared shot out of the booth and rammed into him. The body blow sent him careening toward the broken fish tank. They tipped over chairs and tables in their path.

Meanwhile, Leah snatched up the tall thug's revolver. She almost slipped on the wet floor, but caught her balance. The tall man wasn't so lucky. He blindly staggered around the dining room until he tripped over a chair. He fell down on his knees.

Leah aimed the gun at him, but hesitated before pulling

the trigger. He was incapacitated, defeated. The guy couldn't hurt anyone now.

But apparently, the waitress didn't feel that way. Wiping her tears, the delicate young woman picked up a chair and cracked it over his head.

The man collapsed on the wet floor. A couple of fish struggled and splashed around him in the thin layer of water.

"Son of a bitch!" bellowed the stocky thug—over the clatter of dining room furniture.

Leah swiveled around in time to see him punch Jared in the face. His fist connected with Jared's eye. He staggered back from the blow, but didn't collapse. Wincing, Leah aimed the gun at the big man, but Jared charged him again. Jared slugged him in the gut—a sucker punch.

The chubby man reeled back and grabbed the top of the shattered fish tank to steady himself.

Suddenly, the lights flickered again, and the big man froze. His mouth opened in a silent scream. He started to shake violently as the electric currents raced through his body. Sparks arced out from where he clutched the top of the fish tank.

Jared started to back away. Leah reached out to her fiancé, touching his shoulder. He turned and wrapped his arms around her. Clinging to each other, they tried to catch their breath. But they couldn't yet.

Only a few feet in front of them, the thug stood with his hand seared on top of the fish tank. Spasms racked his body. He wouldn't stop twitching and convulsing, and yet that stunned expression seemed stuck on his oafish face. His skin turned red. Smoke enveloped his feet.

Leah heard a hissing, sizzling sound. It could have been the electrical charges making that noise. Then a new pungently sweet odor wafted through the dining room—just as the stocky man teetered and fell facedown to the floor.

Leah stared at his corpse, and realized what she'd heard—and what she still smelled.

It was human flesh cooking.

Six months later

"With wedding bells and jingle bells on their minds, a Portland, Oregon, couple, Jared McGinty and Leah Dvorak, stopped by their favorite Thai restaurant one night last December for a late dinner. They were making wedding plans . . ." The anchorman punctuated this lead-in with a dramatic pause. The program was *On the Edge*, a prime-time TV newsmagazine. The handsome newscaster, with a tan and premature silver hair, was Sloan Roberts, recently voted one of *People* Magazine's Ten Sexiest Bachelors.

This was a rerun. The man watching the TV program in his Portland hotel room had seen this episode about Jared and Leah before—shortly after the incident had happened, six months ago, around Christmastime. Still, his eyes were riveted to the TV.

The screen-within-the screen just to the right of Sloan's shoulder bore the words: *Movers & Shakers*. Appropriately enough, the letters in these words kept shaking and twitching.

"Jared and Leah had no idea they were about to come face-to-face with death," Sloan continued—in an ominous tone. "On this week's segment of *Movers & Shakers*, Sydney Jordan tells us how Jared and Leah fought the bad guys, fought the odds, and survived—thanks to a little teamwork."

The picture on the TV screen switched to a pretty, thirty-nine-year-old, swaddled in a trench coat. Her wavy, tawny-brown hair blowing in the wind, Sydney Jordan stood under the red awning of Thai Paradise, and spoke into a handheld mike. Her breath was visible that night back in December when they'd originally filmed the segment.

"Jared McGinty and Leah Dvorak are 'regulars' here at Thai Paradise in Portland's charming Hawthorne District," she announced.

The picture switched to Jared and Leah, sitting in front of a fireplace in twin chairs. Except for Jared's black eye, already starting to fade, neither of them showed much sign of the trauma they'd endured just three nights before. "Well, we almost always order the same thing when we go there," Leah said with a timid smile. "Creatures of habit, I guess. The garlic chicken with broccoli and wide noodles is my favorite."

"I usually order the Pad Thai," Jared said, giving Leah a goofy grin. "But Leah always ends up eating most of it."

She laughed, and slapped his arm. "Oh, I guess that's true!"

"Thai Paradise is a family business," Sydney Jordan announced. The cozy image of Leah and Jared together dissolved into a still photo of the owners proudly posing in front of the restaurant on its opening day. "It was started by Som and Suchin Wongpoom, who immigrated to the United States with their nephew and niece, Nuran and Sumalee, just five years ago. Som and Suchin do most of the cooking—old family recipes. Nuran and Sumalee are on the waitstaff . . ."

A lullaby with an Asian lilt provided the soundtrack for a brief montage of old family photos and video clips of the Wongpooms interacting with customers at birthday parties and other special occasions in the restaurant.

"It didn't take long for Portlanders like Leah and Jared to discover the wonderful food and warm atmosphere in this family-run restaurant." The camera returned to Leah and Jared sitting together, zooming in for a close-up of Leah's hand as she caressed his arm. It was hard to miss the diamond ring that sparkled on her finger.

"Leah and Jared were engaged three weeks ago," Sydney Jordan chimed in—over this image. "They still haven't set a date yet . . ."

The picture changed back to Sydney in front of the restaurant again. "The couple were discussing their wedding plans when they stopped in here at Thai Paradise for dinner late last Tuesday night." The brunette reporter gave a nod over her shoulder. "Jared and Leah had no idea that just down the street, parked in a stolen car, two men were hatching a plan of their own . . ."

It was jarring to see the TV screen suddenly filled with side-by-side police mug shots of the skinny, long-haired man and his stocky friend. "Dwight Powell and Harvey Ray Loach were both convicted felons—career criminals—who met while serving jail time at California's Folsom State Prison," Sydney Jordan explained in voice-over. "Police were already searching for the duo in connection to a Portland convenience store robbery in which a twenty-three-year-old clerk was murdered."

There was grainy footage—obviously recorded by the store's security cameras—of the robbery in progress. The two gunmen approached the counter with their guns drawn while a young, gangly clerk raised his hands and backed away from the register. Even at a distance, and even with the poor quality of the videotape, the boy looked scared. *On the Edge* or their *Movers & Shakers* correspondent, Sydney Jordan, had the good taste not to show the terrified young clerk casually—and mercilessly—gunned down.

Sydney Jordan gave an account of what had happened at Thai Paradise that night. She briefly interviewed the busboy, Nuran, his face still bruised, and his sister, Sumalee. They still seemed traumatized. At one point—in the bottom corner of the screen—the camera caught a glimpse of the young waitress clutching Sydney Jordan's hand while she tearfully spoke in her broken English.

More airtime was given to Jared and Leah, who seemed like a sweet couple, very much in love. At one point during the interview, Leah started to cry. "When I heard they planned to—to take us all into the bathroom and shoot us, I was just so scared," she admitted.

Jared put his arm around her, and—on camera, at least—Leah seemed to gather some strength from him. Jared said he managed to stay focused and keep his head throughout the whole ordeal because Leah was there. She claimed the same thing about him.

Sydney Jordan stressed it was *teamwork* that enabled the young couple to overcome the two armed, murderous thugs.

Harvey Ray Loach was pronounced dead—from electric shock—at the scene. Dwight Powell was treated for a mild concussion and second-degree burns on his face and neck. The scalding tea had indeed temporary damaged his eyes, and he was blind for a few days. "But my sources here say Dwight Powell should regain his sight in time to watch this broadcast from his jail cell at the Multnomah County Sheriff's Office, where he's being held without bail." Sydney Jordan announced.

The picture switched to Sydney, walking with the elder Wongpooms through the wreckage of their restaurant. Sydney Jordan was limping slightly. There were close-ups of broken chairs, and all the shattered plates and glass on the water-damaged carpet. The camera pulled back to show Suchin pointing and wincing at the mess. The older woman started weeping on Sydney's shoulder. The reporter gently patted her back. Her voice-over continued, "Som and Suchin's insurance won't completely cover the cost of water damage, the destroyed aquarium and all its fish, as well as business lost while Thai Paradise remains closed for repairs."

They cut to Sydney Jordan flanked by Leah and Jared, and about a dozen other people outside Thai Paradise. Everyone looked chilled to the bone, but they were smiling. "That's why Jared, Leah, and several of their neighbors—all regulars here at Thai Paradise—have so far collected four thousand eight hundred dollars to help offset repair costs for Som and Suchin."

"Oh, Thai Paradise is one of my favorite places to eat," said one middle-age woman, in close-up. "And they're really wonderful people, too."

"My wife and I are regulars," said a forty-something man with a baseball cap. "It's the best Thai food around."

Sydney Jordan turned to Jared and Leah. "Some people might say you two have already done enough to help Som and Suchin and their restaurant. But I understand you don't intend to quit until you've collected eight thousand dollars for them."

Leah snuggled up to her fiancé. "It's the least we can do for these nice people who have had us over to dinner so many times."

The pretty news correspondent turned toward the camera. "I'm Sydney Jordan—with two very special *Movers & Shakers* here in Portland, Oregon. Now back to you, Sloan."

The picture switched to dapper, silver-haired Sloan Roberts at his news desk again. Seated beside him was his pretty blond co-anchor. "Here's an update on that story since it aired last December," Sloan said. "Thai Paradise opened its doors again in early January. If you'd like to eat there, reservations are recommended. It's so popular, Som and Suchin plan to open Thai Paradise II some time next year. As for Jared and Leah, they've set a date and will be married in September."

"Maybe they could have the reception at the restaurant," chirped Sloan's co-anchor.

Grinning, he nodded. "They're sure to get a discount. Thank you, Sydney Jordan—for that moving story. Stay tuned for more as *On the Edge* returns."

A commercial for margarine came on.

The man in the Portland hotel grabbed the remote and

switched off the TV. Funny, they reran Sydney Jordan's *Movers & Shakers* segment with Leah and Jared tonight. He'd started making plans for them shortly after watching that piece when it had originally aired six months ago. He'd been watching Leah and Jared for nearly a month now. He knew the old five-story apartment building where they lived in Portland's Northwest district. He'd learned how to get inside the place undetected. He'd acquainted himself with every inch of it—from the roof to the dark, dank recesses of the basement. He'd even broken into their apartment already, just long enough to study the layout and go through their closets to make sure they didn't keep a gun on the premises. Before making his clandestine exit, he'd left a calling card. He'd peed in their bathroom, left the toilet seat up, and hadn't flushed. He'd imagined Leah later bitching out Jared for being such a pig, and that had made him chuckle. Yet a part of him had wanted them to know someone else had been inside the apartment. Part of him had been *daring* them to figure it out. Last week, he'd been cocky enough to take risks like that.

But not anymore. He had to be very careful now that their *Movers & Shakers* segment had been recycled for *On the Edge*. Jared and Leah were in the limelight again, maybe not for long. But he had to pull back for a while, maybe even delay his plans for a few more days.

Turning away from the TV, he glanced down at the hotel's king-size bed, where he'd laid out his burglary tools—a collection of files, skeleton keys, and wires. He'd used them to break into Leah and Jared's building and their apartment. On the ugly maroon and hunter green paisley bedspread, he'd also set out a pair of gloves, a knife, and a 9-millimeter Glock handgun. And on the pillow was a neatly folded, lightweight, clear plastic rain jacket.

Everything he needed.

Just a few more days, he thought. He could wait. He was a patient man.

And then Sydney Jordan's friends, Jared and Leah, would be on the news again.

"You're clearly limping here in this scene," the hotshot, twenty-something exec said. He had black, spiked hair, designer glasses, and a black designer suit—with no tie. He also had a Bluetooth phone attached to his ear. Leaning back in his chair at the conference table, he unclasped his hands from behind his head to point to the big TV screen for a moment. "See what I mean?"

His assistant, a young East Indian man, worked the DVD remote control. With a flick of the button, he backed up the scene on the big-screen TV of Sydney Jordan assessing the wrecked restaurant with the Wongpooms.

"Yes, I'm clearly limping," Sydney said tonelessly. "It's from an old spinal cord injury, Brad."

Brad was an image consultant the network had hired to review her work. He'd shown the old Jared and Leah story to a test audience, and Sydney had flown from Seattle to New York to hear the test findings. She still had some jet lag. Her hair was swept back in a ponytail, and she wore a blue sleeveless dress.

There was only one other person at the long conference table, a young woman in a power suit from the network's public relations department. She took notes and said nothing.

"Well, people don't want to see you limping, Sydney," Brad said. "The test audience was split right down the middle—the ones who knew about your accident and the ones who didn't. The ones who didn't wondered why you were limping. The ones who knew about your injury didn't want to be reminded of it. Made them feel bad. Plus it's distracting, and not very glamorous."

"In the future, I'll try not to walk when we're taping," she replied. Sydney wondered how much the network was paying this guy. Watching this DVD of her work and getting a blow-by-blow analysis reminded Sydney of her figure-skating days, when her coach used to analyze videotapes of her routines. Those screening sessions, which she'd always loathed, had at least focused on her work from the day or week before and helped her to correct her recent mistakes. But this segment from *Movers & Shakers* was six months old, for crying out loud.

So much had changed in the last six months. Back when she'd gone to Portland to cover Leah and Jared's story, she'd still been based in Chicago and still happily married. Her only real heartaches in life had been her slightly faltering walk and occasionally having to be away from her husband and son while she filmed her stories. Sydney's *Movers & Shakers* segments profiled athletes, inventors, philanthropists, eccentrics, and everyday people who had done something extraordinary. Sydney loved meeting these individuals and profiling them in her video shorts. She'd always searched for subjects and story ideas in Chicago, so she wouldn't have to go on the road. She'd loved her life at home.

Gazing at herself on the TV, Sydney thought about how that woman up there on the screen had no idea her life was about to fall apart.

"The trench coat is good," Brad was saying. "A very classic reporter look, but you've got a nice figure, Sydney. So for this scene inside the restaurant with the old folks, you should have lost the coat. The test audience liked your hair, and thought you looked pretty. I tell you, with high definition, the lines on some of these female correspondents' faces—goddamn, more bags than Louis Vuitton. I know, I know, it's unfair, but people don't expect male reporters to be pretty. Anyway, not to fear, you passed the HD TV test, Sydney. But some time within the next year or two, you might want to go in for a nip and tuck—just for maintenance."

"I'll make a note of it," she said, her nostrils flaring.

"You might even want to devote a segment to it—when you go in for the touch-up, I mean."

She started drumming her fingernails on the desktop. "Are you serious?"

"People want flashier stories from you, Sydney. Think sexy and edgy. After all, this is *On the Edge*. The kinds of stories you do aren't as interesting as they used to be. People don't want tales about these do-gooders . . ."

Sydney glared at him. "No, they want stories about celebrity train wrecks and screw-ups. They want to see who's gotten a DUI, who's in and who's out of rehab, and that way, they can judge them and feel better about themselves. Then they don't really have to aspire to anything. You want me to give the people what they want? How's that going to enlighten or inspire them? Isn't that a reporter's duty—to educate and enlighten?"

Brad touched something on his earpiece, then he held up his index finger. "Just a sec . . . I've got a call here . . . Yeah, well, what do the marketing people say?"

Later that afternoon, Sydney waited for her plane in the VIP lounge at JFK. She had an easy chair over by one of the windows. Outside, they were loading bags into a Boeing 747. Sydney was on her cell phone with her brother, Kyle, in Seattle. She'd already spoken to her son, Eli, who was staying with him. "Anyway, my approval rating could be better, and they think I'm due for a facelift next year," she told him.

"Have your boobs done while you're at it," Kyle recommended. "It's important that all female reporters have a good rack. Screw intelligence and creativity, they're overrated."

Sydney laughed—though a bit listlessly.

"You sound tired," her brother said.

"And homesick," she added.

"Which home have you been sick for? Here or Chicago?"

This jaunt to New York had been Sydney's first overnight trip since leaving her husband, Joe, and moving to Seattle. Somehow the excursion had made her miss her life in Chicago even more. Sydney's plane, leaving within the hour, would be flying over Chicago on its way to Seattle.

"I've missed Eli and I've missed you," she said finally. That much was true. But she also missed Chicago—and Joe. "Anyway, I'll see you guys in eight hours . . ."

After she finished talking with her brother, Sydney took out her laptop computer to check her e-mail. It was mostly junk, a few messages from fans, and one with no subject listed from secondduet4U@dwosinco.com. Sydney opened the e-mail:

Bitch-Sydney,
You can t save them.

She was used to the occasional crank or crazy e-mail. She usually deleted them. "Second duet for you," she murmured, checking the sender's name. "Weird . . . ."

With a sigh, she shook her head and pressed the Delete button.

CHAPTER THREE

The digital timer on the dryer's operating panel indicated thirteen minutes were left in the cycle. Opening the dryer door, Leah pulled one of Jared's sweat socks from the pile of warm clothes. It still felt a bit damp.

Without the dryer's incessant rumbling noise, it was suddenly quiet in the basement laundry room. Though well lit by two fluorescent lights amid the network of pipes overhead, the uncarpeted, dingy room always gave Leah the creeps.

Someone had tried to make the place more cheery with a few cheesy fake plants gathering dust and cobwebs on a shelf above the laundry sink. They'd hung ugly brown and orange plaid curtains on the small, barred window not far below the ceiling. A "Gardens of the World" calendar hung on the graying, paint-chipped walls. Someone had also left several old romance paperbacks and *Better Homes & Gardens* on the card table.

Leah shut the dryer door, but hesitated before pressing the On button again. She could hear the mechanical knocks and humming from the old elevator across the corridor, but it sounded like someone was headed up to one of the floors above the lobby level. They weren't coming down to the basement.

Restarting the dryer, Leah settled back into the folding chair and opened up one of the *Better Homes & Gardens*. She was dressed in a T-shirt, khaki shorts, and sandals. Despite the hot, sticky Fourth of July weather, a little shudder passed through her. In addition to being slightly creepy, the laundry room was also—year-round—the coolest room in the building. Sometimes in winter months, Leah sat on top of the dryer to keep warm.

Just to the left of the washer and dryer was a chain-link, gatelike door to the storage area—a dark annex full of junk stowed in locked cages. There was no outside light switch for it. The few trips she'd taken into that gloomy storage room were with Jared, and she always made him walk in front of her—into the darkness a few steps—where he blindly felt around for a pull-string to the overhead light.

Leah might have been more comfortable if the light were on in that storage area, but she wasn't about to brave the darkness inside there to turn it on. So she did her damnedest to ignore that shadowy nook beyond the chain-link door.

She really shouldn't have been scared right now. It was only six o'clock, and still light out. Over the rumble and roar of the dryer, she heard a shot ring out—and then another. It startled her, but only for a second. *Some idiots with their fireworks*, she thought. They couldn't wait for tonight to set them off. They were probably in the park next door.

She paged through the magazine, and stopped on a feature called, "Newlywed Nests—Affordable Ideas to Upgrade Your Starter Home!" Leah frowned at the two-page spread showing a happy young couple in their well-appointed little love shack.

She and Jared must have looked just as happy and well adjusted to people watching the rerun of *On the Edge* a few days ago. In fact, after that incident in Thai Paradise back in December, she'd sort of fallen in love with Jared all over again. Nothing like surviving a life-threatening situation to make two people feel closer than ever—for a while anyway. They were terrific together, everyone said so. She'd bought into all of Sydney Jordan's *teamwork* talk.

Leah had liked Sydney a lot. For someone who was on TV, she was very down to earth. Sydney had made her feel so relaxed; Leah had almost admitted to the *Movers & Shakers* correspondent that she'd had some doubts about her relationship with Jared. But she'd decided not to spoil the TV-packaged image of this brave, selfless couple who were very much in love.

In fact, it was how Leah wanted people to think of her.

So now she and Jared had set the date. The rerun of their *Movers & Shakers* segment for *On the Edge* only made her feel more pressure from everyone about this damn wedding. That program also produced another strange side effect. Lately, Leah couldn't get over the sensation that someone was watching her.

It wasn't anything she could put her finger on. But lately, while riding the Metro to and from work, or eating her lunch—whether in a restaurant or in the park—she'd suddenly feel someone spying on her. She'd glance around at people in the general vicinity, but Leah never caught anyone staring.

"Oh, you're just picking up on people recognizing you from *On the Edge*," Jared had told her. "It's nothing. Don't be so paranoid."

She couldn't help it. Something very bizarre and unsettling had happened a few days before the rerun had aired. She'd come home from work, and immediately realized someone had been in the apartment. She must have missed him by only a few minutes, because it *smelled* different in there. A stranger's body odor still lingered in the air. Nothing was missing. But the sweaters on her closet shelf were askew, and the clothes in her dresser drawers were slightly messed up. Strangest of all—the intruder had urinated in their toilet and left it there un-flushed with the seat up. She knew it wasn't

Jared. He never did that. Just to be sure, she checked with Jared and their apartment manager and verified that neither one of them had been in the apartment that afternoon.

But later, after Leah had explained her concerns to him, Jared shrugged and said he must have been in a hurry that morning and used the bathroom without flushing.

Leah wanted to have the locks changed, but Jared told her she was being silly. "C'mon, honey, think about it. Why would someone break in, not steal anything, but then pee in our bathroom—and leave it un-flushed?"

"Maybe he *wants* us to know he's been here," she remembered telling Jared. "Maybe he wants us to know he's coming back."

"That's just crazy."

So maybe their intruder was insane. This crazy person had relieved himself in their bathroom as some kind of nasty calling card.

Leah had been on her guard ever since.

The dryer let out a loud buzz, startling her. Leah tossed aside the magazine, got to her feet, and unloaded the warm, dry clothes. She started to fold the pants and T-shirts on the table. Out of the corner of her eye, she thought she saw a shadow move beyond the chain-link door to the storage room. *It's just your imagination,* she told herself. She went on folding clothes, but picked up the pace a bit.

She peered over toward the storage room again—and noticed the shadow once more. It definitely moved. A chill raced through her, and she stood perfectly still for a moment. Clutching a warm T-shirt to her chest, she gazed at the dark room beyond the gatelike door. Leah moved her head from side to side and watched the shadow do the same thing.

She heaved a sigh. "Moron," she muttered. "Scared of your own shadow." Her heart was still fluttering, but Leah forced herself to step over to the chain-link door. In the murky darkness, she could make out the first few storage lockers and the piles of junk inside them—boxes, old bicycles, and things covered with furniture blankets. Leah couldn't see anything past the third set of lockers. The rest of the room was swallowed up in blackness.

She retreated to the table and continued folding clothes. Most of the clothes were Jared's. She should have made him come down here and get his own damn laundry. But he'd stepped out for a few minutes. They were going with friends to watch the fireworks tonight, and he wanted to pick up some beer.

Another shot rang out in the distance, followed by three more. *Get used to it*, she told herself; *they'll be lighting off firecrackers all night and half of tomorrow.* She always felt sorry for the poor dogs and cats traumatized by the barrage of bangs and blasts on July Fourth.

Leah continued folding laundry. She still couldn't shake the feeling that someone else was down there—watching her. Only three more T-shirts, and then she'd get the hell out of there. She could match up the socks once she was safely inside the apartment.

Leah heard the old elevator across the hallway suddenly start up with those mechanical knocks and pings, and then the humming. It sounded like the elevator was headed down to the basement.

She quickly folded her last shirt, then tossed the socks on top of the stack of clothes. The elevator had stopped down at this level, she could tell. But she didn't hear the door open or the inner gate—an accordion-like contraption—clanking. Leah reminded herself that sometimes people pressed the "B" button, but got off on the ground floor instead. That was probably what had happened.

Gathering up the pile of clothes, she headed toward the door. But she hesitated before stepping out to the hallway. Leah gazed down the gloomy little hallway. The elevator door was closed—along with the doors to the stairwell and garage. Carrying the stack of laundry, her chin pressed against the mountain of socks on top, she hurried toward the elevator. She was about to press the button, but didn't have to. The elevator was already on the basement level. With one hand, Leah flung open the door, steadied it with her hip, then pulled at the gate. The whole time, she felt as if someone was coming up behind her.

She ducked into the elevator so quickly that a few socks fell onto the cubicle's dirty floor. She shut the gate. The outer door closed by itself. Leah jabbed at the button for the third floor. The cables let out a groan, and the elevator started moving. She slouched against the wall and let out a sigh. How could she have let herself get so worked up and scared over nothing?

Maybe it was having been reminded so recently about her brush with death. That, and the weird break-in they'd experienced. Perhaps this was some kind of delayed post-traumatic stress syndrome or something.

Creaking and humming, the elevator passed the ground floor and continued its ascent. Leah caught her breath. She managed to balance the load of laundry, then squatted down and retrieved the socks from the floor. She heard another muffled bang. It seemed a little closer than the others. Rolling her eyes, she reminded herself again to get used to it.

When the elevator stopped on the third floor, Leah tugged the gate to one side and pushed the outer door open with her hip. In this very familiar corridor—with its ancient, burgundy swirl-patterned carpet and her neighbor's fake ficus by the elevator—she felt safe again.

But then Leah saw the door to her and Jared's apartment was open a crack. She froze. She'd closed and locked the door before going down to fetch the laundry. Since that bizarre break-in last week, she always locked the door, even when stepping out for only a few minutes.

Jared probably came back, dummy, she told herself. Leah

pushed the door open with her shoulder. “Jared?” she called. “Honey, are you back? Did you get the beer?”

No answer.

Standing in the small foyer area with the stack of clothes in her hands, Leah stared straight ahead at the living room, but she didn’t see Jared. To her left was the kitchen entrance. She poked her head in there. Recently remodeled, the kitchen had green granite countertops and all-new stainless-steel appliances. A six-pack of Coronas was on the counter by the sink, but the grocery bag next to it was on its side, with loose beer bottles spilling out. One bottle had rolled across the counter, and another had fallen onto the black-and-white linoleum floor, although it hadn’t broken.

“Jared?” she called again. “Honey, are you okay?”

She set the laundry on the breakfast table, and then continued to the dining room and living area. The bedroom door was open, but she didn’t see Jared in there. Off the living room a narrow corridor led to the linen closet and bathroom. They had another door to the bathroom in their bedroom.

“Jared? Honey, what’s—” she hesitated.

A musky odor hung in the air. Leah had smelled it before—two weeks ago, when someone had broken into the apartment and left his crude calling card in their toilet.

Leah crept toward the fake hearth and grabbed the poker from the fireplace set. Biting her lip, she moved to the bedroom and peeked past the doorway. On the other side of the bed, she saw the bathroom door—slightly ajar. The light was on.

She thought about calling out Jared’s name again, but remained silent. She cautiously made her way around the bed toward the bathroom. Her legs felt wobbly, and she couldn’t breathe right.

Clutching the poker, Leah pushed open the bathroom door. It creaked on its hinges. Then she saw what was lying on the tiled floor. “Oh, no,” she whispered. “Oh, God, Jared . . .”

Curled up by the base of the sink was her fiancé, his face covered with blood. It matted down his blond hair. He'd been shot in the head. Jared's eyes were still open, and a dazed expression had frozen on his handsome face. On the tiles, a dark red pool slowly bloomed beneath his head. For a moment, it was the only thing that moved in the bathroom.

Leah was paralyzed. She couldn't breathe—or scream.

Then something caught her eye—a reflection in the medicine chest mirror. It was the other bathroom door opening, just behind her right shoulder.

Leah saw the man's reflection. He was wearing a lightweight, clear plastic rain jacket and a shower cap—almost like something a surgeon would wear on his head.

She let out a shriek, and then swiveled around. Instinctively, she raised the poker.

But he had a gun.

Later, Jared and Leah's neighbors would say they'd heard the scream, and then the blast. It had been just as loud and close as the shot a few minutes before. But this was July Fourth, so no one gave those deadly sounds much thought.

CHAPTER FOUR

Seattle

Someone had brought a boom box up to the roof, and it was blasting the *1812 Overture.* The stirring opus accompanied the dual fireworks displays brilliantly. Seattle had two Independence Day fireworks shows that seemed to compete with each other—one over Elliott Bay, and the other on Lake Union. From the rooftop of Kyle's Capitol Hill town house, they had a sweeping view of the Seattle skyline, the city lights, and both firework displays. Over Lake Union, the dazzling bursts of light—some in Saturn, star, and heart shapes—were closer, but the colorful pyrotechnics over Elliott Bay appeared directly above the Space Needle from this vantage point and somehow seemed statelier. The loud pops and blasts punctuated the glittery display. People had gathered on rooftops all over the neighborhood. Their laughter, screams, and applause competed with the *1812 Overture*.

Sydney watched the nine other guests on her brother's roof, their heads turning from one side to another to catch both firework shows. They looked as if they were watching a tennis match. But her twelve-year-old son's head wasn't moving. Dressed in jeans and a long-sleeve T-shirt, Eli leaned against the rooftop's railing. He seemed to be staring at the gap between the dueling shows.

Sydney approached him, and put her hand on his shoulder. "Well, you don't see anything like this—" she hesitated. She was about to say, *You don't see anything like this in Chicago*. But he didn't need to hear that right now. He missed Chicago terribly, and she knew it, because she missed Chicago, too. No doubt, he was sick of her trying to sell him on *their terrific new life in Seattle*. So Sydney just cleared her throat and said, "You don't see anything like this every day."

It was a lame remark. Eli turned and looked at her as if she was an idiot. He'd given her the same look earlier tonight when they'd left for this party. Sydney had her hair swept back in a clip, and she wore a blue sleeveless top, white slacks, and a red belt. "Red, white and blue," Eli had said, deadpan. Then he curled his lip ever so slightly. "Jeeze, Mom, give me a star-spangled break. Did you do that on purpose?"

"Hey, you with the clunky sneakers and the backward baseball cap, don't knock the way I dress," she'd replied. "You live in a glass house."

Eli was a handsome boy with brown eyes, long lashes, and a birthmark on his right cheek. He had beautiful, light brown hair which he'd recently—and quite disastrously—tried to cut himself. Sydney had sent him to the barber to fix it, and the only way to do that was a buzz cut. Actually, he looked good with the new haircut and his summer tan. In fact, it made Eli look very much like his father—so much that Sydney sometimes ached inside when she studied him.

The *1812 Overture* was followed by "It's Raining Men," which prompted several people on the rooftop to howl with laughter. "Well, this is *my* National Anthem!" a flamboyant older man announced, and he started dancing with his hands above his head. Sydney's brother, Kyle, once pointed out to her that no straight man ever danced with his hands above his head. Kyle was gay, and so were most of his friends at the Fourth of July party.

Sydney kept putting herself in her son's shoes—those clunky sneakers. Last year in Chicago, Eli and his dad had spent July Fourth afternoon playing softball with some people in the neighborhood. This was followed by an impromptu water balloon fight in which Sydney got soaked. It didn't matter, because, like everyone else, she was dressed in a T-shirt and shorts. For dinner, they'd barbecued hot dogs and hamburgers, served with chips and baked beans and potato salad. The evening had ended with the fireworks display on Lake Michigan.

Tonight, it had been smartly dressed strangers and smart cocktail-party talk with pita bread, hummus, and couscous. Salmon and chicken had been served off the grill with asparagus and risotto. All the adults there were clearly having a wonderful time. But Eli was the only kid. She knew he was miserable. So was she.

"Look at the smiley-face fireworks over Lake Union," Sydney said, nudging him.

"Jeeze, how dorky can you get?" Eli muttered. He sighed and then peered down over the rooftop railing. Kyle's town house was on a hill, and from this side of the roof, it was a four-story drop down to the garden and patio below.

"Listen," she whispered. "If you're having a horrible time, we can go now and beat the post-fireworks rush. Otherwise, we're stuck here for at least another hour, because Uncle Kyle says the traffic is insane in this neighborhood after the fireworks end. So—speak now, or forever hold your peace, kiddo."

"I'm okay," Eli mumbled. "We can stick around."

She mussed what little hair was left on his scalp. "You sure?"

He nodded and looked toward the showering bursts of light over Lake Union.

Kyle came up to her side. "I'm sorry about Howard," he said under his breath. He nodded toward the older, pudgy, balding man who was dancing round the roof, singing along with "It's Raining Men." He knew all the words. Kyle rolled his eyes. "On a scale from one to ten—ten being totally obnoxious, stereotypically gay—Howard's about a seventeen, especially after he's had a couple of drinks. Is he driving you guys crazy?"

Sydney laughed and shook her head. "Of course not, he's fine."

Compared to some of Eli's father's overly macho business associates, she'd take this flamboyantly gay guy any day of the week.

"He's not your boyfriend, is he?" Eli asked warily.

"Oh, God, no," Kyle sighed, and then he rolled his eyes. "Please."

At thirty-four, Kyle was lean and handsome with receding, sand-colored hair and green eyes. Sydney figured her brother was a great catch. Yet in the six weeks since she and Eli had been living in Seattle, Kyle hadn't been on one single date. All the people at this party were friends or in the real estate business with him.

"I had to invite Howard," Kyle explained in a hushed voice. He led Sydney away from Eli, who stayed by the roof's railing. "He's a big client, and he knows *everybody*. Plus he was dying to meet you."

The party guests had made a fuss over her—and Eli, too—but mostly her. They asked about different *Movers & Shakers* stories she'd done for *On the Edge*. One woman asked if she'd hurt her foot recently or something. Sydney gave the woman her standard answer, "Oh. I just have this limp from an accident years ago." A few party guests asked about Sloan Roberts. How well did she know him? Was he dating anyone? Or as Howard bluntly put it: *"So—Sydney, fess up. Does Sloan play for my team? Is he gay or what?"*

Sydney had to admit she'd met Sloan Roberts only about a dozen times and never had a *private audience* with him. Sloan certainly hadn't confided in her about his personal life. She hated disappointing Kyle's friends, but despite her bimonthly appearance on a top-rated TV newsmagazine show, she didn't have a lot of celebrity connections.

Still, that hadn't stopped her from being the center of attention most of the evening—at least, until the fireworks.

"Is Eli bored to smithereens?" Kyle asked.

With a sigh, Sydney looked over toward the railing, where Eli had stood just a minute before. But he wasn't there anymore. She started to glance around the rooftop.

Suddenly, one of the women at the party let out a shriek, "Oh, my God! Oh, my God!"

There were screams from people on the roof of the apartment building next door, and they weren't looking at the fireworks display. Some of them pointed to Kyle's building.

Sydney raced toward the banister, where one of the party guests stood, gaping down. Sydney glanced over the railing, and for a moment, her heart stopped.

There, suspended four stories above the stone patio, was her son. Eli clung to a storm drain along the roof's edge. He had nothing beneath him to break his fall. The gutter let out a groan—as if it might give and snap off at any moment. Eli looked terrified. Sydney could see him trembling. He had tears in his eyes. With one hand, he tried to grab at the bottom of the railing, but it was just out of his reach.

"It's okay, honey!" she cried out to him. "Don't try to move!"

Without thinking, Sydney immediately kicked off her shoes, then hoisted herself up over the banister. She scooted along the roof's edge until she was almost directly above Eli.

The other party guests didn't seem to know how to help. Frantic, they gathered toward that side of the roof. "Help me get something down there to break his fall!" one man cried. Then he and another guest ducked inside. Howard kept screaming that they should call the police or the fire department. Kyle had gotten down on his stomach and thrust his arms through the bars in an effort to retrieve him, but Eli was too far away.

The gutter creaked again, and Sydney could see it buckling from Eli's weight.

"Oh, God, Mom, help . . . please . . ." he whispered.

"You're going to be all right, honey," she said, crouching down. The heels of her bare feet stuck out over the roof's edge. She gripped a railing bar with one hand, then reached down to her son. Through the bars, her brother grabbed her arm with both hands. Kyle clung to her so tightly, it almost cut off her circulation.

Fireworks lit up the sky, accompanied by loud booms and blasts. But no one was looking up.

"Hold on!" somebody was yelling from a rooftop across the way.

Four stories down, two of Kyle's friends ran out to the patio with sofa cushions and pillows. They made a pile directly below where Eli was dangling. One of them ran inside—obviously for more objects to cushion the impact should Eli fall.

Sydney managed to get ahold of Eli's wrist. The storm drain let out another yawn. She braced herself. "I have you," she said, tightening her grip. "You can let go of the gutter now. I won't drop you, honey, I swear."

Eli bit his lip so hard it started to bleed. He let go of the gutter.

The sudden weight almost pulled her down, but Sydney

held on. Wincing, she started to hoist him up, but Eli was heavier than she thought. For a moment, she thought he might yank her arm out of its socket.

Howard got down on his knees, then reached between the bars and grabbed Eli under his arms. That lightened the load incredibly. Two more partygoers reached out to help pull him up to the railing. Eli was able to swing his leg up to the edge of the roof and then he lifted himself. "Thank you . . . everybody," he gasped, trying to catch his breath. "I—I'm really sorry . . ."

Sydney heaved a sigh of relief. She suddenly felt so depleted and woozy she thought she might faint. But she clung to the banister.

"Are you all right?" Kyle whispered to her. "How's your back? Did you pull anything?" He was referring to her old injury.

Catching her breath, Sydney nodded. "I think I'm okay," she murmured.

Eli took hold of her arm and helped her climb back onto the other side of the railing. Kyle threw his arms around both of them. Everyone on the rooftop broke into applause—as did people on the roof across the way.

"Okay, next on *Fear Factor*," Kyle announced. "Sydney and Eli are going to wrestle with killer cheetahs! Stay tuned!"

The guests laughed. Some continued clapping. Howard declared he needed a drink.

Sydney's heart was still pounding furiously. With one arm around Eli, she waved at the people on the roof across the way. They were applauding, too. No one was looking at the fireworks pageant's big finale.

Nor was anyone looking toward the rooftop of another nearby condominium, where a man stood alone with his arms folded. The building's windows were all boarded up, and except for that lone man, the place looked deserted—and ready for demolition.

Unsmiling, the dark stranger watched Sydney wave and blow a kiss to the people on the rooftop next door.

She didn't look over toward him. Obviously, all this time, she hadn't noticed him there.

No one had.

CHAPTER FIVE

"No, really, I'd like to know," Sydney said, her grip tightening on the steering wheel. "Be honest. What the hell were you thinking?"

Slouched in the passenger seat, Eli stared at the dashboard and said nothing. His lower lip was a bit swollen from biting it too hard earlier tonight. Headlights from an oncoming car briefly illuminated his face, and then he was in the shadows again.

Their lane wasn't moving at all, total gridlock. Kyle had been right. The post-fireworks traffic was a nightmare. But Sydney had been so upset at Eli for pulling that stunt, she couldn't stick around the party and make small talk with people. So they'd bid everyone a hasty good-bye about ten minutes after the fireworks show had ended.

Sydney had the car window open, but there wasn't much of a night breeze. Still, whenever some idiot within four blocks let off a firecracker, she heard it—loud and clear. Though that happened about every two minutes, it still startled her and made her flinch every time. Her nerves were so frayed. "Look at me, I'm still shaking, for God's sake," she said, letting go of the wheel for a moment to show him her tremor-afflicted hands. "Were you trying to give me a heart attack back there?"

"I said I was sorry," he muttered.

'So what exactly were you trying to do?" Sydney pressed, grabbing hold of the wheel again. Traffic started to move—at a crawl. "And please, don't give me that *'I was leaning over too far and slipped'* excuse you gave everyone at the party, because I'm not buying it, kiddo. If you'd really slipped, you'd have yelled. But you didn't. You deliberately climbed over the other side of the railing. Why? And how did you get down to the storm drain?"

Frowning, Eli turned and gazed out his window. He sighed.

Sydney waited for an explanation. She wasn't sure if he'd lowered himself down to that storm drain for some attention or for a dumb thrill. She knew he'd been bored at the party. Perhaps all of Kyle's guests fawning over her had made him feel insignificant—and angry at her. Or maybe he was still upset at her for tearing him away from his home, his father, and his friends in Chicago five weeks ago. He certainly hadn't asked to be relocated to Seattle. And he still had no idea why she'd suddenly decided to leave his dad, a well-respected Chicago cop and all-around terrific guy.

Sydney couldn't tell him why she'd done that, not until Eli was older. If he knew the truth right now, it would wreck him. And the poor kid was already miserable and confused enough.

"Well?" she said, her tone softening. "C'mon, Eli, tell me why you did that, and I'll try to understand. Were you mad at me?"

He shook his head, and then shrugged. "Remember last Friday night, when we went over to Uncle Kyle's and ordered pizza and watched that old movie?"

"*North by Northwest*?" she asked. Eli had said he'd had a great time that night. She didn't understand why tonight he wanted to act out some hostility toward her—or Kyle—for an evening he seemed to have genuinely enjoyed.

"Yeah," he said, nodding. "Anyway, while we were on the roof, I started wondering what it was like to hang off that cliff on Mount Rushmore. So when nobody was looking, I climbed over the railing and lowered myself down—and I guess it was really stupid of me . . ."

Sydney took her eyes off the road to squint at him for a moment. "Let me get this straight," she said. "You decided to hang from that storm drain so you could feel like Eva Marie Saint in *North by Northwest*?"

"I guess," he muttered, shrugging.

Sydney resisted all temptation to ask, *Are you out of your fucking mind?*

She had to remind herself that Eli was an adolescent, and always pushing the envelope. He never walked up or down stairs. He ran—or jumped from one landing to another. It didn't matter how much noise he made or the potential hazards of breaking something—an ankle, leg, or even his neck. If he could leap over something, he leapt over it, and if he could dangle from something, he dangled from it.

His dad knew that about him. It was times like this she really missed her husband. Joe understood Eli. He related to him in a way she never could. She'd foolishly hoped to be both father and mother to Eli here in Seattle, but too often, Sydney realized she was out of her league.

For the rest of the long ride home, she quietly lectured Eli about how he could have gotten himself killed—or gotten *her* killed. And if someone else at the party had tried to save him, *they* could have gotten killed. By the time Sydney pulled into the driveway of their apartment complex, Eli was silent and looking miserable.

Wordlessly, he reached up to the sun visor on his side and pressed the automatic opener device.

Sydney stopped the car and waited for the wrought-iron gate to slide open. They lived in Seattle's Madison Park in a charming two-story Tudor town house on Lake Washington. It was part of a group of town houses called Tudor Court. Narrow stone pathways separated all the units. Practically everyone had flower boxes outside their windows, and the blossoms were at their peak this time of year. The pathways—like the driveway—were gated *"to keep out the riff-raff,"* as Kyle had once remarked, tongue in cheek. The public beach was only half a block away, and there was a lot of foot traffic in the area, especially in the summertime.

While the gate took its sweet time opening, Sydney glanced at her woeful son again. "Well, anyway, you're okay, and everyone survived," she sighed. "It's not the end of the world. Just don't do it again, honey. Okay?"

"Okay, Mom," he muttered. "I—I'll call Uncle Kyle in the morning and tell him I'm sorry."

Smiling, she reached over and gently patted his shoulder for a moment. Then she straightened up behind the wheel and steered the car into their parking spot—a sheltered alcove without a door. There were four more individual parking stalls on this side of the driveway and five more on the other side.

They climbed out of the car, then started down the stone pathway to their town house. It was a balmy, star-filled night. They could hear people screaming and laughing on the beach down the block. There was an occasional pop from a firecracker. "Oh, swell," Sydney muttered, the keys in her hand. "I'm *really* looking forward to listening to that all night long."

She stopped dead at the front door. It was open a crack.

"Eli, did you lock the door when we left for Uncle Kyle's?" she whispered, hesitating on the front stoop. When they'd gotten into the car earlier tonight, he'd suddenly remembered a DVD he'd wanted to return to his uncle, so Eli had run back inside at the last minute.

"Of course, I locked it." He was staring at the door, too. "God, you think somebody broke in?"

Sydney took a deep breath, then slowly pushed open the door. It yawned and creaked. The front hallway was dark. She couldn't see anything yet—just shadows.

"I'm almost positive I locked it," Eli said. "And I know I left the light on—"

Sydney shushed her son, then wedged herself in front of him. Stepping inside, she nervously felt around for the light switch on the wall. She was shaking again. Someone on the street nearby let off a firecracker, and for a second, her heart seemed to stop. At last, she found the light switch and turned on the hall light.

No one was in the living room. Sydney carefully studied the built-in bookcases and the fireplace mantel. When she'd left Joe, she'd taken some old family knickknacks with her. It was the kind of stuff that would go for a small fortune at an antique store. Everything was still there. Nothing had been disturbed.

Still standing in the foyer, she gazed up the stairs, but could only see as far as the landing. Sydney reached over to the wall near the bottom of the stairs and flicked the switch to the upstairs hallway. She didn't see any shadows moving. There were no footsteps, no floorboards creaking above them. Straight ahead was the coved entrance to the kitchen. The light was off in there. Sydney could hear the refrigerator humming.

She moved into the living room. Behind her, Eli opened the coat closet. He pulled out an umbrella and held it as if it were a club. He headed toward the kitchen.

"Honey, wait," Sydney whispered. She turned on a lamp in the living room, then peeked past the alcove entry to the dining room. She flicked the switch to the small chandelier over the dinner table. There was an old, built-in, dark wood breakfront with more family antiques—with several sterling-silver items among them. Nothing had been touched.

One the other side of the room, the louvered door to the kitchen was closed. They always kept that door open. Through the slats, she saw the light go on.

"Oh, Jeez," she heard Eli murmur. "Mom? Mom, you—ah—you better come in here . . ."

Scurrying around the table, she pushed open the louvered door.

With the umbrella still clutched in his hands, Eli stood near the kitchen counter. He gaped at her, then looked down at the shards of porcelain on the slate-pattern linoleum floor. Sydney recognized the floral design on the bits of porcelain. It was her teapot, a wedding gift from her favorite aunt. The thing had been chipped and, on the inside, tea-stained despite lots of scrubbings. Still, Sydney had used it every day for the last fourteen years. She'd left it on the dry rack by the sink this morning. Now it was shattered. Some of the porcelain shards had scattered to the far corner of the kitchen, where Sydney had a tall, glass-top café table and a pair of stools. Beside it was a framed poster from the 1994 Winter Olympic Games in Lillehammer, signed by the entire U.S. figure-skating team. It was probably worth a pretty penny to some collector. But it hadn't been touched.

Sydney stared down at the broken teapot. "Did you—" she started to ask her son.

As if reading her mind, he shook his head. "No, Mom. I didn't touch it, I swear."

Behind him, a cupboard door was open. A box from the shelf lay on its side, and its contents had spilt onto the counter below. Sydney could see it was a box of Minute Rice. A few grains still trickled from the box's side spout onto the pile of rice that had formed on the green Formica counter. "What in God's name . . ." she murmured.

Sydney turned and gazed down the hallway at the back door. It was closed, and the chain-lock set. She poked her head into the powder room, to the left of the back entrance. "Eli, honey, you forgot to flush—and you left the seat up. That's not like you."

"What?" he called.

"Never mind," she said, flushing the toilet and lowering the seat.

Across the hall was a kitchen pantry, which she'd converted into her office. Though the quarters were cramped and a bit claustrophobic, the office had a window with a beautiful view of the lake. If there was anything worth stealing in the house, it was in this room: cameras—both video and still, some sound equipment, a laptop, a fax machine, an iPod station, and a computer with a wide-screen monitor. All of it was still there.

It didn't make sense that only two things—both in the kitchen—had been disturbed.

"Think he's hiding upstairs?" Eli whispered. He still had the umbrella—ready to clobber someone.

They crept up the stairs together and checked her bedroom, Eli's bedroom, and the bathroom. They even peeked in the closets and under the beds.

"Are you sure you didn't leave the door open?" Sydney asked Eli. She kept thinking a squirrel must have gotten in and made that mess in the kitchen.

"I'm positive," Eli said. "I remember jiggling the knob to make sure it was locked."

Sydney called 9-1-1 from the phone in her bedroom. She counted four ring tones, and no answer. All the while, Eli stared at her. He still had the umbrella ready.

She had a spectacular view of the lake from here. She could hear people still laughing and screaming on the beach. A few firecrackers went off. It suddenly occurred to Sydney why it was taking so long to get an answer from the police. It was July Fourth, probably one of their busiest nights of the year. She remembered how much Joe hated having to work on the Fourth of July.

"Seattle Police, 9-1-1," the operator finally answered.

"Yes, hello," Sydney said to the woman on the phone. "Um, I think someone tried to break into my house tonight. My son and I came home and found the front door open. A couple of items in the kitchen were disturbed, but nothing else. I don't think anything was stolen."

"Is the intruder in the house right now?" the 9-1-1 operator asked.

"No. We've checked every room and every closet. I'm fairly certain my son and I are alone." Sydney glanced at Eli again.

Standing by her bed, he still had that stupid umbrella clutched in his hands as if it were a saber. Sydney covered the phone's mouthpiece for a second. "Honey, you can put that down now, okay? You don't need it."

"Are you reporting a robbery?" the operator asked briskly.

"It's more like an attempted break-in," Sydney said. "I'm not sure if—"

"Was there any property damage?"

"Um, just a teapot that got broken in the kitchen," Sydney explained, feeling silly. "And a box of food was tipped over—"

"Was there any damage to the *property*?" the woman cut in, sounding impatient.

"You mean like the lock on the front door? No. No, they didn't do any damage to the house, at least nothing we've noticed so far. We've only—"

"Name please?" the operator interrupted.

"Sydney Jordan." She kept thinking—on this busy 9-1-1 night, she was probably wasting their time with her call about this botched *burglary attempt*—if that was even what it had been. Despite Eli's insistence that he'd shut and locked the front door earlier, she couldn't totally trust him tonight—not after what he'd pulled at Kyle's place. In all likelihood, he'd accidentally left the door open, and something had gotten in the house.

"Could you verify your address for me?" she heard the operator ask.

"One minute, please," Sydney said. Then she covered the mouthpiece again. "Eli, could you switch off the lights in your bedroom and in your closet? Our electric bill's going to be enormous." She didn't want him hearing what she'd decided to tell the operator. As soon as he left the room, Sydney got back on the phone. "Sorry. Listen, I—I don't want to report anything. But if you could send a patrol car to check for any suspicious activity around the Tudor Court Apartments on Forty-first Street, I'd appreciate it."

She figured if someone had actually broken into their house and he was still around, a police presence might discourage him from trying again tonight.

"We'll check it out," said the woman on the phone.

"Thanks very—" Sydney fell silent at the sound of a click on the other end of the line. She realized she was talking to no one. Sighing, she hung up the phone.

She worked up a smile for Eli, who now stood in her doorway. At least he'd stopped brandishing the umbrella as if it were a weapon. Now he held it as if it were a walking stick. "They're sending a patrol car to check out the general area," Sydney said, moving to her dresser. "If someone did try to break in, I doubt he'll be back. I think we're okay, honey."

"It's weird nothing got stolen," Eli said, squinting at her. "Do you think it was our ghost?"

From the dresser drawer, Sydney pulled out a pair of long pajama bottoms and a T-shirt. She rolled her eyes. "You blame that *ghost* for everything."

"Well, *something* was screwing around in the kitchen," Eli said. "Think we got rats? I mean, after all, we're right on the water. They say rats like the water."

"I'd rather it be the ghost. Let's go back to that one." Her nightclothes slung over her shoulder, Sydney paused in front of him. "Move it, buddy."

Eli stopped playing with the umbrella and stepped aside. Sydney patted his shoulder as she brushed past him, then she ducked into the bathroom. She heard the floorboards squeak outside the door. He was retreating toward his bedroom. Sydney shed her sleeveless top and started washing her face.

Their *ghost.* For Eli, she always tried to shrug it off as an amusing little curiosity.

In truth, there was some kind of *other presence* in this place. It was why she'd been able to get a six-month lease so cheap. Even with her respectable salary from the network, Sydney couldn't have afforded any of the other apartments in Tudor Court. But this unit was different. Under Washington state law, the property management company was required to tell potential renters about the suicide here in Apartment 9. Sydney didn't get any details, just that a woman had killed herself in the unit about thirty years ago. Sydney used to wonder exactly how the woman had ended her life—and in which room.

Kyle had had misgivings about her moving in there. But Sydney had considered this beautiful, charming place—ready for immediate occupancy—a godsend. She and Eli had been living with Kyle for two very rough, emotional weeks after leaving Chicago. Sydney was eager to get on with their lives and settle in somewhere. And as much as her brother had insisted they were no imposition, Sydney knew they were. Kyle was used to living alone. She slept in his guest room, and Eli had the sofa in the TV room. Half their stuff cluttered up Kyle's immaculate apartment, and the other half was in storage. Sydney figured her brother would urge them to take the first place she didn't *hate*—just to get his life back to normal. Instead, Kyle was cautious.

He used his real estate connections and did a little digging around about Tudor Court's Apartment 9. He didn't uncover anything about the suicide, but he learned that in the last twenty-plus years, that apartment had had the highest turnover rate of all ten units in Tudor Court—and the longest vacancy stretches.

"Some rich doctor from Denver had it as his second home for several years," Kyle told her while barbecuing on his patio one warm night in mid-May. Eli was in the TV room, out of earshot. Sydney didn't want him to know someone had died in their prospective new home. "The Denver doctor wasn't actually there much," Kyle explained, flipping the hamburgers on his gas grill. "But the place is bad news. The guy I talked to on the QT at Tudor Court's property management company said the last renter endured it for only four months. And—get this—the renters before her, some incense-burning Birkenstock couple, they even hired a certified shaman to do a house blessing and exorcise whatever's in there. But I guess it didn't take, because Mr. and Mrs. Birkenstock got the hell out a few weeks before their six-month lease was up."

"So you're saying this place is haunted?" Sydney asked, setting place mats, napkins, and utensils around the umbrella-covered glass-top table near the grill.

"I'm just telling you what the property management guy told me, Syd."

She shrugged. "Well, maybe we can hire that short, little lady with the funny voice from *Poltergeist*. We'll have her throw some tennis balls in a closet, or whatever they did to fix their ghost problem. Listen, Kyle, I really like this place. Plus we can move in right away. If the place is truly haunted, I could always—"

"Pack up again and go back to Joe?" he said, finishing for her.

She frowned, and set down the utensils. They clattered against the glass tabletop. "I wasn't going to say that."

"Yeah, but you were thinking it," Kyle replied soberly. "Let's face it, you're miserable, Syd. All this time, you've been hoping for some excuse to make up with Joe. And hell, maybe you'd have one—if the son of a bitch ever bothered to call you. I really don't think he gives a damn. He probably wouldn't even be talking to his own son if Eli didn't *call him* every day. That's another thing. I used to think Joe was such a great dad. I can't believe he didn't put up more of a fight to keep Eli with him."

"You don't know the whole story," Sydney muttered.

"I know he *hit* you. That's enough for me. That makes him an asshole in my book."

"Can we switch the subject, please?" she said, gazing down at the tabletop.

Kyle was silent for a moment. He flipped the burgers again. "So nothing I've told you about this freaky *Blair Witch* apartment in Tudor Court has changed your mind," he said, finally. "You're still moving in anyway, aren't you, Syd?"

She sighed. "I signed the lease this afternoon."

Sydney didn't know what to expect their first few days and nights in the apartment. She wondered if she'd hear strange voices—faraway moaning, laughing, or crying. Maybe the walls would start bleeding or something. Perhaps the lights would flicker for no reason.

If some kind of *spirit* resided there, it allowed her and Eli to move in their stuff without making its presence known. None of the new pieces from Macy's, Ikea, or Georgetown Furniture Liquidators suddenly toppled over in the night. Doors didn't open or shut by themselves. There was no unexplainable tapping from inside the walls.

The only disturbances were from *outside*—the occasional

late-night drunken swimmers, screaming and laughing on the beach. Sydney would crawl out of bed and glance out her window. Often the clandestine swimmers were naked or in their underwear though it was too far away for her to really see anything. No cheap thrills. Still, it made her heart ache for Joe when one night, she spied a young, amorous couple skinny-dipping in the moonlight.

She also understood why Eli—who shared pretty much the same view of the beach she had—suddenly wanted binoculars for his birthday.

They had been in the apartment a little over a week and had unpacked the last of the boxes when it happened. Sydney had just switched off her bedside light to go to sleep one Tuesday night. Down the hallway, Eli had already gone to bed. His door had been closed—and the light off—for at least an hour.

"Mom?" His voice was muffled.

She sat up, uncertain whether or not he was talking in his sleep.

"Mom, is that you? Mom?" he repeated, louder and more panicked than before. Then there was a loud crash.

Sydney switched on the light and jumped out of bed.

"Oh, God, Mom!" he yelled. Dressed in his T-shirt and undershorts, Eli threw open his bedroom door. He almost tripped bolting out of there. "Were you just in my room, Mom?" he asked, catching his balance—and his breath. He braced himself against the corridor wall. "Were you just in there?"

Bewildered, Sydney shook her head.

"Someone came in there—like thirty seconds ago—"

"Honey, it was probably just a dream—"

"I wasn't asleep!" he insisted. "Somebody's in the house! He came in my room and sat down on the end of my bed. I felt it, Mom! He brushed against my foot. I felt the weight on my bed . . ."

They searched the apartment, both upstairs and downstairs, including the closets. There was no sign of a break-in.

Eli kept insisting that he'd been awake. He'd heard her using the bathroom about ten minutes before this *person* came in his room. He'd thought it had been her at first. He hadn't seen anything, because it had been too dark, but he'd felt someone hovering. Then the person had sat down on the end of his bed. In his panic, Eli had knocked over the Homer Simpson lamp on his night table while trying to turn on the light.

Homer had survived the fall, but the bulb had gotten smashed. Eli slipped into his jeans and shoes and helped her clean up the glass. It took him another hour to settle down for bed again. But after that night, he wanted the hallway light on and kept his bedroom door open. The last time Eli had needed a light on so he could go to sleep, he'd been eight years old.

Sydney didn't tell him the place had a vague history of weird occurrences. She didn't have to. He figured it out on his own a week later, after a second, similar late-night episode in his bedroom. He claimed he also heard voices this time—a soft, undecipherable muttering and a woman crying. Eli bought himself a night-light. Sydney thought about doing the same thing. She had her own *night visitor*. She didn't hear voices, but otherwise it was just as Eli had described it—an inexplicable sensation that someone was *hovering* over her as she lay in bed. It had happened enough times that Sydney tried to discern a pattern in the erratic visits. Was it a certain day of the week—or a particular time of night? Not really. Was the bedroom window open or closed that last time she'd been spooked out? She couldn't be sure. She became very superstitious, a slave to certain illogical bedtime rituals to ward off whatever was haunting her and Eli—until another unnerving *night visit* proved those rituals meaningless.

She went online and researched how to deal with a ghost. Apparently in some haunted houses, a happy cohabitation of the living and the spirit residents was quite possible. The Web sites recommended acknowledging the ghost, talking to it, and asking it to leave—even shouting at it if necessary.

"Okay, dude, I'm going to bed now," Eli had taken to announcing some nights—right after brushing his teeth. "I gotta have my sleep. You need to leave me the hell alone for the next eight hours." From her study downstairs, Sydney would hear him some nights going through his bedtime monologue. They tried to make jokes and shrug it off as a minor annoyance—just one of those things that came with living there.

But it was still unnerving.

The bathroom seemed to be the center of this paranormal activity. Sydney had a framed Georgia O'Keefe print on the bathroom wall. For no logical reason, it fell to the floor on three different occasions—the glass shattering twice. She finally put the print away and left the wall blank. Twice, water started gushing out of the bathtub faucet on its own—both times late at night. She'd had to crawl out of bed and switch off the valve under the sink. Eli called the occurrences *water raids*.

Sydney suspected her son might have exaggerated some of his own brushes with the supernatural, and maybe—out of boredom or resentment toward her—he'd been triggering the water raids himself.

But one night last week, Sydney had felt that otherworldly *presence* while in the bathroom. Washing her face, she half-expected to catch a glimpse of something in the medicine chest mirror—a dark figure lurking behind her or a strange light. By the time she'd dried off her face and switched off the bathroom light, Sydney had managed to give herself a thorough case of the creeps. She was just down the hall, about to step into her bedroom, when she heard the water start in the tub. A chill raced through her. That made three times. She waited in the corridor and listened. The gushing only lasted a few moments, and then there was a steady drip. She crept back to the bathroom, and switched on the light. "Oh, God," she whispered. One of the towel racks was bare; the two bath towels that had been draped over it were strewn across the floor.

The door to Eli's room had remained shut the entire time.

Sydney often thought the woman who killed herself in this apartment years and years ago must have done it in this bathroom.

Drying off her face, Sydney glanced down at the old, chipped powder blue and white tiled floor and wondered if the body had been discovered here, curled up by the toilet. She knew when people overdosed they sometimes died on or near the toilet. Or perhaps the woman had cut her wrists in the sink or in the bathtub.

Was that why their *night visitor* kept coming back to this bathroom?

A sudden, loud pounding on the door startled her.

"Mom?"

"What? What is it, honey?" she called back, a hand over her heart.

"The phone light's blinking," Eli said. "You got a message. I checked caller ID. I thought it might be Dad, but it looks like someone in New York."

"You have one new message," the computerized recording told her ten minutes later. Sydney had taken the cordless phone out of the kitchen and now sat at her office desk. Nearly all the wall space was taken up by shelves and cabinets full of books, files, and equipment. But there was a small space beneath her window that had framed family photos—and Joe was in some of them. There wasn't one of just him alone.

Eli had the TV on in the living room. Sydney could hear him channel surfing with the remote control. She'd already checked the caller ID. Eli had been right; the call had been from New York. Someone from the network had phoned—probably about an assignment. She was supposed to be on a summer vacation, but that had never stopped them before.

"Friday, July Fourth, ten-twelve P.M.," the recording continued. Then there was a beep tone. "Hi, Sydney, this is Judy Cavalliri in the news office. Sorry to call so late. I have some pretty awful news. I thought you should know, since we recently reran the story you did about that Portland couple, Leah Dvorak and Jared McGinty. It just came over the AP. They were killed tonight, shot in their apartment. It looks like a burglary gone from bad to worse. A bunch of their stuff was missing. A neighbor found both bodies in the bathroom. There's a chance we'll show part of your *Movers & Shakers* piece tomorrow on the network news. They might want a comment from you, too. Anyway, Sydney, I thought I'd give you a heads-up. I'm terribly sorry. They seemed like such a nice couple."

Dazed, Sydney listened to the beep, then she slowly put down the phone.

She'd gotten to know Leah and Jared pretty well when she did the story on them last Christmas. She and Leah had sent Christmas cards to each other and there had been a few e-mails back and forth in January, but they hadn't had any further correspondence. That was typical of her work. She became close to nearly all of her *Movers & Shakers* subjects while working on their segments. Then a week later, she was already involved in her next story and her next subject. She was in and out of these people's lives so quickly. Way too often, she didn't hear about any of them again—not until something awful happened.

She just couldn't believe Leah and Jared were dead.

Slumped in her desk chair, Sydney remembered something. She told herself there was no connection, and yet she still thought about that cryptic e-mail from a few days ago.

"*You can't save them,*" it had read.

CHAPTER SIX

"Hang on, Eli! Hang on!" she called to him.

Four stories above her, Eli clung to the storm drain on Kyle's roof. Screaming, he helplessly dangled in the air. Kyle's town house was on fire. Flames shot out the windows of the top floor, licking at Eli's feet.

"I'll catch you!" she called to her son. "I'll break your fall!"

Eli's clothes started to catch on fire. His screams turned to agonizing shrieks. He let go of the gutter, and his body plummeted down toward her.

Sydney suddenly sat up in bed.

Her heart was racing. She started to reach for the light on her nightstand, but hesitated. Sometimes it was easier just to sit there in the dark and face her fear. She knew she was alone right now, no *ghostly visitor*. If she turned on the lights, then switched them off later, she'd just have to get used to the dark again.

Sydney settled back down and rested her head on the pillow. She glanced at the digital clock at her bedside: 2:11. She heard some firecrackers popping in the distance. The Fourth of July celebration was still going on for some people.

She rubbed her eyes. That dream had everything screwed around, of course. It wasn't Eli who had fallen from a burning building. It had been another boy.

The incident had been a pivotal chapter in her bestselling autobiography from fourteen years ago. But the paperback original had been out of print for years. Not many people remembered it or the hokey TV movie based on the book. The people who only knew her as the pretty correspondent for *On the Edge*, the ones who asked if her slight limp was from a recent injury, those people didn't know Sydney was once an awkward, homely girl whose legs worked beautifully. In fact, they worked wonders.

Ever since she was seven—with her Dorothy Hamill wedge-style haircut—Sydney had dreamed of skating in the Olympics someday. From the Jordan's home in Seattle's Queen Anne district, her mother drove Sydney to the Highland Ice Arena in Shoreline three times a week so she could practice. If Sydney did enough household chores, her mother rewarded her with an extra trip to the ice arena. Once she was old enough, Sydney took the bus there: a seventy-minute trek both ways with a transfer—six days a week.

She had a long, awkward puberty: bad skin, frizzy hair, and braces. In family photos, Kyle was always the cute one, damn him. She was shy, and hopeless around guys. But on the ice, she felt beautiful and confident—for a while at least.

Sydney's high school physical education teacher recommended a private coach for figure skating, and Mr. Jordan hired her. Donna Loftus coached several girls who competed nationally. Two of her former pupils had ended up on the U.S. Olympic teams—in 1984 and 1988. She was a thin, homely woman with rank body odor that reminded Sydney of bad vegetable soup. Sydney never saw her crack a smile. She practiced and practiced until her ankles were ready to snap. She felt lucky to be working with such an accomplished coach, but nothing she did seemed to please Ms. Loftus. Sydney finally asked her what she was doing wrong. Was it her spirals? Her landings?

Leaning against a post at the rink's sideline, Ms. Loftus folded her arms and heaved a sigh. "I don't think you're right for figure skating," she frowned. "I probably shouldn't have taken this job. You've got a lot of talent, and you're not afraid of hard work. You're very graceful on the ice, but your looks are awkward. I don't mean to be cruel, but most people expect figure skaters to be pretty."

Sydney was devastated. But she didn't give up. She was going to dazzle Ms. Loftus if it killed her. But before she had a chance to prove herself to her, Ms. Loftus quit. She told Mr. Jordan, "Sydney just doesn't have the right look for a figure skater. There's no nice way to put it. She's rather plain and awkward."

Sydney's father was furious. "That woman—who looks and smells like the backside of a horse—she said *you* weren't pretty enough?" He immediately hired another coach, and Sydney worked even harder—just to prove Dog-Face Donna wrong.

Her Olympic dream took over and dominated the whole family. Sydney's mother found temp work to help pay for Sydney's trainers. When he wasn't working overtime, her father worked closely with her trainers on weekends. They entered Sydney in local and statewide competitions. The family scheduled their lives around her practice sessions and those competitions.

"You wanted to skate like Dorothy Hamill, and I wanted to skip down the yellow brick road like Dorothy Gale," Kyle once pointed out. "I mean, how many eleven-year-old boys save up their allowance to buy their own copy of *Judy at Carnegie Hall*? But Mom and Dad didn't even notice that I was *different*. They were too busy planning for your big

Olympic moment. God, sometimes I thought I'd barf if I had to sit through one more dinner-table conversation exclusively devoted to the subject of you and your double axels."

By the time Sydney was nineteen, people compared her to her idols, Dorothy Hamill and Peggy Fleming. She'd also turned into an attractive young woman, and not just on the ice. The braces came off, her complexion cleared up, and she had developed a toned, taut body. No one would ever call her awkward-looking again. She moved up from junior to senior level and shined in the U.S. Nationals. She didn't make the Olympic team for the 1992 games in Albertville, but she came in at thirteenth place and was written up in several newspapers and magazines.

She graduated from the University of Minnesota, where she'd majored in broadcasting. Sydney's respect for good reporters came through whenever she was interviewed or profiled, and those reporters loved her. They predicted she'd come home from the 1994 Lillehammer Games with a medal.

There was a lot of pressure on her. The dreams of that driven homely little kid with the Dorothy Hamill haircut had touched so many people—the reporters, her trainers, and her family. She started receiving fan letters and e-mail from total strangers. All these people had gotten caught up in her dream, too, and she didn't want to disappoint them. Sydney trained harder and harder. She kept thinking about how much her family had sacrificed and what she'd given up, too.

Sydney was profiled in *Sports Illustrated* and had a page and a half in *People* during the fall of 1993. *The Seattle Times* wanted to do an interview. They planned to put her on the cover of their Sunday magazine section. Hoping to look decent for her first magazine cover, Sydney made an appointment at a chic beauty salon downtown. She kept thinking Donna Loftus might see that magazine cover—and be sorry as hell.

It was a beautiful, crisp, sunny autumn afternoon, and she'd decided to walk to the beauty salon from a friend's apartment on First Hill. Tall trees lined the residential area's parkways, and as she strolled along, Sydney gazed up at the leaves—so vibrant with their autumn colors.

That was when she saw the smoke.

It came from a slightly dilapidated, beige brick apartment building a half-block away, close to a busy intersection. Yet she was the only one on the street who seemed to notice something wrong.

Black clouds billowed out of an open window on the fourth floor. Sydney thought she heard screams.

She ran across the street—almost smack into a moving car. The car's brakes screeched and its horn blared. The driver continued down the street, screaming out at her, *"Stupid idiot! Want to end up in the hospital?"*

But Sydney was gazing up at the building. Smoke continued to belch from the open window. In one of the windows next to it she saw the curtains on fire and flames licking at the glass.

Sydney tried to wave down another car for help, but the driver sped past her. Panic-stricken, she raced back across the street to the building's entrance. She pressed random buttons on the intercom. "Hello?" she said loudly. "Is someone there?" Finally, two or three people answered at once. "There's a fire on the fourth floor!" Sydney said, the words rushing out.

"What?" one person said.

"Who the hell is this?" another tenant replied.

"There's a fire on your fourth floor!" Sydney repeated. "Call 9-1-1!"

They all seemed to reply at once: *"Is this a joke?"*

"What?"

"Hello—"

But someone buzzed her in. Sydney pushed open the door. The tiny lobby was a bit seedy and neglected. She could smell the smoke even down here. She saw the fire alarm by the old-fashioned mailboxes. There was no glass to break; it was just a lever in a red box with the words, *FIRE—PULL,* on it. Sydney tugged down on the switch, and suddenly a shrill alarm rang out.

For a second, she wasn't sure she'd done the right thing. She'd never in her life pulled a fire alarm. Would she somehow get into trouble for this?

Past the alarm, she could hear doors opening in the first-floor hallway and people lumbering down the stairs. She found a rubber door-stopper on the floor near the front entrance and used it to prop the door open. Then Sydney hurried outside. She kept wondering if she'd overreacted. Maybe the smoke had subsided. She ran across the street for another look.

By now, two other pedestrians had stopped to see what was happening. A car had pulled over, too.

The smoke continued to pour out of that fourth-floor window. Sydney noticed a phone booth by a small parking lot on her side of the street. She frantically dug into her purse for some change. *Did she have to deposit money to call 9-1-1?* She didn't know. Her hands shaking, she pushed thirty-five cents into the slots and punched 9-1-1.

Across the street, people started to wander out of the old building. They appeared annoyed and confused. One of them, an old woman swaddled in a bathrobe, gazed up and then her mouth dropped open. She pointed to the smoke for one of her neighbors.

On the phone, the 9-1-1 operator answered on the second ring: "Police Emergency."

"Yes, hello," Sydney said, trying to keep calm. She glanced up at that same window again. "I need to report a fire on the—on the fourth floor of an apartment building on First Hill. I just went into their lobby and rang their alarm. It's—um, on the corner of Terry and—and—" Sydney fell silent as she noticed another window open up beside the one emitting smoke. A young boy started to climb out to the ledge.

"Oh, God, there's a kid . . . I think he's going to jump!" Sydney told the operator. "Th-th-the building is two blocks north of Madison—on Terry. Please, hurry!"

"Your name?"

"Sydney Jordan," she said. She meant to hang up the phone, but the receiver fell off the hook and just dangled there. Sydney didn't notice. She was already racing across the street.

More tenants had drifted out of the building, but they just milled around by the front entrance. A few wandered across the street to look at the fire. But no one seemed to know what to do about the poor boy trapped on the ledge.

Sydney ran up to a gaunt young woman who had a pierced nostril and short, spiked green hair. She stood near the front door, gnawing at her fingernail and looking up at the boy.

"Do you know what apartment he's in?" Sydney asked her, shouting over the fire alarm.

She shrugged. "He's Aidan Somebody on the fourth floor someplace. I don't know for sure."

Sydney started to brush past her toward the door.

"Shit, don't try to go up there," the girl said. "Are you nuts?"

Sydney hesitated, then looked up at the boy. Flames shot out of the window beside him. He recoiled in terror and almost fell off the ledge.

Pushing past the dazed tenants, Sydney made her way along the narrow lawn in front of the building until she was directly under the boy. He was thin with dark hair and a handsome, almost angelic face. He wore jeans and a long-sleeve denim shirt that looked too big for him. Soot covered the shirt, and smudge marks marred his forehead and cheek. Sydney guessed he was about ten years old. He precariously stood on the tiny ledge, his back pressed against the beige brick edifice. Sydney could only imagine how hot those bricks were. Just a foot away from him, flames lashed out of the window, along with thick, black clouds of smoke. Trembling, he stared down at her.

"Aidan?" she called to him, over the incessant alarm. She thought she heard a siren in the distance. "Aidan, is there anyone else in the apartment with you?"

Frozen on the ledge, he just gazed down at her. He opened his mouth to speak, but it seemed he couldn't get any words out.

"Honey, hang on!" she called. "I think the fire department's on the way! Do you have any brothers or sisters? Is anyone else in there?"

Finally, he shook his head.

The smoke started to obscure her view of him. But she heard him coughing—and then the shrieks.

"Aidan! Can you hear me, honey?" Sydney glanced over her shoulder. She didn't see the fire trucks yet. The building alarm nearly drowned out the sirens—still too far away.

The smoke cleared for a moment, and she saw him up there. His shirt was on fire. Choking and screaming, he tried to pat down the flames. He went to grab on to the side of the open window to keep his balance. But his hand went right into the flames.

"Let go!" Sydney called to him. She automatically put her arms out in front of her. "I'll catch you, honey! I'll break your fall! Aidan, let go!"

His shirt was still on fire. He pushed himself from the ledge—away from her.

But Sydney ran under him, her arms outstretched. She didn't know what she was thinking—or doing. She acted on sheer gut instinct. She just needed to break his fall.

Sydney saw the boy's thin body as it plunged toward her.

Someone screamed. Sydney didn't see who it was. She was already blinded.

All of his weight came crashing down on her. Something snapped in her neck—or her spine—she wasn't sure which. But she heard it—a loud, horrible crack.

Then there was nothing.

For a very long time, there was nothing.

Later, they told Sydney that when she'd briefly regained consciousness in the hospital that night, the first thing she'd asked had been: *"Is the boy alive? Is he okay?"* Sydney didn't remember; she'd been doped up on painkillers and medication that first week. For a while, she was on a respirator, and the doctors thought the injury to her spinal cord might leave her paralyzed. Emergency surgery helped save her punctured lung, and they inserted a rod and some screws for her shattered femur. The other leg was fractured. She'd also broken her left arm, sprained the right one, and dislocated her shoulder. It seemed no organ or appendage escaped injury—from spleen trauma to a sprained ankle.

The doctors still weren't sure she'd ever walk again. One thing for certain, her skating days were over. Sydney's dream of competing in the Olympics and all those years of sacrifice and hard work had been snuffed out in just a few moments. It was all gone.

Sydney kept telling herself the boy would have died if she hadn't broken his fall.

Eleven-year-old Aidan Cosgrove had it even worse than she did. In addition to his crippling back injuries, he suffered second- and third-degree burns on his arms, torso, and neck. After two days, they moved him from Swedish Hospital to the University of Washington Burn Center at Harborview.

It turned out that Aidan's mother had also been in that fourth-floor apartment. Sydney remembered calling to him and asking if anyone else was in there; but he'd shaken his head. She figured the poor kid was probably confused—and terrified. He probably hadn't even heard what she'd been saying to him.

According to *The Seattle Times* and the local TV news, the fire had started in the mother's bedroom. Miraculously, Rikki Cosgrove survived, and her burns were minor. But she'd sustained respiratory damage from smoke inhalation. An unemployed single mom on government assistance, Mrs. Cosgrove admitted to the press that she might have fallen asleep with a cigarette going.

Only two other apartments in the building were damaged by the inferno, and no one else was injured. Yet the fire made national news. One passerby had a video camera with him. He'd caught Sydney's valiant rescue on tape. It was just the kind of harrowing, dramatic stuff the public ate up.

"Mom and Dad cry every time that home video is played on TV," Kyle told her during a visit. "So that means they've cried like—seventy-eight times just this week. It's a regular waterworks at home. Don't you feel sorry for *me*, having to put up with it? You can't possibly know my anguish. I'm really suffering."

"Huh, I'll pray for you." Sydney murmured. Lying in the hospital bed, she cracked a smile. "Don't make me laugh, you dip-shit. It hurts too much."

Kyle had visited her every day, but this was the first time she was lucid for more than just a few minutes. "Seriously, when are you getting out of here?" he asked. "The phone hasn't stopped ringing. You're all over the newspapers and TV. I taped the programs for you and saved the clippings. Anyway, you're famous, Syd. About a zillion people want to interview you. In fact, someone from *Oprah* even called us this morning. They want you on the show. So I repeat, when are you busting out of this joint?"

The doctors told her it would be at least six weeks. Sydney surprised them all by getting around in her "touch-control" wheelchair by the second week. She'd made up her mind not to feel sorry for herself. There were so many people in this hospital who were worse off than her. The fifteen-year-old girl in the room next door had fallen off her bicycle and landed headfirst in a ditch. Her name was Carol, and she would spend the rest of her life a paraplegic. Next to her, Sydney's shattered dreams seemed like pretty small potatoes—at least, she told herself that. She spent a lot of time visiting Carol and others in the intensive care unit.

Updates on her remarkable recovery made the news. Someone on the hospital staff leaked that she spent time boosting the morale of other patients, and the press ate it up. All the attention embarrassed Sydney. The reports made out like she was Mother Teresa or something. The truth was, she visited her fellow patients to forget her own pain and agony and to help boost her *own* morale. It must have worked, because she was healing a lot faster than the doctors had expected.

Sydney's story became an inspiration for others. While still in the hospital, she had three different publishers wanting to handle her autobiography—with the help of a ghostwriter, of course. If one more agent described her tale as a "lemonade from lemons" saga, Sydney thought she'd throttle them with her crutches. At first, she turned down all the offers.

But her parents had gone into debt paying her trainers, and her medical bills were already staggering. So Sydney finally accepted one of the publishers' deals. They wanted a rush job, because a quickie, *unauthorized* biography was already in stores, selling quite well: *Picking Up the Pieces: The Sydney Jordan Story*.

Her advance was $125,000, and Sydney donated $25,000 of it to Aidan Cosgrove and his mother. After a while, Rikki Cosgrove became a real pain. She seemed to be a strong believer in the old Chinese proverb that once you save someone's life, you're responsible for them. She was forever asking

Sydney for favors and hitting her up for money. And Rikki wasn't exactly Mother of the Year either—as the ghostwriter for Sydney's autobiography discovered while doing her research. But none of it was included in the book.

Sydney discovered that publishing a book meant making a lot of compromises and concessions. She loathed the title the marketing people came up with: *Making Miracles: My Own Story.* But the book spent three weeks on the *New York Times* bestseller list. A made-for-TV movie was quickly thrown together.

By the time *Making Miracles: The Sydney Jordan Story* aired on Lifetime, Sydney was out of the hospital and walking with a cane. Hired to do color commentary for a televised figure-skating event, she made such a great impression that the network put her in their broadcast booth for other women's sports tournaments. Sydney ended up going to the Olympic Games in Lillehammer after all.

She won raves from viewers and critics for the short films she put together and narrated about certain athletes, coaches, and even the people working at the event (a woman who ran a concessions stand in the main auditorium, a maid at a nearby hotel, and the man who operated one of the scoreboards). Pretty soon, the network assigned her to make her video shorts about interesting people for their nighttime news magazines. That was how *Movers & Shakers* got started.

One of her *Movers & Shakers* pieces was about a handsome young, Chicago cop named Joe McCloud. While off duty and on his way to a Cubs game, he'd restrained a man who had gone berserk on the El. The man had shot his girlfriend in front of dozens of horrified commuters on the train. He had then taken a child hostage and threatened to execute her—as well as everyone in the car. *"I thought we were all going to die,"* one middle-aged woman commuter testified in Sydney's video short. *"People were crying and getting sick.*

And then this—this good-looking guy stepped up and started talking to the gunman, and he distracted him . . ."

Joe McCloud managed to overpower the deranged man. He even gave mouth-to-mouth resuscitation to the man's wounded girlfriend, saving her life.

Joe was six feet, three inches tall, with straight blond hair and soulful green eyes, and Sydney was smitten. On top of everything else, he was a hero. During the interview, he confessed something to Sydney: "When the network said they wanted to interview me, I told them okay—as long as they sent you to do it."

"Why me?" she asked.

With a crooked little grin, he shrugged. "Well, ever since I first saw you on TV about a year ago, I've had a little crush on you."

Her parents weren't crazy about her marrying a cop, and it meant her moving away to Chicago. But they ended up falling in love with him, too. It was just the kind of story they would have had her cover for *Movers & Shakers*: the handsome hero cop and the semicelebrity correspondent who profiled him were now getting married. Photos of their wedding ran in *People* magazine.

The doctors had warned her that the spinal injuries might cause some fertility problems. So finding herself pregnant five months after they were married took Sydney by surprise. Oddly, she had trouble conceiving *after* Eli. Joe helped her get through the huge disappointment when the doctors said her chances for another child were less than five percent. Sydney really leaned on Joe again when her father died in 2002, and then again when her mom passed away three years later.

Sometimes Joe caught flack at work from certain fellow cops, because his wife was on TV. *"Mr. Sydney Jordan,"* they called him.

"Oh, they're just jerks," Joe said. "They don't bother me." At least, that was what he told her.

Eli openly hated it when Sydney's *Movers & Shakers* stories took her on the road for days at a time, and so did she. Joe didn't hold it over her head that he often had to be mom and dad to Eli while she was away. Sydney kept busy on these trips, running herself and her crew ragged during the day. Yet she'd still have a tough time falling asleep alone in her bed at the Hyatt, Marriott, or Red Lion. She missed having Joe beside her, spooning her. She was always worried something might happen to him while she was on the road. As a policeman's wife, Sydney knew she had to prepare herself for the possibility that she could lose him at any time and without any warning.

But she didn't lose him that way. It didn't happen that way at all.

As she lay alone under the covers, Sydney figured she might as well have been in a strange bed at the Hyatt, Red Lion, or Marriott. She felt lonely and homesick. She missed Joe. Down the hallway, her son was sleeping—with his night-light on.

She heard another pop in the distance. People were still setting off firecrackers.

With a sigh, Sydney threw back the covers and then switched on her light. She padded down the hall to use the bathroom. This was one of those nights when the *extra presence* in the apartment scared her. Sitting on the toilet, she warily glanced over toward the tub. The closed shower curtain fluttered a little. She told herself that it had moved when she'd shut the bathroom door earlier. There was nothing on the other side of that plastic, map-of-the-world curtain. She was alone in here.

Staring down at the tiled floor, Sydney thought about Leah and Jared. A grisly image crept into her head of two corpses lying there on the tiles, a pool of blood beneath them.

"A neighbor found both bodies in the bathroom," her friend in the newsroom had said.

Sydney closed her eyes and rubbed her forehead. What had happened to poor Leah and Jared was just too bizarre, sad, and senseless. It still hadn't quite sunk in that they were dead—and *how* they'd died. It baffled her.

She flushed the toilet, washed her hands, and retreated to her bedroom. Crawling back into bed, she switched off the light.

Sydney lay there in the dark for a few moments. Then instinctively she knew she wasn't alone. Even with the windows open and a breeze wafting in from the lake, the bedroom suddenly felt warm. She could hear breathing. The room seemed to get darker. This was how it always happened. Yet Sydney didn't think she'd ever get used to it.

She clutched the bedsheets up to her neck. A shadow passed over her. Something brushed against the side of her face—by her ear. It felt like a kiss. For a brief moment, she thought of Joe and wished he were there. Then maybe she wouldn't be so scared.

But it wasn't Joe.

It was only a ghost.

The picture quality was poor, and the sound fuzzy. On the TV screen, Amanda Beck, the perky brunette actress best known for her popular late-eighties sitcom *Get Out of Here!*, was taking a dramatic turn in this old Lifetime Movie. She didn't look very perky—or pretty—as she lay unconscious in a hospital bed, hooked up to a respirator. A tube tugged down one corner of her mouth, a nasty bruise marred her forehead, and her hair looked greasy. The respirator made a constant *whoosh-whoosh-whoosh* sound. The eleven-year-old boy she'd saved from the fire before the last commercial now maneuvered himself in his wheelchair to her bedside. It was night, and no one else occupied the hospital room with them. With dogged determination and all the strength he could muster, the poor, pathetic, bandaged boy pulled himself out of the wheelchair just long enough to kiss her cheek and whisper in her ear. "Thank you for saving my life. Sydney Jordan, you're my hero."

"That scene with the boy late at night in the hospital never happened," Sydney told *TV Guide* when the TV movie first aired in 1994. The maudlin segment wasn't in her autobiography either. They'd invented it for the film.

Another commercial came on. The clock on his DVD/VCR player read: 3:45 A.M. He could hear a series of pops outside. People were still lighting off firecrackers. He poured a shot of Courvoisier, sat back in his chair, and watched the rest of *Making Miracles: The Sydney Jordan Story.*

It was on a medium-quality videotape he'd bought on eBay. Intermittent static nearly ruined the final scene with Sydney's color commentary of the Olympic Games in Lillehammer. The music swelled while they showed all the people whose lives Sydney had touched in the hospital now watching her on TV, including young Aidan Cosgrove. It was a real tearjerker.

But he was dry-eyed.

He had to finish packing for his trip tomorrow afternoon. But instead he watched once again some *Movers & Shakers* segments he'd recorded over the past several months. For closure, he viewed the Jared and Leah piece one more time. A set of silver candlesticks from their dining room now sat on the same shelf as his TV. And a fancy sterling-silver plate on display in their living room was serving as a coaster for his glass of Courvoisier. He'd also taken forty-seven dollars out of Jared's wallet and another sixty-two dollars from Leah's purse—along with their credit cards. He'd already cut up the credit cards. He didn't really need the money. He just needed the scene at Leah and Jared's place to look like a robbery gone bad. Still, the silver items and the cash were a sweet little bonus.

Glancing over at his open suitcase on the living room floor, he decided to get back to his packing. He ignored the TV for a few minutes. The segment now showing he'd watched so many times recently, he knew it word for word and shot for shot. Sydney was interviewing Ned Haggerty, a rail-riding transient, who had seen a Burlington Northern yardman trip and fall on the tracks. Ned had emerged from his makeshift temporary home in a boxcar to save the unconscious yardman from being sliced in two by an oncoming freight train. Ned was quite a colorful character, but after the umpteenth viewing, his pontificating on what was wrong with people and the current administration no longer amused.

Throwing an extra T-shirt and pair of socks into the suitcase, he shoved a pair of work shoes into a plastic bag, and placed it on top of the clothes. He already had the new work uniform in there. He wouldn't need his skeleton keys or his burglar tools this time. There would be no break-ins.

He had two jobs on this trip. If he carried them out as planned, he wouldn't need his rain slicker and shower cap. It was ironic, too, because he anticipated both kills would be extremely messy.

There would be a great deal of blood, but not a drop of it would touch him.

It would be on Sydney Jordan's head.

If anyone had noticed a stranger coming or going last night, it would have been Sally Considine, the fifty-something divorcee in Apartment 8. Despite the fact that the chateau-style town houses looked alike and often had the same kind of flowers in the window boxes, Tudor Court's occupants usually kept to themselves. Sydney knew Sally Considine well enough to chat politely in passing, and Sally had twice praised her *Movers & Shakers* reruns when they'd aired recently. She'd also asked Sydney if she knew how to get tickets for *Oprah*.

This was the first time Sydney had rung Sally's doorbell. She knew Sally was home. Her windows were open, and she could hear the radio going.

It was a hot morning, the mid-eighties. Sydney wore khaki shorts and a pink blouse. She'd tried to look halfway presentable for her neighbor. She'd been on TV long enough to know that one bad hair day out among the public could start a chain reaction of gossip about what an utter slob she was. It had been particularly hard trying to look pretty this morning. She hadn't gotten much sleep at all last night.

The phone had started ringing at 6:35 this morning. The network—along with a few news services—had wanted a quote from her about the deaths of Leah and Jared.

She'd had three cups of coffee while checking the Internet this morning. There had been several articles on Leah and Jared, but no new developments except for the rather lame quote she'd given them two hours before:

> "It's all so senseless and tragic," said *On the Edge* correspondent Sydney Jordan, whose *Movers & Shakers* profile on McGinty and Dvorak brought them national attention. "They were a very sweet, selfless couple, genuine heroes. Jared and Leah should have had many happy years together ahead of them. It's very sad indeed."

The Portland police still didn't have any leads.

Sydney kept thinking about that strange e-mail she'd received a few days before. *"You can't save them,"* it had said.

She wondered if the person was talking about Leah and Jared, or had it been just some crank, screwing around with her head?

She clicked RECENTLY DELETED EMAIL in her mail file. It took her a few moments to find it among the seven days' worth of deleted messages. There was no subject header, but Sydney recognized the sender's address. She remembered *duet* had been in the e-mail moniker: secondduet4U@dwosinco.com.

She clicked RESTORE, and stared at that cryptic message again. Sydney hesitated before clicking the REPLY icon. Did she really want to respond to the nutcase who had written this message and addressed her as *Bitch-Sydney*? She took a deep breath, then her fingers worked over the keyboard: *"Who are you?"* was all she wrote. Sydney didn't even include her name. As she clicked SEND, Sydney felt as if she were opening up a can of worms.

Just a moment later, she heard a click, signifying incoming mail. She opened up the mailbox:

MAILER-DAEMON . . . Returned Mail
User Unknown: secondduet4U@dwosinco.com

"Just as well," Sydney muttered to herself, sipping from that third cup of coffee. She hadn't received any follow-up e-mail from that *duet* person and figured maybe it was best to just leave it that way.

All that coffee had done a number on Sydney's stomach. Plus her arms and back ached horribly from hauling Eli from that storm drain last night. She was limping pretty badly this morning, too. She hoped Sally Considine wasn't averse to the smell of Bengay—if she ever answered her door.

Sydney pressed the doorbell again.

"Coming, coming!" she heard Sally call.

A moment later, the door flung open. Sally was a large,

buxom woman with a pretty, oval-shaped face and close-cropped auburn hair. She wore a white sleeveless blouse, plaid shorts, and sandals. A smile lit up her face. "Well, hi, Sydney!" Then she immediately seemed to regret it, and covered her mouth. "Oh, I just read online about that nice couple from Portland you interviewed. I'm so sorry. How awful! Would you like to come in for some coffee?" She opened the door wider.

"No thanks," Sydney replied, a hand on her queasy stomach. "That's sweet of you, Sally. I don't want to take too much of your time. I was just wondering. Were you home last night?"

Sally stepped outside. "Well, yes, as a matter of fact. I was a regular couch potato. I stayed in and watched the fireworks on TV."

"You didn't happen to see anyone—any strangers—out here in the courtyard, did you?"

"Last night? No, I didn't notice anybody. Why?"

"Well, it might be nothing. But when my son and I got back from my brother's last night, we found the front door open—"

"Oh, my goodness," Sally murmured. "Was anything missing?"

Sydney shook her head. "Not a thing. There was a small mess in the kitchen, a broken teapot, and some food from the cupboard was spilled onto the counter—nothing else."

Sally blinked at her. "Maybe you accidentally left the door open and a squirrel got in or something."

"That's what I thought. But my son swears he closed and locked the door when we left." Sydney felt like an idiot for double-checking with her neighbor, but she wanted to give Eli the benefit of the doubt. She sighed. "Sorry to take up your time, Sally. Maybe it was a ghost or something." She started to walk away.

"Funny you should mention that," Sally said. "How are you folks getting along in the apartment?"

Sydney turned and half-smiled at her. "Are you asking if we've had some things *go bump in the night*?"

Her neighbor hesitated. "Um, maybe . . ."

"Then you know about it," Sydney said.

"I wanted to say something sooner. But the property manager would have killed me if I'd blabbed. They've had a hard time trying to rent out that place . . ."

In a hushed tone, his mother started to describe some of their *night visits*. From his open bedroom window, Eli could only hear snippets of what she was saying. He peeked past the edge of his curtain down to the cobblestone courtyard, where his mother and Sally stood by Sally's front door. He couldn't see their faces, just the tops of their heads.

"My brother's in real estate and he told me about some of the previous tenants and the high turnover rate," his mother said. "I gather they had experiences similar to ours."

"Well, I've lived here three years," Sally said. "And the people in number nine have usually moved in and out so fast I've never gotten to know many of them. But I became chums with this gal, Nancy Abbe, who lived here a while back. She was very cute, very fun. Anyway, Nancy told me that in the upstairs hallway, she once spotted a woman in a long robe. Only she could see through the woman. She said the woman was there for only a few seconds. At the time, I thought Nancy might have been pulling my leg. But since then, I've heard other stories about things going on in that apartment, and now I don't think she was kidding. You know, Sydney, if what happened to you last night is because of this *ghost* or whatever you want to call it, then it's a real first."

"What do you mean?" Eli heard his mother ask.

"Well, from what I've heard, all the disturbances have occurred on the second floor," Sally explained. "But you said the mess was in your kitchen."

Eli bit his lip. Their neighbor was right. Until last night, there hadn't been any *night visits* on the first floor.

Sally scratched her head and shrugged. "I always figured the disturbances happened upstairs, because that's where they found the bodies."

"Bodies?" his mother repeated.

Eli leaned closer to the window opening. He saw Sally take a step back. She put a hand over her heart. "Oh, dear, the woman who showed you the apartment told you, didn't she? She's required by law to tell you—"

"Yes, she said a woman committed suicide in there. It was supposed to have happened back around the mid-seventies."

"That's right, but—"

"Listen, Sally," his mother said, lowering her voice again. "I'd appreciate it if you didn't mention anything about this suicide to Eli. He doesn't know. He's already well aware that the place is haunted. I don't want to pour gasoline on that fire."

Frowning, Eli watched Sally just nod. She didn't say anything.

"You know, for a minute there," his mother continued. "I thought you said *bodies*."

"I did say *bodies*, Sydney," their neighbor whispered.

Eli felt a chill race through him.

"The woman who committed suicide in your apartment had a son," Sally explained. "Before killing herself, she murdered him—in his sleep."

Chapter Seven

Chicago—Three nights later

She'd managed to slip out of Houlihan's without him noticing. Angela Gannon hurried across East Michigan toward the eighteen-story office building where she worked as a paralegal. It was 9:45 on a sultry Tuesday night. Angela still had on her work clothes: a black skirt and a mint-green blouse that complemented her tan and her shoulder-length ash-blond hair. She was thirty-one, and what she lacked in natural beauty—Angela always thought her nose was too long and her chin too weak—she compensated for with a toned, trim body and lots of panache. Still, Angela was always surprised when a guy told her she was *beautiful*. And sometimes, she fell for that guy, even though he was a mega-jerk.

Kent, the man she'd stealthily abandoned at a table for two in Houlihan's, was the most recent example of that "whatever did I see in this asshole?" phenomenon. He worked in the same building, but on sixteen, two floors above her. They had started out flirting in the elevator, then had a few brushes in the lobby, and finally a date for lunch. Her friends at the law firm warned her that he was a shallow pig—and *married* to boot. And if she took a good look at his gorgeous wavy brown hair, she'd notice early signs of male pattern baldness.

Angela convinced herself she just wanted to be friends with this cute, married guy who thought she was beautiful. He was a total sweetheart and very much a gentleman all through their lunch date.

Too bad he wasn't the same way at Houlihan's. She'd been wary about having drinks with him after work anyway. A harmless lunch was one thing, but this was different. After two Tanqueray and tonics, he turned into an utter creep. He was rude to their waiter. He made two calls on his cell phone while she just sat there, bored to smithereens: one to a buddy to schedule a racquetball game and the other to someone about scoring tickets to a White Sox game. *The White Sox?* It would have been bad enough if her Cubs-crazy family ever found out she was seeing a married guy—*but a White Sox fan*? They'd have disowned her.

The last straw had been when Kent—with a smarmy grin—had made an innuendo about checking out the view from one of the upper-floor suites in the Hyatt down the street. After that, Angela had tried to leave, but he'd insisted she stay for just one more drink. She'd waited ten more minutes before saying she had to hit the ladies' room, excusing herself, and then slipping out of the restaurant.

Hurrying into the lobby of her office building, Angela figured she had about five more minutes before Kent caught on that she'd ditched him. She didn't see the night guard on duty as she hurried through the lobby to the garage elevator. She jabbed the button, and the door opened immediately. The building was older—with only three underground parking levels. Angela pressed C, leaned against the elevator wall, and caught her breath. The elevator let out a groan as it made its descent.

She'd get the "I told you so" look from her friends when she let them know about tonight with Kent. Well, she had it coming. After all, the guy was married. What was she thinking? *His poor wife . . .*

The overhead light in the elevator flickered for a second, and a little panic swept through her. She could feel the elevator still moving. It was just the light, and it was okay now. Still, that flickering unnerved her for a moment. She was grateful when the elevator stopped and the door whooshed open on Parking Level C. She stepped out of the elevator and started to hunt through her purse for her keys.

Whenever Angela went for drinks with friends after work, she always volunteered to drive people home—partly out of kindness, but also because she hated venturing down to this creepy garage alone late at night. It wasn't so bad in the morning and at quitting time, because there were other people around. But at this hour, she was the only one down here—at least she *hoped* she was the only one down here. There was no garage attendant on duty, just an emergency phone and a keypad device near the exit for a code that opened the garage door.

Angela found the car keys, and had them out and ready—even though she was still quite a ways from her car.

She'd never been in a submarine, but Angela was pretty certain it would be a lot like this gloomy, old parking garage—the low ceilings with so many exposed pipes, the gray walls and floor, little wire cages around the lights overhead—and yet it was still dark with shadowy nooks everywhere. A click, click, click from her high heels on the concrete floor echoed as she made her way to her Toyota Camry. She saw only two other cars on this level, and they looked as if they'd been there for weeks.

Angela quickened her pace as she approached her car. While unlocking the door, she glanced through the window into the backseat. No one. It was okay.

Climbing inside the car, she shut the door, locked it, and started up the ignition. She sighed. She wasn't usually this nervous, but that flickering light in the elevator had disturbed her—and then she couldn't shake the feeling something was wrong. That jerk, Kent, certainly wasn't worth all this angst. It was what she got for succumbing to his "you're so beautiful" line.

Angela shifted to Drive and pressed on the accelerator.

The car started to move, but then it lurched forward. All at once, the left rear side slammed down on the garage floor with a loud bang. Angela gasped at the sudden jolt. The car's left underside scraped across the concrete, and a severe grating noise reverberated through the garage.

Panic-stricken, she stomped on the brake. The car skidded for a second, then stopped.

Angela's heart pounded furiously, and she tried to catch her breath. She heard a tinny clattering sound. Out her window, she saw her hubcap rolling across the garage floor—five spaces over. She glanced in her side mirror. "Jesus Mary Joseph," she gasped.

The back tire had fallen off. A thin haze of smoke crept up from beneath the car. Angela quickly switched off the ignition.

"Okay, Angie, calm down," she murmured to herself. Unlocking the door, she stepped out of the Camry. She was a little shaky on her feet. She stared at her crippled, lopsided car—at all the mangled steel and structural damage around where the tire used to be. "What the hell?" she said under her breath.

She pulled her wallet from her purse, and found her AAA card. Then she took out her cell phone and dialed. No answer. She couldn't get through, and realized there wasn't any reception down here on the garage's bottom level.

She remembered the emergency phone by the garage door. But that was three floors up, and she wanted to get out of this creepy garage. Angela decided to try AAA again from the lobby. She was still shaking. She took a deep breath and started toward the elevator bay.

But she heard something, and stopped. The elevator let out a *ding*, and the door whooshed open.

Angela couldn't quite see the elevator from where she stood—only part of the annex. She waited for someone to emerge from that alcove. She listened for footsteps. But there was nothing.

"Hello?" she called. "Is anyone there? I could use some help. Hello?"

No reply.

Angela was afraid to take another step. Paralyzed, she gazed at the alcove and saw a shadow moving.

"Who's there?" she called.

The shadow swept across the gray wall by the elevator area, then disappeared.

"Who's there?" she repeated, louder this time. But her voice quivered.

Again, no response.

Unnerved, Angela retreated back to her disabled car. She ducked inside and quickly locked the door. She couldn't quite see the elevator bay from the front seat of her car, but she kept her gaze fixed in that direction. She was still trembling as she pulled out her cell phone again and dialed Triple-A. No luck. She gave her brother's number a shot. Nothing. She even tried Kent's cell, figuring at least he was close. But her phone just wasn't working.

All of the sudden, she caught sight of someone out of the corner of her eye—just as he tapped on her window. Angela let out a startled yelp. A hand over her heart, she gaped at the handsome janitor standing on the other side of her window. He gave her a sheepish smile. "Looks like you could use some help!" he said loudly—so she could hear him inside the car.

Angela immediately felt embarrassed for gasping. Still, she didn't roll her window down more than a few inches to talk to him. "Ah, yeah. I was trying to call Triple-A, but my cell phone doesn't work down here."

He walked over toward the back of her car and collected some articles from the garage floor. "Lug nuts," he said, studying them in his hand. "They couldn't have all gotten loose at the same time. I don't mean to scare you, but it looks like someone sabotaged your car."

Angela sighed. "Well, I'm pretty scared enough already. That's why I'm sitting in here with the door locked."

He nodded. "Smart. The kook who did this could still be hanging around here." He stepped back and took another look at the left rear side of her Camry. Then he returned to her window. "If you have a jack in the trunk, I'll raise her up and put the tire back on for you. But I think you're better off getting a tow. Looks like a lot of damage back there."

Angela just nodded. She still kept the door locked and the window up most of the way. She'd never seen this janitor before, and it was strange how he'd shown up just when he had. Still, he was friendly enough—and quite attractive. And there was no one else offering to help her.

"We can go up to the lobby, and I'll keep you company until the tow arrives," he offered. "I don't know the night watchman very well. I'm new here. But he strikes me as kind of squirrelly. I wouldn't trust him if I were you."

She hesitated. "Well, if it's not too much trouble . . ."

"Trouble?" he said. "Are you kidding me? I know this is a nightmare for you, but it's a lonely night janitor's dream come true. I get to help a beautiful woman out of a jam."

Smiling up at him, Angela felt herself blushing. She unlocked the door.

He opened it for her. Angela grabbed her purse and stepped out of the car. He closed the door after her. "You're going to think this is a line," he said. "But you look really, really familiar."

She shrugged. "You've probably seen me around in the building."

"No, that's not it," the custodian said. "I just started working here a few nights ago."

They headed toward the elevator alcove. Angela glanced back at her disabled Camry. "Will it be okay there?"

He nodded. "I don't think anyone's coming down here any time soon—except for the tow, God willing." He took a few more steps, and then stopped abruptly. "Wait a minute. I know where I've seen you before. Weren't you on TV a while back? That *Movers & Shakers* story from *On the Edge*? I remember now . . ."

Angela let out a little laugh. "So—you saw that, huh?"

"God, yes." The handsome janitor snapped his fingers. "Y'know, I didn't make the connection. But now I realize—it happened in this building. When I first hired on here, the woman in personnel told me an employee here tried to commit suicide a while back. He climbed out to the ledge on the fourteenth floor, or something. But I didn't connect it to you—and that *Movers & Shakers* story. I can't believe it's you. This is amazing! You're the one who talked him back inside. You saved that guy's life."

Angela felt embarrassed—and yet also excited that he'd recognized her from her one and only TV appearance, nine months ago.

"It's no big deal," Angela told him. "I really didn't do much."

Most of what had happened was a blur when she tried to remember it now.

But she remembered Archie. He'd been the nervous, nerdy, high-strung office clerk. Archie's biggest responsibility was running the copy machine, and he routinely screwed that up. He was in his mid thirties with pale skin, greasy brown hair, and a slight paunch. Angela used to think he could have been good-looking with a makeover, some crunches, and a new wardrobe that *didn't* include clip-on ties and short-sleeve shirts. Angela's friends at the firm used to tease her because Archie had a crush on her.

That Friday nine months ago, she'd heard during lunch that Archie was being fired—after only six weeks on the job. Angela felt sorry for him. He was such a loser, the poor guy.

She was emerging from the restroom when a fellow paralegal ran up to her. "My God, Archie's on the ledge! He climbed out the window in Weymiller's office. He's gonna jump!"

One of the younger lawyers was racing down the hallway. "I called 9-1-1!" he yelled. "Jesus, I don't know how he got out there . . ."

Mr. Weymiller came around the corner, and he motioned at her. "Angie, thank God! Listen, we need you to talk to Archie until the police get here. He likes you—"

"But wait a minute!" she cried, confused. "What do you expect me to say to him?"

That was when the whole thing became a blur—all these people talking and screaming at her at once—someone pulling her toward Weymiller's office; and then leaning out that window while Mr. Weymiller held her around the waist so she wouldn't fall. She remembered the chilly November wind whipping through her hair, and Archie, tears streaming down his face as he clung to the side of the building. His ugly fake tie flapped in the breeze. The whole time, Angie tried not to look down—fourteen stories to the traffic below on Michigan Avenue. Car horns were honking and a siren wailed in the distance. But mostly she just heard the wind and her own voice as she tried to talk to Archie.

She didn't even remember what she said exactly. She fought her vertigo and just kept talking. All the while she was terrified that at any minute Archie might leap off the ledge.

Angela found out later from her coworkers what she'd

said. Sydney Jordan had interviewed them for *Movers & Shakers*. Apparently, she'd told Archie about the times when she felt lost, lonely—and even suicidal—only to feel better days later. She'd claimed that she would really miss him, and had been hoping to stay in touch with him after he stopped working there at the law firm. She'd asked him several times to come in off the ledge and admitted to him that she was very, very scared.

Angela didn't remember any of it.

She had no idea how long she'd been half-hanging out of that fourteenth-floor window. She hadn't realized when the police arrived—or when the traffic below stopped on Michigan Avenue. She hadn't noticed the man in the building across the way, recording the whole thing on his cell phone's video camera.

That dramatic footage was later shown on the news and in the *Movers & Shakers* segment.

"What I do remember," Angela told Sydney Jordan for the piece, "is never losing eye contact with Archie. I just held my breath when he finally started to make his way toward me. I prayed and prayed he wouldn't slip. Then I finally grabbed his hand. I nearly collapsed when we pulled him back inside. I was just so relieved."

She didn't tell Sydney how the cops on the scene had pounced on Archie once he'd climbed back through that window. They'd grabbed him and started frisking him. And someone else had whisked her away.

On the *Movers & Shakers* segment, she'd wished Archie well. But she hadn't seen him since that Friday afternoon in November, nine months ago.

"So—what was Sydney Jordan like?" the janitor asked. "I've always figured her as kind of a phony."

Having been lost in thought, Angela blinked at him and smiled. "Actually, she's just the opposite—very nice, very genuine."

They started toward the elevator annex again. The janitor didn't say anything, and for a few moments, there was just the click, click, click of her high heels. They turned into the alcove, and she noticed him pull out his janitor keys. He stepped up to the service elevator and inserted a key into some mechanism and then pressed the button.

Angela wondered why they didn't just ring for the regular elevator, but figured he was probably accustomed to using this one. She didn't say anything.

He nodded to the service elevator door. "This will take us all the way to the roof if we want. The other one just goes as far as the lobby."

"But we only need to go as far as the lobby," she pointed out.

"I know," he nodded. "Tell me something. Do you know whatever happened to that guy you saved?"

Angela gave an uneasy shrug. "Last I heard he was still in the hospital with all sorts of mental problems. It's really very sad."

The handsome janitor frowned. "Kind of makes you wonder if he'd have been better off jumping." He turned toward her. "Ever stop to think maybe you shouldn't have interfered?"

Bewildered, Angela stared at him.

A *ding* sounded, and the elevator door opened. "Here we are," the janitor announced.

Angela hesitated for a moment, but then he took hold of her arm and guided her into the cubicle, which was lined with heavy, quilted, dark gray blankets—the kind movers used to wrap up antiques.

She watched him press the button for the fourteenth floor, then he pulled out the key again and switched on the Express lock.

"Wait . . ." Angela said, just as the door shut. She turned toward him. "I thought we were going to the lobby."

The elevator made a humming noise as it started its ascent.

The janitor stared at her, his eyes narrowed. "No, we're going to fourteen," he said coolly. "I didn't fuck up your car so we'd go only as far as the lobby."

Angela shook her head. "Oh, God no—" she cried, recoiling.

But he still had ahold of her arm. He suddenly twisted it around her back.

Angela let out a shriek.

He slapped his hand over her mouth. She struggled, but he was too strong for her. It felt as if he were about to snap off her arm.

Helplessly, she watched the illuminated numbers above the elevator door as they climbed higher and higher.

"You're going up to fourteen, Angela," he whispered, his lips brushing against her ear. "You're going back to that same ledge. But you won't be there very long."

She frantically dug into her purse for her cell phone. Twenty-six-year-old Dominique Chandler walked at a brisk clip down Michigan Avenue. Attractive, with close-cropped hair and a flawless cocoa-colored complexion, she was accustomed to guys coming on to her and making passes. But this was too much.

She'd just left the Hyatt bar, her favorite after-work watering hole. She wore a sexy red wraparound dress. A couple of guys had hit on her in the Hyatt's bar, but she wasn't interested. She'd had her fill of happy hour hors d'oeuvres and cocktails, and said good night to her coworkers at 10:15. She'd wanted to catch the 10:24 CTA.

She'd walked only a block in the direction of her bus stop when she'd heard someone call to her: "Hey, wait up, pretty baby!"

Dominique had furtively glanced back at the pest but hadn't gotten a good look. If the police asked later about the man who had attacked her, she could only say that he was a tall, skinny white guy with black hair.

"Hey, baby, don't you tease me!" he yelled, following her. "I know you want it, bitch!"

Dominique had the cell phone in her hand now. She was walking even faster. She hoped there would be people at her bus stop—but that was three more blocks.

"Leave me alone!" she screamed—as loud as she could. She pressed the button to activate her cell phone.

"Dominique?" he called. "Dominique, wait up!"

She wondered how the hell he knew her name. But she didn't slow down. Her thumb was already pressing 9-1-1 on the cell phone's keypad. She broke into a sprint and was about to cross the street.

"Dominique, it's me, Zack!" she heard him yell. "I'm just messing with you, for God's sake!"

She glanced over her shoulder and suddenly realized her tormentor was actually a pal from work, Zack, the cute young guy in the mailroom. Dominique stopped near the curb in front of an older, eighteen-story building on Michigan Avenue. She swiveled around. "Oh, my God, Zack!" she screamed, laughing. "I was about to call the cops on your ass. You scared the shit out of me, you son of a—"

Before she could finish, Dominique heard a piercing scream from above.

She looked up to see something descending on her. She almost stumbled into the street as she backed up to avoid it. Dominique dropped her cell phone.

With a loud, hollow thump, the body hit the pavement a few feet in front of her. Dominique was splattered with the woman's blood.

She shrieked.

* * *

Fourteen stories up, the man dressed as a janitor didn't have a drop of blood on him.

He had kept his word to Angela Gannon. She hadn't been on the ledge for very long.

CHAPTER EIGHT

Sydney had no desire whatsoever to drive twenty-five miles to the grand opening of a ValuCo store in Auburn, but she was one of four local celebrities scheduled to appear at the event. That Saturday afternoon, they were throwing a fun fair in the store's parking lot, and there would be a food court, too. All the profits were going to charity.

She'd practically browbeaten Eli into going with her. It was ironic, too, because she was always feeling guilty for not spending enough time with him—and here she was, forcing him to spend time with her. She was dressed—*"fun/casual"* the publicist's memo recommended—in a dark blue sleeveless top and white capri pants, and ready to go. But Eli was still up in his room, getting ready.

While waiting, Sydney retrieved their mail and sat down at the dining room table. A bill, two credit card offers, *Entertainment Weekly*, a personal letter/card from someone with a Portland, Oregon, address, and a letter from Joe.

Sydney felt a little pang in her stomach as she recognized his handwriting. It was addressed to her, not Eli.

Some slightly masochistic part of her decided not to open Joe's note first. Or maybe she was just too proud to admit to herself how much she still cared. Whatever the motive, she tore open the envelope with the Portland address first. Inside was a white card with silver embossed fancy script that said *"Thank You"* on the cover. Sydney opened the card. The penmanship was somewhat sloppy, but decipherable:

Dear Sydney,

Thank you so much for your kind note about Leah & Jared. It brought comfort to all of us at this very difficult time. Leah was so very fond of you. The video short you made about our daughter & Jared is a beautiful tribute to them that we will cherish always. Thank you also for the lovely flower arrangement. Your thoughts & prayers are very much appreciated.

With Kindest Regards,
Peggy & Robert Dvorak

Sydney was touched by the note and surprised at how quickly Leah's parents wrote back to her. But she was confused, too. She'd mailed them a card on July 5th, but hadn't sent any flowers. She figured someone at the network must have sent the flowers in her name.

For the last seven nights, she'd checked the Internet for any possible new developments in the police investigation into Leah and Jared's deaths. But there was nothing.

Sydney now wished she'd opened Joe's letter first, because it still mattered—too much—what he had to say, even after reading this heartbreaking note from a woman whose daughter was just murdered a week ago. She was still thinking about Joe.

She had no idea why he was writing to her. Was he begging her to come back? She didn't dare hope for that. If he truly missed her, he would have let her know by now.

Sydney opened the envelope and pulled out a folded piece of paper. It was his stationery from work—with

Chicago Police Department printed along the top, beside the star-badge logo. The first thing she thought was, *it looks so damn official*. Sydney started reading:

Dear Sydney,

While these past six weeks have been very hard for me, I realize you were right to take Eli and move to Seattle. You & I are better off apart for a while. This separation is the best thing for us right now.

We haven't discussed divorce yet, and I hope we can keep the situation status quo for a few more weeks. I need this break from you & Eli. Thank you for not trying to contact me. I don't know if you even wanted to, but you've made the right choice with your silence.

I hope you & Eli are doing well.

Joe

P.S. Your dentist's office called. You & Eli are both scheduled for teeth cleaning on 7/14. I went ahead & canceled.

"Asshole," she murmured, her eyes filling with tears. Could he have been any colder and passionless? He never even mentioned missing her or Eli. She felt as if he'd just sucker-punched her in the gut. The son of a bitch wanted to *keep the situation status quo?*

She started to cry, and crumpled the letter in her fist. But then she heard Eli—jumping from the top step to the first landing, and then again from the first landing to the second landing.

Sydney quickly wiped her eyes.

"Can I at least check out some of the rides while you're

giving your speech?" he asked, stepping into the dining room. "I don't have to be up on some stage with you, do I?"

Sydney stashed the crumpled letter back in its envelope. But she was too late; he'd already seen the envelope and no doubt recognized his father's handwriting.

"Hey, is that a letter from Dad?" he asked eagerly.

Sydney pressed the envelope to her chest. "It's for me, okay? It doesn't concern you." She glanced at Eli and frowned. "That's the same shirt you wore yesterday, and it has a stain on it. Go upstairs and put on a clean shirt. Okay, honey? Please?"

Eli rolled his eyes at her, shook his head, and then retreated toward the stairs. "Jeez, fine," he muttered.

"And could you hurry it up a little?" she called after him. "We're going to be late."

Sydney wiped her eyes again, then turned in her chair, opened the bottom drawer of the built-in breakfront, and stashed Joe's note under some papers. It was already becoming a junk drawer—with their lease, some stuff from her new bank, and insurance. There were also receipts from the furniture stores and appliance shops. Sydney figured he wouldn't go looking for his father's letter in there. She didn't want him to find it—and read it.

She didn't want Eli to know that his dad was an uncaring son of a bitch.

Eli had paused on the stairway at the first landing. There was a mirror on the living room wall that allowed him to see around the corner into the dining room. Frowning, he watched his mother hide the letter from his dad in the built-in breakfront's bottom drawer.

* * *

"That was a letter from Dad, wasn't it?" Eli asked.

"Yes, it was," Sydney admitted. She looked over her shoulder as she backed the car out of the shelter. "But like I told you before, it doesn't concern you, honey."

"Well, I don't get it. Why don't you want me to see the letter?"

Shifting into drive, she heaved an exasperated sigh. "Eli, what part of *it doesn't concern you* is failing to register here? Could you hit the button for the gate, please?"

Frowning, he poked at the automatic gate-opening device, which was clipped onto the passenger sun visor.

"Thanks," Sydney said, slowing down while the driveway gate slowly opened. "Honey, it's a personal letter—addressed to me. When your dad writes to you, I don't ask to read it, do I?"

"I figured that's because you don't care," he said, folding his arms.

"I do care," she said emphatically. The gate was finally open, and she pulled forward. "But I also respect your privacy. What's between you and your father is none of my—"

A man walked out in front of them. Sydney slammed on her brake, and the car's tires let out a screech. At the same time, her arm shot out to brace Eli. The gate-opening device fell off the sun visor and landed in Eli's lap.

Catching her breath, Sydney gaped at the stranger. He was in his late twenties with black hair, a swarthy complexion, and a lean build. He wore a navy blue T-shirt with a silver *59* stenciled across the front of it. As he glared at her, Sydney noticed something was wrong with one of his eyes—a broken blood vessel or something. The white part was all red.

"I'm sorry!" Sydney called.

But he shook his head and kept moving.

"Well, if looks could kill, I'd be six feet under right now," she mumbled.

"I didn't see him," Eli said, clipping the gate-opening device back onto the sun visor.

"This trip's off to a great start," she muttered, turning onto the street. "Anyway, thanks for coming along, Eli. I really didn't want to do this thing alone."

"Who are the other celebrities there?" he asked, slouching in the passenger seat.

"They've got David Beckham, J-Lo, Brad Pitt, Angelina Jolie, and me."

Eli stared at her. "Yeah, right."

"Okay, it's Gil Sessions from *PM Magazine,* Terri Tatum from *What's Cooking, Seattle?,* that obnoxious guy who does the weather for channel 6, and moi." Sydney watched the road ahead. "Tell you what. When we get there, I'll give you twenty-five bucks, and you can go on as many rides as you want. Just don't throw up. Is it a deal?"

He didn't say anything. Eli's short hair fluttered in the wind as he pensively gazed out the window. He looked so sad.

"What's going on?" she asked. "What are you thinking?"

"Don't you miss Dad?" he asked quietly.

"Of course I miss him."

"Then why can't we go home?

She tightened her grip on the steering wheel and watched the traffic ahead on Madison Street. "We've been through this before, Eli. It's not as easy as that. There are a lot of reasons why your dad and I are apart right now. None of it has to do with you. We both love you very much. That hasn't changed at all. You continue to drive us crazy, and we continue to love you."

Sydney glanced over at him. He didn't even crack a smile.

She reached over and patted his shoulder. "I'm kidding," she said. "Eli, honey, for the umpteenth time, the problem is between your dad and me. It's the kind of stuff we might discuss with a marriage counselor, but not with our son. So—please, quit asking. Even if your dad and I resolve things, and we move back to Chicago, I'm still not telling you what's private between your dad and me."

"If we go home to Dad, I won't ask anymore."

But he doesn't want us back, she thought. Joe had told her so in his letter, "I need this break from you and Eli." But she couldn't repeat that to their son.

What was she supposed to tell him?

It had started four months ago with a phone call from *Polly*. Usually, she and Joe screened their calls. But that Tuesday night back in March, Joe had gone out on a special assignment, which could have been anything from what he called "desk-jockey duty" to busting a narcotics ring. Whenever he was out on a special assignment she worried about him and always answered the phone—even when the Caller ID read UNKNOWN. She ended up having to talk with a lot of telemarketers on those dreaded nights. So when the call came in UNKNOWN at 9:20 that evening, Sydney snatched up the receiver. "Yes, hello?" she said.

"Joe McCloud?" the man said, sounding haggard and edgy. "Is Joe McCloud there?"

"I'm sorry. He can't come to the phone right now," Sydney said. "Who's calling?"

"This is a friend of his. If he's there, tell him Polly's on the phone. I really need to talk to him."

"Well, as I said, he can't come to the phone, but if you'll leave me your number—"

"Is this Mrs. McCloud?"

"Yes—"

"Listen, Mrs. McCloud, I gotta talk to him *now*. He's not picking up on his cell. So you know how I can reach him?"

She didn't like hearing that Joe wasn't answering his cell right now. "Um, no. Do you want to leave a number?"

"Jesus," he muttered. "I'm in a phone booth. I lost my cell, and can't go home. It isn't safe. They're probably . . ." he trailed off. "Um, listen, have Joe call me at home and leave a number where I can reach him, okay? It's urgent. I'll keep checking my voice mail. This is Polly. He knows my home number, but—but let me give it to you anyway. Got a piece of paper?"

Sydney copied it down: *Call Polly—773-555-4159*. "I'll give him the message," she told the man.

"Thanks, Mrs. McCloud," he said. "You're a nice lady." Then he hung up.

She tried Joe on his cell, but Polly was right. He wasn't picking up. She left Joe a message about Polly's call. "And after you phone this Polly guy," she said, "buzz me and let me know you're all right."

Then Sydney hung up and waited.

Two excruciating hours later, Joe phoned to say he was on his way home. He'd been on some kind of surveillance project. "Same old, same old, a waste of time," he reported.

"Did you call that Polly person?" she asked him on the phone.

"That's a waste of time, too," he replied. "Honey, don't you know the score by now? How many times have I told you to hang up on calls like that?"

"He sounded like he was in trouble," Sydney said.

"These jokers are in trouble all the time. He was probably stoned. Did he sound like he was high?"

"He sounded scared," she replied.

"A lot of them are paranoid. If he ever calls again, just hang up on him."

He called again—two nights later. Joe was home, watching *My Name Is Earl* with Eli. Sydney was washing the dinner dishes when the phone rang. She checked the caller ID: 773-555-4159—ARTHUR POLLARD.

Though she didn't recognize the name or remember the number, Sydney picked up. "Yes, hello?"

"Mrs. McCloud?" said the man on the other end of the line. "It's Polly—from the other night? Remember me? Is Joe home tonight? I really gotta talk to him."

She hesitated. "Um, I—I'll see if he can come to the phone. Hold on for a second." Sydney put down the receiver, and hurried into the family room, where they'd switched off most of the lights. Joe, in sweatpants and a Chicago Bulls T-shirt, was in his recliner. Eli was stretched out on the floor in front of the TV. They were both laughing.

"Honey, there's a call for you," Sydney said. "It's that Polly character who called on Tuesday night."

Joe glanced at her, and the smile ran away from his face. Getting to his feet, he brushed past her on his way out of the room. "I'll take it in my office," he muttered. "Can you hang it up for me, babe?"

Sydney listened to him lumbering up to the second floor. His office was a small room at the top of the stairs. She went back to the kitchen, picked up the receiver, and listened. "Okay, I got it, thanks," Joe said on the other extension.

Sydney hung up, and then wandered over to the bottom of the stairs. She could hear Joe talking quietly, but the words were undecipherable. Only once did he raise his voice. *"Polly, I'm sorry!"* he said loudly. *"Goddamn it, I'm in no position. . . ."*

She didn't feel right eavesdropping. Retreating to the darkened family room, she stood in the doorway and watched TV with Eli. A minute later, she heard Joe come down the steps. Sydney glanced over her shoulder at him. "So—was he a crank?" she asked, under her breath.

"He has no business calling here," Joe growled. "If he calls again, hang up on him."

He settled back down in his lounge chair. Something happened on the show that sent Eli into fits of laughter. Sydney glanced over at her husband—the light from the TV flickered across his handsome face. He didn't even smile.

Polly didn't call again.

The following Saturday morning—two days later—a headline on page three of *The Chicago Tribune* caught her eye. Sydney read the newspaper every morning for any human interest stories that might make for a good *Movers & Shakers* segment. She didn't know why she decided to read the article. It wasn't exactly the kind of subject matter she covered in her *Movers & Shakers* reports:

SHOOTING VICTIM FOUND IN WOODLAWN DUMPSTER

Murder Could Be Drug-Related, Say Police

CHICAGO: Rochelle Johnson, 23, a clerk at E-Zee Mart Liquor on Martin Luther King Drive, made a grisly discovery Friday afternoon while emptying the garbage in a Dumpster behind the store. "I saw this hand sticking out of a big garbage bag," said Johnson, who immediately called the police.

Arriving at the scene at 3:20 P.M., Chicago police found the body of a Cicero man, Arthur Pollard, 30. He had been shot three times. Early reports from the Cook County Coroner's Office estimate that Pollard had been killed sometime between midnight and 7 A.M. Friday.

Pollard, a part-time bartender at Anthony's Cha-Cha Lounge in Cicero, was well known to Chicago Police. Since 2001, he had been arrested nine times and convicted twice . . .

The article went on to list Arthur Pollard's criminal record, which included a stint in Illinois State Penitentiary in Joliet for breaking and entering, and another at Stateville Correctional Center for possession of narcotics with intent to sell. The narcotic in this case was heroin. Most of Arthur Pollard's arrests were drug-related.

According to the article, the police were following several leads.

Sydney wondered if Joe was involved in the investigation. If so, why didn't he say anything to her? She couldn't get over the fact that Polly had phoned their home Thursday night at eight o'clock, and a few hours later, he was dead—with three bullets in him.

Joe was cleaning out their garage that Saturday morning. He was always in there; they probably had the cleanest garage on North Spaulding Avenue.

Sydney threw on a sweater and took the newspaper outside with her. She found Joe on a ladder, rearranging boxes of Christmas decorations on the top shelf of a storage area he'd built in the garage. "Honey, did you know about this?" she asked.

"Know about what, babe?" he replied, climbing down the step ladder.

She gave him the folded *Tribune*, and pointed to the article at the bottom of page three. "Isn't that the guy who called here the other night?"

He glanced at the article for a few moments. Then he sighed, and handed the newspaper back to her. "Yeah, I heard about it yesterday afternoon. I knew sooner or later that sorry son of a bitch would get himself killed." He glanced at his wristwatch. "It's a quarter to eleven. When does Eli need to be picked up at school?"

"Basketball practice goes until 11:30," she answered numbly. "You've got plenty of time."

Joe folded up the ladder and leaned it against the wall. "Think I'll grab a shower."

Sydney looked at the newspaper again. "So why did he call here the other night?"

"Who?" Joe asked, wiping his hands on his pants.

"Arthur Pollard . . . *Polly,*" she said. "I keep thinking about how scared he sounded. When he called the first time, he was afraid to go home."

Joe kissed her cheek as he walked past her. "Honey, I deal with this kind of stuff all the time at work. The guy was thirty-one flavors of trouble, and most of it he'd brought on himself. You shouldn't let it concern you."

"But he called here, Joe. It sounded like he wanted your help. Did he—"

"Can we just drop it?" Joe said, cutting her off. He shook his head. "Christ on a crutch, it's the weekend. I don't want to think about this shit right now. And it doesn't even concern you."

Her mouth open, she watched him turn away and stomp into the house.

Sydney remembered thinking at the time that Joe was hiding something from her, something horrible.

"It doesn't concern you."

She used that same line whenever Eli asked why she and his father were apart now. Funny, she hadn't been satisfied with that answer. She'd gone behind Joe's back, and started digging up what she could about Arthur "Polly" Pollard. And what she'd found wrecked their lives.

What in the world made her think "It doesn't concern you" would work on Eli?

She glanced at her son in the passenger seat. He'd put in his earphones and was listening to his iPod, completely tuning her out.

Sydney saw the temporary sign posted along Auburn's Highway 167. Balloons tied to the sign fluttered in the summer breeze:

VALUCO GRAND OPENING!
Fun Fair, Refreshments + Rides!
Celebrity Guests!
NEXT RIGHT

Sydney switched on her turn signal.

"Shit," she muttered, knowing Eli couldn't hear.

* * *

"I'm really thrilled to be here today," his mother announced. Thanks to the mike, her voice carried across ValuCo's vast parking area to the fun fair in the neighboring lot—over all the music, the people laughing and screaming, and the incessant honking of several car horns. Parking was a nightmare. His mom stood on a platform near the store's front entrance. Behind her sat the other local celebrities drafted into this shindig. They had some television news cameras aimed at her. Eli guessed about two thousand people were there, and among those, at least three hundred were listening to his mother. He wasn't one of them.

He clicked his iPod back on, and wandered across the lot to the fun fair. His mom had given him twenty-five bucks to go on as many rides as he wanted. He'd already tried their Crack the Whip roller-coaster ride, and it had been kind of scary at times—but not very fun alone, and certainly not worth five bucks. Plus he'd felt kind of pathetic, standing in line for ten minutes with no one to talk to, so he'd decided not to waste his money on any more rides.

The smell of hot dogs and ice cream waffle cones wafted through the air. The hot sun beat down on Eli as he wandered among all the strangers and listened to the Rolling Stones (his dad's favorite rock group) on his iPod. He roamed past toss-and-win booths, refreshment stands, and even a video game arcade tent. But none of it appealed to him. It just wasn't any fun doing that kind of stuff alone. He missed his friends—and he missed his dad terribly. It had been nearly seven weeks, and he still hadn't gotten over this homesickness. He still cried in bed some nights, but he buried his face in his pillow so his mom wouldn't hear. Weird, he didn't hesitate to convey his anger at her half the time, but he'd be damned if he let her know how sad he was. He didn't want her trying to comfort him. He knew he was acting like a jerk and didn't like himself very much for it. Still, Eli figured if he made his mom miserable enough, she'd finally give in and they'd go back home to Chicago. Then he'd get to sleep in his own bed again.

He stopped in front of a booth, where a gaunt woman sat at a card table, with a mangy-looking German shepherd curled up at her feet. Eli guessed she was about fifty years old. She had black hair and a pale, ruddy complexion. She wore sunglasses and puffed on a cigarette. There was something witchlike about her appearance. Eli wondered if she was blind—what with the dark glasses and the dog; plus one of the lower buttons of her purple blouse wasn't fastened in the right hole. The sign along the top of the booth read:

PSYCHIC READER
Love? Career? Happiness?
Answers about Your Past, Present & Future
Ask MARCELLA – $5.00 a sitting

Eli switched off his iPod and took out his earpieces. His mother wasn't talking anymore. Now he heard some man's voice booming from the ValuCo parking lot.

He stared up at the psychic woman's sign. He certainly had some questions about his future. But the lady's name was kind of weird. Wasn't *Marcella* a certain breed of chicken or something? And five bucks? It sounded like a rip-off. Still, he felt sorry for the lady, because she was blind.

"For five dollars, I'll tell your future!" the woman called to him.

Startled that the lady could actually see—and she was addressing him—Eli quickly shook his head and started to move on.

"I'll give you a discount!" the woman persisted. "I'll read your fortune for only three dollars. I can see you have many questions!"

"I'm sorry, thanks anyway!" Eli replied. But he paused for a moment.

"C'mon in, and I'll give you a free reading," she called, waving him into the booth. "It's slow anyway." As she raised her voice, the old German shepherd slowly got up on its feet to see what the hubbub was about. "Sit!" Marcella said.

Eli wasn't sure if she was talking to him or the dog, but he stepped around the front counter and sat down in the folding chair across from her. It was hot in the tent booth, and smelled like cigarettes. Sitting this close to Marcella, he could see she was sweating. "When were you born?" she asked.

"August 29th, 1995," he answered.

"Virgo," she said, stubbing out her cigarette and reaching for his hand. "Your planet is Mercury. I should have known you were Virgo the minute you said, 'No thanks,' to me. You didn't want the strange lady to read your fortune. You're cautious, a classic Virgo trait. You're also intelligent, but a bit too critical of other people." She studied his hand—both sides, as if it were a piece of fish in the marketplace. "Relax," she said, focusing on his palm now. "You have a long life line, but there are several breaks—many different lives. You'll be doing some traveling in the near future . . ."

Eli wondered if that meant they'd be moving back to Chicago soon. Or was that just some standard line she gave everyone?

"You're going through a lot of changes right now, difficult times, but you should be okay."

Once again, he wondered if she was really seeing something, or if she was giving him the same reading she'd use on any teenager. *Lots of changes, difficult times*, well, sure, duh.

She looked up from his palm and into his eyes.

It made Eli nervous to be scrutinized like this. He was aware every time he blinked. The German shepherd, curled up on the floor, wagged his tail and it slapped against Eli's feet.

This close, he could see Marcella's eyes narrowing behind the dark glasses. "You're an only child, aren't you?"

He nodded.

She kept staring at him. "You have three letters in your first name," she said finally.

Eli felt the hair stand on the back of his neck. "Yes. My name's Eli."

She just nodded, very matter-of-fact. Then she held her hand directly over his head for a few moments. "You're in touch with the spirit world, aren't you?" she asked.

Eli hesitated before he said anything. He thought about the ghost—or maybe *ghosts*—in their apartment; the former occupant who killed her teenage son and then herself.

"Yes—yes, you are . . . very spiritual," she said, answering for him. She suddenly pulled her hand back, as if she'd touched something extremely hot. The German shepherd lifted his head from the ground for a moment.

"What is it?" Eli asked. "Do you see something that's going to happen to me in the future?"

"It's been happening to you for a while now. But you've been very secretive about it."

Eli shifted a bit in the folding chair. What was he being secretive about? He wondered if she was talking about all the time he spent whacking off lately. Maybe she could see that he was a major pervert or something. He broke eye contact with her to glance at the people passing by Marcella's booth. He saw these two older teenage girls pass by. They glanced at him, whispered something to each other, and then laughed. Eli felt embarrassed. He turned his attention back to Marcella.

He figured she was just jerking him around, waiting for him to reveal something about himself so she could claim she'd seen his *aura* or something. "I don't know what you're talking about," he said finally. "What do you think has been happening to me?"

"You already know, Eli," Marcella said, staring at him from behind those dark glasses. She took hold of his hand again. "Someone dead is communicating with you."

* * *

"I have one last question here—and it's for Sydney Jordan!" Gil Sessions announced, checking an index card. Gil, the host of *PM Magazine*, was the MC at this event. After everyone had their brief "it's great to be here" speech, they had to answer questions certain audience members had written down ahead of time. As he read off the queries, Gil asked the questioner to raise his or her hand. But only about half of those people were still in the area. The rest had obviously lost interest in the celebrity appearances and wandered into the store or to the fun fair in the neighboring lot. It made the interview session pretty pointless, but Sydney, Terri Tatum of *What's Cooking, Seattle?,* and the obnoxious weatherman from Channel 6 had bravely gone through the motions. Sydney had kept her responses humorous and brief.

"This question's from Tammy Milsap of Federal Way," Gil announced. "Tammy, are you out there? Tammy?"

From the audience, a pretty blond woman waved.

"Hi, Tammy, looking good!" Gil said into his handheld microphone. Then he turned to Sydney and glanced at the index card. "Sydney, Tammy would like to know: *'Are you and your family making the Seattle area your new home?'"* He glanced up from the card. "Your husband is a Chicago police detective, isn't that right?"

Seated between the Channel 6 weatherman and Miss *What's Cooking, Seattle?* Sydney kept a smile plastered on her face and got to her feet. She moved to the standing mike at the front of the platform. She'd already developed a standard answer to questions about her recent move to Seattle sans her handsome, hero-cop husband. The topic had already come up a few times—in interviews with *Seattle Magazine, The Seattle Times,* and some online articles. "That's right, Gil," Sydney said into the mike. "Joe's a Chicago cop, and obviously, he doesn't work undercover."

This got a few chuckles from the crowd. Sydney scanned

the sea of faces for Eli, but she didn't see him. "I'm originally from Seattle, so I've always thought of this area as my home. My son and I are here for the summer, not a bad time to escape the sweltering Chicago heat . . ." Sydney hated lying to all these people in front of her son. She kept expecting to see Eli's scowling face among the crowd. Instead, she saw someone else. "Um, Joe, my husband, he might be joining us next month—if he can get away from his—um, police work. . . ."

She couldn't take her eyes off the lean, swarthy man with sunglasses and a baseball hat. He stood a few yards away. A woman directly in front of him stepped aside for a moment. Now Sydney could see his blue T-shirt—with a silver *59* on the front of it.

She froze at the microphone.

An hour ago—and thirty some-odd miles back in Seattle—she'd almost plowed into that man in her driveway. And now he was here, watching her. At least, she was almost certain it was the same man. The T-shirt was definitely the same. Had he followed them all this way from their apartment complex?

"Sydney?" Gil said into his mike. He chuckled. "Did we lose you for a second, Sydney?"

She suddenly remembered to smile. "Um, I was just thinking, Gil—how great it is to be back in the Seattle area. There's no doubt about it, the Puget Sound area is one of the most beautiful places in this great country of ours. I've really missed it. Tammy, thanks for that question."

The crowd applauded. Sydney slinked back toward her chair. She'd sounded like an idiot. *This great country of ours?* What, was she running for office or something?

As she sat down, Sydney looked at the man again. Was he stalking her? Up until now, her being married to a cop had discouraged the stalker types. Then again, maybe her minor-celebrity status just hadn't warranted stalkers—until this

Number 59 guy. She couldn't get over the fact that he'd followed her and Eli in their car for thirty miles. Why? She remembered his scowl as he'd passed in front of her car in the driveway. *"If looks could kill . . ."*

Sydney shifted in her chair. This guy obviously knew where they lived. He was hanging around there today. Had he been there on the night of July Fourth as well? Maybe he's the one who got inside their place. She had to remind herself to sit straight and keep smiling.

One small solace, as long as she could see the man, she knew he wasn't preying on Eli. But right now, Sydney wished she could see her son out there somewhere.

"Do you know who this dead person is?" Eli asked the psychic woman.

Gazing at him from behind her sunglasses, she held onto his hand and said nothing for a few moments.

Though the booth was open in front, no breeze came in—just heat. Eli began to sweat. Curled up under the table, her mangy dog's tail still slapped at his feet occasionally. Eli waited for Marcella to say something.

"Your father isn't—he isn't dead, is he?" she asked finally.

Eli shook his head. "No, my dad's fine."

"But he isn't with you. You're separated from him."

"Yeah," Eli replied, leaning forward in his chair. "But it's just temporary, and my dad isn't dead." He glanced at his own hand, trying to figure out what she was picking up from it. "Um, do you know who this dead person is I'm communicating with?"

Marcella touched his forehead, and her hand lingered there for a few moments. Her fingers smelled like an ashtray. Eli tried to sit still. He had a pretty good idea about this dead person. He just needed Marcella to confirm it for him.

Someone dead is communicating with you.

Eli had heard the muffled voices at night. They had seemed to come from within his bedroom walls. He'd felt the weight of some *other presence* sitting on his bed—or touching his cheek as he tried to fall asleep. Eli didn't need to overhear the neighbor woman talking the other day about the murder/suicide in their unit. He already knew a teenage boy had once lived in their unit—and met a violent death there.

Not long after a *second night visit*—during which, for a few minutes, Eli had been utterly certain someone had crept into his room—he'd finally gotten a night-light. He'd also gotten his mom to acknowledge that their apartment was indeed haunted. Not long after that, he'd bought a Frisbee and a Ouija board at a neighborhood yard sale. *Real smart.* In order to use either one, he needed another person. Except for his mom and his Uncle Kyle, he didn't even know anyone in Seattle. And he'd have rather been shot than be seen playing Frisbee with his *mother*.

His uncle wasn't a big Frisbee fan. "Eli, I'll give you ten dollars *not* to play Frisbee catch with you," his Uncle Kyle had told him. "That thing is a bent-back finger or a Marcia Brady broken nose just waiting to happen. I hate Frisbee."

That left the Ouija board. There wasn't much public humiliation in trying out the Ouija with his mother—in the privacy of their kitchen on a rainy afternoon a few weeks back. She asked lame questions like, "Should we go out for dinner tonight?" and "Will Eli have a girlfriend a year from now?" Both times, the Ouija's movable indicator (his mother said it was called a "planchette") gradually moved over to *YES*.

Then it was Eli's turn. They both had their hands on the planchette. Eli closed his eyes. "Are we going to move back to Chicago and be with Dad by August?"

The indicator didn't move. Eli opened his eyes to see his mom frowning. "Honey, I don't think it's such a good idea to ask that. I don't want you getting your hopes up."

"But I let you ask what you wanted!" he argued. "God, you're so unfair—"

"All right, all right," she sighed and rolled her eyes. "Ask it again."

Eli repeated the question, and he felt the indicator under his fingertips as it slowly inched over the board. "You're moving it," his mother said.

"I'm not, I swear!"

When the indicator ended up on *YES*, Eli shoved his fist in the air. "All right! We're gonna go back to Chicago and be with Dad!"

His mother winced, and shook her head again. "Eli, I told you, don't get your hopes up. This is just a game. It doesn't mean anything. Back when I was in junior high, my best friend Rachel Porter had an Ouija board. If what it told me turned out to be true, right now I'd be a millionaire, have an Olympic Gold Medal in figure-skating, and be happily married to Michael Schoeffling. This is just a game, honey."

"Who's Michael Schoeffling?" he asked, squinting.

"He played Jake in *16 Candles*, and I was in love with him." She set the disc back on START again. "Go ahead, and ask another question."

Eli rested his fingertips on the planchette again, then closed his eyes. "Who is the ghost in this house? What is his or her name?"

"Nope, no way," his mother said, shaking her head and pulling her chair away from the table. "We have enough *otherworldly* excitement around here. I think we should just leave it alone. I'm not up for a séance right now. Let's ask it something else. Ask for the name of this girlfriend you'll have."

"What? Are you scared?" he asked, laughing.

"Yes. I don't want to stir things up with whatever's *going on* around here," she admitted. "Bringing a Ouija board into the equation is taking too much of a chance. I don't want to push our luck. Some people believe Ouija boards can be dangerous. That's why I think you shouldn't ask it anything too serious. Call me a chicken, I don't care."

"A minute ago you were telling me it's just a game and it doesn't mean anything."

She got up from the table. "I'm sorry. I just don't feel like summoning the dead right now. Besides, we should wrap this up anyway. If we're going out to eat, you should wash up and change your clothes."

Eli stayed up late that night. He waited until his mother had gone to bed, then he pulled out the Ouija board. He felt so sneaky, almost like he was digging out the one *Playboy* he owned (bestowed on him by his best friend in Chicago, Brad Reece, who had inherited it from his college-age brother) from its hiding place in his desk's bottom drawer. His mother hadn't discovered the *Playboy* yet. And he didn't want her discovering him *summoning the dead* with the Ouija. He locked his bedroom door and then set the Ouija board on the spare bed.

Eli had two twin beds in his room. He didn't think he'd be living there long enough to make any friends—at least, no one he'd know well enough to invite overnight. He wondered why his mom had wasted her money on the extra bed. There was a lava lamp on his desk, and his Homer Simpson lamp on the nightstand. From his old bedroom he had a lighted Dad's Root Beer clock, two Chicago Bears posters, and another one from the Will Farrell movie *Anchorman*.

Eli also had a ghost, and he wanted to know more about it.

He sat on top of the spare bed, placed the movable indicator on the board's starting point, then gently rested his fingertips on it. "Does the *undead* person dwelling in this house have a name?" he whispered.

Eli listened for the muffled voices. He waited for the room to get warmer—always a sign he was about to have a *visit*. But he didn't hear or feel anything. All he heard were the waves rolling onto the shore at the nearby beach. He must have waited at least two or three minutes before the indicator started to move. He felt a chill race through him. He wasn't moving it. He expected it to gradually move over to the *YES* sign. Instead it started spelling something: *C-A-R-L*. Then the planchette moved to *GOOD BYE* at the bottom of the board.

"Carl?" Eli whispered. "Your name is Carl? Are you here right now?"

He closed his eyes this time, because he didn't want to cheat. When he felt the indicator move, Eli kept his eyes shut tight—until it stopped. He glanced at the board. He thought the indicator would be on *YES*, but it was on the letter *I*. Eli's hands started to shake, but he kept his fingertips on the indicator. The planchette inched over the board again—to the letter, *M,* and then to the word *GOOD BYE.*

"*I-M?*" Eli murmured. "Oh, my God, *'I am.'* You're here right now. Your name is Carl, and you're here with me now. Did you die in this house?"

Eli wasn't sure if it was his imagination, but it felt as if the room was getting warmer. The planchette seemed to move on its own now. He was barely touching it. Eli watched the indicator move to *YES*.

Eli didn't even wait for *GOOD BYE*. "Did you die in this room?" he asked.

The indicator moved to *YES* again.

"How old were you when you died?" Eli whispered.

Then the planchette seemed to stall on him. Finally Eli gave it a nudge toward the row of numbers. He knew he was cheating, so he closed his eyes. The first number the indicator stopped on was *1*. Then it moved to *4*, and then *GOOD BYE*.

A fourteen-year-old named Carl had died in this bedroom. "How?" Eli asked. "How did you die?"

The planchette slowly skimmed across the board to the

letter *L*, and then *A*. It seemed to take forever for it to move from letter to letter. After eight letters, Eli wondered if it was ever going to make sense: *L-A-C-E-R-A-T-I.* But the disc kept moving until it spelled out the word: *L-A-C-E-R-A-T-I-O-N*. Then it said *GOOD BYE*.

Eli climbed off the bed and went to his desk. He grabbed his Webster paperback dictionary, and looked up the word. He found something under lacerate. "To tear roughly," it said.

He glanced up at his Dad's Root Beer clock and realized it was 3:40 in the morning. The bedroom didn't feel so warm anymore. Eli figured that last *GOOD BYE* from Carl would be for a while.

His mother was wrong about the Ouija. Instead of stirring up their ghost, that long session with the Ouija board seemed to have made *Carl* more docile. The next few nights went by without any *otherworldly* incident, though Eli felt more scared than ever—sleeping in that room where someone was murdered. He tried to get more information from the Ouija about fourteen-year-old Carl and exactly how he'd died. But it was frustrating, nothing at all like that first night. When he didn't come up with letters that spelled gibberish, Eli knew he was controlling the planchette himself. So he wasn't sure about Carl's last name, who had *lacerated* him, and how long ago it had happened.

His mom used to say that he quickly grew tired of his toys. And the Ouija wasn't much different. After a few days, the Ouija board went up on his closet shelf and stayed there.

Then on the night of July Fourth, when they'd found the front door open and that strange mess in the kitchen, Eli had figured Carl was back. It had been their first *unexplainable incident* in a while—unless his mother had been keeping something from him. Eli realized the next day—when he'd overheard her and the neighbor lady talking outside—she'd been doing exactly that. Obviously she'd known all along about a suicide in the apartment, but she hadn't told him. Eli wondered what else she was hiding.

Well, he could keep secrets, too. His mom didn't know about Carl. The whole thing started to make some sense to Eli. The woman who had lived in this apartment years and years ago had *lacerated* her fourteen-year-old son, Carl, before killing herself. Eli still wasn't sure what that meant, and he casually asked his mother at the breakfast table the other morning.

"Lacerate?" she repeated. "Oh, it means to tear something up, cut it up."

"You mean—like cut it with a knife? A knife could give someone a *laceration*?"

She nodded over her coffee cup. "That's right. Why do you ask?"

"No reason. Somebody used the word on a TV show yesterday, and I wasn't sure what they were talking about." He went back to eating his Honey Nut Cheerios.

Eli wanted to find out more about Carl and his mother. But he didn't even know their last name—or when they'd died. He'd tried to google *Tudor Court, Seattle, murder-suicide,* but his search results had been a weird mix of real estate listings for the apartment complex and articles about different unrelated murders in the Seattle area.

He'd thought about asking his neighbors in Tudor Court about the murder/suicide, but he was worried it might get back to his mother.

Eli hadn't been sure how he could learn more about Carl—if that was indeed the kid's name—until he'd heard Marcella say just a few minutes ago: "Someone dead is communicating with you."

Her hand was still on his forehead. "I see a person very much like you," she said finally.

"Is it a teenager?" Eli asked. "Is the dead guy a teenager—like me?"

She took her hand away, sat back, and sighed. The dog

lazily got to its feet, then rested his head on her thigh. She scratched him behind the ears. "It might be you in a past life, Eli. I can't be sure. Do you have any reoccurring dreams? Sometimes, that's your past life trying to communicate with you." She lit up another cigarette.

"So you're saying this dead guy who's communicating with me is actually *me* in a past life?"

Marcella took a long drag from her cigarette and nodded.

It sounded pretty screwy to Eli. "Well, do you know what my name was in my previous life?" Earlier she'd figured out his name had three letters. Maybe she could tell him something about the name of this dead teenager. "Does his name start with a *C*?"

"The answer is in your dreams, Eli," she said cryptically. She set her cigarette in the ashtray, then reached across the table. "Give me your hand again."

Eli obeyed. He glanced outside the booth. The sun had disappeared behind some clouds. He didn't hear any more speeches from the guest celebrities over by the mega-store. His mom was probably looking for him.

Marcella set his hand down on the table, palm up, then stroked it. "I usually don't tell people bad news unless they ask to hear it," she said. "In your case, I think I can help you. Shall I tell you what I see here?"

His mouth open, Eli nodded.

"You're in danger. I see dangerous forces all around you, Eli. And I'm sorry, but you will face a loss—very soon."

Eli stared at her. He felt a sudden tightness in the pit of his stomach—like a warning. He tried to tell himself that she was just jerking him around. But lately—ever since the Fourth of July—he'd felt something bad was going to happen. Maybe it had to do with their ghost; maybe not. But the danger was there.

Even if he didn't want to believe Marcella's prophecy, in his gut Eli knew it was true.

* * *

Sydney tried not to lose sight of the man with the blue *59* T-shirt, but it was difficult. They'd finished up the interview portion of the program, and placed a long table in front of the celebrity guests. This setup gave audience members had a chance to come up on the stage and get an autograph or chat privately with her, Terri, and the Channel 6 weatherman. People kept crowding in front of her on the other side of the table, blocking her view. Then someone would step to one side or move their head a little, and she'd see the swarthy man again—among the audience, just a bit closer to the platform each time.

The network had sent a stack of her latest 8 x 10 glossies publicizing *On the Edge*. She signed about a hundred of those. She couldn't believe that some people still had 8 x 10 photos of her from her figure-skating days. She even signed a few old copies of *Making Miracles: My Own Story*. All the while, she kept an eye on that stranger in the blue T-shirt. He'd been getting closer and closer to the celebrity platform, and now he stood in line right by the platform steps.

It made her a bit nervous. But what could he do to her in front of all these people?

"Sydney, can I come around there and get my picture taken with you?" asked a large forty-something woman with honey-blond hair.

Nodding, Sydney got to her feet. "You bet. What's your name?"

"I'm Shirley!" the woman squealed. "Oh my God, this is so exciting! I love your *Mover & Shaker* stories!"

Sydney shook her hand. "Well, thanks, Shirley. Get on back here."

While the woman eagerly trotted around to her side of the table, Sydney stole another look at Mr. *59*. He was standing on the platform steps now.

She and Shirley put their arms around each other, while

Shirley's friend took three different photos. Shirley asked for an extra autograph for her daughter, who wanted to be an Olympic figure skater. Sydney signed it: *To Audrey, Best of luck on & off the ice.* Shirley thanked her over and over, then gave her a hug and moved down the line.

Sydney stole another look toward the other end of the platform. She didn't see Mr. *59* on the steps or in the line of people. She gazed out at the crowd dispersing in front of the store. She tried to catch a glimpse of him. That blue T-shirt should have given him away. But Sydney didn't see him anywhere. It was as if he'd disappeared.

"Hi, Sydney," a woman was saying to her. "I don't watch your show, but I'd really love an autograph."

"Um, sure," she said. She scribbled her name on one of the 8 x 10s, then handed it to the woman. "There you go. Excuse me."

She walked around the table. Several people in line said hello to her. She smiled and nodded back, but she kept glancing out at the parking lot—and beyond. Eli was probably on one of the rides over by the fun fair area.

Gil had given up the mike and was signing autographs. Sydney asked one of the big-shots with ValuCo if she could use the microphone to make an announcement. "Um, my son was supposed to meet me here fifteen minutes ago," she explained.

The middle-aged man, sweating in a business suit, nodded. "Help yourself, Sydney."

She went to Gil's mike, and switched it on. "Eli McCloud!" she said, trying not to sound too shrill. She kept thinking, *he's really going to love this.* "Eli McCloud, please meet your mother at the platform by the ValuCo front entrance . . ."

She repeated the announcement, all the while gazing out at the parking lot for the stranger in the blue T-shirt. There was still no sign of the man.

Sydney hoped she'd find him—before Eli did.

* * *

"What exactly do you mean?" Eli asked timidly. "What kind of danger am I in?"

Marcella stroked the palm of his hand and said nothing.

Finally, Eli pulled his hand away. "You—you can't just tell me something like that, and expect me not to freak out. When you say I'm—*facing a loss*, do you mean somebody I know might die?"

Marcella nodded. Her expression was unreadable behind those dark glasses. "Someone close to you," she said. "It may be prevented, though. I know a way to help you."

The German shepherd stirred a bit as Marcella hoisted a big cloth purse off the floor and plopped it in her lap. She fished out a pencil and a notepad. "Write down your address," she said.

Eli wasn't sure if the woman planned to send someone over to rob them later or what, but he scribbled down their address at Tudor Court.

"I will create some good luck for you," Marcella said. "But you must help me. In order for this to work, you need something valuable. Do you have a twenty-dollar bill on you?"

Eli stared at her and blinked. "Um, I'm not sure," he lied. He still had a twenty from the twenty-five bucks his mother had given him.

"It can work with a ten-dollar bill," she sighed. "But a twenty is better—the stronger the value, the stronger the luck. You don't have to hand it to me, Eli. I just need to *see it*."

Reluctantly, he reached into his pants pocket and found the twenty. He showed it to her, folded up. He wondered if she'd suddenly lunge for it.

Instead she leaned back in the chair, took her cigarette from the ashtray, and puffed on it. "Unfold the bill and show me the front side."

Eli was obedient. But he balked as she reached over and

touched the top right corner of the bill. "Tear that corner off—so the twenty mark is separated from the rest of the bill," she said.

Eli hesitated.

"Go on. Do what I tell you. It'll bring you luck. Tear it off, and stick the torn piece inside your pocket. You'll need to keep that in a special place for the next twenty days."

Eli figured he could always tape it up later. He carefully tore the top right corner from his mother's twenty-dollar bill, then tucked the detached piece into his shirt pocket.

"Now, let me tear off the opposite corner," she said, reaching for the twenty.

Eli held the bill very tightly while Marcella ripped off the bottom-left-corner 20 mark. She held that corner piece to her heart for a moment and lowered her head as if in prayer. Eli could see her lips moving. Then she gave him the torn-off little section. "You need to put that in another special place, Eli. Keep it there for twenty days."

He slipped the second severed corner into his shirt pocket. Something about all this didn't feel right.

She glanced at his address scribbled on the notepad, tore it off the piece of paper, and slapped it down on the table. "Fold up the twenty-dollar bill, set it on top of this paper, and then fold over the paper so you can't see the bill anymore. The bill needs to be completely covered."

Eli squinted at her. "Are you going to make my twenty bucks disappear?"

She sighed. "I'm trying to help you, Eli—"

He pushed his chair away and quickly got to his feet. "I'm sorry," he said. He shoved the mangled twenty back in his pants pocket. The knot in his stomach got even tighter. "I—I'm not comfortable with this. I've got to go."

The dog suddenly stood up and let out a bark.

"Don't put the bill back together for twenty days!" Marcella warned. "It's bad luck!"

But Eli didn't stop to listen. "I'm sorry!" he called, hurrying out of the booth. He only glanced back to make sure the dog wasn't chasing him. It was all clear; no sign of Marcella or her German shepherd.

As he turned forward again, Eli almost slammed right into a lean twenty-something man with a dark complexion. He looked Italian or Latino; Eli wasn't sure. "Sorry!" he said.

But the man said nothing. He wore sunglasses, a baseball hat, and a light summer jacket, which he must have just bought—or stolen—from ValuCo, because it still had part of the sales tag sticking out of the sleeve. It was weird how on this hot day, the guy wore the beige jacket zipped all the way up to his neck.

"Sorry," Eli repeated, edging past the man.

He made his way through the crowded fairgrounds toward the parking lot. Eli looked over at the ValuCo store and tried to catch a glimpse of the celebrity stage by the front door. But he was still too far away. Four older teenagers walked past him: two pretty girls and their loud, dumb-ass, cigarette-smoking boyfriends. The girls were holding balloons.

Eli looked over his shoulder at them. What he saw made him stop.

The man in the beige jacket stood a few feet behind him.

The teenage foursome walked past the man. One of the guys popped the girls' balloons with his cigarette. The two loud bangs were followed by a piercing shriek from both girls. Everyone in the area stopped to look at them except for the man in the beige jacket. He didn't turn around at all. He just kept staring in Eli's direction—his eyes shielded by the dark glasses.

"Who—" Eli started to say. But he couldn't get the words out. He was too scared. He swiveled around and hurried toward the parking lot. Threading through the mob of people, he kept glancing back to see if the man was following him. Eli didn't spot the guy among the crowd, but he couldn't be sure.

He remembered what Marcella had told him: *"I see dangerous forces all around you, Eli."* Now he wondered if he should have given her the damn twenty bucks.

Up ahead in the distance, he saw the celebrity stage platform by the ValuCo store, but a bunch of people were milling around on it, and he couldn't see his mom among them.

At the edge of the parking lot, Eli paused and looked back again. He tried to catch his breath. He didn't see the weird guy in the beige jacket anywhere, but Eli took another minute to survey the crowd. His heart was pounding furiously.

Then he recognized his mom's voice coming over the loudspeaker: *"Eli McCloud, please meet your mother at the platform by the ValuCo front entrance . . ."*

He let out a grateful laugh. Ordinarily, he would have been utterly humiliated to have his mother paging him this way. But right now, he smiled at the sound of his mom calling out for him.

Eli took one last long look at the fairgrounds. The smile disappeared from his face. He saw someone duck behind a phone pole at the edge of the lot—someone in a beige jacket.

"Leave me alone!" he screamed—with what little breath was left in his lungs. *"I can see you! Stop following me!"*

A moment later, a woman in a beige pullover emerged from behind the phone pole. She was waving out a match and puffing on a cigarette. Apparently, she didn't hear him, thank God. She didn't even look his way, though several people in the parking lot did.

Eli felt like an idiot. But he wasn't any less scared, not after what Marcella had told him.

His mother made the announcement again. Her words boomed over the speakers posted throughout the parking lot and fairgrounds. He knew she was somewhere on that crowded makeshift stage, calling for him.

Eli turned and ran like hell toward the sound of his mother's voice.

CHAPTER NINE

Sydney checked her rearview mirror again.

She wasn't sure what she expected to see behind her on Highway 167. When she'd pulled out of the ValuCo parking lot fifteen minutes before, at least a dozen cars were leaving at the same time. The man in the navy blue *59* T-shirt could have been driving any one of those cars. If he was following her right now, she wouldn't have been able to recognize his car anyway. Besides, she and Eli were headed home, and the olive-skinned stranger had originally been lingering outside their driveway gate. Trying to elude him wouldn't do any good. He already knew where they lived.

Her grip tightening on the wheel, Sydney glanced over at Eli in the passenger seat and tried to smile. He wasn't listening to his iPod, for a change. The Moody Blues played on an oldies station on the car radio, and he seemed to enjoy "Nights in White Satin."

To Sydney's utter amazement, Eli hadn't given her any flack for paging him at the fair. Earlier, when she'd spotted him in the parking lot headed her way, she'd hurried down from the stage and hugged him. He hadn't balked or asked why she was acting so weird. Instead, he'd hugged her back. He'd seemed kind of relieved to see her, too.

Later, on their way to the car, Eli had dug into his pocket and tried to give her the three dollars and some-odd-cents left over from the twenty-five bucks she'd given him for fun fair rides.

"Keep the change, honey," she'd told him, patting his shoulder. "I didn't feel like driving all the way out here by myself. Consider it mommy-sitting money."

Sydney didn't want to think about what might have happened if she'd left him alone at home this afternoon—what with that man loitering around the place. She would have to warn Eli about this potential stalker character.

Swell, she thought. The poor kid had enough troubles—what with his parents separating, and living in a strange, new place that was *haunted*, for crying out loud. Now she had to tell him about this possible nutcase.

Sydney looked over at him again. Slouched in the seat with his knees on the dashboard, Eli pensively gazed out the windshield.

"Are you feeling okay, honey?" she asked.

"Yeah, I'm fine," he answered listlessly.

Sydney sighed, then turned her attention to the road ahead. She couldn't tell him about this stalker business right now. Maybe she'd invite Kyle over for a pizza tonight and he could bring one of his DVDs. Then she could break the news to Eli later.

She glanced over at him once more. "You sure you're all right? I've seen that look before. You're worried about something."

"Or some*body*," he said.

"Who's this *somebody* you're worried about?"

"Dad," Eli murmured. He sighed. "I know you're probably sick of me talking about Dad."

"I'm not, honey. Go ahead. Why are you worried about him?"

"Well, I got to thinking earlier. Remember how you used

to get all bent out of shape every time he had to work at night on one of his special assignments? I mean, you used to pretend you weren't nervous, but—c'mon, duh—I could always tell you were kind of scared something might happen to him."

Sydney cracked a sad little smile. She kept her eyes on the traffic.

"Anyway, now that we're living here, we don't even know when he's on a special assignment. He could be on one right now, doing something really dangerous. Anyway, I'm worried about him. If Dad got hurt or something, how would we find out?"

"The same way we'd find out if we were still living with Dad in Chicago. Someone would notify us right away. Listen, Eli, if you're worried about Dad, then give him a call when we get home."

"Okay. But he wouldn't tell me if he was in trouble," Eli murmured.

Sydney sighed. "He wouldn't tell me either, sweetie."

They drove in silence for a while.

Sydney remembered back in March, when Joe had refused to admit anything was wrong. So she'd started her own investigation into the death of Arthur "Polly" Pollard. She searched the Internet for more stories about him, but there wasn't any follow-up to that first *Tribune* article about Polly Pollard's body being discovered in a Woodlawn alley Dumpster.

Two days after Joe had told her, *"It doesn't concern you,"* while Sydney was out shopping at Dominick's, she used a pay phone in front of the supermarket to call the Woodlawn police precinct. She asked if they had any updates on their investigation into the March 14th murder of Arthur Pollard.

"Who's calling, please?" asked the cop on the other end of the line.

"Um, Ellen Roberts with the *City Beat* section of the *Tribune*," she lied.

"I'll connect you with Lieutenant Mullen."

But Sydney got Mullen's voice mail and hung up. She couldn't leave a number for him, not without giving herself away. She made four more calls from pay phones over the next two days and always got Lieutenant Mullen's lousy voice mail.

"Hey, hon?" she casually said to Joe while he was in the shower. She stood in front of the bathroom mirror in her slip. Her cosmetic clutch was on the side of the sink. They were getting ready for the wedding of Joe's cousin, another cop—in Evanston. "I was just wondering, did they ever find out who killed that Polly character, the one who called here?"

She saw Joe's nude silhouette behind the foggy shower curtain. He stopped scrubbing his chest for a moment and turned toward her. "What?"

"Arthur Pollard," she said, "the one who called here a while back. Did they ever find out who shot him?"

"I don't know, and I don't care. It's not my case." He went back to washing himself.

"All right already, you don't have to bite my head off."

"Well, I really wish you'd leave it alone."

"You make it sound like I'm needling you," she called, putting down her mascara wand. "I haven't even broached the subject since the poor guy was dumped in that Dumpster last week." She stared at the shower curtain again. "I'll be honest with you, honey. You're acting awfully strange about this, very touchy. It makes me think you might be in some kind of trouble." She paused. "Are you—in any kind of trouble?"

The shower went off with a squeak, then he pulled a towel down from the rack and started drying himself. "Arthur Pollard was a pain-in-the-ass petty crook with drug problems," Joe said finally. "He was messing with the wrong kind of people and wanted my help. But I couldn't help him, and I feel bad that he's dead."

"Why did he approach *you* for help?" Sydney asked, her eyes still on his movements behind the fogged curtain. "Did he know you, Joe?"

"He knew my reputation as a sap who always tries to help people."

Sydney smiled a little. That much was true. She turned toward the mirror again and wiped some steam away.

"Anyway, I feel like shit I didn't help him," Joe admitted. With a whoosh, the shower curtain opened. Joe was still drying himself off as he stepped out of the tub.

Sydney realized something he'd said that didn't make sense. She turned toward him. "Honey, if you feel so badly about Polly's murder, why aren't you interested in who might have killed him?"

"What?"

"A minute ago you said that you didn't care."

Shaking his head, Joe wrapped the towel around his waist. "Y'know," he muttered. "I'd really appreciate it if you'd just fucking drop this."

Her mouth open, Sydney stared at her husband as he stomped into the bedroom.

Eli had been invited to the wedding as well, and he failed to notice that his parents didn't talk to each other all night long.

Sydney did, however, talk to Sharon McKenna at the reception. Sharon's husband, Andy, was Joe's best friend on the force. Their oldest, Tim, hung out with Eli and his pal, Brad Reece. "The Three Musketeers," Joe called them. Sydney liked Sharon, a petite, pretty, freckle-faced woman with short red hair. She caught a few minutes alone with Sharon in a corner of the reception hall.

"You look gorgeous, Syd—as usual," Sharon said, raising her champagne glass. "You must be feeling better."

"Feeling better?" she asked.

"Yeah," Sharon said, sipping her champagne. "We invited

you folks to dinner last weekend, but Joe said you had the flu." Sharon stared at her for a moment. "Joe didn't mention it to you? I was going to make lasagna, because I know Eli loves it."

Sydney just shook her head.

"You weren't sick, were you?"

"I'm sorry, Sharon," she murmured. "I don't know what to say. I can't imagine why Joe . . ."

"He's been really distant with Andy lately," Sharon frowned. She finished the rest of her champagne. "I don't know if you've noticed or not, but Joe has said about five words to Andy since we arrived here. He's managed to avoid me altogether, because he knows I'll tell him what I'm thinking. You don't just freeze out your friends like that."

Sydney gave a hopeless shrug. "Sharon, I'm so sorry. All I can tell you is Joe hasn't been himself lately. This whole last week, I've been worried about him."

"Andy's been worried about him for at least *two weeks* now," Sharon said. "That's when Joe started to give him the cold shoulder."

"Do you know—" Sydney hesitated. "Has Andy mentioned someone named Polly?"

Sharon's eyes narrowed at her.

"Polly's a man, Arthur Pollard," Sydney explained. All the while, she had a nagging feeling she ought to keep her mouth shut. But she had to find out if Joe's best friend knew something. "Andy hasn't mentioned anything about *Polly*? He was killed last week."

"No, Andy never talks about work at home. Besides, he wouldn't be on that case. He and Joe haven't worked on a case together in five years. You know that."

"It's not Joe's case either," Sydney said. "Listen, Share, don't mention any of this to Andy. Please, forget I said anything. I'll talk to Joe, and—get to the bottom of this."

But she didn't try talking to Joe.

Sydney felt she'd already crossed a line by asking Sharon about Arthur Pollard. She crossed another the next day when she went through Joe's desk drawers in his home office. Unlike her office in the basement, full of expensive video and audio equipment, Joe's second-floor study was more like another family room—with framed photos of them on the wall, a sofa, and a smaller TV set. The only thing *official* about his office was a display case full of his police awards from the City of Chicago and the computer monitor on his desk.

Sydney didn't find anything useful in his desk drawers except a stack of old birthday cards and love notes she'd given him, along with scores of postcards she'd sent him while on the road for *Movers & Shakers*. She got into his computer and checked his e-mails and recently deleted e-mails. But there was nothing about Arthur "Polly" Pollard.

She kept checking the *Tribune* and Google for any news on the investigation into Arthur Pollard's murder, but came up with nothing. She re-read and re-read the March 15th *Tribune* article about the discovery of Polly's corpse. One sentence stuck with her:

> Pollard, a part-time bartender at Anthony's Cha-Cha Lounge in Cicero, was well known to Chicago Police.

Anthony's was a cruddy corner saloon with cheap-looking faux-brick siding from the sixties. During the long drive to Cicero, Sydney prayed she wouldn't discover anything there that might incriminate her husband. As frustrated as she'd been by her fruitless search for clues in Joe's study, Sydney had also been relieved not to find anything.

They needed her to go to Atlanta to cover a possible *Movers & Shakers* story, but she'd lied and told them she was sick. She couldn't leave right now. If Joe had been involved in anything dishonest or shady, it could ruin the whole family. Both of their careers would be in shambles.

She kept thinking he must have gotten into some awful trouble to have frozen her out—along with his best friend, Andy. For someone with a reputation for rescuing others, Joe never asked for help himself. In times of crisis, he often pushed away those closest to him. Sydney wondered if his reluctance to talk with her about this Polly business was because he was protecting someone else. That was so much like him, and she desperately hoped it was the case here.

Even with sunlight streaming through the front window—which had a filthy-looking grass-skirt-type valance—it was seedy and depressing inside Anthony's Cha-Cha Lounge. The interior design was a luau theme. But all of the tiki-style accents looked dusty and decrepit from the stuffed fish and barnacles in the nets on the walls to the fake plants and palm trees. Years of smoke and sun bleaching must have caused their plastic leaves to turn that ugly, light gray color.

Another grass valance hung over the bar, where a large, goateed man with a cigarette dangling out of his mouth poured drinks. He wore a Hawaiian shirt. Neil Diamond's "Cracklin' Rosie" resonated on the jukebox; in the corner, two guys who looked like ex-bikers silently played a game of pool. A few people sat at the bar, and Sydney spotted a couple quietly talking in a booth.

She took a seat at the bar, away from the others, and ordered an Old Style light beer. As the bartender set the full pilsner glass in front of her, Sydney worked up a smile for him. "Hey, I used to know a bartender here named Art Pollard. *Polly?* Do you know him? Does he still work here?"

A few barstools down, a forty-something woman with straight platinum-colored hair and black roots looked up from her drink. She wore jeans, a tube top, and a gauzy, see-through flower-patterned blouse—unbuttoned with the shirt-tails tied around her slightly bulging midriff. She stared at Sydney, and then a look passed between her and the bartender.

He turned toward Sydney and shook his head.

"So—you don't know him?" Sydney asked. "Or he doesn't work here anymore."

"I knew him," the bartender grunted. "And he doesn't work here anymore. He's dead."

Sydney feigned surprise. "My God, how did he die?"

"Stupidity," the heavyset man grumbled.

The blonde slapped the edge of the bar. "Hah! You're a real shit, Phil."

Ignoring her, the bartender stared at Sydney. "Want to start a tab?"

"I'm not sure yet," she said.

A few stools down, the blonde cleared her throat. "What's your name, honey?"

Sydney hesitated. "I'm—Sharon." She worked up a little smile.

The woman slid off her bar stool and took her drink over to where Sydney sat. "I'm Aurora. I was a good friend of Polly's." She raised her glass. "God rest his soul. Somebody shot him two weeks ago."

"Oh, no," Sydney murmured. "That's horrible."

"How did you know Polly?" she asked.

"Um, I came in here a few nights some months back. My mom lives in the area, and she was sick. I remember Polly was really sweet and helped cheer me up. He didn't get fresh or anything. He was just nice. Anyway, my mom's real sick again, and I came here, hoping to see Polly. Do they—um, do they know who killed him?"

Aurora tilted her head to one side and gazed at her for a moment. Sydney wasn't sure if Polly's friend believed her or not.

"Phil?" Aurora called, not breaking eye contact with Sydney. "Phil, honey, start a tab for her, and put a Seven and Seven on it. Okay?" She smiled at Sydney. "Okay?"

Sydney nodded.

"Let's go sit where we can talk," Aurora said. She grabbed her drink and sauntered toward a booth.

Sydney followed her, and slipped into the booth with her Old Style Light. The brown Naugahyde cushioned seat had black duct tape on one corner. The table was overly lacquered, and decorated with cigarette burn marks and an unlit hurricane lamp.

"So—did they catch whoever killed Polly?" Sydney asked.

Frowning, Aurora shook her head.

"Do they have any clue who shot him?" Sydney pressed.

"Well, his pals here at Anthony's have their own theories," she said, draining the rest of her glass. "Polly was sweet. But he also pissed off the wrong people. So—it could have been a mob hit. That's the popular theory around here. But some of us think it's the cops who killed him. He was—"

Aurora fell silent as the stocky, goateed bartender came by with her Seven and 7. He set it on the table and took her empty glass.

"Thanks, Phil, you're a peach," she said, not really looking at him. Then Aurora waited until he was back behind the bar. She pushed her colored blond hair back behind her ears. "Polly was a snitch. But of course, you probably already knew that."

Sydney stared at the woman and shook her head. "I don't understand—"

"He was a snitch, a police informant," Aurora whispered. "He gave them information about drug deals and small-time jobs, and they gave him money."

"Oh, I see," Sydney replied numbly. "A *snitch*, of course." She figured that must have been how Joe had been acquainted with him. Even the newspaper article said Polly was *"well known to Chicago Police."*

Aurora sipped her Seven and 7. "That's a sweet story about how you met Polly," she said. "Did you just make it up on the spur of the moment? Or did you dream it up on your way here?"

"What?"

Aurora leaned back in the booth and smiled. "You're name isn't Sharon. You're Sydney Jordan, and I recognized you the minute you walked into this dump. You're married to a cop, aren't you?"

Sydney took a minute before she could answer. "Yes, that's right," she said, finally.

"So—what the hell are you doing here, *Sydney*? And please don't try to tell me you're doing a *Movers & Shakers* story on Polly, because you don't profile fuck-ups on that show. And sweet as Polly could be, he was a major fuck-up. Did your husband send you here?"

Sydney shook her head, then gulped down some beer. "Joe doesn't even know I'm here. You—you're right about Polly being an unlikely subject for *Movers & Shakers*. The truth is, he called my house twice, and when I read about his murder, it really disturbed me. The newspaper article made him out to be this shiftless ex-con with a drug problem. They more or less indicated he got what was coming to him. But I thought about this guy, Polly, who sounded so nice on the phone, and I wondered what happens to the friends of someone like him. Okay, so he had a criminal record, and he had some troubles—he also had friends, didn't he? I'm sure Polly made a difference in the world and touched several people's lives in a positive way. I know my husband felt bad about his death. He didn't know Polly very well, but suggested—if I wanted to do a story about Polly—I should talk to some of his friends. So—here I am."

With one elbow on the table and her chin in her hand, Aurora sat across from her and stared. Sydney wasn't sure if she believed a word of this. "What does your husband say about him?" Aurora asked.

"Joe and I have a rule. Neither one of us can talk about

our work at home. Besides, Joe didn't know Polly very well. At least, that's what he said." Sydney waited to see if Aurora would contradict her.

Aurora uttered a sad little laugh. "Well, I can tell you Polly was good to his cat. It's this half-deaf, half-blind, old bag of bones named Simon. I inherited the thing, lucky me. Is that the kind of shit you're looking for?"

Sydney nodded. *So Joe didn't know Polly very well, thank God.* "Yes, little human touches like that," she said. "And of course, I'd like to include something about the work he did for the police. Without Polly's help, they probably wouldn't have been able to crack several important cases. Am I right?"

"Yeah," Aurora replied over her Seven and 7. "In fact, I figured it was his part in that drug bust at the pier three weeks ago that got him killed."

"What drug bust?" Sydney asked.

"Huh, you weren't shitting me earlier," Aurora said. "You and your old man really don't talk about his work. It happened about three weeks ago. A couple of small-timers were moving some cocaine at Fort Jackson Pier when the cops arrived. The two schmucks ended up burning to death in their RV, along with most of the stuff—or so the cops claimed. Polly was the snitch on the deal. He told me there was up to half a million worth of coke involved. The four cops who pulled off the raid recovered something like thirteen thousand dollars' worth, and claimed the rest went up in smoke. I think the newspapers estimated forty-some-odd thousand went poof, but that's bullshit. And Polly knew it." Aurora sipped her drink, then gave her a wary sidelong glance. "So—this is all news to you?"

Sydney nodded.

"Well, honey, then this must be news to you as well. Your husband was one of the four cops who pulled off this drug bust—though I'd call it a *heist*."

Sydney shook her head. "My husband would never get involved in anything like that. Joe's a good guy. He's an honest cop. He—"

"Huh, Polly used to think so, too," Aurora said, cutting her off. "He knew these guys were after him, these hit men. Polly wasn't sure if it was payback from someone connected to those two schmucks who fried in their RV or if the cops had hired these guys to shut him up permanently. Whoever it was, Polly knew he was a dead man. I've never seen him so sick with worry. He called your husband at least six times, begging for help."

"But I didn't think he knew Joe very well," Sydney said.

"Not very," Aurora agreed. "Polly never snitched for your husband. For the Fort Jackson Pier deal, he dealt with one of the other cops. But Polly knew your husband. He knew Joe McCloud's reputation as a good guy who went out of his way to help people in trouble." Aurora drained the rest of her glass and loudly set it down on the table. "Well, your nice-guy hero-husband didn't lift a fucking finger to help Polly. He let him down—and he let him die."

Sydney squirmed in the booth seat. "Why are you telling me this?"

"Because I don't believe a goddamn thing you've told me—except the fact that Polly called your house, and your husband doesn't talk to you about his work. It's why you came here, isn't it, Sydney? You wanted to find out why your big hero-husband was associating with a small-time hood like Polly. Well, now you know. He was involved in a heist—and murder. And then he let a sweet guy get shot to death. Why don't you do a story on that, Sydney?"

Dazed, she just shook her head.

"Anyway," Aurora muttered. "If your darling Joe gives you a beautiful new mink coat or a sparkly diamond bracelet on your next birthday, now you'll know where the money came from."

Sydney felt sick to her stomach. "Why haven't you told any of this to the police investigating Polly's death?" she heard herself ask.

Aurora leaned forward. "How old do you think I am?"

Sydney hesitated. She could feel the color draining from her face.

"I'm forty-three," Aurora answered for her. "And I'd like to live to see my forty-fourth birthday. I'm not saying the cops checking out Polly's murder aren't honest. But why take a chance, y'know?" She gazed at Sydney, her eyes narrowed. "Say, you don't look so hot."

With a shaky hand, Sydney pulled two twenties out of her purse. "This ought to cover my tab," she murmured, setting the money on the tabletop. "Don't worry. It's not my husband's money. It's mine. Thank you for your time."

Her legs felt unsteady as she got up and moved to the door. She was nauseous and dizzy. Staggering out of Anthony's Cha-Cha Lounge, she didn't even make it to her car. Sydney grabbed hold of a light post, braced herself, and then threw up on the sidewalk.

She still felt queasy driving home. Even after drinking half a bottle of Evian water and sucking on a peppermint from her purse, she still had an awful taste in her mouth—and a sore throat. She knew Aurora's story was probably true. Three weeks ago, she'd been in Boston on a *Movers & Shakers* story. For one of those nights while she'd been away, Eli had slept over at Brad's house. That had probably been the night of the raid—or *heist*, as Aurora called it.

"Please, God, let it not be true," she kept whispering during the long drive home. She tried to convince herself that there was an explanation, some reason Joe couldn't tell her what was going on. By the time Sydney turned down North Spaulding, she was crying. Something so dear to her had died back there inside that crummy bar in Cicero.

As she approached the house, she noticed a strange car in

their driveway. Sydney pulled in and parked behind it. She took another Kleenex out of her purse and wiped her eyes and nose. When she looked up, she saw Eli shuffling out the front door. He gave her a listless wave.

She quickly checked herself in the rearview mirror, wiped her nose again, then climbed out of the car. She glanced at the white Taurus in front of her. Sydney had been on the road enough to recognize a rental car when she saw one. But the Hertz logo on the frame around the back license plate left no room for doubt. She gave Eli a quick kiss. "Hi, Eli," she said. "Whose rental car is that?"

Eli shrugged, and kicked the tire. "I dunno. This weird guy's in the living room, talking to Dad, and they asked me to leave."

"What?" she murmured.

Eli followed her into the house. She saw Joe standing in the living room with a can of Budweiser in his hand. He still had his tie on from work, but it was loosened. He appeared startled to see her. "Oh, hi, honey . . ."

She squinted at him. "Do we have company?"

Frowning, he heaved a long sigh. Then he nodded in the direction of the kitchen. "It's this joker from Seattle, who hasn't seen you in a year. He says he's your brother."

Kyle came around the corner from the kitchen, and Sydney let out a gasp. She threw her arms around him and started crying. Her brother hugged her. "It was all Joe's idea," she heard Kyle say. "He's been hatching this for a while. He even insisted on paying for my flight. Hey, Joe, next time, first-class might be nice . . ."

She turned and embraced Joe. "Thank you, sweetie," she said, past her tears.

"I've been such an unbearable grouch lately," he whispered, kissing her. "I'm going to start making it up to you, honey."

Sydney just nodded. She thought about what Aurora had

said: *"So if your darling Joe gives you a beautiful new mink coat or a sparkly diamond bracelet on your next birthday, you'll know where the money came from."*

She couldn't stop crying. But she told herself it was all right. She wasn't giving herself away. Her family probably thought they were tears of joy.

That week while Kyle stayed with them, Sydney couldn't help wondering if Joe had planned the visit just so she'd be distracted and preoccupied—and less likely to pursue this Polly business any further. If that was Joe's plan, it sure as hell worked. Kyle's visit put everything on hold. Her brother kept asking her if she was okay, and saying she looked tired. Was she sleeping all right lately? She couldn't tell him the truth. Kyle thought Joe was wonderful.

"Okay, let's see," Kyle said, over drinks at a gay bar called Sidetracks. Joe had insisted she and her brother have a night on the town together while he looked after Eli. They sat at a counter by the window. Nancy Sinatra was singing "These Boots Are Made for Walking," and Kyle had to shout over the loud volume. "Joe does the laundry, and folds it better than Mom used to. He helps with the dishes. He doesn't bitch or moan about having to take care of Eli while you're away. Plus, he's so cool about me being gay. It's such a *non-issue* with him. And looks-wise, on a scale from one to ten, he's about a twelve plus. Plus he's still crazy in love with you after all these years, any fool can see that. Could I clone him, please? I want a Joe of my very own."

"Well, you haven't been exposed to him in the morning, while he's eating his Cheerios," Sydney argued, raising her voice to compete with the music. "He has to make sure every piece of cereal gets dunked in the milk, and he keeps clanking his spoon against the bowl between shoveling the cereal in his mouth. All that clanking, it's enough to drive you nuts. God help that man if a dry morsel of cereal passed his lips. And at night, when he's getting ready for bed and he takes off his wristwatch, *he smells his wrist afterward!* How gross is that? I don't know if he's sniffing for sweat or the leather wristband smell against his skin. But it's weird—and disgusting."

"I'd put up with that," Kyle told her.

Put up with that? Though she was complaining, she secretly loved those idiosyncrasies. Those were the weird, quirky little things about Joe that no one else knew. She cherished them—beyond his good looks and good deeds. And if she thought about it too much, she couldn't help crying, because this man she loved so dearly had obviously done something vile and deplorable.

But she couldn't admit any of this to Kyle.

When her brother had to go back to Seattle at the end of that week, Sydney cried inconsolably. Yes, she was going to miss him, but there was another reason for her tears. There would be no more distraction, no more stalling. She would have to face this awful thing Joe had been hiding from her.

At the time, Sydney had thought she wouldn't see Kyle for at least another year. She'd had no idea when she'd put her brother on a plane at O'Hare, she would be seeing him again—and temporarily moving in with him—in only five weeks.

Sydney glanced in her rearview mirror as she turned down their street. Eli wordlessly reached up toward the sun visor to press the gate-opening device for the Tudor Court Apartments. She didn't think that gate would keep Number 59 out. If he was the one who had broken into their apartment on July Fourth, he could certainly get in again.

She didn't want to call the police about this guy, not until she was positive he was stalking her. She'd already phoned

9-1-1 about their possible break-in last week; she didn't want to call them again about a possible stalker. They'd think she was a nut.

Turning in to the driveway, Sydney stopped to watch in the rearview mirror as the gate closed behind them. "What do you say to a pizza tonight?" she asked Eli, trying to sound nonchalant about it. "I can call Uncle Kyle and see if he's free. Maybe he can bring over a DVD."

Eli shrugged. "Sure."

He didn't sound too thrilled about it. Then again, it wasn't like one of his friends was coming over. Sydney had gotten in touch with Sharon McKenna to see if Tim could fly out and spend a week with his pal; she'd done the same thing with Brad's parents. She'd offered to pay for the flight. But the McKennas and the Reeces each had misgivings about putting their twelve-year-old on a plane by himself. And in the case of the McKennas, they were friends with Joe once again, and she was the villain for taking her son and moving away.

Approaching the front stoop with the keys in her hand, Sydney couldn't help worrying that she'd find the door unlocked and open again. She'd experienced that same apprehension several times since coming home on July Fourth. The door was closed and locked, thank God.

Eli followed her inside, then headed upstairs to the bathroom. Kicking off her shoes, Sydney went into the kitchen, where she checked the back door to make sure it was closed and locked. No break-in. It only made sense. If Number 59 had followed them to Auburn and back, when would he have had time to break into their apartment?

She phoned Kyle and got his machine. "Hey, it's me," she said to the recording. "This is kind of last minute, but I would love it if you could come over tonight. Color me needy. I'll buy the pizza if you bring the DVD. Call me when you get this. Bye."

She was checking her voice mail when she heard Eli bounding back down the stairs, jumping from landing to landing.

On her voice mail, there were three hang-ups, and no messages. Ordinarily, she wouldn't have given the hang-ups a second thought. But she was already unnerved by this potential stalker situation. Moreover, the person calling each time stayed on the line long enough for Sydney to hear people talking in the background. She checked the last call return, and the automated voice told her: *"The number called cannot be reached."*

Sydney told herself that it was just a telemarketer.

It sounded like Eli was in the dining room. She heard a drawer squeak open.

Sydney headed toward the refrigerator, but remembered stashing Joe's letter in the breakfront's bottom drawer.

She swiveled around and hurried into the dining room. "What are you doing in there?" she asked, surprised at her own, almost-shrill tone. "Get out of there—"

Startled, Eli glanced up at her. He was crouched down in front of the built-in breakfront. He had the bottom drawer open. "What's wrong? What'd I do?"

"What are looking for?"

"The charger for my iPod," Eli answered, squinting at her as if she was crazy. "Jeez, what's the big deal?"

Sydney took a deep breath, then stepped over to the drawer and closed it. "Your charger's in the kitchen drawer, top right hand, where it always is."

"Well, thanks," he grumbled. He brushed past her and headed into the kitchen. "God, you don't have to bite my head off."

"I'm sorry, honey. I didn't mean to snap at you," she called after him.

She listened to him open and shut one of the drawers in the kitchen. "Did you find it?" she called.

No answer. She heard him stomping toward the stairs.

Swell, now he's mad at me—again. She should have just let him see the damn letter from Joe, and then he would have known just how much his dad cared about them. But she couldn't break his heart like that.

Sydney stooped down and opened the breakfront's bottom drawer. She found the letter in the back of the drawer, where she'd originally stashed it under a pile of loose papers and bills.

She heard the front door slam. "Eli?" she called, shutting the breakfront drawer. "Honey, are you there?" She didn't want him going outside, not when that stalker could be lurking around. "Eli?" she repeated, running to the front door. She opened it and called out his name again. He wasn't in the courtyard.

"Eli? Honey, where are you?" In her bare feet, she hurried toward the garages and gazed down the driveway. The gate was still closed. She didn't see him anywhere.

"Oh, God," she murmured, tears stinging her eyes. Her son had no idea this potential nutcase was out there—watching and following them. "Eli, honey, answer me, please!" she screamed.

But there was no answer.

Sydney obviously had no idea he was studying her every move right now.

From an alleyway off the courtyard—within the gated premises—he'd seen Eli bolt out the front door. The boy had ducked into the shadows of a little alcove, where the caretaker's unit was. He'd stayed there while his mother called out his name again and again.

He couldn't help smiling. Her son was hiding from her. He hated his own mother.

Sydney looked so upset—*unhinged*. Even this far away, he could see the tears streaming down her cheeks. A hand over her mouth, she kept glancing around the courtyard. Each time she called out for her son, her voice became more warbled and strained. She looked so scared and pathetic, wandering out there barefoot, crying for her son. It amused him to see her suffer.

And he hadn't even really started in on her yet.

CHAPTER TEN

Eli listened to his mother calling out for him. She seemed awfully panicky, considering he'd just stepped out less than a minute ago. What was her problem? It was barely twilight, not even dark yet.

"Eli? Honey, can you hear me?" she called out, her voice shaky. *"Oh, God . . ."*

He kept his back pressed against the brick wall in an arched alcove to the caretaker's unit. There was a light above him, but none of the outside lights had gone on yet, so Eli was shrouded in darkness. It sounded like his mom was crying. Part of him felt bad for her, but he was angry at her, too.

Okay, so she'd caught him searching for that letter from his dad. She didn't have to get all snippy about it. Could he help it if he missed his dad?

Eli waited until he heard her go back inside the apartment. Then he slowly emerged from the shadows to make sure she'd gone. On the opposite side of the courtyard, he thought he saw someone in the alley. A dark figure darted behind some Dumpsters.

Eli gazed at that alley for another moment. Nothing moved. He told himself it must have been his imagination.

He glanced over toward their apartment. He thought about

sneaking out of the courtyard and walking for a while—maybe along the beach. He just wanted some time to calm down—and yeah, maybe keep her wondering about him a little bit longer. It was pretty dumb, really. Here he was, twelve years old, and *running away from home*. Some home. He didn't think he'd ever call this place home.

He really did need to be alone for a while right now. He kept thinking about what that psychic lady had told him—about the danger around him, the loss he would have to face, and his communication with someone dead.

Reaching into his pocket, Eli pulled out the twenty-dollar bill with the two corners ripped off. He felt a little pang in his gut. His mom had given him this money to go on rides and have fun, and now he'd made her cry. What a little shit he was.

Eli figured he'd better go back inside and let her know he was all right. But then he saw something move in the alley again. He hesitated, then ducked back into the alcove. Keeping perfectly still, he studied the alleyway, especially around the Dumpsters. But he didn't see anything. He wondered if it had been a crow or something.

Maybe there were ghosts *outside* their apartment, too. Maybe Carl wasn't the only *undead spirit* haunting Tudor Court.

Eli glanced at the caretaker's door. If anyone knew about their ghost—and the murder-suicide in their unit—it would be Larry, the caretaker.

Eli figured his mom would be okay for another minute or two. In fact, that was all she probably needed to realize he'd just stepped out to blow off some steam. He was coming back. No reason for her to freak out about it.

He rang the caretaker's bell—then listened at his door. Larry's studio apartment was in the basement. Eli heard someone coming up the stairs. He stepped back from the door as it opened.

"Mr. Eli McCloud in Unit Nine," Larry said. "What can I do you for?"

About thirty, with a pale complexion, dark eyes, and a crooked little smile, Larry was handsome, but also kind of crazy looking. When they'd first moved in, Larry's black hair had been in a ponytail, but he'd recently cut it all off so he was practically bald. He was friendly enough, but a bit of an oddball. He'd come to the door in a thin, yellowish, tight T-shirt, pale blue shorts, and brown socks with sandals. Thick, black hair covered his pale arms and legs.

"Sorry to bother you," Eli said. He shot a glance over his shoulder. "I wanted to ask you a few questions."

"Didn't I just hear your mother calling out for you?" Larry asked.

"Yeah, she found me," Eli lied. "Everything's okay. Um, do you have a few minutes?"

"Sure. My dinner's in the oven, but it won't be ready for a while. C'mon down."

Eli followed Larry down a short flight of stairs toward his apartment. He hadn't been inside Larry's place before, and had only glimpsed it passing by the basement windows sometimes. It seemed like a really cool place to live. But now, as Eli walked down the steps to a dark corridor, it felt like a dungeon. Whatever Larry was cooking had an overly sweet, spicy, meat odor that filled the studio apartment. It wasn't the kind of smell that was welcome on a hot day. But at least Larry's place was a bit cooler.

"Have you had dinner yet?" Larry asked, leading the way into his combination living room and bedroom. "I'm cooking rabbit. There's enough for two. It's mighty tasty. I have a whole freezer full. My buddy's a hunter."

"Oh, gosh, thanks anyway," Eli managed to say.

For someone who kept the Tudor Court's grounds so neat, Larry was a slob at home. Clothes were strewn over the unmade bed as well as the back of an easy chair that was losing its stuffing. Random pictures Larry had torn from magazines were haphazardly taped to the beige walls: lots of pretty girls (Eli recognized Cameron Diaz in three photos); some race car shots; nature scenes; and quite a few pictures of the Beatles. In the corner, he'd spread some newspapers beneath the cage holding a canary that wouldn't stop chirping. Just enough light came through the small, high windows for Eli to see how dirty and dusty the place was.

"So what did you want to ask me?" Larry said, heading into his kitchen.

Eli stopped in the kitchen doorway. Dirty dishes were stacked in the sink, and a portable TV sat on Larry's battered, old wooden breakfast table. A Princess Di commemorative plate was being sold on the Home Shopping Network. Larry had it on mute.

"Um, I was wondering if you knew anything about the lady and her son who used to live in our place," Eli said.

Larry stirred some greasy-looking potatoes and cabbage cooking on the stove. "What lady and son?"

"The ones who died there, back in the seventies," Eli said.

"Oh, them," Larry nodded. "Well, I wasn't here then, sport. Hell, I wasn't even born yet." He opened the oven and checked on his rabbit.

"Still, I figured you might know something about them though, maybe like how they died or something."

Larry was silent for a few moments. Eli listened to his canary chirping away in the next room.

"Listen, I'd like to help you out," Larry said, finally. "But if the property manager ever got wind I was flapping my mouth off to you about what's gone on in Unit Nine, I'd get shit-canned in no time. Then Anita and I would be out on our tails."

"Who's Anita?"

"She's my girl," Larry said.

Eli stepped aside as the pale, hairy caretaker walked back

into the messy living room. He opened the birdcage. "C'mon, Anita, girl. There's my boopie-boopie. That's my nickname for her. Hey, boopie-boopie!" The canary jumped on his finger, and Larry carefully took Anita out of her cage.

"My mom and I already figured out the place is haunted," Eli said, watching him play with his bird. "Plus one of the neighbors told us about the lady who killed her son in there and then killed herself. I just thought you might know more. I won't tell anyone you said anything, I swear."

Larry pursed his lips at the canary and cooed at it. Then he gave Eli a wary look. "You rat on me, and I'll have Anita peck your eyes out."

"I wouldn't," Eli murmured.

"Ha, I'm messing with you," Larry grinned. He put the bird back in its cage, then fussed with the water and feeder trays. Eli heard some seeds spill onto the newspaper. "I really don't know that much about it, sport," Larry said. "I do know they replaced the tub upstairs in that unit."

"The tub?" Eli repeated.

Larry nodded. He seemed focused on his chores with the birdcage. "Yeah, that's where she shot herself after she slit the kid's throat."

"The mother shot herself in the bathtub?" Eli said, blinking. He thought about all the weird disturbances in their bathroom.

"Yep," Larry replied. "They found her in the tub with a bullet in her head and the gun on the bathroom floor. They replaced the tub for the next tenant. Everything else in there is the original fixtures."

"And the son," Eli said numbly. "Where did they find him?"

"In his bed," the caretaker answered, still tinkering with his canary's cage. The bird wouldn't stop chirping. "I think she killed him in his sleep, but I'm not sure."

Eli nervously rubbed his forearms and felt gooseflesh. He

was thinking about what the Ouija board had told him. It had said the boy died in his bedroom. It had spelled out *L-A-C-E-R-A-T-I-O-N*. "She cut her son's throat?" Eli heard himself ask.

"That's what I hear."

"Do you know how old the son was?" Eli asked. The Ouija board had said Carl was fourteen.

"A young teenager, I think," Larry replied with a shrug. "Probably around your age."

The sweet, spicy smell of that rabbit cooking started to make Eli sick. "Um, do you know when this happened?" he asked. "What year?"

"Some time in the mid-seventies."

"Did you—did you ever get their names?"

"Nope," Larry said, wiping his hands on the front of his pale blue shorts. He peeked into the cage. "Okay, boopie-boopie, all cleaned up," he cooed to Anita. The bird kept chirping.

"Is there any way to find out their names and when they lived here?" Eli pressed. "I mean, the management company must have some kind of records, right?"

Larry reached under his yellowish T-shirt and scratched his pale, hairy stomach. "Nope, sorry, sport." He shook his head as he walked past Eli and into the kitchen again. "They tossed out all the old documents when the apartment complex changed ownership back in 1987." He stirred the potato concoction on the stove, then turned up the heat.

"Do you think any of the neighbors here might know more about them? The kid and his mother, I mean. . . ."

"I doubt it," Larry said, opening the oven to peek at his rabbit again. "Most of the people who were living here when it happened in the seventies are long gone now."

"Do you know if any of them still live in the neighborhood?" Eli asked.

Larry shut the oven door, leaned over the stove, and scratched his chin. "Shit, what was that old lady's name?" he muttered—

almost to himself. "Vera something, she moved away two years ago. Wait a sec, I know . . ."

Larry brushed by him as he moved back into the living room. He opened up the middle drawer of an old rolltop desk. "She sent me a Christmas card last year. It's in here somewhere. Good thing I don't throw anything away. Vera something, she was still pretty much on the ball for an old lady, only her legs were giving out. So she moved into this rest home. Sucks to get old. Here it is . . ." He pulled out an envelope. "Cormier, Vera Cormier," he said, reading the preprinted return address label. Then he handed the envelope to Eli. "Go ahead, you can keep that if you want."

Eli glanced at the shaky penmanship on the front of the envelope and the Christmas wreath return address label:

Vera D. Cormier
Evergreen Point Manor
7711 Evergreen Court, N.E.
Seattle, WA 98177-5492

"Do you know where this Evergreen Point Manor is?" Eli asked.

"It's this rest home up in north Seattle," Larry said. "Not too far, about a fifteen-minute drive."

There was a hissing sound, and Larry rushed to the stove to turn down the heat on his potato dish, which was boiling over. Now a burning smell competed with the sickly sweet waft from the roasting rabbit.

"Did you want to keep the card?" Eli asked, pulling out the Christmas card. It had a cheesy painting of a bird on a holly branch on the cover.

"Read what she says, will ya?" Larry replied, tending to his potatoes and cabbage.

Under the preprinted *Merry Christmas,* she'd scribbled something in her frail hand. "Um, *'Happy Holidays to you and all my Tudor Court neighbors,*" Eli read aloud. "'*I keep busy, busy, busy here. Miss you, Larry. Hello to Anita. Best Wishes for the New Year. Vera.*'"

"Keep it," Larry said, still toiling over the stove. "Anyway, if you want the real lowdown on that murder-suicide, Vera's your lady. She was living right next door in Number Ten when it happened."

Eli politely turned down Larry's second offer to dine with him. Larry cut off a piece of his roasted rabbit, then wrapped it in tinfoil, and stuck it in a plastic store bag for Eli to take home with him. "I promise you, you haven't tasted anything like this," Larry said with a wink.

"Well, thanks," Eli said. *And I promise you, I'm not going to taste it*, he thought.

He was glad to breathe fresh air again as he stepped out to the courtyard. Slipping Vera's Christmas card back into the envelope, he folded the envelope and shoved it in his pants pocket. Eli held onto the plastic bag with the roast rabbit part in it. Though tempted to toss it in the Dumpster, he didn't want Larry finding it tomorrow and getting his feelings hurt.

A cool wind came off the lake, and Eli shuddered. He suddenly had a weird feeling. It was the same sensation he sometimes got in his bedroom at night—when he wasn't quite *alone*. He felt this invisible *other presence*, like someone or something was there watching him.

Glancing around the courtyard, Eli didn't see anyone. He stopped to stare at that alley again. But no one was there.

He still felt a little sick to his stomach, but it wasn't something left over from the smell of that rabbit cooking. It was a feeling of dread he couldn't shake.

Eli nervously patted the envelope in his pocket, and he hurried toward the apartment.

* * *

"Eli?" his mom called, when he came in the front door. "Honey, is that you?"

He didn't even have time to answer or shut the door. She scurried out of the kitchen. "Oh, thank God," she said, hugging him. "You gave me such a scare. Where were you?"

He gently pulled back from her. "I just went for a short walk, that's all. What's the big deal? Why are you acting so weird?"

She glanced at the plastic bag in his hand, the one holding Larry's roast rabbit section, wrapped in tinfoil. "What's that?" his mom asked.

"I got some candy at the store," he lied.

She put her hand on his shoulder. "Listen, honey, I'm sorry I snapped at you earlier. Sit down for a second, okay? I have to tell you something that might help explain why I'm *'acting so weird . . .'"*

Eli sat on the stairs, the third from the bottom step, and his mother leaned against the banister. She asked if he remembered the guy she'd almost hit with her car while pulling out of the driveway earlier that afternoon. Eli had barely caught a glimpse of him. His mother gave a long description of the man: medium build, black hair, olive skin, possibly a Latino, one eye had an infection of some kind, and he wore a navy blue T-shirt with a silver number *59* on the front. She explained how she'd spotted the same man an hour later in the audience at the ValuCo event, only he'd had on sunglasses and a baseball cap. At least, she was almost positive it had been the same man, and he'd had on the same T-shirt. "Did you notice anyone with a navy blue *59* T-shirt when you were wandering around the fun fair?" she asked.

"No, Mom," Eli said, shaking his head. "But y'know, the Seattle Mariners' team colors are navy blue and silver, and 59 is probably a real popular number because of Felix Hernandez. You sure it wasn't two different guys in the same T-shirt?"

His mother just stared at him for a moment. Then she

rubbed her forehead. "Oh, good Lord, you must think your mother's a crazy woman." She sat beside him on the stairs. "That didn't occur to me about the shirt. But it did look very much like the same man. And if both guys were one and the same, it means he followed us all the way out to Auburn. He knows where we live. Can you see why I'm a little concerned? I keep thinking about that weird break-in on the Fourth of July."

"So you figure you got a stalker?" Eli asked.

"It's a possibility," she said soberly. "Anyway, do your crazy mother a favor, and keep a lookout for someone fitting that description. If you want to step outside, let me know where you're going and when you'll be back. Let's err on the side of caution for the next few days, okay? Humor me. Maybe I'll give you that cell phone you've been wanting."

Eli nodded. "Okay." He managed to smile at his mother. "Sorry I took off like that, Mom," he murmured, patting her shoulder.

She kissed his forehead, then rubbed her hand over his scalp. "Your hair's starting to grow out again. It looks nice."

"Well, I'm gonna wash up," he said, standing. "What time is Uncle Kyle coming over?"

"I don't know. I haven't heard back from him yet. But I'm hoping we can eat soon. Don't eat too much of that candy and spoil your appetite."

"I won't," Eli said. He started up the stairs, but paused on the landing and glanced back at his mother. She moved over to the front door and double-locked it.

He continued up the stairs and stopped in the second-floor hallway. Switching on the bathroom light, Eli stood in the doorway for a few moments. He gazed at the bathtub, the one they'd replaced after that woman had shot herself in the old tub.

Eli retreated to his room, closed the door, then dumped Larry's rabbit-doggie-bag in the trash can. Something shiny on his desk caught his eye—a tiny metal train engine. It looked like a Monopoly token, only his Monopoly set didn't have a train token.

"Who would . . ." he started to whisper.

He knew the Monopoly tokens had changed over the years. Maybe they had train tokens back in the seventies.

Back when that kid was murdered in this room.

Sydney didn't hear any water churning in the second-floor bathroom as she climbed the stairs. "Eli, honey, if you're not going to take a shower right now, I might jump in ahead—"

She stopped at the top of the stairs, and set her purse on the half-table in the the hallway.

Eli stood in his bedroom doorway with something shiny in the palm of his hand. "Hey, Mom, did you leave this on my desk?"

She looked at the Monopoly train token, and shook her head. "No, honey."

"Well, it was on my desk," he said. "And I didn't put it there. Do you think your stalker guy broke in and set this on there?"

Sydney hesitated before answering him. *Terrific*, she thought, *I've made my son a nervous wreck*. She worked up a smile and shook her head. "I don't think so. The front door was locked when we got back from Auburn, and so was the back door. I checked."

"But maybe he broke in like he did on the Fourth of July, only this time, he locked up after himself."

"I doubt it, honey. I mean, if the man I saw at the ValuCo event is indeed stalking me, he was in Auburn when we were there. He couldn't have gotten back here that much sooner than us." She stroked Eli's arm reassuringly. "It was probably on your desk earlier, only you just didn't notice."

Eli looked like he was about to say something, but hesitated. He frowned at her. "Fine," he muttered finally.

"If you're not going to use the bathroom, do you mind if I pop in the shower?" she asked.

He headed for his room. "I don't care," he said, his back to her.

Sydney watched him close the door. He almost seemed *disappointed* that they hadn't had a break-in. Of course, she couldn't blame him. To a bored, suddenly friendless, twelve-year-old boy, a potential break-in was something exciting.

Reaching back for the zipper to her top, Sydney headed into her room. She walked through the doorway into a wall of warm air. This room usually didn't cool down until nighttime. A fly darted in front of her—and then another. Sydney stopped to shoo them away. Their buzzing sound seemed to fill the bedroom. She glanced over toward the open window, where a few more flies scurried around against the sunlight. Some stopped to crawl over the windowpanes.

"My God," she murmured. There were at least a dozen flies in her bedroom.

It didn't make any sense. Except for one side window, which was open only a few inches, all of her windows had screens.

Then she noticed something on her pillow, something dark on the pale blue and white sham that matched her quilt bedspread. A swirl of flies buzzed around it.

Her mouth open, Sydney stared at the small dead bird. It looked like a robin—with its mousey brown feathers and reddish chest. The poor thing was perfectly centered on her pillow as if laid to rest there.

Dazed, she took a few steps back and bumped into her dresser. "Eli!" she screamed. "Eli, could you come in here, please? Now?"

He'd left here mad at her, then returned with something in a rolled-up plastic bag. But she couldn't believe he'd do something this sick, no matter how angry he was at her.

"What is it?" he called.

She grimaced at the sight of all the flies picking at the dead robin on her pillow. "Um, come in here, please," Sydney repeated. She was getting so upset, she couldn't breathe right. "I need you to look at something . . . *now*."

Eli came to her door. "What's going on?"

Sydney pointed at her bed. "Are you responsible for this?"

He glanced over at her pillow and winced. "Oh, God, gross!"

"You didn't put it there?" she pressed.

He scowled at her, "No, of course not!" He looked at the dead robin again. "Jeez . . ."

"Well, it didn't just fall out of the sky and land there dead," she argued. "You sure you didn't put that there?"

"Of course I'm sure! God, stop asking me that!" Eli glared at her and shook his head. "You think I killed a bird?"

"I didn't say you *killed* it. But maybe you found it outside someplace, already dead. I know you were mad at me—"

"I didn't leave that fucking bird there!" he yelled, cutting her off. "God, I can't believe you'd think I'd do something like that! This is so fucked!"

Sydney was stunned. Eli had never used language like that in front of her. She saw tears in his eyes. She took a deep breath. "Okay, I'm sorry, but—"

"God, I hate you!" he screamed over her. He spun around and stomped toward his room. "This really sucks!" he yelled, his voice choked with tears. "I want to live with Dad! I can't stand living with you!"

Sydney heard his bedroom door slam.

Frazzled, she marched out to the hallway, grabbed her purse off the table, and dug out her cell phone. "Well, that's just fine with me!" she screamed. She put the cell phone down on the floor, by his threshold. "Go ahead! Call him! I just left my cell phone by your door. Call your father and tell him you want to stay with him. And while you're at it, tell him you just used the f-word in front of me *twice*! I don't care how angry you are, you don't use that kind of language in front of your mother. If you pulled something like that in front of your dad, he would have nailed your hide to the wall! Go stay with him! I'll even help you pack! I'm so sick of you moping around and blaming me for everything! Do you think I like this?"

Eli's bedroom door opened a crack. He glared out at her.

Sydney felt tears stinging her eyes. Her throat was sore from screaming. She took a deep breath. "I'm sorry I accused you of putting that dead bird on my bed," she said in a scratchy, strained voice. "But you left the house mad at me, then returned with something in that old plastic bag and came up here. I didn't know what to think. Anyway, Eli, I'm sorry, I know you'd never do anything that—that *creepy*."

He stared at her through the narrow door opening. Crouching down, he swiped her cell phone off the floor.

Then Eli shut the door.

"Hi, you've reached the McClouds," his mother's recorded voice said. His dad still hadn't changed the greeting. *"Sorry we missed you. Leave a message for Joe, Sydney, and Eli after the beep. Bye!"*

"Hello, Dad?" Eli said, after the beep. He swallowed past the tightness in his throat. He didn't want his father to know he'd just been crying. "You home? Are you there? It's me—"

There was a click on the other end of the line. "Hey, buddy," his father said. "I was just call-screening . . ." He lapsed into his Arnold Schwarzenegger impression for a moment: "I am *The Screenanator*." Then he went back to his normal voice. "So what are you up to, sport?"

"Nothing much," Eli said. He sat down on the edge of his bed. "I went to some stupid store opening with Mom today.

She had to give a speech. How are you, Dad? What have you been doing?"

"Oh, work, tinkering around in the garage, trying to keep busy—same old, same old." There was a pause. "How are you doing, Eli? You don't sound so good."

"I'm not," he admitted, his voice cracking. "I miss you, Dad."

"Oh, hang in there, buddy. It'll get easier."

"No, it won't," he argued. "I want to move back and stay with you. I hate it here. Mom's so tense all the time, and we fight—like every day."

"That's because you two are so much alike. You guys are just adjusting—"

"I want to move back with you. Please, Dad? Mom said I could. She said she'd even help me pack."

He heard his father let out a little chuckle on the other end of the line. "It sounds like she was mad at you about something. Are you guys in the middle of a fight?"

"Kinda," Eli replied. "Dad, please, I can't stand living with her. And she's sick of me, too. She just said so."

"You know she doesn't mean that," he said. "You two are just mad at each other right now. Be patient with her, okay? She's really trying. I know she must have felt bad that Timmy McKenna and Brad Reece couldn't come out and visit. But you'll be making friends there—"

"Wait," Eli interrupted. "What are you talking about? Timmy and Brad were going to come out here?"

"She didn't tell you? I figured you knew. She was trying to do it for you. The McKennas mentioned it to me. Your mom phoned them, offering to pay Tim's way to Seattle so he could stay with you guys a few days. I guess she tried the same thing with the Reeces, trying to get Brad to visit. But—you know, the guys got baseball and they just couldn't get away."

"Mom was trying to do that—for me?" Eli whispered. He suddenly felt so awful for screaming at her.

"She's doing the best she can, Eli. You just have to hang in there. It wouldn't work out if you moved back with me right now. They have me jumping through hoops at work, and I'm awfully busy. You'd be alone in the house most of the time. You're much better off with your mom in Seattle. Give it another few weeks."

Eli said nothing.

"It was ninety-nine degrees here today," his father said. "Believe me, you're better off where you are. Listen, I should scram. You go make up with your mother now, okay?"

"Why can't *you* make up with her?" Eli asked quietly.

"It isn't as easy for adults," his father muttered. "And you and I have been over this before, sport. Now, I better go. I love you, Eli."

"I love you, too, Dad."

"G'night," his father said. Then he hung up.

Eli clicked off the cell phone. Wiping his eyes, he wandered to his door. He opened it—just wide enough to put the cell phone down on the floor.

He closed the door again, then lay facedown on his bed. Eli buried his face in the pillow so she wouldn't hear him crying.

CHAPTER ELEVEN

Sipping pinot grigio from a Speed Racer jelly glass, Sydney sat in a patio chair by the kitchen door, which she'd propped open. There was a railing in front of her, and just beyond it, Lake Washington. She always felt as if she were on a ship's deck back here on this little stretch of concrete behind the town house. The lake was still. Moonlight revealed only a few silver ripples. She listened to the night swimmers on the beach next door, laughing and splashing. It made her feel so lonely, she wanted to cry. In the distance, she could see the headlights of cars on the 520 floating bridge.

She'd wrapped the dead robin in some paper towels, then put it in the garbage can on the other side of the kitchen door, just behind her. She'd found a can of Raid in the broom closet and sprayed in her bedroom, all the while thinking about ozone depletion. After vacuuming up the dead flies, she'd stripped off the pillow shams and quilt, then stuffed them in a big plastic bag. The bag would take up most of her closet floor—covering her sneakers, sandals, and slippers—until she hauled it to the dry cleaner on Monday.

Maybe by then, Eli would have decided to come out of his room and speak to her. She'd ordered a small cheese pizza for him around eight o'clock and left it outside his room, along with some napkins and a cold can of Mountain Dew. Then she'd knocked on the door. "There's pizza here by your door, honey. Don't let it get cold. And don't starve yourself just because you're mad at me."

She heard his portable TV going when she checked an hour later. The Jet City Pizza box was where she'd left it, but when she opened the box, only one piece remained. The Mountain Dew can was empty. At least he was eating.

She was the one self-starving. She'd thrown together a salad, but only had a few bites of it before reaching for a jelly glass and the bottle of pinot grigio, then heading outside.

This was her second glass.

Sydney wondered how that robin had gotten in her bedroom. She hadn't noticed any loose feathers while vacuuming up the flies, so it was highly unlikely the poor thing had flown in through the small opening in the window and then died on her bed somehow. And to land right in the center of her pillow like that? This hadn't been any freak accident.

If Eli hadn't put it there, who had? Was it her stalker? She'd already answered that question earlier while talking with Eli about his Monopoly token. If Mr. 59 had indeed followed them to Auburn this afternoon, when would he have had time to break in and plant that little avian surprise?

Sydney wondered if it was their ghost—or whatever it was haunting this apartment. Freakish, unexplainable things had been happening in there. Why not this bird death?

It was a silly notion, one Eli might fancy. He was too angry to talk with her right now. But once on speaking terms with her again, he'd probably come up with some pretty fantastic notions about ghosts and birds and Monopoly tokens. Then again, maybe he wouldn't say a thing to her. He could be very secretive at times.

It was a trait he'd inherited from her and his dad—but mostly her.

She remembered back in May, waiting until Kyle had left for Seattle before she'd checked the story on the Internet. She needed to confirm what Polly's friend, Aurora, had told her about that drug bust at Fort Jackson Point Pier. She remembered it must have been during the first part of March, because she'd been in Boston, covering a *Movers & Shakers* story. Otherwise, she would have found out about it—if not from Joe, then from the Chicago papers.

Sydney used her computer in her basement office. The keywords *Fort Jackson Pier Drugs Police Raid,* yielded several Google results. She clicked on the first one, and an article came up from *The Chicago Tribune*, dated March 6th:

2 SUSPECTS DIE IN CAR FIRE DURING POLICE RAID

Officers Seize $12,800 in Narcotics at Fort Jackson Pier

> CHICAGO: A police raid Tuesday on a narcotics operation near Fort Jackson Pier turned deadly as fleeing suspects opened fire on the arresting officers. The suspects, Ahmed Turner, 28, and Derrick Laskey, 23, both perished in a fiery explosion as their minivan, carrying an estimated $43,000 worth of cocaine, spun out of control and crashed into several drums containing highly flammable creosote residue.
>
> Turner, who had been driving the vehicle, was shot in the neck by police returning fire. Laskey, in the passenger seat, reportedly died in the ensuing fire . . .

The article confirmed everything Aurora had told her. Sydney stopped in the middle of the fifth paragraph. She felt an awful tightness in her chest as she saw something she'd hoped not to find. It was Joe's name, listed with the three other cops who had participated in the raid gone awry.

His name came up again a few paragraphs later:

> "We had no choice but to return fire on the perpetrators," said Detective McCloud, a 16-year Chicago Police veteran. "My fellow officers acted responsibly and very professionally."

According to the article, the $12,800 worth of cocaine recovered had been left behind in a backpack by one of the fleeing suspects. Both Ahmed Turner and Derrick Laskey had a long list of prior arrests.

Sydney googled both their names for any articles about a follow-up investigation into what had happened that night. But there were none.

She had to talk to Joe—even if he got testy. She had every right to ask her husband about something he did that was reported in the newspapers, for God's sake. The rest of the day went by without her finding the right time and opportunity to broach the subject.

She couldn't sleep worth a damn that evening. After an hour under the covers with Joe, she thought about getting up and reading in the family room for a while. Then she felt him nudge her, and his arm went over her. "What's with you tonight, babe?" he mumbled, his face against the back of her neck as he spooned her. "You've got the fidgets something fierce. I feel like I'm in bed with a whirling dervish."

"I ran into Adele Curtis in the vegetable aisle at Dominick's today," she lied. It was the "casual" lead-in she'd been planning all day to use. "She—um, asked how you were and said she read about you in some drug bust at Fort Jackson Point Pier a few weeks back. Adele said a couple of guys were killed. I felt stupid not knowing anything about it."

Joe's arm slipped away as he turned on his other side. "It happened while you were in Boston, covering that cancer survivor story," he muttered. "By the time you got back, it was old news. I didn't think it was worth going into."

"Not worth going into?" she repeated. "Honey, in the last thirteen years you've only fired your weapon—what, four times? Two guys were killed, and you didn't talk to me about it . . ."

"You were editing and scoring your cancer story," he said. "I knew you had to stay focused on that. I didn't want to distract you with *my* problems."

Sydney said nothing for a moment. Considering how often she went on the road to cover a story, leaving Joe to play bachelor-dad with Eli, he was usually pretty good about it. Only once in a while did he make her feel guilty, and this was one of those times. She rolled over toward him—only to stare at the back of his head. "I'm sorry I wasn't there for you," she whispered. "Do you want to talk about it now?"

"Talk about what, the drug raid? It was a routine raid on a small-time operation. It got screwed up and two career criminals fried in their getaway car. It happened nearly a month ago, and no thanks, I don't want to talk about it."

"And you wouldn't have wanted to talk about it when it happened either," she pointed out. "So—don't try to make me feel bad because I was away when it happened."

"Fair enough," he grumbled.

She studied the back of his head. "Is there any connection between this drug bust and that Arthur 'Polly' Pollard person who was shot?"

He sighed, but didn't flinch at all. "Not that I know of," he muttered.

"Did they ever find out who shot him?" she pressed.

"I think it was a mob hit. But they haven't nailed down any suspects yet. They probably won't. Polly had more enemies than friends." Joe yawned. "Listen, why don't you take a pill if you can't sleep?"

Sydney didn't take a pill, and she didn't sleep much that night. Three days later, she went to Madison, Wisconsin, to cover a Spam-carving contest. Despite the "wacky" festivities, she was in a somber mood during the two-day trip. She had to fake her frivolity for the contestants and the cameras. All the while she was in Madison, Sydney thought about Polly and this drug raid. She wondered if she could just drop it and choose not to know any more. In order to survive, some husbands and wives turned a blind eye to their spouses' extramarital affairs or crooked—even nefarious—business deals. That was how they stayed married. The trouble was Sydney didn't know if she could be one of those wives.

When Sydney returned home, there was a surprise waiting for her in the family room. Joe put his hands over her eyes, and Eli led her by the hand. And when Joe took his hands away from her eyes, Sydney was watching a scene from *Superman Returns* on their new big-screen, high-definition TV. "We're going to see *Movers & Shakers* in HD, sweetheart!" Joe declared. Eli couldn't wait to see *Lord of the Rings* in HD. But Sydney just stared at the beautiful, sharp picture on that huge, state-of-the-art TV screen and felt sick to her stomach. She knew where the money for it had come from. "Can we afford it?" she murmured.

"No, but I figure it's a tax write-off for you," Joe said. "We'll work it out."

The next day, she neglected the editing and scoring of her Spam-carving piece so she could rifle through Joe's desk and check the e-mail in his computer again. There was nothing. She called Visa; the charge for the TV had gone on their joint card. They had barely enough in their checking account to cover it. Joe wasn't the type to spend money he didn't have. So where was the extra money? Where had he hidden his cut from this drug bust—or correction, this *heist* that had cost three people their lives? Did he have a secret bank account somewhere?

In her earlier searches she would have noticed a bank passbook or checkbook among Joe's things. So she went through his closet and the pockets of his clothes. Sydney checked under the rug and behind the framed photos in his study. Then it dawned on her: *they had the cleanest garage on North Spaulding Avenue.* He was always working in there. If Joe needed to hide something from her, the garage was where he'd stash it.

Sydney stormed the place, rifling through his built-in work desk and cabinets. She accidentally yanked one drawer out all the way, spilling a bunch of bolts and screws on the garage floor. But she didn't care. She ransacked the contents of two different toolboxes. In his cabinets, she shoved aside old paint cans to make sure they weren't hiding a bankbook or some incriminating document. "Where is it, Joe?" she kept whispering. "What are you hiding from me?" From the shelves he'd installed, Sydney tossed work gloves, coveralls, and paintbrushes aside so she could get a better look at what might be concealed behind them or beneath them. She scoured through boxes of Christmas decorations, finding nothing.

Dirty and sweating, she paused for a moment and gazed up at the top shelf, where he stored a rolled-up paint tarp. Sydney dragged a ladder over to the shelf and climbed up to reach the tarp. It started to unravel. Frustrated, she finally pushed it off the shelf. The big heavy cloth landed in a heap on the garage floor—around the bottom of the ladder. The shelf was empty now—except for a third toolbox. It looked new. "Oh, no," Sydney murmured, feeling her stomach turn.

Trembling, she took another step up the ladder and grabbed the handle of the tan metal box. It wasn't as heavy as the other two toolboxes she'd examined. She could tell he didn't have any tools in there. Sydney almost tripped on the tarp as she climbed down from the ladder, hauling the metal box with her. Setting the box on the hood of her car, she unfastened the latches. Her hands were shaking as she opened the lid.

Receipts.

He'd stashed old receipts for paint, power tools, and yard equipment in there. Sydney let out a grateful little laugh. It looked like a whole boxful of receipts—until she picked up a few to examine them even closer. That was when she saw part of a twenty-dollar bill under the pile of loose papers. She dug past those old receipts and saw more twenties. There were stacks of them, banded together. "Damn it, Joe," she cried. "Damn it, damn it to hell . . ."

She didn't count the money. But Sydney estimated there was at least twenty thousand dollars in that metal box.

As she stacked the money back into the metal receptacle, Sydney couldn't stop crying. She covered the stacks of bills with the old receipts. If Joe had the receipts in any kind of special order to detect if someone had gotten into the box, she didn't care. She would tell him tonight that she knew and that their marriage was over.

She couldn't live with this secret. She couldn't look at Joe the same way ever again. He'd once been her hero, and now he was a lying, corrupt cop who let three people die for a little bit of money. And he'd forever ruined three more peoples' lives: his son's, hers, and his own.

Sydney rolled up the heavy tarp and hoisted it back onto the top shelf, once again concealing the metal box. She moved the ladder back to its original spot. Still sobbing, she swept up the bolts and screws she'd spilt from his work desk drawer. Her face was filthy because she kept wiping away tears and snot with her dirty hands.

She wouldn't blow the whistle on her husband. For now, his secret was her awful secret, too. But she wasn't going to stay with him, either. She couldn't be associated in any way with his crime—and neither could Eli. They needed to put as much distance as they could between themselves and him. These thoughts weren't new to Sydney. For the last few weeks, ever since she'd learned of Arthur Pollard's death, she'd tried to prepare herself for this.

But it still devastated her.

Sydney's head was throbbing by the time she wandered out of the garage. In the kitchen, she took three Tylenol, and then glanced at her wristwatch: 4:25. She had to pick up Eli from basketball practice at school in a half hour.

It was strange, walking into their bedroom and undressing to take a shower. Suddenly, the room seemed different somehow, like it wasn't hers anymore.

Even under the warm, pulsating shower, Sydney still didn't feel clean. She turned off the water and began to dry herself. Wrapping the towel around her, she opened the bathroom door, and a shadow swept in front of her. She gasped. Someone was in the bedroom.

Then she saw it was Joe. "My, God, you scared me!" she said, a hand over her heart. "What are you doing here?"

He stood near the foot of their bed in his "plainclothes": blue blazer, tie, and khaki slacks. "We need to talk," he said soberly.

Sydney nodded. "I know. But I have to get dressed, and pick up Eli at school."

"Sharon McKenna's picking up Eli, and taking him back to their place for dinner."

"That's nice," Sydney murmured. She ducked behind the bathroom door, took her pale blue jacquard silk robe off the hook, and put it on. Then she tossed her towel over the shower curtain rod. "It's nice that you're talking to Andy again, too," she said, emerging from the bathroom again. She tied the waist sash of her robe.

"I heard you were asking Sharon at the wedding if she knew about Polly," he said. "That was really careless, Syd."

"I asked you first—several times. I needed an answer."

"All you did was put a big spotlight on the situation," Joe said. "Today, I had to hear from someone that you were sniffing around a Cicero bar, asking questions about Polly."

"Who told you?" she asked, running a hand over her damp hair.

"Never mind," he grumbled. He plopped down on the bed, rubbed his forehead, and sighed. "The point is, you're linking my name with his. You don't know how much damage you're doing, Syd."

"What about the damage you've done, Joe?" she asked, pointedly. "I know about the money. I found it today in the garage—in that metal box you've hidden. It's your cut of that drug-bust swindle, isn't it?"

His mouth open, Joe just stared at her.

Sydney felt tears welling in her eyes. "The minute you took that money, Joe, you ruined our marriage. You ruined this family."

"You don't know the circumstances."

"Fine. Look me in the eye and tell me you've switched to Internal Affairs work and this is all some undercover thing. I'll believe you, Joe. I *want* to believe you. Tell me this money doesn't have blood on it. Tell me I'm wrong, and in a month or so all of this will be switched around and you're going to be my hero again—instead of some low-life corrupt cop on the take."

He gave her a wounded look. "Is that what you think I am?"

"What am I supposed to think? Every time I've asked you about this sordid business, you've been evasive or you've snapped at me, or you've lied to me. So what really happened, Joe? It can't be any worse than what I've imagined."

He gazed down at the floor, then rubbed his eyes.

"I'm thinking you and the three other cops killed those two guys," Sydney answered for him. "Then you set fire to their van to make it look like an accident—but not until you'd already unloaded the drugs. How much did you get for the cocaine? Did Polly demand a cut? Is that why he was killed?"

"You're not very far off," he said quietly. "Sydney, I didn't know what the other guys were up to until it was too late. If I hadn't gone along with them, they would have shot me right there."

She gazed at him. "Did *you* kill anybody?"

He turned and looked her in the eye. "No, honey, I didn't."

"How much did they steal?"

"Over half a million's worth," he muttered.

"And how much was your cut?"

"Thirty-two thousand," he answered. "But I wasn't going to spend any of it. You can go look in that metal box again and count it if you want. It's all still there. I'm thinking of anonymously donating the whole wad to charity."

"No, you aren't," she argued. "You might have convinced yourself of that on the surface. But I know you, Joe, and you don't spend money you don't have. We can't afford a big-screen, high-definition TV, but you bought one because you knew you had some money to fall back on in a pinch. You're spending it already, and you don't even know it." She shook her head at him. "Why didn't you just turn around and give the money to Len? He's your superior officer. You trust him. If you were really coerced into this swindle, why didn't you go to Len and explain it to him? Why not go public with this?"

"Believe me, I couldn't," he said, exasperated. "It's too complicated to explain. Once I took that money, I was screwed. But if I hadn't taken it, they would have killed me. Would you rather have me dead right now?"

Sydney just stared at him. He was being evasive again.

He let out a cynical laugh. "Huh, of course you'd rather have me dead. Just think what that would do for your ratings if you were the widow of a murdered cop."

His words stung. She continued to glare at him. "And just think of how fast my career would go down the toilet if news of your involvement in this heist ever got out. Think about Eli, and how this would devastate him." She moved to a stuffed chair in the corner of the room and sat down. Sydney nervously rubbed her leg. She felt her whole body tensing up. "Joe, I—I've been wondering what I should do—if all this was true. I'll keep your secret, but I can't stay with you. I'm sorry, but you crossed a line when you took that money and hid it. You crossed it when you lied to me and made me ashamed of you. This isn't some little scandal. I'd stand by you if it was something like that. But people were killed, Joe. And I—I can't pretend that didn't happen."

He gazed down at the floor. "So what are you going to do? Where will you go?" He shook his head. "Because I'm not moving out of this house, that's for sure."

She was surprised at the sudden anger in his tone. "School ends next week," she said steadily. "I'll take Eli, and we'll stay with my brother in Seattle for a while—at least until I figure out something more permanent."

Joe got to his feet. "You know, this didn't have to happen," he grumbled. "If only you'd kept your fucking mouth shut and believed in me. You never gave a crap about my work until this. And now, thanks to your snooping around, they're breathing down my neck. These guys have it out for me. But go ahead, desert me, *sweetheart*. Hell, I'm used to it. Maybe if you were *home for a change* while all this shit was going down, I might have had some support. Maybe I wouldn't be in this bind right now."

Sydney stood up. "Don't try to blame this on me—"

"Why wait until next week to leave?" he yelled. He flung open her closet door, then yanked her two suitcases off the shelf. "Why don't you find yourself a nice hotel tonight, huh?" He flung her suitcases on the bed. "Start packing. I don't want to see any of your shit in here tonight. Anything you leave behind I'll throw in the fucking garbage. And don't worry about Eli. You never did before. I'll call the McKennas and ask them to put him up for the night. Then he can stay with you tomorrow, and he'll see what it's like to be on the road with his mom for a change."

She moved toward him. "Joe, stop being this way. Don't you think—"

But she didn't finish. He hauled back his fist and hit her across the face.

The blow sent Sydney flying back, and she slammed into the dresser. She landed in a heap on the floor. Stunned, she couldn't see anything for a few moments. A high-pitched ringing filled her ears. Her head felt like it was going to explode, and then the side of her face started throbbing.

Sydney caught her breath and blinked a few times until he came into focus.

Joe stood over her, his hand still clenched in a fist. But he had such a tormented look on his face, she thought he might start crying. Tears welled in his eyes, and he shook visibly. "Just get out," he whispered.

Then he turned and stomped out of the bedroom.

Sydney did what Joe told her to do. She packed two suitcases and two boxes and spent the night at a Holiday Inn. She phoned Kyle and asked if she and Eli could stay with him the following week. Kyle kept saying she sounded terrible, and Sydney admitted that Joe had hit her. She didn't tell him anything else.

She refilled her ice bucket twice—for the homemade cold compresses she applied to her face most of the night. Not surprisingly, she didn't sleep well. She was worried about Eli and how his parents separating would destroy the poor kid. He wouldn't want to leave Joe. They were so close.

At one point in the evening, Sydney finally got out of bed

and wandered to the window. She pushed the curtain aside a bit and peered outside at her car, parked just a few feet away. Three spaces down from that was Joe's Honda Civic. Sydney wasn't sure why he was there. Did he plan to kick down her door and beat her up some more? He'd never hurt her before tonight. It was like he was a different man. She didn't know what he might do.

The light from the green Holiday Inn sign illuminated the front seat of his Civic. He sat at the wheel, looking miserable and staring off in another direction. Even in the distance, she could tell he was crying.

He wasn't there when she woke up in the morning. But his older sister, Helen, was. A stocky brunette with a pretty face, Helen was divorced, and lived in Evanston with her twin seventeen-year-old sons. Sydney liked Helen, despite her habit of telling everyone what to do. "You and Eli are staying with me and the boys until you work this thing out with Joe," she announced in the doorway of Sydney's hotel room.

"Oh, Helen, I don't think Joe and I have much chance of working things out," she admitted. Her hair a mess and her face badly bruised, Sydney was still in her robe. "How did you know where to find me?"

"Joe told me. He isn't a detective for nothing. So you'll stay with us until you come up with Plan B, whatever that is. I won't take no for an answer. Eli should be with you right now, but not here in some hotel. He should be with family. The boys will keep him entertained and distracted. If you're moving out of the house, I'll help you find some movers who aren't going to rip you off."

Sydney squinted at her. "Why are you doing this?"

"Because you and Eli are family," Helen answered matter-of-factly. "And my kid brother is acting like a *dickhead*—if I can borrow a term my boys overuse. I hope you slugged him back."

The temporary living arrangement with Joe's sister and

her teenage sons should have been awkward, but it was oddly ideal for everyone. Eli had his cool older cousins to help buffer the blow of his parents' impending separation. They'd been through it before when Helen had thrown their dad out of the house for the final time three years before. Eli asked his mother about her bruised left cheek, which makeup didn't quite conceal. She told her son that she'd run into a door, and he believed her.

Between Joe's visiting Eli at Helen's house, and Sydney's trips back and forth as she finished all the packing at North Spaulding Avenue, running into each other was unavoidable. Other people were usually around, so Sydney and Joe were civil to each other. But every time she saw him, he looked so forlorn.

"Let him suffer," her sister-in-law advised her.

Sydney didn't tell Helen the reason she'd decided to leave Joe. She had a hunch that perhaps her sister-in-law already knew. It didn't really matter. Sydney was grateful to Helen for helping her survive that miserable week in limbo.

Sydney had moved all of her things out of the North Spaulding house—along with everything that originally belonged to her family. Eli had taken about forty percent of his stuff, mostly things he would need over the summer. Unlike her, Eli would be coming back for visits—court appointed, once they'd started divorce proceedings.

"We haven't discussed divorce yet," Joe had written in that awful letter she'd received today. *"And I hope we can keep the situation status quo for a few more weeks. I need this break from you and Eli . . ."*

Sydney took another sip of pinot grigio from the Speed Racer jelly glass. She stared at the headlights of cars on the 520 floating bridge in the distance. A cool wind came off the lake. She touched the side of her face that had been black and blue for several days back in May. For a while, she'd thought it would never stop hurting.

That damn letter. Eli obviously knew where she'd stashed it. She'd caught him prying into that breakfront drawer earlier tonight. It was what had started this latest fracas.

Getting to her feet, Sydney carried her glass of wine inside, then closed and double-locked the kitchen door. She stepped into her office and switched on her computer. It always took a moment to warm up; so she headed into the dining room. She dug Joe's letter from the built-in breakfront's bottom drawer, then returned to her little office and sat down in front of the computer. Her new e-mail messages popped up: a bunch of spam from Macy's, AOL, Amazon.com, and others, and what looked like a fan e-mail: *"Thank You"* from prettylizg@gilfordcorp.com.

She deleted the spam e-mail, then glanced at Joe's letter again. She could understand him not wanting to see her, but why brush off poor Eli, who adored him?

Sydney ripped up the letter. She was about to toss the torn pieces away in the trash can by her desk, but hesitated. She imagined Eli going through her trash later, finding the scraps and taping them back together again—only to discover that his beloved dad needed a *break* from him.

Leaving the scraps of Joe's letter on the corner of her desk, she decided to toss them in the garbage outside after she checked her e-mail. She clicked her mouse to open up the thank-you message:

Dear Sydney,

It was so thoughtful of you to send those beautiful flowers. I m still in shock over Angela's death. It hasn't sunk in yet that my sweet older sister is gone. I got the terrible news late Tuesday night, and your flowers arrived the very next afternoon, before anyone else's condolences. The roses were perfect. They were Angie s favorite flower. Thank you for your kindness.

Yours Very Truly,
Elizabeth Gannon Grogen

PS: I found your business card among Angie s things, and it only had your e-mail. Please forgive the e-mail Thank You, but I didn t have your regular address.

Baffled, Sydney had no idea who Elizabeth Grogen was. It took her a moment to connect her to Angela Gannon, the paralegal who had talked that suicidal man in from the fourteenth-story ledge of her office building in Chicago.

"Angela's dead?" She reread her sister's e-mail, but there was no mention of how Angela had passed away.

It had happened again—another one of her *Movers & Shakers* people had died suddenly, and someone had sent flowers to a surviving family member, signing her name on the card.

When she'd read that note from the Dvoraks, thanking her for a flower arrangement she *didn't* send, Sydney had assumed they were confused. But no, obviously someone with the network must have been sending these flowers for her. It was strange they hadn't notified her about what they were doing on her behalf.

Sydney's fingers worked furiously over the keyboard. She went to Google, and typed in the keywords *Angela Gannon Chicago death.* Several articles appeared. "Oh, God, no," she whispered, covering her mouth as she read the first search result:

The Chicago Tribune - Front Page News
Woman Plunges to **Death** from . . . Victim Had Intervened . . .
Chicago: Dominique . . . The victim was **Angela Gannon**, 31, a paralegal at a law firm on the 14th floor . . .
www.chicagotribune.co/news/womanplunges/070908 - 14k

She clicked on the search engine, and anxiously read the article. The date was July 8th, last Wednesday, the same afternoon her flowers were delivered to Elizabeth Gannon Grogen's front door.

WOMAN PLUNGES TO HER DEATH FROM 14TH FLOOR OF MICHIGAN AVE. OFFICE BUILDING

Victim Had Intervened with a Suicidal Coworker at the Same Window 9 Months Ago

CHICAGO: Dominique Chandler, 26, was talking with a friend, Zackary Ross, 24, outside the Dexter Building on Michigan Avenue at 10:20 Tuesday night when they heard a scream from above. "We both looked up and saw this thing hurtling down at us," said Chandler. "It took me a moment to realize I was looking at a human being, a woman. It was as if the poor thing just fell out of the sky. Then her body hit the sidewalk curb with an awful thud. It was terrible."

The victim was Angela Gannon, 31, a paralegal at Gaines, McCourt and Weymiller, a law firm on the 14th floor of the building. Investigators on the scene discovered Gannon's purse beside an open window in the law office. No suicide note was found.

Just eight months ago, on November 14, Gannon had intervened when a disgruntled coworker had attempted to jump from a ledge outside that same 14th floor window. She managed to talk the man into climbing back inside, a feat that won her brief national attention when the story was profiled in a "Movers & Shakers" segment for the primetime TV newsmagazine, "On the Edge."

"I worked alongside Angela all day on Tuesday, and she was in a great mood," said Margarita Donovan, a coworker and friend. "I have a difficult time believing only hours later, she took her own

> life." Police are questioning another friend, Kent Blazenvich, 36, who had drinks with Gannon in the bar at a nearby Houlihan's Restaurant. Gannon left the bar alone at 9:40. Blazenvich remained there until approximately 11:30 . . .

Sydney read the article, hoping to find something more conclusive about Angela's bizarre death. Obviously, at press time, the police hadn't yet determined if it was a murder or suicide. They'd discovered Angela's car in the Dexter Building's underground parking garage, and it had been vandalized. Sydney wondered if this business with the car might have somehow triggered Angela's suicide. Sydney had sunk into horrible moods over less; sometimes one little thing could push a person over the edge, and a vandalized car was a pretty big deal.

Sydney had interviewed Angela back in November but hadn't corresponded with her since then. Still, she'd liked Angela's sense of humor. She had a lot of panache—and probably a lot of boyfriends, too. Had one of them been angry enough about her date that night with Kent Blazenvich that he'd vandalized Angela's car, dragged her up to the fourteenth floor of the Dexter Building, and hurled her out a window?

Clicking back a page on the Internet, Sydney tried to find another article on Angela's death that would give more information or an update of some kind. But none of the other articles offered anything new. Each story carried that same quote from the woman who had seen Angela's body plummet: *"It was as if the poor thing just fell out of the sky."*

Sydney rubbed her forehead, then switched off the computer. It was strange—first Leah and Jared, and now Angela Gannon. They'd died—violently—only four days apart. And their deaths, as far as she knew, were still unsolved.

Sighing, Sydney got to her feet and collected Joe's torn-up letter from her desktop. With the scraps of paper clutched in her fist, she wandered to the back door and unlocked it. She was thinking about Angela and Jared and Leah. Those kind of tragedies always happened in threes. Was that already three, or would someone else die?

A light breeze came off the lake as she stepped outside. The lid to the garbage can was stuck, and she had to jostle it a bit before she could open it.

"Oh, shit," Sydney whispered, startled. She'd forgotten about the dead robin in there. It must have rolled out of the paper towels when she'd moved the garbage can lid. Now the poor dead thing lay there in the moonlight.

Sydney still wondered how the dead bird had ended up on her pillow. She tossed the scraps of Joe's letter into the garbage. Then she very gingerly picked out a sheet of the paper towel and covered up the frail little feathered corpse again.

"Poor thing," she said to herself.

Then she thought of Angela, and a chill raced through her.

"It was as if the poor thing just fell out of the sky."

CHAPTER TWELVE

Sydney frowned at her slightly puffy reflection in the bathroom medicine chest mirror. *This is what you get for that third glass of pinot grigio last night,* she thought. She'd already gone downstairs and started up the Mr. Coffee machine. She'd also phoned the network.

George Camper was a head honcho in publicity. Forwarding fan letters and handling special requests were among his department's responsibilities. If someone from the network had sent Elizabeth Grogen and the Dvoraks flowers on her behalf, George would have known about it.

But the network was operating with a Sunday skeletal staff this morning, and nobody knew anything. They'd given her George's home phone number. Sydney had called there and left a message.

With her hair pulled back in a scrunchie, Sydney put some Visine drops in her eyes and then washed her face. She was still haunted by the thought she'd had last night—that perhaps there was a connection between the dead robin on her pillow and Angela's bizarre death.

Drying off her face, she heard the water dripping and glanced over at the sink. The hollow dripping sound wasn't coming from there. She gazed at the closed shower curtain with the map of the world on it. The curtain billowed in and out slightly—almost as if it were breathing. The dripping sound got steadier—then abruptly stopped. Sydney pulled back the curtain and saw the beaded water drops around the tub's drain. One last drop clung to the faucet. Suddenly, something crept out of the drain.

Sydney gasped and bumped into the sink as she recoiled. It took her a moment to realize it was a medium-size spider. But the black crawly thing had still scared the hell out of her. With a shaky hand, she gathered up some toilet paper, then swiped up the spider and flushed it down the toilet. She gave it a second flush, just to be sure.

She wondered if maybe that dead bird had more to do with this creepy town house than with Angela Gannon's death.

Opening the bathroom door, she hadn't expected to see anyone, and there stood Eli in his pajama bottoms and a T-shirt. Sydney gasped. "Good God, Eli, you scared the *you-know-what* out of me."

"Sorry," he muttered sleepily.

She caught her breath. At least he was talking to her now.

"You done in there?" he asked, rubbing his eyes.

She nodded, but remained in the bathroom doorway. "Are we okay?"

"I guess so," Eli replied. "Sorry about dropping those f-bombs on you last night."

She let out a stunned little laugh. "You're just lucky you didn't end up with a mouthful of Dial. I've never heard you use that kind of language." She patted his shoulder. "Anyway, I'm sorry I accused you of putting that bird on my bed. It really unnerved me to find it there. Maybe that sort of thing happens when you live this close to the water—or in a friggin' haunted house."

Eli cracked a smile. "So *friggin'* is okay to use?"

She kissed his forehead. "Only in front of me—and sparingly. Anyway, we're all forgiven, right?"

Eli nodded, then he slid his arms around her. "I called Dad last night," he said. With his face in her shoulder, his voice was slightly muffled. "He told me you tried to get Brad and Tim out here for a visit. Thanks for trying, Mom."

Sydney held him tightly. "Well, I'm sorry I wasn't able to pull it off."

After a few moments, Eli squirmed a little. "Mom, I got to pee."

She pulled away and mussed his hair. "How about homemade waffles for breakfast? I haven't broken out the waffle iron in months."

"Sounds good, Mom," Eli replied, ducking into the bathroom.

Sydney's first attempt at making a waffle in three months was a disaster. One side was burnt black, the other side nearly raw. She unplugged the waffle iron. "Eli?" she called. "Honey, a little delay to breakfast! It'll be about another fifteen minutes."

"No sweat!" Eli answered from upstairs. "Don't knock yourself out, Mom, because I really don't think . . ." She couldn't hear the rest, because his voice was fading, and the phone rang.

She checked the caller ID and saw it was George Camper, calling back. She grabbed the cordless. "Hello, George?"

"Hi, Sydney."

"Thanks for getting back to me. Sorry to bother you at home."

"No problem, Sydney. What can I do for you?"

"I wasn't sure if you knew anything about this or not, but last week this couple from *Movers & Shakers*, Leah Dvorak and Jared McGinty, the ones who stopped the robbery at the Thai restaurant—"

"Yeah, I heard they were murdered," George finished for her. "That's just awful. What a tragedy . . ."

"Yes, well, last night I found out Angela Gannon committed suicide, at least the police seem to think it might have been a suicide. She's the woman I interviewed who talked that man out of jumping from that office building ledge in Chicago."

"Oh, sure, I remember that story. The girl's dead?"

"Yes," Sydney said. "You didn't know?"

"No, I hadn't heard anything, Sydney. God, that's terrible. In one week, you lost three of your *Movers & Shakers* people. Were you—um, thinking about doing some kind of posthumous tribute or something?"

"No." Sydney hesitated. He'd already answered her question: he didn't know about Angela's death. Still, she had to ask. "Listen, George, do you think someone in your office might have sent flowers to the Dvoraks and to Angela's sister on my behalf?"

"I'm not sure I understand, Sydney."

"I've gotten notes from the Dvoraks and Angela's sister, thanking me for the flowers—and I didn't send any. Do you think someone in your department—or any other department—might have sent flowers to these people and signed my name on the card?"

"Not in my department," George replied. "I can't think of anyone at the network who would have done that. The folks in Legal have names and addresses on file from when your interview subjects sign the waivers making sure we don't get sued. But I really doubt anyone in Legal sent the next of kin flowers. Besides, they wouldn't have the addresses of the *relatives*."

"No, of course they wouldn't," Sydney heard herself say.

"Is there anything else I could do for you, Sydney?"

Numb, Sydney sat down at the tall café table in the corner of her kitchen. If no one from the network had sent flowers in her name to the Dvoraks and Angela's sister, then who had? Who would have the addresses of the deceased's relatives?

"Sydney, are you still there?"

"Yes, George," she said. "Um, thanks for your help."

"No worries," he said. "I'm sorry about your *Movers & Shakers* friends. Let me know if there's anything I can do."

"I will. Thanks, George," she murmured. Then Sydney clicked off the phone.

She sat there in a stupor for a moment until she could smell bacon burning. She put down the cordless phone, quickly got to her feet, and hurried to the stove. "Eli!" she called, removing the bacon from the grill with a set of tongs. "We're having our bacon extra crisp! Is that okay with you?"

There was no response from upstairs.

"Honey? Eli?"

Switching off the stove, she headed up the hallway to the foyer. Sydney stopped abruptly when she saw a piece of paper taped to the banister newel post:

I didn't want to bug you while you're on the phone. I decided to go to the beach like I was telling you. I'll get something to eat at the bakery. Be back around 3.

Love, Eli.

Dressed in khaki shorts, gym shoes, and a white T-shirt that had CHICAGO POLICE and their insignia on it, Eli carried a backpack as he shuffled along the sidewalk. It was a beautiful, sunny day, and Madison Park beach was a mob scene. A few boom boxes competed with the ice cream truck that played "Twinkle, Twinkle, Little Star" over and over. Eli couldn't see any grass on the sloping lawn leading down to the water—just blankets and people, lots of nearly naked people. He noticed one cute teenage girl in a yellow bikini that he liked. She was doing a sexy little dance and squealing—very loudly. Then he saw she had a cigarette in her hand, and he decided between the squealing and the smoking, she was probably a jerk. So Eli moved on, bypassing the beach—even though in his backpack he had a beach blanket, his trunks, and a tube of sunblock.

Passing restaurants, shops, and then the bakery, he walked to the bus stop. His timing was perfect. Eli could see the Number 11 coming up the street. He dug into his pocket for bus fare and Vera Cormier's Christmas card.

The bus came to a stop in front of him and then the door whooshed open. Eli stepped aboard, and dropped his fare into the receptacle. He showed the bus driver Vera's Christmas theme return address sticker on the envelope. "I need to go to this address," Eli said. "Could you tell me where I should transfer and on what line?"

The driver was a thin black woman in her late thirties. She had auburn hair and wore sunglasses. "Sure, handsome," she said with a smile. "Just park it right behind me there in the handicapped area, and I'll tell you what to do. I know that place. It's nice. Visiting a grandparent?"

A dark-skinned man with a green Izod polo shirt and sunglasses stepped in after him. The man threw some money into the machine and then brushed past Eli. He took a seat near the back of the bus.

Eli glanced at him for a moment before he sat down in the handicapped area. "Um, yes," he said to the driver, as the bus started moving again. "I'm visiting my grandmother. And I've never been there before."

Eli had called Evergreen Point Manor early this morning, while his mother had been downstairs in her office. He'd asked if Vera Cormier still lived there. The operator had told him yes, and would he like to be connected to her extension?

"Um, no thanks," Eli had whispered into the phone. "I'd

like to surprise her. How—um, how's she doing, by the way?" He'd imagined going all that way to meet with some loopy old lady who couldn't even talk. "Is she okay?"

"Vera? Oh, Vera's great. She'll outlive us all."

Eli had thanked the operator, then hung up. It might have been easier to talk with the old lady on the phone, but he remembered something his mother had told him about interviewing people. She'd said online and phone interviews were okay in a pinch, but it was best to do it in person, one-on-one.

He glanced around at some of the other passengers on the bus, and his gazed stopped on the man with the green shirt seated near the back. He looked so familiar. With his dark hair and olive complexion, he looked like an Italian actor in *The Sopranos*.

Gazing at him, Eli remembered something else his mother had said—about her stalker. He was an olive-skinned man, possibly Latino, medium build, and with an eye infection of some sort. This guy on the bus still had on his sunglasses. He wasn't wearing a Felix Hernandez Mariners shirt, but otherwise the guy totally fit the description of this stalker.

Eli kept studying the man, who stared out the bus window. Eli hadn't seen the guy in the Mariners number 59 shirt yesterday. So why did this man on the bus seem so familiar?

Suddenly, the man turned and faced him.

Eli quickly looked away. He remembered him now: the man he'd almost collided with at the fun fair, the one who stood and stared at him. For a while, Eli had thought the guy was following him. He'd even screamed at someone else in a beige top, thinking it had been that man. Then he'd realized his mistake and figured if that man had indeed been following him, he must have given up.

Eli stole a glance at the stranger near the back of the bus, and he realized something.

The man hadn't given up at all.

* * *

"MARCO . . . POLO! MARCO . . . POLO!" The kids were screaming in the shallow water near the shore. Shrieking, flailing their arms, another swarm of wet children raced by her, and she was sprinkled with water.

Sydney wandered along the shore, looking at all the swimmers, as well as the sunbathers on the grass. The beach was packed, but she didn't see Eli anywhere. There had been a few false alarms, boys who looked like Eli from behind or at a distance, but no Eli.

Craning her neck, Sydney stood on her tiptoes for a better look at a large raft tied to poles in the deep water. It was crammed with people, many of them standing in line to use one of the two diving boards. She couldn't tell from here if Eli was among them.

"Attention, swimmers!" a lifeguard announced into a bullhorn. He got up from the little bench on his observation perch. *"Eli McCloud, please report to the lifeguard station at the beach house. Eli McCloud, please report to the lifeguard station at the beach house."*

Sydney waved and mouthed *thank you* to the lifeguard, and he waved back at her. Then she threaded around all the blankets and sunbathers over toward the beach house. If only she'd caught a glimpse of Eli as he'd left the apartment. Then she would have known which pair of swim trunks he had on, and it might have been easier to spot him.

She felt so frustrated—and anxious. She couldn't really be angry at Eli for leaving the way he had. Obviously, when he'd called down to her while she'd been on the phone, he must have said something about skipping the big breakfast for this beach trip. Why wasn't she listening to him?

She'd warned Eli last night about her stalker. But he hadn't taken her too seriously. And why should he have? He didn't know she was worried about more than just this stranger in a Mariners number 59 T-shirt.

In his note, he'd said he would return at three o'clock. That was two and a half hours from now.

Standing by the lifeguard station, Sydney shielded her eyes from the sun. She scanned all the faces and body types, thinking there was still a chance she'd see Eli. She kept hoping that he'd emerge from the crowd and come toward her.

But she had an awful feeling Eli wasn't anywhere near here.

Eli waited for the swarthy man in the green shirt to take off his sunglasses. He wanted to see if one of his eyes was infected. But the man's glasses stayed on.

Eli remembered a ValuCo price tag had been sticking out of the sleeve of the guy's beige jacket at the fun fair yesterday. Obviously the guy had picked it up in a hurry so he could cover his Mariners 59 T-shirt. Maybe he'd grabbed the baseball cap, too; anything to alter his appearance—just in casc his target had started to catch on to him.

The closer they got to downtown Seattle, the more the bus filled up, and now people were standing. The bus driver announced they were in a free-ride zone, and people started getting on and off through a door closer to where that man sat—as well as the one up front.

No one had asked Eli to give up the handicap seat, thank God. He'd been able to sit there while the driver told him where to transfer for the bus to Evergreen Point Manor.

A woman in the back pulled the Stop cord for the driver. Eli watched her get out of her seat and waddle over to the bus's back door. Eli stood up. "This isn't your stop yet, honey," the driver told him.

"I know," Eli whispered. He held onto a pole and leaned close to her. "There a creepy guy in a green shirt back there. He's got sunglasses on. I think he's been following me."

Her eyes searched in the rearview mirror. "Looks normal

enough," she said. "What—is he a pervert or something? Want me to radio it in?"

"No, but I'd really like to lose him."

As she pulled over to the next stop, Eli moved closer to the door. Casually glancing back, he saw the man get to his feet. He shuffled past a few passengers in the aisle, then stood behind the woman at the back door.

No one was at the stop as the bus ground to a halt. And no one stood behind Eli at the front door. It whooshed open. He took another step toward the door, then crouched down and turned to the driver. "Has that guy stepped off yet?" he whispered.

Her focus shifted up to the rearview mirror. She kept one hand on the door lever. "One second . . . okay . . ."

Eli heard that whoosh sound again, and the doors closed right behind him. He felt the draft on the back of his legs.

Grinning, the bus driver started to pull into traffic. The man in the green shirt pounded on the rear door to get back in. Eli spied him through the window. He looked so pissed off. He was running alongside the bus.

"Hey, stop!" yelled a woman passenger. "Stop, driver! Somebody wants to get on!"

The driver picked up speed. "Like the song says, 'It's Too Late, Baby!'"

"Thank you," Eli whispered, and he returned to his seat.

The transfer stop to the Number 41 was only a few blocks from where they'd ditched the creepy guy in the green shirt. So while Eli waited in the bus shelter, he kept a lookout for the strange man. He felt bad for not taking his mom more seriously when she'd said she might have a stalker. But his mom was wrong about one thing: this weird guy wasn't stalking her; he was stalking *him*.

The bus driver on the Number 41 wasn't nearly as nice as the lady driver on the Number 11. He was a pasty-faced guy in his forties. When Eli asked if this was the bus to Evergreen Point Manor, the driver nodded tiredly. "Your stop's Northeast 125th· You'll walk three blocks north from there."

"Um, how will I know if—"

"I'll announce it," he interrupted. "You got about twenty minutes. Take a seat."

Eli did as he was told. He found an empty seat. But at the first stop on I-5, the bus filled up with a score of noisy, obnoxious teenagers who kept screaming and laughing. A big woman with BO ended up sitting next to him, and she talked loudly on her cell phone the whole time. It was all Eli could do not to rip it out of her hand and hurl it out the window. The noise died down when most of the people got off at Northgate Shopping Mall. His stop was two stops later.

It was an industrial park area bordering on a big forest. The buildings housed medical and dental offices, as well as some insurance company branches. Every building looked the same: cold, sterile, and boring—each with a big parking lot. Eli couldn't find Evergreen Court Northeast. He wandered around for fifteen minutes until he saw a bus pull into another parking area beyond some trees. Then he noticed the big stone slab with raised lettering on it at the edge of the lot:

EVERGREEN POINT MANOR
A Seniors Community Since 1998

There was also a sunflower carved in the stone. That must have been their symbol, because the same sunflower was stenciled on the orange awning over the front door. The drab three-story building was beige with tan trim and a lot of balconies—probably with views of the boring industrial park. A couple of woman with walkers slowly lumbered toward the front entrance. Eli was amazed to see one bundled up in a sweatsuit, and the other had a sweater on—in this warm weather. Two elderly men sat on a bench by the door. One wore a hat and a sweater; his buddy appeared to have dressed for a golf game, only his shirt was inside out and he held onto a cane. "Hey there, sport!" the hat-wearing old man on the bench called to him. His friend with the cane waved and smiled.

Eli was waiting for the two ladies with walkers to make it through the door, which opened automatically. He smiled and waved back to the guy on the bench. "Hi, how are you?"

"Finer than frog's hair!" he replied. "And it's a beautiful day!"

When the old ladies finally made it inside, they turned and smiled at him and said hello. They seemed nice and so happy to see him. It was weird being in this strange place in a city he still wasn't used to. This whole trip had been pretty scary. He felt so grateful for the friendly smiles. He even started to tear up a little, and he wasn't sure why.

At the front counter, there was a sign, BINGO 2-NITE! 6:30—ACTIVITIES ROOM. Beside it was a Latino woman with shoulder-length hair and orange scrubs that had the sunflower logo on it. She smiled at Eli and asked if he needed any help.

"Yes, I'm here to see Vera Cormier," he said.

She reached for the phone. "I'll see. I doubt she's in her suite."

Eli's heart sank a little. Had he come all this way for nothing?

"Are you Vera's grandson?" the young woman asked. She had the phone to her ear. "I didn't think Vera had any kids."

"Um, my mom's a friend of hers," Eli lied.

She hung up the phone. "No answer." She turned toward the doorway to a room behind her. "Hey, Noreen, have you seen Vera? She isn't in her digs. Do you know where she might be?"

"Three guesses!" called the woman from the back room.

The pretty receptionist nodded, then smiled at Eli. "She's in the garden, honey—"

"You guessed it," said the woman from the back room.

The receptionist told Eli to go straight down the hall to another set of doors that led outside. The garden was just to the right of the flagpole. He couldn't miss it.

As Eli headed down the corridor, a slightly putrid smell filled his nostrils. He passed a few people in wheelchairs parked in the hallway. Some of them were in their robes or nightclothes, and they looked pretty out of it.

He breathed easier outside. The lawn in back was bordered by the forest. A winding path snaked through the yard and the garden area. Several benches flanked the path, most of them occupied by the elderly residents. A few nurses in scrubs were pushing folks in wheelchairs.

Eli headed to the garden, dense and cluttered with tall plants, flowers, and blooming bushes. Someone had set a bunch of different lawn ornaments in the garden—a birdbath, a fake deer, a couple of gnomes, a Cupid, and even a small replica of the Statue of Liberty. It reminded Eli of a miniature golf course.

A blond woman was on her knees at the edge of the garden, planting some pink, purple, and white flowers. She wore a straw hat and gardening gloves. On the back of her tan sweatshirt was a drawing of some flowers over the words: COMPOST HAPPENS.

"Excuse me, ma'am," Eli said, approaching her. "Are you Vera?"

The sweet-looking old lady turned and gaped up at him. "Am I under arrest?" she asked.

Eli was confused for a moment, then he looked down at his CHICAGO POLICE T-shirt. "Oh, um, no."

"Well, that's a relief," she said, with a grin. Holding the hoe, she dabbed her brow with her sleeve. "For a minute there I thought I'd forgotten to pay a parking ticket back in 1973 or something. Do I know you, dear?"

"No, we—we haven't met," Eli said, a bit nervously.

Setting down the hoe, she took off a gardening glove and

held out her hand to him. “Well, I’m Vera, resident tiller of the soil here.”

Eli shook her hand. “I’m Eli. I—um, I like your garden a lot.”

She frowned at the fake deer. “Personally, I think some of this tacky stuff can go, but I’ve been outvoted. These new petunias ought to be nice. They’re such a cheery flower.” She looked him up and down, then smiled. “Eli, that’s a nice name. So what did you want to see me about, Eli?”

“I live in the Tudor Court Apartments with my mom,” he said. “We moved in about five weeks ago. We’re in apartment number nine.”

The smile ran away from her face. “Oh.”

“We’ve had some pretty weird things happen in there.” Eli squatted down so they were face-to-face. “We figured out the place is haunted. I hear this woman killed her son in there, and then she shot herself. I was talking to the caretaker, Larry, and he said you were living next door in number ten when it happened.”

A slightly pained look on her face, she nodded again. “How is Larry? Does he still have the canary?”

“Yeah,” Eli said. “Larry’s fine.”

“A nice man,” Vera said. “Bit of an odd duck, but a nice man and a hard worker.”

Eli could tell she didn’t want to talk about the murder-suicide. She was changing the subject on him. “Anyway,” he said. “I was hoping you could tell me something about what happened with that woman and her son. No one seems to know what really went on. No one even remembers their names and when it happened.”

With a long sigh, the old woman glanced down at the box with three more petunias in plastic pots. The rest of the box held empty pots. “You know, these petunias can tolerate a lot of heat,” she said. “But this afternoon sun is a bit strong for yours truly. Why don’t we sit over there in the shade?” Pulling off her other work glove and dropping it on the ground, Vera nodded toward a nearby bench—beneath a sycamore tree. "First, help an old lady up. These knees aren't what they used to be."

Eli took her by the arm and helped her up from the kneeling pad at the garden's edge. He noticed she had some trouble walking, and she clung to him until they sat down on the bench. "Whew!" she said, taking off her hat and fanning herself. "So—you want to hear about Loretta and her boy?"

"Loretta? That was the mother's name?" Eli asked, sitting beside her.

Vera nodded, then she squinted at him. "Say, why don't you just look up all of this on the Internet World Wide Web or whatever?"

Eli shrugged. "Because I don't know their names—or when it happened."

She stopped fanning herself with her hat. Her mouth twisted into a frown. "You know, Eli, you and your mother should just find another place to live. Ever since Loretta and her son died there, something's been wrong with that apartment."

"Do you remember the son's name—and how old he was?"

She nodded. "He was about your age, fifteen."

"I'm going to be thirteen soon."

She smiled at him. "Well, you're very mature for your age. Earl, he was a *young* fifteen."

"Earl," he repeated. The Ouija board had said that the boy's name was *Carl* and he was fourteen—just one letter and one year off.

"You remind me of him," Vera said. "Your names are similar, too, Earl and Eli. He was a good-looking boy, too, and very sweet."

"What was their last name?" Eli asked. "Do you remember?"

She nodded. "Sayers, Loretta and Earl Sayers." She slowly fanned herself with her hat again. "They moved to Tudor Court in July 1974. Loretta had just left her husband, an older man who lived in—um, Magnolia, I think. And he had some older children from a first wife who died." She ran her bony fingers over her mouth. "I can't for the life of me remember his name. He and Loretta weren't married for very long. His name wasn't Sayers. That was the name Loretta went back to. Earl was her son from a previous marriage, this Sayers fellow. I don't know what happened there."

"What was she like?" Eli asked.

"Oh, she was a very beautiful girl—or I should say, *woman.* She was in her late thirties and a bit withdrawn—moody at times. Maybe she was just lonely. I never saw her with a friend or a boyfriend."

"What about Earl?" Eli asked. "Did he have any friends?"

"Only one that I ever saw, but he was over quite a lot," she answered. "I forget his name, but he was a little older than Earl. He had to be at least sixteen, because he usually drove over, and ended up blocking my car in the garage. It really got my goat, the way he'd just leave his car right in front of mine for hours on end. I don't know how many times I had to call Loretta and ask Earl's friend to move his silly car . . ."

"When did they die?" Eli asked. "Do you remember?"

"November, that same year," she replied. "The shot woke me up. It was around three in the morning. I thought someone had lit off a rocket-bottle on the beach."

"Bottle rocket," Eli said. "Did you call the police?"

Vera shook her head. "No, but the next morning, her husband came by—I don't think they'd officially divorced yet. He got the super to let him in, and they found Loretta and Earl upstairs. A lot of people talked about how the murder-suicide looked *staged*. I don't see how they could say anything like that, because the police sealed off that place right away. So no one saw anything in there except for the authorities. But there was some gossip that maybe the husband had murdered them both, only he'd set it up to look as if Loretta had killed Earl and then herself. I suppose I did as much to fan those flames. The police asked me about him. He visited there quite a lot, especially during the first month or so. It was late summer, and with the windows open, I could hear them arguing. For such a quiet little thing, Loretta's voice sure got loud at times. I'd hear her screaming at him on the phone sometimes, too. I got the distinct impression he didn't want to let her go—at least, not without a fight. And fight, they did."

"Did you ever hear him threaten her?" Eli asked.

Vera let out a little laugh. "You sound just like the police." She pointed to his T-shirt, "You look like one, too. Well, Eli, I'll tell you what I told them. I tried not to eavesdrop, but it wasn't easy when their voices were coming right through my window. I never once heard him threaten her. But some of the other neighbors, I guess they heard differently, because the newspapers at the time reported he'd threatened to kill her on more than one occasion."

Vera glanced up at the darkening sky as the sun went behind a cloud. "The police couldn't find enough evidence to make a case against the husband. But that didn't stop people from gossiping. If you ask me, I believe the official story. Loretta seemed to have a lot of emotional problems. I think she slit her son's throat while he was sleeping. The newspapers said she even tucked him in afterward. Then she got undressed, got into the bath, and shot herself through the head." She shuddered. "Well, there's just no polite way to talk about it, is there?"

Eli just nodded. He felt a little numb. He didn't know what to say.

"So—you've been having some strange problems in the upstairs bathroom," Vera said. "Am I right?"

"In my room, too," Eli murmured.

"Oh, of course, that only makes sense. All the different people who have moved in and out of that apartment always reported strange goings-on in the upstairs bath. But most of them used Earl's room as a guest room, and they wouldn't have been in there very much." She patted his arm. "You poor boy, having to stay in that room where Earl—" She shook her head. "Well, I've talked too much."

"No, I asked to hear it." Eli put his hand on top of hers. "Thank you."

She nudged him. "You and your mom shouldn't be living there."

"Right now, I'm trying to get her to move back to Chicago," he admitted. "But I don't think it's working."

Vera glanced up at the sky again. "Looks like we're losing our sun. And I've been sitting down too long." She was a bit unsteady as she got to her feet. Eli tried to take her arm, but she pulled away. "Nope, thank you, dear, but I need to walk on my own."

He walked alongside her until she reached the garden's edge. "I'm moving like molasses in January, I know." She groaned as she got down on the kneepad. "It's no fun getting old, but it beats the alternative."

"Thanks for talking with me," Eli said.

"I hope you don't have nightmares thanks to me," Vera said. She put her gardening gloves back on. "Come back any time, Earl."

He balked. "Um . . ." He was about to say, *'I'm Eli,'* but instead, he just said good-bye to the nice lady. Then he walked away.

Chapter Thirteen

Dear Elizabeth,

I really enjoyed working with Angela on Movers & Shakers last November. Spending time with your sister and getting to know her was a lovely experience. She had such a wonderful spirit. I was so sorry to hear about her death. In my book, she was a true hero and a very special human being.

I got your kind e-mail today. I'm glad the flowers arrived. Do you by any chance know the name of the florist who delivered them? I'm sorry to bother you with this during such a difficult time, but . . .

"But *what*?" Sydney muttered to the computer monitor. What kind of excuse should she use in this e-mail to Angela's grieving sister? How could she explain her interest in the local florist that had delivered the roses *she'd never sent*? She hoped somehow to trace whoever had put in the order by talking with the people on the delivery end.

But it didn't seem right, bothering Angela's poor sister about this. She was still in shock—and mourning. How devastating to lose a family member in such a violent, bizarre way.

To lose a family member.

Sydney looked at the clock again: 2:40. She sat back in her chair and sighed. Eli had said he'd be back by three. She still had twenty minutes before she went into panic mode. Sydney glanced out the window at the gray clouds forming over Lake Washington. The beach had to be emptying out. Why wasn't he home yet?

The phone rang, giving her a start.

Sydney jumped up from her chair and raced into the kitchen to answer it. She didn't even bother checking the caller ID box first. "Hello?"

"You sound haggard," her brother said on the other end.

"I am, totally," she muttered.

"I figured something was up. Three messages since yesterday afternoon and you sounded more and more frazzled in each one. I was out with friends last night, and by the time I got home, it was too late to call you."

"So—did you get lucky at least?" she asked, a bit of cynicism creeping into her tone.

"Yeah, I found a dime on the sidewalk. God, I can tell you're mad at me—"

"I'm not," she insisted. And she wasn't, really. Her brother had a life of his own. She hated herself for being so needy and demanding of his time lately.

"Syd, I was out with work people at this lame-o play and then a late dinner. I dragged my ass home alone at twelve-twenty. I didn't call back because I thought I might wake you guys. I slept in and almost missed opening an open house at nine. That just ended, and now I'm finally calling you back. Okay?"

"Okay," she said, rubbing her forehead. "I'm sorry I'm Needy Nelly and left you three messages, but I'm freaking out here."

"'*You kids, and all the bickering!*'" he said, imitating their late mother. It was scary the way Kyle could sound just like her. Then he lapsed back into his own voice. "So—what's going on? Why are you freaking out?"

Kyle already knew about Leah and Jared. Sydney told him about Angela Gannon's death, and how—for the second time—someone had sent flowers to the next of kin in her name. "It's nobody from the network, I checked," Sydney said.

"It isn't someone on your film crew?" he asked.

"No. That wouldn't be like them. We pass the hat whenever we have to buy someone a birthday cake. If one of them was sending flowers in my name, they'd let me know."

"That's really screwy," he said. "No wonder you're freaking out."

"Oh, that's just for starters," Sydney said. She recounted her brush with the stranger in the Mariners 59 T-shirt, the dead robin on her pillow, and the blow-up with Eli last night. She took him right up until three hours ago when Eli had gone off to the beach. "He didn't answer the lifeguard's page. Maybe he didn't hear it. But with everything that's been happening, I don't want him roaming around by himself."

"I understand why you're going into meltdown territory, Syd," Kyle said. "But Eli's very smart and very mature for his age. He'll be fine. Nothing is about to happen to him in the middle of the day on a crowded beach. He's all right."

Sydney let out a shaky sigh. "Kyle, let me remind you that in the middle of a hot July day on a crowded beach—by Lake Sammamish—Ted Bundy abducted two of his victims."

Kyle was silent for a few seconds. "That kind of creeps me out," he admitted. "Okay, now I'm officially worried, too."

She glanced at the microwave clock again. "If Eli's not back in ten minutes, I'm going to the beach again. It should be less crowded. I ought to have a better shot at finding him—" Sydney heard a beep on the line, another call coming in. "Oh, maybe that's Eli right now," she said. "I'll call you back."

"Okay," Kyle said, and then he hung up.

Sydney clicked the Flash button on her receiver. "Hello?"

"Is this Sydney Jordan?" It sounded like a woman, her voice weak. But the nasally whine was very familiar. Sydney hadn't heard that voice in over ten years. She cringed, and her grip tightened on the phone.

"Sydney? Is that you? Hello?"

"Yes, this is Sydney," she said.

"It's Rikki Cosgrove, Sydney." There was a pause, in which it seemed she struggled for a breath. "I saw you on the five o'clock news last night—at that ValuCo thing in Auburn. I had no idea you were back in town. Shame . . . shame on you for not calling me."

"I'm sorry, Rikki," she said. She glanced at the clock again. "I've just been very busy. How are you? How's Aidan?"

"Oh, I'm not doing so well. I've been seriously ill, Sydney . . ."

Rikki Cosgrove had always had problems—and demands. Sydney didn't want to hear them now. For the last thirteen years, she'd managed to avoid Aidan's mother. Unfortunately, that had meant losing touch with Aidan.

"Well, you do sound very weak, Rikki. I can barely hear you."

"Oh, it's true. I can't even get out of bed . . ."

Sydney wondered if Rikki was still smoking in bed. They say that was how the fire had started. Even with all her respiratory problems, she hadn't quit smoking.

With the cordless phone to her ear, Sydney wandered to the front door, opened it, and stepped outside. She gazed at the courtyard and the gate at the end of the driveway. All the while she listened to that raspy, whiny, weak voice: ". . . haven't been able to get around for quite a while now. The doctor says there's not much they can do . . ."

Sydney remembered back when she'd been recuperating in the hospital, trying to keep her spirits up by visiting the other patients. But the one patient she'd missed seeing was the boy whose life she'd saved. So Sydney had arranged a trip—by ambulance—to Harborview Hospital's Burn Center. She'd made arrangements on the phone with Aidan's mother, whom she hadn't met yet either. How was she to know that Rikki Cosgrove had decided to transform the private visit into a media event?

After they'd arrived at Harborview, instead of escorting Sydney to Aidan's room in the ICU, the orderlies took her by wheelchair into the lobby, where two slick-looking hospital PR people met her. They rolled her to the stage entrance of the hospital's small auditorium. Dozens of reporters, photographers, and TV cameramen clogged the aisles and crammed into the first few rows. At least another two hundred people filled thc seats. Sydney thanked God she'd had her hair washed recently, and before leaving for Harborview, she'd applied a little makeup and donned a not-too-humiliating, dark-blue sweatsuit. Still, she was wearing a plastic neck brace and one of those halo contraptions with the screws in her forehead. She also had a cast on her right leg, and her arm was in a sling.

Some hospital bigwig with glasses and a blue suit greeted her as she was wheeled onstage. Flashbulbs blinded her, and the audience broke into applause. They even gave her a standing ovation. Sydney worked up a smile, all the while thinking how pathetic she must look in that neck brace. She used her workable arm to wave. Still, it hurt.

The bigwig stepped up to the podium. He talked about Sydney's figure-skating career and what an inspiration she was to so many youngsters. And now she was even more of an inspiration, a genuine hero. The orderly hadn't turned her wheelchair around to face the speaker, and Sydney couldn't move her head to look back at him. So the whole time, she was staring at the audience, trying to smile, and feeling like a total idiot while the man sang her praises. Worse, she desperately had to go to the bathroom. Bladder problems were just one of the many side effects of a spinal injury. She'd thought this would be a ten-minute private visit; and assumed she could hit the bathroom at any time. Instead, she was trapped on this stage with this well-meaning windbag.

The lights dimmed, and two big-screen TVs were rolled out on either side of the stage. The orderly turned her wheelchair toward one of the television sets. They started to play the home video of her rescuing Aidan. Until now, Sydney had managed to avoid seeing the clip.

Sydney watched herself in the slightly shaky, slightly grainy home video. She weaved through the crowd and called up to Aidan Cosgrove. The camera kept tilting up and down—from the boy to her. It pained Sydney to see that poor, sweet handsome boy on that ledge again. A collective murmur and a few gasps came from the audience as Aidan's shirt caught on fire. They gasped even louder as he jumped from the ledge and plummeted down toward Sydney. Her arms were outstretched in an effort to break his fall. She winced at the sight of him crashing down on her. Small wonder they both weren't dead. Sydney could almost feel her bones and organs being crushed all over again.

There was an awkward silence as the video clip ended and the lights came back on. It was like watching the Zapruder film; obviously, no one wanted to applaud. But they didn't even whisper or cough.

"Sydney," the big shot said at last. "There are two people here who would like to thank you for your courage and your selflessness."

The orderly was a bit slow picking up his cues, and she still had her back to the speaker while the bigwig was addressing her. He finally turned Sydney's chair around in time for her to see Rikki Cosgrove emerge from behind the left curtain. Aidan's mother rolled onto the stage in her mechanized wheelchair. It had a small sidecar attachment that held a respiratory device. She took a brief hit of oxygen from a mask, and then set the mask in her lap. Rikki was about forty with a pale, careworn face and coppery-auburn hair that was cut in an unflattering bob with bangs. She wore a shiny lavender and powder blue jogging suit and slippers. She had an anguished look on her face—as if every breath she took hurt. And it probably did, Sydney figured.

Rikki Cosgrove rolled up beside Sydney and rested a hand on her arm—the one in a cast. Aidan's mother had tears in her eyes. Another orderly brought a microphone and set it close to Rikki. Then he lowered the mike so she could make her statement from the wheelchair.

"Sydney," she said, in a strained, almost whiny voice. She seemed to struggle for a breath. "I—I wouldn't be here right now if it weren't for you—and—and your *humanity*." She took a moment to catch her breath again and then started to cry. "I want to thank you for my life and the life of my son."

Sydney put her hand over Rikki's and squeezed it. The audience cheered and flashbulbs popped. Rikki kissed Sydney's hand and held it to her cheek. Sydney was so overwhelmed, she couldn't speak.

The orderlies wheeled Aidan—in a portable bed—onto the stage. Staring at that poor, damaged little boy, all Sydney could think was: *It's too soon for him to be put on display.* The white bedsheets covered him up to the waist and he wore no shirt. There were no bandages hiding the horrible burns and blisters on his arms, stomach, and chest. A clear salve coated the blood-red and pink scarred skin, making the wounds look moist and greasy.

Several people in the audience gasped at the sight of this beautiful boy who was so disfigured. He seemed in terrible pain, but managed to give the crowd a brave smile. One of the orderlies grabbed the mike, and held it in front of Aidan. He didn't say anything for a moment. He seemed nervous and scared. Finally, he looked over at Sydney. "Thank you, Sydney Jordan," he murmured. "You're my hero."

The crowd applauded and cheered. One orderly moved the microphone back to Rikki while the other man wheeled Sydney to Aidan's bedside. More flashbulbs popped as she reached over and stroked his brown hair. Some of the hair along his right temple had been burned off and hadn't grown back yet. She could see he was trembling. "I kind of hoped we could get together in private," she admitted, under her breath. "I know you're in a lot of pain, honey. I'm—so sorry. I hope you feel better soon."

"You, too," he whispered. The brave smile ran away from his face. "I really, really tried not to land on you. I didn't expect you to catch me."

"That doesn't matter," Sydney said. "All that matters is that you're alive, and you'll get better soon."

No one else heard what was said between them, because Rikki was addressing the audience. Sydney just heard snippets, something about *people touching people's lives*. She mentioned how difficult it was raising a child on her own and taking temp jobs. She thanked the hospital for everything they'd done for her and Aidan. But the cost of their medical care would be enormous, and she welcomed donations through the hospital from people who wanted to *touch their lives* the way Sydney Jordan had. "You can be a hero—like Sydney Jordan," she concluded in her strained voice. "We're not asking for a handout—just a helping hand."

There was a polite smattering of applause from the audience while the orderly whisked the mike away from Rikki and set it in front of Aidan again. He nearly banged the thing against Sydney's halo-encircled head in the process.

Once again, Aidan seemed intimidated by the microphone. "Please, be a hero, and give what you can," he said meekly.

The audience applauded again.

Sydney suddenly didn't like any of this. The poor kid had been fed those lines ahead of time. He was obviously in horrible pain, and yet they'd wheeled him under these hot stage lights to perform—all so his mother could raise money to pay their hospital bills. Sydney realized desperate times called for desperate measures, but her heart broke for Aidan and she felt like a pawn in this whole venture.

The hospital bigwig started speaking again. Sydney waited until they moved the mike away from Aidan. "I don't know about you, but I'm awfully tired," she whispered to him. "How are you doing, Aidan?"

"Everything hurts," he murmured. "I just want to go back to my room."

Sydney still felt the need to rescue him. She touched his cheek, and it felt hot.

"*. . . I'm sure you'd all like to hear from Sydney Jordan,*" the hospital's representative was saying. The orderly set the mike down beside her, and readjusted the height level.

She waited for the applause to die down. "Hi," she said into the mike. "I want to thank Aidan and Rikki Cosgrove for coming," she said. "It's wonderful to see Aidan again. He's an incredibly brave young man. I understand his doctors want him back in his room right now. So we're saying good-bye to Aidan and his mom . . ."

Blinking, Rikki Cosgrove appeared confused—and a bit perturbed—for a moment. But Aidan gave Sydney a furtive, grateful smile. No one on the stage moved.

"So—*good-bye* for now," Sydney repeated. "I hope we can get together again very soon."

Finally, the orderlies got the hint and started to move Aidan's bed toward the right curtain. With a pinched smile,

Rikki waved to the crowd, then turned her wheelchair around and trailed after the orderlies.

"I'm unable to applaud," Sydney said, moving her one good arm. "But I hope you'll give Aidan and Rikki a hand for me—in more ways than one."

A few people in the audience chuckled at her lame pun, and everyone applauded as Aidan and his mother made their exit together.

Once the clamor died down, Sydney made a brief, off-the-cuff speech, thanking everyone for their cards, encouragement, and prayers. She still desperately had to go to the bathroom, so she announced that she was very tired, and quickly wrapped it up.

As the orderly rolled her out stage left, a thin, balding man she'd never seen before approached her. Wearing a cheap pale blue suit, and carrying a clipboard, he blocked their way. "That's not how the program was supposed to go!" he hissed. "Rikki still had another speech to give, and the kid had some more lines. You screwed up the whole thing!"

Sydney just glared at him. "Get the hell out of my way," she growled.

And he did.

She often thought about that guy, though she never saw him again. She wondered if Rikki had hired him to help raise money. That was the only misgiving Sydney had had about donating $25,000 of her book advance to the Cosgroves. Were the funds being well managed?

Though she never got to spend any time with Aidan alone, Sydney could see they were taking good care of him in the hospital. So she recorded a thirty-second radio spot for their charity, the Aidan Foundation. She also—rather stupidly—signed some document allowing them to use her image for the charity. Sydney cringed at what Rikki Cosgrove's reps came up with: a heavily retouched composite, showing her and Aidan. She hovered at his bedside, but they'd altered a photo taken at the Harborview visit-turned-press-conference. Smiling bravely, Aidan was shirtless and scarred. Beside him, Sydney was no longer in a wheelchair. They'd airbrushed out her halo contraption. They also put her face on someone else's body—a model in a figure skater's leotard with miniskirt. It appeared as if she'd briefly stopped skating to pose for a minute with this poor, mangled, crippled child. It was a ridiculous image, and so airbrushed, she almost looked like a cartoon. Sydney had to tell herself if the stupid ad-photo made money to pay for the Cosgroves' medical expenses, why should she care?

While still in the hospital, Sydney worked on her autobiography with a ghostwriter named Andrea Shorey. About fifty, with glasses and wild, curly gray hair, Andrea was very thorough in her research. She discovered that for a while Aidan Cosgrove was a child model, and a successful one, too. "You know the picture of that cute toddler in all the ads and on the sales tags of those kids' clothes, *Toddels*?" Andrea asked, during one of their editing sessions in the hospital's lounge. "Well, that's Aidan. He's the *Toddels* toddler. He was a moneymaker for Rikki until the modeling agency called child protective services on her. During a photo shoot, the photographer's assistant helped Aidan change shirts and noticed all these bruises on his back. Rikki's boyfriend at the time was beating him up. It says "father unknown" on Aidan's birth certificate. Rikki's had a history of bad relationships and lousy taste in men. She has also had problems with drugs and booze. Oh, and did I mention that she's still smoking—even with all her respiratory ailments from the fire? Anyway, Mother of the Year, she isn't. Though I understand from the friends and neighbors I interviewed she's been trying to turn her life around these last few months. Do you want any of this in the book?"

"My God," Sydney murmured, "that poor kid."

She felt so horrible for Aidan Cosgrove—and couldn't

help being angry at his mother. She hated thinking this way, but if that stupid woman—*that crummy mother*—hadn't fallen asleep with a cigarette going, none of this would have happened. Sydney wouldn't have ended up in this wheelchair with this halo contraption screwed into her skull.

"Well, do you think we should use it in the book?" Andrea pressed.

"We're going to have to check with Rikki, first," Sydney answered with a sigh. "Painting that kind of picture of her could really sink the Aidan Foundation, which I know is legit. I don't want to be responsible for that."

Rikki allowed them to divulge her struggles with alcohol and drugs, and even provided some candid quotes about those *dark days*. But she drew the line when it came to any discussion of child abuse, which she insisted *never happened*.

While the TV movie *Making Miracles: The Sydney Jordan Story* was in production, Sydney heard from Rikki's lawyer. Rikki demanded a share of the movie-deal money. Sydney's dad was furious. *"The nerve of that woman!"* he protested. *"I can't believe she's asking for another handout. She's got more balls than a Christmas tree, considering her antics are what put you in the hospital for so long."*

Sydney settled with Rikki's lawyer, even though Rikki was merely mentioned in the film. As far as Sydney was concerned, it wasn't worth the hassle. The network asked her to make some promotional appearances with Aidan, but the boy was still in and out of the hospital for surgery on his back and skin grafts to repair the scars. Sydney didn't want to put the poor kid on display. Besides, any association with Aidan meant dealing with Rikki, and Sydney was pretty tired of her. She was always *seriously ill* or *in pain,* and always needing money.

Sydney wrote to Aidan, but the responses always came from Rikki, usually hitting her up for a favor or more money.

Sydney never got a chance to sit down and talk privately to the boy whose life she'd saved.

After marrying Joe and moving to Chicago, she was glad to have Rikki Cosgrove out of her life—even though it meant losing touch with Aidan. But in truth, she'd never really been able to get together with him anyway. Rikki had always been there, running interference.

". . . and as you know, my lungs haven't been the same since the fire." Sydney listened to Rikki's weak, nasally drone. "Aidan's coming up from San Francisco to visit me tomorrow. He's been up the last several weekends. I truly think this will be our last visit. I just can't see me hanging on for another week. I'm so—tired . . ."

"I'm very sorry to hear that, Rikki," Sydney said. Ordinarily, she would have asked the person, "Is there anything I can do?" But this was Rikki Cosgrove, perpetually ill, perpetually manipulative.

Sydney was now sitting on the front stoop with the phone to her ear. A few neighbors had come through the gate and passed by. She'd worked up a smile and nodded at them. But there was still no sign of Eli.

"Sydney, I really need you to do something for me . . ."

Well, here it is, she thought. "Um, what is it I can do for you, Rikki?" she asked.

"Could you come by my apartment tomorrow? I'd really like you to sit down and talk to Aidan while he's here. I'm so worried about him. He—he says he's doing all right down in San Francisco, but I honestly don't know . . ."

"How's he feeling? How's his back?" Sydney asked. He'd had two corrective surgeries fourteen years before.

"Oh, his back's much better. He met this woman in San Francisco. She's older. She's become his *sponsor* or something." There was a pause on the other end of the line, and then some labored breaths. "Um, this woman, she paid for an operation on his back last year—and skin grafts, too. He doesn't have the scars anymore. He—he's his old handsome self—from before the fire, I mean." There was another pause—with some sickly coughing this time. "Anyway, he wants to be an actor. He's already done a play and some TV commercials. I don't know how steady that line of work is. He could probably use some advice, some kind of direction. I was wondering, since you're on TV. . . ."

"Of course, I'll talk to him, Rikki," she heard herself say. This was one favor she wouldn't mind doing for Rikki Cosgrove. It would be her first real opportunity to sit down and talk with Aidan. "I don't know how helpful I'll be, but I'd be happy to answer any questions Aidan might have."

"Oh, that's wonderful . . ." Sydney heard some wheezing. "Are you—are you free around one o'clock?"

"Um, I'm not sure yet." She ducked back inside the house and hurried into the kitchen. She glanced around for her address book. "Let me get your phone number, Rikki—and your address while I'm at it." Taking the cordless into her office, she saw her purse by the computer monitor. She fished her address book out of it, then sat at her desk and wrote down Rikki's contact information. As long as she had the book open to the C's, she asked for Aidan's address and phone number, too. Sydney figured it would be nice to connect with him some time—without his mother being involved.

There was a frail sigh on the other end of the line. "Oh, it's a new address, and I'm honestly too weak to get out of bed and look it up right now. You can get it from Aidan tomorrow, when you come by. I'll expect you around one."

"Um, like I said, Rikki, I'll call you back and confirm with you."

Sydney glanced at the clock in her office: 3:20. Still no Eli.

"Rikki, I need to scoot," she said into the phone. "It—it was nice to reconnect with you. I hope you feel better. I'll let you know about tomorrow. Okay?"

"All right, and I do hope to see you tomorrow, Sydney. It's very, very important."

"I'll let you know," she said. "Good-bye, Rikki."

Sydney clicked off the phone; then she closed her address book and stuck it back in her purse. She would give Eli ten more minutes, then she'd go to the beach again and have the lifeguard make another announcement.

There was no point in calling Kyle back just yet. She glanced at the e-mail she'd been writing to Angela's sister. She reread the second paragraph:

> I got your kind e-mail today. I'm glad the flowers arrived. Do you by any chance know the name of the florist who delivered them? I'm sorry to bother you with this during such a difficult time, but . . .

If no one from the network or her crew sent the flowers in her name, who had? Who would have had access to the addresses of Leah and Jared's parents as well as Angela's sister?

Sydney gazed at the address book sticking out of the top of her purse. She remembered the newspaper article about Angela's death. They'd found her purse by that open window on the fourteenth floor of that office building in Chicago. Was Angela's address book or Blackberry in her purse?

Jared and Leah had been murdered in their home. It couldn't have been too difficult to find Leah's parents' address—in a notebook or computer somewhere in their apartment.

Until then, Sydney had clung to the notion that someone she knew had meant well by sending those flowers in her name. But the person sending those flowers must have been with the victims at the time of their violent deaths, and he hadn't meant well at all.

* * *

Eli knew his mother was probably worried about him.

The next Number 11 bus left at 3:26 from a bus stop not far from where he was right now: the Seattle Public Library on Fourth Avenue.

He'd always thought the ultramodern glass and steel building was cool looking from the outside when he went on trips downtown with his mom or Uncle Kyle. But he'd never stepped inside its doors until an hour ago. The bus from North Seattle had dropped him off downtown, and he'd decided to try the library to look up Loretta and Earl Sayers on the Internet. He didn't want to use his mom's computer for this kind of research.

Eli was temporarily distracted—and fascinated—by the angles and grids of the library's interior, the high ceilings, and the way the sun reflected off the glass walls. He took a tall escalator up to the computer room, where a librarian helped him get online. She was a pretty young Asian in her late teens with short black hair that had a pink streak in it.

"This place is awesome," he murmured to the librarian.

Eli tried the keywords *Loretta Sayers, Seattle, suicide* on several search engines. But the search results he got were mostly about an actress, Loretta Sayers, born in Seattle in 1911, died 1999—not a suicide. The keywords *Earl Sayers, murder, Seattle* brought him articles about Seattle author Earl Emerson and his murder mysteries. Nothing else was even in the ballpark. He tried altering the way he spelled their last name: *Seyers, Seayers, Seiers, Sayrze.* Nothing. Eli wondered if Vera hadn't remembered their names right.

He felt so frustrated. The talk with Vera had only made him hungrier for more details about what had happened in that haunted apartment. He desperately wanted to see a photo of Earl, the fifteen-year-old boy whose spirit still occupied that bedroom—thirty-some-odd years after he'd had his throat slit in there. Did he really look like him?

Eli glanced at his wristwatch: almost 3:20. He had only six minutes to catch that bus.

"Shit," he said under his breath. Clearing the computer screen, he grabbed his backpack and got to his feet. As he passed by the librarian's desk, he nodded and worked up a smile for the pretty girl with the pink streak in her hair.

"Find what you were looking for?" she asked in a quiet voice.

"Not really," Eli admitted, shrugging.

"Well, maybe I can help you. What are you trying to look up?"

Eli approached the desk. "I wanted some information about a murder-suicide here in Seattle, back in 1974. This woman Loretta Sayers killed her kid and then herself."

She said, "Hmmm, you're probably better off going into the microfilm files for old *Seattle Times* and *Post-Intelligencers*. We have those here. Do you know *when* in 1974?"

"November," Eli said.

She nodded. "Well, it might take a little digging, but you ought to find something on microfilm."

"Gosh, thanks," Eli said. "Are you guys open tomorrow?"

"Until nine. And *gosh, you're welcome*." She smiled.

Eli knew he had sort of a dumb, grateful-smitten grin on his face. He gave her a salute, and said, "Okay, see you!"

Seconds later, hurrying toward the escalator he wondered why the hell he'd *saluted* her. Could he possibly be any more of a dork?

However embarrassed he was about the way he'd acted with that cute girl, Eli still felt elated about returning tomorrow. He'd been incredibly bored and lonely all summer. This murder-suicide was the first thing in weeks that he cared about here.

On the bus, Eli realized he had to make another stop before going home. It meant five more minutes. His mother would probably have a major cow when he got home anyway. Five more minutes wouldn't make a difference now.

When the bus let him off at his stop, Eli hurried to the beach. It wasn't very crowded anymore. He ducked into the beach house men's room. Off to one side was a single shower, along with a small changing room with a bench; on the other side were the urinals, a toilet, and a sink. In the changing room, Eli started peeling off his shirt and shoes. He unzipped his backpack and pulled out his towel and trunks. He hoped no one came in while he was naked because he felt very self-conscious about his body lately. He was too skinny and just starting to get pubic hair, so he felt like a freak. Plus he had a farmer tan.

He figured it would be faster and easier to wet his swim trunks, then put them on. He ran them under the shower. Then just as Eli pulled off his shorts and underpants, a little black kid with a buzz cut in red trunks appeared in the changing room doorway. With a finger in his mouth, the wide-eyed boy gaped at Eli as if he were an alien.

"C'mon, we're going home!" boomed his father's voice.

Naked and trying to step into the wet trunks, Eli looked up in time to see the kid's father take him by the arm and lead him out of the restroom. Eli finally got his legs through the trunks and then realized he had them on backward. He had to step out of them and start over again.

A shadow swept past the changing room, and Eli figured it was the kid coming back for another look at the skinny naked guy with the farmer tan. Still struggling to step into the wet trunks, he glanced up and froze. He locked eyes with the man in the green polo shirt—the one from the bus. The man paused in the doorway and glared at him. He wasn't wearing his sunglasses.

Eli felt his stomach tighten. His mom was right. The white part of the man's left eye was bloodshot.

The man turned away and moved toward the toilet stall.

Rattled, Eli almost tripped pulling up his swim trunks. He couldn't breathe right. His hands were shaking as he gathered up his clothes and shoes. He shoved them in his backpack, threw his towel over his shoulder, and hurried out of the beach house men's room. Barefoot, he raced across the sand, threading around blankets and sunbathers. He stepped on a few rocks or pebbles but didn't stop—not until he got to the wrought-iron front gate of the Tudor Court complex. Then he had to dig into his backpack for the keys—inside his pants pockets. He glanced over his shoulder but didn't see the man with the green shirt. Eli fumbled for a few moments as he tried to get the key in the lock. Finally, he heard it click, then he pushed open the gate, ducked inside, and shut it behind him. Hearing that lock click again, he felt better. He pulled out his CHICAGO POLICE T-shirt and his shoes, put them on, then hurried toward the apartment.

"Eli?" his mother tentatively called when he stepped inside. It sounded like she was in her office. "Is that you?"

"Yeah, Mom," he called back. "Sorry I'm late—"

"Oh, thank God!"

Just as he'd figured, she'd been worried. Now he knew why. That creepy man with the weird eye was very, very real. Part of Eli wanted to tell her right away about his two brushes with the guy. But he didn't say anything. He didn't want her to know he'd lied about going to the beach.

He was starving. In the kitchen, he dumped his backpack on the tall café table, then helped himself to two fruit roll-ups and a Rice Krispie Treat. His mom poured him a glass of milk.

He felt bad when his mother told him that she'd gone down to the beach, looking for him. "I even had the lifeguard page you," she said.

His back resting against the kitchen counter, Eli stopped

chewing his food for a moment. "Guess I didn't hear you," he said finally. "Sorry, Mom."

He apologized for losing track of the time, too, and then the lies started. The water was really great—just the right temperature. And he met another kid his age there. "Um, I told him I'd see him there tomorrow," Eli added, eying his mom to see how she would react. He needed an excuse so he could sneak off to the library tomorrow. "I think he's a pretty cool guy."

"Oh, I don't think the beach is such a good idea, honey," his mom said, wincing. She sat down at the table. "I told you about this stalker character. Well, there may be a lot more to it than just some weirdo following me around."

"What do you mean?" Eli asked. He stopped eating. "Who is he?"

She gave an uneasy shrug. "I'm still trying to figure that out."

Eli thought once again about telling her that he'd seen the man, but he hesitated. He really wanted to go to the library tomorrow. He'd given that guy the slip twice now; he could do it again tomorrow. "You think he's really dangerous?" he asked.

She sighed. "I'm not sure yet. But in the meantime, I don't want to take any chances. I'm sorry, but I don't want you going off on your own while this guy is out there."

"Oh, please, Mom," he moaned. "You're always telling me I should get out more! This is the first person my age I've met out here. And my buddy is coming with his dad and his older brother tomorrow. I'll stick with them the whole time. I'll be real careful . . ."

"Well, I'll think about it," she said.

"Thanks, Mom," he replied. "I'm gonna go wash up." He kissed his mother on the cheek, then started to head out of the kitchen.

"Honey, about this new friend of yours," she said.

Eli turned in the kitchen doorway.

"What's your buddy's name?" his mom asked.

Eli worked up a smile. "Earl," he said. "His name's Earl."

As she stepped back into her office, Sydney could hear Eli up in his room—with a U2 CD blasting. The bass was *boom-boom-booming*. She would tell him to turn it down in a little while. For the moment, she was just glad he was home.

Sitting at her desk, Sydney reread the second paragraph of her note to Angela Gannon's sister on the monitor screen:

> I got your kind e-mail today. I'm glad the flowers arrived. Do you by any chance know the name of the florist who delivered them? I'm sorry to bother you with this during such a difficult time, but I was out of town on business when I heard about Angela. I stopped by a florist and put in the order. But I don't think they billed me. Anyway, I don't have a receipt or the name of the florist. I'd like to pay for those roses. If you could tell me who delivered them, I can work backward and figure out where I placed the order. Thank you for your time, Elizabeth. I really appreciate it.
>
> Once again, you and your family are in my thoughts and prayers.
>
> Sincerely,
> Sydney Jordan

Sydney typed her home and cell phone numbers at the bottom of the e-mail. Then she clicked SEND.

She hated bothering Angela's grieving sister, but if someone had indeed murdered Angela, this might be one way to help track him down.

Hunched over the keyboard, Sydney pulled up another e-mail—one she'd deleted and restored a while back:

Bitch-Sydney
You can t save them.

She'd tried to respond to it on July 5th, but the address, secondduet4U@dwosinco.com, had bounced back as invalid. Maybe she'd just encountered a glitch the last time. She clicked the REPLY icon, and typed the same response she'd used before: *Who are you?*

Biting her lip, Sydney hit Send.

A moment later, she was almost relieved to hear the click, indicating an incoming e-mail. It was another MAILER-DAEMON delivery failure notification.

Had the person used that e-mail account name just that once—for her? If so, the moniker he'd chosen meant something—the same way that dead bird on her bed must have meant something. Were the murders of Leah and Jared a *duet*?

If that was what he'd been telling her, then Leah and Jared weren't his first. He'd killed two people together before—if not together, than at least on the same day: *second duet for you.*

The telephone rang. Sydney jumped up, ran into the kitchen, and grabbed the cordless. She checked the caller ID. It was her brother's cell phone number. She clicked on the phone: "Hi, Kyle."

"Is Eli back yet?" he asked. It sounded like he was in the car.

"He just came in about fifteen minutes ago," Sydney said. "I was about to call you, but I got distracted. Sorry."

"You really had me all wound up. I kept imagining Eli's photo on a milk carton."

"No, he's fine, thank God. He's up in his room with Bono

blasting as we speak. I think he made a new buddy at the beach today."

"Oh? Then things are looking up."

"He wants to go back there tomorrow, but I'm not so sure it's such a terrific idea—what with everything that's going on right now." Sydney told her brother she was about to dive into her *Movers & Shakers* files, and look at the couples she'd profiled in the last year or two. She needed to see if any of them had recently died under suspicious circumstances. She was looking for that first *duet*—before Leah and Jared.

Her brother was silent on the other end of the line for a moment.

"Kyle?"

"Yeah, I'm here," he said. "I just think you've accrued a lot of *ifs* there: *if* the message was supposed to be about your Portland friends; *if* the sender made up the e-mail account exclusively for you; and *if* someone is indeed bumping off your *Movers & Shakers* people. I don't know, Syd. Maybe this *duet* guy is just some music lover who dropped his account name after sending you that crank e-mail and calling you a bitch. Maybe he meant you can't save the whales. You might be freaking out over nothing."

"I hope you're right," she said. "But I still think it's worth checking into."

"Well, knock yourself out," he sighed. "Listen, I have to wine and dine another client tonight. Are you going to be okay? I can cancel and come spend the night with you guys if you're scared."

"Thanks, but I think we'll be okay," she replied.

Yet moments later, after she'd hung up the phone, Sydney realized she'd been lying to her brother—and maybe to herself, too. She didn't really think they'd be okay.

And she was very, very scared.

CHAPTER FOURTEEN

New York City—Monday, 1:22 A.M.

He'd established eye contact with Troy about ten minutes before, and now they made a game of glancing and smiling at each other across the crowded bar. Troy seemed to think he looked pretty good in those jeans and the white V-neck T-shirt that showed off his toned torso and muscular arms. A tall, handsome guy, he had short, spiked, straight sand-colored hair and a five o'clock shadow.

It was a look Troy had had for at least eight months now. In fact, when he'd appeared in a *Movers & Shakers* segment for *On the Edge*, he'd had the exact same haircut and stubble-length.

He'd been watching Troy for an hour tonight. But he'd watched and studied him many other nights as well. In fact, this wasn't the first time he and Troy had flirted with each other across the bar at Splash.

He wasn't bad looking himself. He'd already had a few Chelsea muscle boys approach him this evening—along with one drag queen. But he'd politely dismissed each one. Splash's Sunday Disco Tea Party was winding down. Yet the bar was still crowded with sweaty men—and pulsating to the beat of Laura Branigan's "Gloria."

He watched a handsome jock-type nuzzle up to Troy at the bar. It looked like the guy was trying to strike up a conversation.

From across the bar, he imagined the questions: *So what's your name? What do you do?*

He was Troy Bischoff, a thirty-one-year-old struggling screenwriter and full-time waiter at Ting, a trendy SoHo restaurant. *And he's not interested in you, buddy*, the man across the bar thought.

It looked as if the jock was asking Troy to dance, but Troy shook his head. Mr. Jock patted him on the shoulder and moved on. Troy checked out the guy's butt as he walked away, but then his gaze totally shifted direction—across the bar at *him*. He grinned.

Troy's smile seemed to say, *Look what I just passed up for you.*

He smiled back, picked up his beer from the tall table, and moved in for the kill.

In for the kill, he thought.

"Hey, I'm Joe," he said—loudly, over Laura Branigan's singing.

Troy nodded. "I've been wondering how long it would take you to walk over here." He raised his martini glass. "I'm Troy. You look familiar, Joe."

He chuckled, and leaned in close so he could be heard over all the noise. "Well, we've been in this same situation before here, only then, I didn't have the nerve to approach you—too much competition at the time. That was about two months ago. Maybe you remember me from then."

"Maybe," Troy allowed. He looked him up and down, then right into his eyes.

At that moment, he knew Troy was his.

Thelma Houston's "Don't Leave Me This Way" began churning over the speakers. Troy moved his hips in sync with the music. Sipping his martini, he cocked his head to one side and grinned. "So tell me, Joe. What do you do for a living?"

"Believe it or not, I'm a cop!" he shouted over the music.

"No shit!" Troy said, laughing.

"I shit you not. NYPD."

Troy touched his shoulder, then his hand slid down to his chest and lingered there for a moment. "Well, I've never made it with a cop before."

He caressed Troy's arm. "So what is it you do?"

"I'm a waiter. And I'm pretty sure you've made it with a waiter before." He laughed at his own remark, then took another sip of his martini. "But I'm also a screenwriter. I have several people in the industry looking at my latest screenplay."

"Wow, that's really cool." Then he put on a perfect look of jaw-dropping revelation. "Hey, wait a minute. I know where I've seen you before. Last time I was here, I kept wondering why you looked so familiar. That's one reason I kept staring at you—that and the fact that you're so damn cute. You were on TV—*Movers and Shakers*. You're the waiter who saved that rock star from choking to death in the restaurant . . ."

Rolling his eyes, Troy nodded. "Yeah, *Via*. It's my big claim to fame. I gave Via the Heimlich."

"You work in that vegetarian restaurant, Tang."

"*Ting*, and it's vegan," Troy said with a tiny frown.

"I remember you on that *Movers and Shakers*. It was aired back in October, right?"

Troy nodded over his martini glass.

"I remember thinking that if you didn't sell a screenplay; you'd probably get some offers to work *in front of the camera*, because you're so hot-looking. Did that *Movers and Shakers* help pave the way for anything?"

Troy sighed. "Not really. Sydney Jordan shot a lot of footage interviewing me, but didn't use much of it. She ended up spending eighty percent of the story profiling the woman I took the Heimlich and CPR classes from, Caitlin Something. I forget her last name."

"That sucks, man!" he shouted over the music. "You're the one who saved Via's life. You should have been in that segment more. You know, I always figured Sydney Jordan was a bitch."

"She's not bad," Troy said, shrugging. "At least, I thought she was cool—until I saw how little of me there was on that *Movers and Shakers* bit."

"Well, I would have liked seeing a lot more of you." He stroked Troy's arm again, and gave him a coy smile. "So is there a chance I can see a lot more of you tonight?"

"I think that can be arranged," Troy said. "I don't live too far from here."

Yes, I know, Eighth Avenue, he thought.

"And my roommate's out of town," Troy continued, leaning in for a kiss.

He pulled away—just slightly. "My ex is here," he explained. "Not that he'll go psycho on us or anything, but I don't want him to see us leaving together. Would you mind leaving first? Then I could meet you in five minutes?"

"This is pretty silly," Troy said.

"I know, indulge me. Then I'll indulge you later. C'mon, meet me on the corner of West Seventeenth and Sixth. I won't keep you waiting long."

Nodding, Troy grinned. "Okay, Officer Joe, I'll see you in five minutes. Don't forget to bring your nightstick." Troy waved to the bartender, and said good-bye to two more people in the bar. Troy was a regular here at Splash. He made his way to the door, glanced back at him, and smiled.

Then Troy left his favorite bar—for the last time in his life.

* * *

He wondered if his name was really *Joe*, and if he was really a cop.

But right now, it didn't matter too much to Troy, because Joe was in his apartment, and he was really hot. They'd already thrown their shirts off. From the way Joe pulled back a little each time, Troy figured he didn't like to kiss—at least, not on the mouth. He'd been with guys like that, and some of them just needed a little warming up.

Fondling and groping each other, they made their way toward Troy's bedroom. His roommate, Meredith, wouldn't be back from Pittsburgh until midmorning. Troy wondered if this Joe guy would be a member of his "breakfast club." Those were the guys he let sleep over. He wasn't sure yet.

"You got some porn?" Joe asked, biting at his earlobe. He glanced over at the TV across from Troy's bed. "I like having porn on when I'm doing it."

Troy kissed his neck—safe territory. "Um, I got some old DVDs, yeah."

"Put one on," Joe said. He playfully bit his shoulder, then pushed him away. Troy had a one-station home gym in the corner of his bedroom. Joe sat down on the stool—under a bar for pulling weights. He started to take off his shoes and socks.

Troy grinned back at him and made a tiger-growling noise as he walked across the bedroom. Squatting in front of the TV, he pulled a few DVDs from the cabinet underneath it. "Um, I got *Drill Bill . . . Below the Belt.* How about *Dawson's Crack*?"

"Anything," Joe said, unzipping his jeans. "You pick it. I just like having the music and all that copulating noise in the background."

"Hmmm, the cop likes his copulating noise." Troy switched on the TV, and popped one of the discs into the DVD player. He hit the chapter selection so it was right in the middle of a sex scene. Then he raised the volume a bit. The music was churning, and both guys in the movie were groaning and grunting.

He turned and saw Joe standing by the bed in only his white briefs. Sweat glistened off his arms and chest. Troy unfastened his own belt.

"No, let me do that," Joe said. He walked up behind him, reached around and ran his hands over Troy's stomach. He tugged at the belt, slowly pulling it past all the belt loops on his jeans. Troy shuddered gratefully as the guy gently slid the belt buckle's metal tongue up his back. He loved that mild scratching sensation. Joe was breathing in his ear.

On the TV, the music and the guys seemed to be reaching a crescendo. It got louder and louder.

Joe was now teasing him with the leather belt strap, wrapping it around his neck as he pushed his pelvis up against him from behind. Troy chuckled. "Oh, man . . . police brutality . . ."

Suddenly, the belt tightened around his throat. Troy's head snapped back. He tried to yell out, but he couldn't. His hands came up and frantically clawed at the other man's fists. His face was turning crimson.

Oh, God, if this is a game, he has to stop, Troy thought. He opened his mouth, but he couldn't get any air. *Please, God, no . . . this isn't happening . . .*

The man squeezed the belt around Troy's neck even tighter. A fold of pinched flesh protruded over the leather strap.

There was a loud scream. But it wasn't Troy—or the man choking him. It was one of the actors in the porn movie.

Troy couldn't scream at all. In fact, he'd already taken his final breath.

* * *

She heard the waves rolling onto the beach. At her open window, the sheer curtains billowed. And on her nightstand, the digital clock said 3:11 A.M. Sydney was wide awake.

Yet she was exhausted, and her eyes were still sore from all the reading and Internet browsing. Delving through her files for the twenty-eight *Movers & Shakers* video shorts she'd filmed last year, she'd found six that had profiled couples—seven, if she'd counted Leah and Jared. Among them were a husband and wife in Columbus, Ohio, who trained service dogs for people with spina bifida, and a Kalamazoo couple who rescued four kids from a school bus after it plunged off a bridge into the Kalamazoo River. Sydney didn't just limit her search to traditional couples either. She included two teenage brothers in Winnetka, Illinois, who started their own Designated Driver service and made $3,000 in one semester, and two women, both mothers of leukemia victims, who had bought a vacant lot in their hometown outside Indianapolis and built a playground in the memory of their kids.

Sydney remembered all of them. She dreaded the notion that one of these amazing *duets* may have been killed recently. But to her relief—and from what she could tell from her search on the net—all of these *Movers & Shakers* were still alive and well.

She wondered if perhaps Kyle had been right. Maybe she'd been overreacting.

She remembered how full her life had been last year when she'd worked on those stories. It was strange, but she'd felt so independent while still with Joe; without him, she felt scared and needy. She'd been tempted to call him tonight several times

After all, who better to talk with about all of this business than a Chicago police detective? Angela had been killed in Chicago. Maybe Joe knew something about the case that hadn't been mentioned in the newspapers—or online. She told herself that Joe would listen to her, and maybe *do* something.

But each time she'd almost picked up the phone to call him tonight, she'd thought about that damn letter of his and decided against it.

She and Eli had gone out to dinner tonight: a five-block walk up Madison to Bing's for hamburgers. She didn't see any sign of Mr. 59. It was still light out both coming and going to the restaurant, so she felt safe. It was a good dinner, and a nice change of pace from cooking for two and eating with Eli in front of the TV, usually some movie or show she tolerated for his sake.

Tonight, they'd actually talked. Eli had admitted he still missed his dad, his friends, Cubs games, Vienna Beef hot dogs, really good pizza, fireflies, and thunderstorms. At the same time, he'd gone on about all the cool places in Seattle he would have liked to show his buddies, Tim and Brad: the beach, the mountains, Pike Street Market, Broadway, the bus tunnel; even the library was awesome—at least from what he saw on the outside. He didn't talk much about his new friend, Earl. But Sydney realized Eli was starting to feel more at home here than she did. Of the two of them, she was the one having a tough time being happy.

She glanced at the nightstand clock again: 3:27.

She heard a muted hum, followed by a mechanical sound of something shifting.

Sydney climbed out of bed and crept over to her bedroom door. The noise came from her office downstairs. She realized it was her fax machine. Rubbing her arms, she padded down the hallway and switched on the downstairs foyer light. In her pajama shorts and T-shirt, Sydney stole down the steps. She eyed the front door—double locked, with the chain fastened.

She'd heard a story once about a murderer breaking into a house, then switching on the clothes dryer in the basement to lure a woman down there for the kill. She wondered if someone was just updating it a bit with a fax machine. Who would be faxing her something at 3:30 in the morning?

Sydney opened the closet door at the foot of the stairs and pulled out an umbrella, the same one Eli had brandished for their elusive intruder the night of July Fourth. She made her way to the kitchen, then switched on the overhead light. Nothing had been disturbed. The chain lock was still on the kitchen door. The fax machine let out a beep, indicating it was finished with the job. Sydney poked her head in her small office and turned on the light. She leaned the umbrella against her desk.

She saw something in the fax receiving tray. The top page was blank—except for some printing at the top:

Page 3 of 3 KINKOS/FEDEX 202/555-0416
STA 7-071408 06:32AM

"New York City," she murmured, checking the phone number area code. Was someone from the network working early? But why would they go to Kinko's when they could fax her from the office?

Sydney looked at the next page: Page 2 of 3. On it were six squares, each with a simple illustration on how to give the Heimlich maneuver. The figures in the drawings were like the international symbols for men's and women's washrooms—mere faceless forms in different lifesaving positions.

Page 1 was a cover sheet addressed to her, but the sender line remained blank. The Kinko's/FedEx outlet showed an address on Seventh Avenue. The time was on there as well. Who would be sending her this diagram from New York City and at 6:32 A.M. Eastern time?

The phone rang, giving her a start. Sydney hurried back into the kitchen and grabbed the receiver on the second ring. "Yes, hello?"

No response. But she could hear traffic noise in the background. She still had the fax pages in her other hand. "Hello?" she repeated.

Sydney heard a click, and then the line went dead. She glanced at the caller ID box: CALLER UNKNOWN.

The phone rang again, and Sydney snatched it up once more. "Yes, hello?" she said, an edge to her voice.

Nothing, just the background traffic noise, but she waited a beat. "I got your fax," she said steadily. "Who are you? Damn it, who—"

There was a click, and the connection went dead again.

His hand lingered on the pay phone receiver for a moment. He stood outside the Kinko's/FedEx on Seventh Avenue. The fluorescent light from the store seemed a bit muted from outside now that morning was breaking. They'd already turned off the streetlights, and the city traffic grew more congested.

Of course, he hadn't slept at all last night, and he was dead tired. He had the burning eyes and dry throat that came from sleep deprivation. But his adrenaline was still pumping, and he felt elated, too.

He hailed a cab. "JFK Airport," he said, climbing into the backseat. "And I'm in a hurry." He had an 8:05 flight to catch.

The back of the cab was stuffy, and he rolled down the window. He could still smell Troy Bischoff's cologne and sweat on him. Some people relished the scent of their partner on them after sex; they enjoyed smelling like they'd just screwed somebody.

He felt a bit like that right now. Though he hadn't really had sex with Troy, he still carried his scent. He rolled up the window again, so he could savor it longer. That musky, pungent smell reminded him that he'd just killed somebody.

* * *

Sydney counted four ring tones until someone finally picked up: "Kinko's/FedEx," the woman said in a flat, tired voice. "Please, hold."

"Um, wait—" But it was too late, they'd already stuck her in Hold limbo. An instrumental version of "Band on the Run" came on, periodically interrupted by a chirpy woman's recorded voice explaining the benefits of shipping FedEx.

Setting the fax pages on the kitchen table, Sydney kept the cordless to her ear and moved to the refrigerator. She took out the opened bottle of pinot grigio and pulled a wine-glass down from the cabinet. Sydney filled up most of the glass.

"Kinko's/FedEx," the same tired-sounding woman came back on the line. "How can I help you?"

"Hi, yes. I just received a fax from your store about five minutes ago. My name's Sydney Jordan, and my fax number is—"

"One minute," the woman said. Then Sydney heard her ask in a loud voice: "Ronny, did you just send a fax? Did anybody just send a fax?"

Sydney sipped her wine while she waited.

"Nobody behind the counter sent you a fax. It must have been a customer using one of the self-service computer-fax machines."

"Well, this guy was just in there five minutes ago," Sydney explained. "Did anybody there see him?"

There was a pause on the other end of the line.

"Please, it's very important."

"Ma'am, we've got eight computer stations here, and right now, seven of them are in use. We're awfully busy. Early Monday mornings are pretty crazy around here—"

"Your self-serve machines are activated with a credit card, aren't they?" Sydney asked.

"Yes . . ."

"Well, if you could please just tell me the name of the person who sent a three-page fax at"—she glanced at the printing along the top of page 2—"at six thirty-two this morning from one of your self-service machines, I'd be very, very grateful."

"I'm sorry, I can't give out that information," the woman replied. "Now, I have customers waiting."

"Please, don't hang up!" Sydney said. But she heard the click on the other end of the line.

After another hit of pinot grigio, Sydney phoned them back and asked to talk with the manager on duty. The man named Paul with a Bronx accent was friendly enough, but he had to stick with company policy. They weren't responsible for the content of faxes or e-mail sent from their store. It sounded like he was reading it from a rule book. Even when Sydney explained that the fax was *threatening,* he wouldn't budge.

She even resorted to using the "I'm Sydney Jordan from *On the Edge,* maybe you've heard of me" card, and the guy still wouldn't cave. But he admitted he watched the show and was a fan.

"Listen, Paul," she said, exasperated. Her wineglass was already half empty. "Could you do me a huge favor? Can you ask around and find out if anyone there just saw a man in his late twenties using one of the self-serve computer-fax machines? He's got a dark complexion. He's fairly good-looking, but one of his eyes is infected and all blood-shot. Could you ask your employees if they saw someone like that leaving the store about ten or fifteen minutes ago?"

He didn't answer for a moment. "Sure, Sydney," he said finally. "Hold on."

The woman's recorded voice came on the line again, the same FedEx pitch. Then a dentist-office version of Van Morrison's "Moondance" serenaded her.

"Sydney?" the manager came back on the line. "Sorry,

nobody here noticed anyone fitting that description. I even asked a few of the customers."

"Do you have surveillance cameras in that store?" she asked.

"Yeah. One near the counter."

Sydney frowned. That wouldn't do her any good. The person who sent the fax wouldn't have needed to go up to the counter if he'd used the self-serve machine. "Listen—Paul, all I need is his name from the credit card record. I hate people who always want to be the exception, but could you please ignore the rules this time?"

"Sydney, if I gave you his name, and you wanted to charge this guy with anything, the charges wouldn't stick, because the way you got the goods on him wouldn't be legit. You really want to track down this guy who's sending you these threats? You should call the police. Get a cop in here, flashing a badge, and we'll give him this wacko's credit-card info. Okay?"

Defeated, Sydney thanked the Kinko's manager, then clicked off the line. Setting her near-empty wineglass on the counter, she pulled the pinot grigio out of the refrigerator again. As she refilled her glass, she heard a noise outside.

Glancing up, Sydney thought she saw someone in the window above the sink. She gasped, knocking over her glass and spilling wine across the counter. Then she realized it was her own reflection in the darkened window. "Stupid," she murmured.

Sydney frowned at the mess she'd made on the countertop. At least her glass hadn't broken, just some spilt wine—and her cue that she'd probably had enough to drink for tonight. Grabbing a sponge from the sink, she started to wipe up the puddle of wine. It extended to the green Formica backsplash. As she wrung out the sponge, Sydney noticed a few grains of rice in the perforations. She was ashamed at her own sloppy housekeeping. The rice must have been hidden at the far edge of the counter since that box of Minute Rice had mysteriously tipped over on the night of July Fourth.

As she plucked pieces of rice out of the sponge and tossed them in the sink, Sydney realized something. The mess in the kitchen that night hadn't been an accident. It had been deliberate—as deliberate as that dead bird on her pillow and now this faxed diagram of the Heimlich maneuver.

Why hadn't she seen it before? She'd walked through Thai Paradise with Som and Suchin Wongpoom surveying the damage to their restaurant. It had still been a crime scene at the time, and they hadn't been able to clean it up. She'd seen the shards of glass, the smashed plates, and spilt food on that damp, moldy carpet. She'd noticed several steel teapots and spilt bowls of rice on the floor by a bus table that had been knocked over. Rice and tea, staples in almost every Thai restaurant.

On the night of July Fourth, the same night Leah and Jared had been murdered, someone had broken into this apartment and arranged that "accident" in the kitchen. The smashed teapot and the spilt rice were cryptic reminders of the Thai restaurant where Leah and Jared had become heroes. The intruder had returned to the apartment again on Saturday, planting a dead bird to show what had happened to Angela Gannon.

Sydney stared at the fax on her breakfast table. With a shaky hand, she picked up the crudely illustrated Heimlich maneuver instruction sheet. No intruder had broken into the apartment tonight. He was in New York right now. Yet he'd still found a way of getting inside—through the fax machine and her phone.

The last *Movers & Shakers* story she'd done in New York had been in November—about the people who decorated the big Christmas tree in Rockefeller Square. But before that, she'd shot a story about a woman who taught classes in CPR and the Heimlich maneuver in Chelsea. Sydney remembered her name was Caitlin, and she was a great subject—very down to earth, very funny. At one time, she'd been homeless and she ended up putting herself through nursing school.

"Oh, my God," Sydney murmured. "Caitlin . . ."

Wiping her damp hands on the front of her pajama shorts, she hurried into her little office. Frantically she clawed through her files for the final quarter of last year. She found the one labeled: *Episode: Choke Detector—Airdate: 10/17/07*. She opened up the file, and found all her paperwork for putting together the five-minute segment. That included records of expenses accrued during the trip, her editing and scoring notes, lists of the locations used, and schedules and contact numbers for her interview subjects.

Sydney found Caitlin Trueblood's phone number. She accidentally knocked the file folder off her desk as she ran back to the kitchen. Papers scattered on her office floor, but Sydney didn't care. She snatched up the cordless and dialed Caitlin's number. Someone answered after two rings: "Well, God bless caller ID. I wouldn't have picked up for anyone else at seven o'clock in the morning. Ms. Sydney Jordan, to what do I owe the pleasure?"

"Caitlin?" she said, even though she recognized her voice. She needed to make sure. "Is that you? Are you okay?"

"Yes, I'm doing great, Sydney," she replied. "Are *you* okay? You sound a little keyed up. My caller ID shows a 206 area code. Isn't that Seattle?"

"Yes—"

"Well, it's four in the morning there. What's going on?"

"Someone from New York just sent me a fax with this illustration of how to give the Heimlich maneuver. I thought you might know something about it, Caitlin."

"No, I'm sorry, I—"

In the background, Sydney heard a doorbell.

"Just a second, Sydney," Caitlin said. "I've got someone at my door—"

"No, wait, wait!" she interrupted. She couldn't help thinking that perhaps this phantom stalker was just now paying Caitlin a visit. "Are you expecting somebody?"

"Yes, my neighbor, Debi," she said. "We always take the subway together. Just a sec . . ."

Biting her lip, Sydney listened to her opening the door. "Hi!" she heard Caitlin say to her friend. "The coffee's ready. Guess who I'm talking to, Deb? Sydney Jordan!"

"Oh, come off it," Sydney heard her friend say.

"Here, Sydney Jordan, say hello to Debi Donahue."

"Hello?" Caitlin's friend came on the line. "Sydney Jordan? For real?"

Sydney sighed with relief. "Hi, Debi Donahue."

"Oh my God, it's really you. Hey, is Sloan Roberts really as handsome in person as he is on TV?"

"Gimme," Caitlin was saying in the background. "Pour yourself a cup and open the doughnuts." Then she came on the line. "Sorry, Sydney. Anyway, I didn't send you a fax. I don't know anyone who would either. I can ask around in my class and at the high school."

"That's okay," Sydney said. "But you're doing all right? Did the TV appearance lead to any nutcases calling you or stalking you? Sometimes that happens."

"No, in fact, thanks to your *Movers and Shakers* piece, my class is twice its size. And remember how just after the segment aired we started getting all these donations? Well, I just found out last week, we have funding for the next three years."

"Well, that's terrific news," Sydney said. "Listen, I don't want to keep you, Caitlin . . ."

As she wrapped up the conversation, Sydney told Caitlin to be careful, but she didn't say why. Caitlin would be taking the subway with her friend, and then she'd be teaching the CPR class at Chelsea High School in SoHo. She would be all right for the next few hours. Maybe she wasn't in danger after all.

After hanging up, Sydney wandered back to her office and started picking up the scattered papers from her *Choking Detector* file.

The network had assigned her to do this story because the rock star Via had choked on something while dining at a trendy SoHo vegan restaurant. One of the waiters had saved her with the Heimlich maneuver. Via couldn't be bothered with an interview, and Sydney had found the waiter to be not a very good subject—photogenic as all get-out, but slightly vapid and dull. She'd scrapped most of his interview footage and instead focused the piece on Caitlin, who had taught him the Heimlich and CPR in her class. At the time, those classes were about to be canceled due to lack of funding. Sydney had kept Via in the forefront of the piece, stressing that if it wasn't for Caitlin's class, the pop star would have choked to death.

Sydney found the contact number for the lifesaving waiter, whose part in the video short had been reduced to thirty-five seconds. His name was Troy Bischoff. If that strange fax wasn't about Caitlin, perhaps it was alluding to the death of the other *Mover & Shaker* in that segment.

It was 7:15 New York time, and Troy was a waiter who worked at night. He was probably sleeping, but Sydney took a chance and phoned him anyway. After four rings, an answering machine clicked on, and then a recording: *"Hi, this is Troy and Meredith,"* the man and woman said in unison, cracking up a little. *"We're out—and about—so leave a message! Ciao!"* The beep sounded.

"Hi, I'm calling for Troy," Sydney said. "This is Sydney Jordan. Sorry to be bothering you so early. Troy, I was—ah, thinking of a follow-up piece to that segment I did for *On the*

Edge last October. I wanted to talk with you again. Could you call me as soon as you get this message? I'd really appreciate it . . ."

Sydney left her home and cell phone numbers, then clicked off the cordless. She set the phone on her kitchen table, and sat on one of the tall stools.

Though a lousy interview subject, Troy had enjoyed the attention. It hadn't been very nice to lying to him and getting his hopes up, but Sydney figured her proposing to him another shot on network TV would prompt a quick callback.

Unless Troy was already dead.

Sydney stared at the cordless phone in front of her. The manager at Kinko's had suggested she call the police. Where, in New York? And what would she tell them? That she wanted them to investigate who faxed a Heimlich maneuver instruction sheet to her in the middle of the night?

Joe was the only one she could turn to. He had friends all over. He probably knew another cop in New York who owed him a favor. He could find out if there were any new developments in the investigation of Angela Gannon's apparent suicide. Most important of all, if she told Joe about what was happening she wouldn't feel so all alone in this.

She glanced at the microwave clock: 4:18 A.M. Joe was up, probably showered already. For normal workdays, he always set his alarm for 6:07. That was her birthday, June 7th. She wondered if he'd changed his wake-up time since she'd left.

Grabbing the phone, she dialed her old home number. Strange, she'd just made two urgent, potential life-or-death situation calls, but this one made her the most nervous. Sydney's mouth was suddenly dry. She counted the ring tones.

After the third, she heard someone pick up on the other end: "Hmm, yes, hello?"

It was a woman's voice.

Sydney quickly hung up.

Dazed, she set the cordless phone on the tall café table's glass top. Sydney couldn't move. The woman had sounded as if she'd just woken up.

Sydney checked the last number dialed. It was home, all right. She hadn't misdialed. Even after everything that had happened she couldn't picture him in their bed with another woman.

She didn't think Joe would return the call unless his *friend* told him about the hang-up, and he checked the caller ID. *He told you he didn't want to hear from you*, she reminded herself.

She truly didn't expect Joe to call her.

Yet for the next half hour, Sydney did nothing but sit and stare at the phone.

Chapter Fifteen

Meredith O'Malley lumbered up the stairs, lugging her medium-size suitcase, her purse, and a bag full of books she'd taken from her old room at home, among them, her high school yearbooks. She couldn't wait to show them to Troy.

Twenty-eight years old, Meredith was plump, with a sweet, dimpled smile and beautiful, wavy red hair. She'd just spent the weekend from hell at her parents' house in Pittsburgh. Her mother had driven her crazy. The only silver lining was that once she started telling Troy some of her mom's latest insanities, she'd be laughing about it. Maybe she'd get lucky and find that Troy had been *un*lucky last night. She didn't want one of Troy's "breakfast club" conquests hanging around the apartment this morning.

Meredith hoped to find him still in bed and very much alone. Then she'd crawl under the sheets with Troy and they'd talk the rest of the morning. Maybe after that, they could go out for brunch together. They both had the day off.

During one of her many rants over the weekend, Meredith's mother had asked, "How long do you intend to keep up this *Will and Grace* thing with Troy?"

As long as I can, Meredith had thought. She knew it was

only temporary with Troy. All it would take was a certain guy to come along, and she would lose him.

She reached the third-floor landing and caught her breath. At the door, she put down her suitcase and bag, then pulled the keys out of her purse. Slipping the key in the door, she realized it was unlocked.

Frowning, Meredith opened the door and peeked inside. All the shades were drawn, and the air-conditioning was off. Stepping into the dark, sweltering apartment, she noticed Troy's T-shirt and sneakers on the living room floor. The place smelled like a bar near closing: rank, smoky, and sweaty.

She figured Troy must have had a wild night if he'd forgotten to lock the door—and he was still asleep in this suffocating heat.

Meredith retrieved her suitcase and bag, then set them inside the door. She adjusted the window blinds and switched on the air conditioner. Swiping Troy's T-shirt from the floor, she couldn't resist sniffing it. One solace, it was just *his* T-shirt. His date from last night was long gone. She glanced over toward his bedroom door. It was open.

She headed into Troy's room. "Well, somebody was a real slut last night. I just hope—"

The next word got caught in Meredith's throat.

She saw the TV was on—stuck on the main menu of a porn movie. Troy's jeans and underwear littered the floor, along with the porn DVD cover.

Naked, Troy slumped forward under the suspension bar of his home gym. The bar held a pull-beam for some weights. And at the moment, it also held him dangling and lifeless. Wrapped around Troy's neck, his belt was twisted in knots and buckled over the support beam.

At his feet—on the floor—was a lemon cut in half and a bottle of lubricant.

Paralyzed, Meredith couldn't quite comprehend what she was seeing. Troy's handsome face was a bluish color, and his tongue protruded over his lips. His dead, half-closed eyes seemed to stare at the floor.

Though she didn't realize it then, Meredith had been right about her and Troy. It had ended just as she'd figured it would.

A certain guy had come along, and she'd lost Troy.

"Well, you packed up, took his son and moved to Seattle two months ago," Kyle said. "You didn't take a toothbrush, Syd. You had furniture shipped here. Did you expect Joe to put his life on hold for you all this time? I mean, this isn't just a little break. You have a six-month lease here. You've officially left him, Syd . . ."

They stood outside the kitchen door—along the railing that overlooked Lake Washington. The building provided some shade, but it was still warm along that little stretch of concrete behind the apartment. They'd stepped out there so Eli wouldn't hear them. He was watching TV in the living room.

Her hair pulled back in a ponytail, Sydney looked tired, and knew it. She hadn't gotten much sleep last night, and had been inside all morning. She wore some knock-around tan shorts and an old green print top.

It was now 1:30 in the afternoon. Troy Bischoff still hadn't phoned her back yet. She'd put in another call to Caitlin Trueblood a half hour ago to make sure she was still all right. Caitlin probably thought she was crazy. Sydney had even considered getting ahold of one of Via's representatives to make sure the superstar hadn't suddenly met a grisly demise. But then she'd gone online and read that Via was in the middle of a European tour.

Of course, she'd never heard back from Joe. Then again, why should she? Her brother had a good point. She'd left him, and he was moving on with his life. Hell, he probably didn't even know that she'd called.

She'd gotten ahold of Kyle an hour ago, asking if he could take Eli to the beach. She didn't want to leave the house in case someone called her back. Despite thunder-showers in the forecast, it was sunny right now, in the high eighties, and Eli was going crazy. This was the first time he'd actually found something fun to do in Seattle, and this Earl he'd met yesterday was his very first friend here. Just because she was scared and miserable, it didn't mean her son had to suffer.

Kyle had shown up in an old oxford shirt and black swim trunks. She'd told him about everything that had gone on in the wee hours of the morning—from the Heimlich maneuver fax to the aborted call to Joe.

"Listen, why don't you just call the son of a bitch again?" Kyle now asked. "You know you want to, or are you afraid of hearing that he has indeed moved on?"

Sydney glanced out at the glistening lake and said nothing.

"I don't know why you'd still want anything to do with him," Kyle went on. "The guy hit you. I know there are extenuating circumstances you won't talk about. But can you tell me this much? Was it something *you* did? Is that why he hit you? You didn't have an affair while you were on the road or anything like that, did you?"

Sydney rolled her eyes. "Lord, no, Kyle. You know me better than that. I didn't do anything."

"Then he's the one who did something wrong, and it must be pretty god-awful, because you won't talk about it. You spilt the beans about him belting you, but you won't talk about this other—*thing* he did. And yet, you still want to go back to him, so much that you even . . ." Kyle shook his head. "I better shut my pie-hole. I don't want to piss you off."

Crossing her arms, she stared at him, eyes narrowed. "Go ahead and say what you were going to say."

Kyle sighed. "Okay. I think you've built up these *Movers and Shakers* deaths as some kind of threat so you have an excuse to go back to Joe. Don't get me wrong. These deaths are tragic and disturbing. But you didn't find a *first duet* among your *Movers and Shakers* people, did you? And to imagine someone is leaving you little signs and souvenirs is just a bit much. Tea and rice, some dead bird, and now this weird fax—and it's all supposed to mean something? I'll tell you what it means. It means someone sent you a fax, probably while drunk, and forgot to write their name on the cover sheet. It means Tweety flew into your bedroom and croaked on your pillow Saturday afternoon. It means some critter got into the kitchen on the Fourth of July. Or shit, maybe it's because this place is haunted. Weirder stuff has happened inside haunted houses. I told you not to rent here, but you wouldn't listen to me. You're acting crazy, Syd. And you're even contradicting yourself."

"What do you mean?" she asked.

"You don't believe it's safe for Eli to go to the beach by himself—a block and a half away—because some guy is after you. But apparently the same guy was also in New York sending you a fax at six-thirty this morning. You've got your stalker in two places at practically the same time, working both coasts. Or do you think there are *two* guys after you?"

Sydney frowned at him. "He sent the fax at six-thirty, New York time. He could be here by now. It's quite possible."

"Good God, Syd, listen to yourself." He slumped against the porch railing. "If right now you were back in Chicago with Joe, and all this weird stuff was happening, would you be giving it this much thought? Tell me the truth."

"Probably not," she admitted. "But what about the flowers in my name sent to the next of kin?"

"That's bizarre, I grant you. But it's not exactly grounds

for pushing the panic button or calling in the FBI." Kyle shrugged. "But I'm guessing—as far as you're concerned—it's grounds for calling Joe."

Sydney sank down in the patio chair and rubbed the bridge of her nose. "You're probably right, damn you."

Kyle patted her shoulder. "I'll take Eli to the beach. Why don't you catch a few winks? And if you can't sleep, call Joe and get it over with. The sooner you figure out he's moved on, the sooner you'll get on with your life, too."

The telephone rang, and Sydney sprang from the chair and hurried into the kitchen. She grabbed the cordless and switched it on. "Yes, hello?"

Silence.

"Hello?" Sydney repeated.

"Is . . . this . . . Sydney?" The frail voice was barely audible.

"Yes. Who's calling?"

"It's—it's Rikki, dear. Could you come over . . . please? I'm so, so sick. I'm afraid of dying alone—before Aidan gets here. I phoned him in San Francisco earlier this morning, when—when this last spell came over me. I told him to hurry . . ."

"Oh, um, Rikki, I'm sorry," she said. "I forgot to call you back—"

"Please . . . come . . . I'm so afraid."

Perplexed, Sydney wasn't sure whether or not Rikki was just being her old manipulative self. Whenever she used to call for money or a favor, Rikki had always sounded as if on the verge of crying—or dying. The voice Sydney had heard on the phone yesterday had sounded weak and sickly. But this one almost had a death rattle to it. If Rikki was putting on an act, it was a pretty damn good one.

"You do sound very weak. Maybe you should call an ambulance, Rikki," she said. "Or let me call one for you."

"No, please . . . I'm scared. Just—just come over, Sydney. Can't you, please?"

Sydney glanced at Kyle, standing by the sink and staring at her.

"Okay, Rikki," she said, a bit exasperated. "I'll come by. In the meantime, can you call a neighbor to come sit with you? If you're really that weak, someone else will need to buzz me in. I'm leaving right now." She paused. "Rikki?"

There was no response. It sounded like she might have dropped the phone.

"Rikki?" Flustered, Sydney hung up.

"Is that Rikki Cosgrove?" Kyle asked. "Icky Rikki?"

Grabbing her purse from the kitchen chair, Sydney nodded. "I forgot to tell you, she called yesterday. She sounds really sick."

"She always sounded sick."

Sydney checked to make sure she had her address book in her purse. "I need to get over there. She says she's dying."

"Oh, yeah." Kyle rolled his eyes. "Better make sure you have your checkbook with you. That's what she really wants."

Scowling at him, Sydney pulled her checkbook out of her purse to show him that she had it with her. "Just do me a favor and take my son to the beach. I won't be long."

"Sucker," he murmured.

Before she'd left to go see some sick old lady, his mom had told him to wear sunscreen, not to wander off too far with his new friend, and to keep checking in with Uncle Kyle.

Wearing a blue T-shirt with Bart Simpson on it, and khaki shorts over his yellow trunks, Eli walked alongside his uncle toward the beach. He had a beach blanket, sunscreen, and a paperback copy of *The Sword of Shannara* in his backpack. He'd slipped the Number 11 bus schedule inside the book. The next bus downtown was at 1:50.

Eli thought about confessing to Uncle Kyle that he had no

desire to go to the beach today, that he really wanted to go to the library and find out more about the murder-suicide in their apartment back in 1974. But Eli didn't want it getting back to his mother.

Madison Park Beach wasn't quite as crowded and noisy as it had been yesterday, and it was easier to see that certain people flocked to certain areas. Gay men seemed to occupy the majority of the north section. The section south of the beach house was crowded with families, kids, and teenagers. The middle section became sort of a smorgasbord of people. The water was choppy, and waves crashed against the concrete steps leading down to the lake. Only one boom box in the area was blaring, and it competed with all the screams and laughter from the swimmers.

The sun beating down on them, Eli and Kyle stopped in the north area amid many a tanned and toned male body. "So I guess you want to pitch our blankets here, huh?" Eli warily asked his uncle.

"Okay, okay, I get it," his uncle said. "You don't want to sit in Homo Heights. Well, I'm not dying to camp out amid all the families with those wet kids running around screaming. The beach is one of the only places where I really can't give someone a filthy look if their kid is making too much noise. Let's compromise. We can sit in the middle section."

Eli squinted over toward all the families in the south section. "Hey, I think I see my buddy from yesterday," he lied. He waved in that direction. "That's him, that's my friend, Earl . . ."

"Where is he?" his uncle asked. Adjusting his sunglasses, he gazed toward the crowded south section.

Eli kept waving—to nobody. "He's over by that lady in the purple swimsuit under the umbrella."

"I still don't see—"

"Can I go sit with him, Uncle Kyle? Please? Then you can sit with the gays."

"Is he the skinny pale kid in the red trunks?"

"No, he's just a few people over," Eli lied. He pulled on his uncle's arm. "It looks like he's going into the water. I need to catch up with him. Please, Uncle Kyle . . ."

"Okay, fine," Uncle Kyle nodded. "I'll be right around here. Check in with me in forty-five minutes."

"Forty-five minutes?" Eli repeated, crestfallen. It would take almost that long just getting back and forth from the library. "Give me an hour and a half, at least. How do you expect me to have any fun if you make me check in every forty-five minutes?"

Uncle Kyle lowered his sunglasses for a moment and glared at him. "Okay, an hour, that's my final offer, bub." He glanced at his wristwatch. "And if you don't check in with me by the time the lifeguard announces it's three o'clock, I'll hunt you down and drag you home. Then I'll sic your crazy mother on you. Understand?"

He nodded. "Okay, Uncle Kyle." Eli ran toward the south section of the beach. He remembered to wave and even yelled, *"Hey, Earl, wait up!"* for his uncle's benefit.

Weaving around blankets, dodging and sidestepping all the other beachgoers, Eli kept running until he figured he was out of his uncle's range of vision.

He only had a few minutes to catch the 1:50 bus downtown.

Sydney found Rikki's apartment building on Thirteenth Street in Capitol Hill. It was a slightly run-down, ugly nine-story concrete edifice with old aluminum-frame windows. She found parking close to the building, hurried up to the front door, and found *R. Cosgrove—808* on the intercom panel. Sydney pressed the button, and then waited.

No answer.

She buzzed the apartment number again. Still nothing.

Sydney caught her own haggard reflection in the fingerprint-smudged glass door. She tugged at the handle. Locked. Then she shielded her eyes and moved close to the door. The stark, slightly grimy lobby was empty.

She buzzed a few other apartments on the eighth floor. For a moment, she remembered the first time she'd randomly buzzed the apartments of Rikki Cosgrove's neighbors, trying to alert them about the fire.

"Yes? Who is it?" someone finally answered.

Sydney leaned in close to the intercom. "I'm trying to get ahold of Rikki Cosgrove in 808. I think she's sick. Could you buzz me in?"

There was no response.

"Hello? Are you—"

The front door let out a low mechanical drone.

"Thank you!" Sydney called—probably to no one. Then she pulled open the door. Hurrying into the lobby, she rang for the elevator. She wasn't sure how to get inside Rikki's apartment if Rikki wasn't answering the intercom. Maybe this was no false alarm. Maybe Rikki was seriously ill this time.

It smelled like someone had thrown up in the elevator, which made her ride up seem even longer. As Sydney stepped off on the eighth floor, she saw an older woman with glasses, a pink sweatsuit, and a three-pronged cane standing in the hallway. She was knocking on the door marked 808. "Rikki!" she called. "It's Arlene from next door! Can you hear me?"

Approaching the woman, Sydney noticed a hearing aid in her ear. "Aren't you having any luck?" she asked.

Startled, the old woman turned and gaped at her.

"Rikki phoned me about twenty minutes ago," Sydney explained to the woman—loudly. "Is the building manager in? Is there anyone who might have a passkey?"

Arlene shook her head. "I already tried calling them."

Sydney pounded on the door, and rattled the knob. "Rikki!" she yelled. "Rikki, it's Sydney Jordan!"

"Rikki phoned me, too, about ten minutes ago," the woman said. "She sounded horrible. She mentioned something about expecting her son this afternoon. Then it sounded as if she'd fainted or something."

Sydney took her cell phone from her purse, then dialed 9-1-1.

"I'm trying to get inside the apartment of a very sick woman," she told the operator. "She's not answering her door. I think she might need an ambulance. I'm at . . ." She glanced at Arlene. "Um, what's the address here again?"

The old woman told her, and Sydney repeated it for the 9-1-1 operator. The ambulance would be there in five minutes, the operator said. Sydney had a feeling they were already too late.

Putting away her phone, she pulled her wallet from her purse and dug out a credit card. Her hand shook as she tried to jimmy the lock. She kept jiggling the doorknob at the same time. She wondered if this was all in vain. Maybe Rikki had dead bolted the door. "Rikki? Rikki, are you in there?" she called.

She felt the credit card slip through, and she turned the knob. A click sounded.

As she opened the door, Sydney was hit with a wave of heat and stench. The window blinds were open, and sunlight streamed into the messy living room—catching all the dust floating through the air. Several magazines and newspapers littered the stained beige carpet around a well-worn easy chair. The chair seemed aimed at the television, and beside it stood a cluttered TV table and a bathroom wastebasket with a rose pattern on it overflowing with garbage. Flies buzzed around the room.

The counter that separated the kitchen from the living area was full of dirty plates and glasses. Most of the food on those plates remained uneaten. Empty frozen food boxes, microwave trays, crumpled napkins, and a barrage of prescription bottles also cluttered the counter.

"Rikki?" Sydney called. She tried to hold her breath. The place smelled of sour milk, rotten fruit, and shit.

She realized the source of that last smell when she stumbled into the dark, sweltering bedroom. The shades were drawn. Sydney almost ran into a wheelchair. Beyond it, an emaciated Rikki lay motionless on top of the bed in a soiled nightgown. The bedsheets were covered with excrement. Flies hovered around her.

"Oh, my lord," the old woman gasped. She was standing behind Sydney. "I had no idea she'd gotten this bad . . ."

On Rikki's nightstand were three water glasses, some prescription bottles, and a telephone with the receiver off the hook. The pulsating alarm tone could be heard across the room.

"We're too late," Sydney murmured, approaching the bed.

Rikki's eyes were closed, and her mouth was open. A fly landed on her lip. Her face looked like a skeleton's head with gray-tinged skin stretched across it. Sydney could see right through the thin mousey-brown hair to her scalp. Rikki's hands and arms were bony with signs of decay already eating away at the flesh.

Sydney tried not to gag. One shaky hand covering her mouth, she reached toward the nightstand with the other. Picking up the receiver, she replaced it on the phone cradle. Then she turned to glance once again at the corpselike thing on the bed.

Rikki's eyes opened.

He found something. He'd been sitting at a computer desk between racks of newspapers, magazines, and other periodicals in the central library's reference room for forty minutes now. Eli was using the digital scanner to search through the microfilm files of old *Seattle Post-Intelligencers* starting on November 1, 1974.

The last time he'd looked at the clock, it had been 2:50, and the next bus to Madison Park was at 3:07. He was already in a heap of trouble.

Maybe if he apologized enough to his uncle for being late, all would be forgiven. Or maybe Kyle would forget about the three o'clock check-in. Was that too much to hope for?

In fact, Eli had been about ready to give up any kind of hope when he spotted the headline on page 2 of the Monday, November 11th edition:

MURDER-SUICIDE SHOCKS
MADISON PARK RESIDENTS

Teenage Boy Slain While Sleeping,
Mother's Shooting Self-Inflicted, Police Say

Eli studied the grainy newspaper photo of Loretta Sayers posing with Earl in front of a church. *"HAPPIER TIMES,"* said the caption. *"Victims of what police call a 'possible murder-suicide,' Earl Sayers and his mother, Loretta Sayers, celebrate her wedding to Robert Landau of Seattle on May 26, 1973. Sayers and Landau separated earlier this year."*

Loretta looked attractive in her frilly white dress, with a crown of flowers in her hair. Her shoulder-length hair appeared blond in the black-and-white picture. She had her arm around Earl, who was as tall as his mother. His hair was the same light shade as Eli's—only it was long and messy. His outfit was pretty goofy-looking, too: a dark suit with a dark shirt and a fat white tie. Earl grinned as if he were about to laugh. Eli could see a resemblance between Earl and himself—if he had a real dorky haircut.

He couldn't help thinking about reincarnation. Didn't Marcella mention something along those lines? Is that why he felt this weird connection with Earl?

He anxiously scanned the article:

> SEATTLE: An elegant, lake-view town house apartment in affluent Madison Park became a grisly death site early Sunday morning as police discovered the bodies of residents, Loretta Sayers, 38, and her son, Earl, 15, in an upstairs bedroom and bath. The teenage boy was stabbed while sleeping in his bed. His mother was found in the bathroom with a fatal gunshot wound. A revolver, registered in her name, was found near her body. Police discovered a bloodied knife in the upstairs hallway by the boy's bedroom . . .

Eli kept reading. Except for saying Earl had been "*stabbed,*" the two-page article was pretty close to what Vera Cormier had told him. He figured maybe they didn't want to say *"throat slit"* in the newspaper. Either way, it was still a laceration.

Loretta's estranged husband—and Earl's stepfather for less than a year—was fifty-three. Robert Landau had three children of his own, their ages ranging from eighteen to twenty-six. Landau's first wife had died in an auto accident. Eli wondered if Robert Landau had done something to his first wife's car. Maybe he'd "staged" the car accident the same way he could have staged the murder-suicide scene later. Or had Loretta Sayers indeed killed her son and herself?

The article quoted a friend of Earl's, Burt Demick, sixteen. He must have been the one who had often parked in the driveway, blocking Vera's car. He'd had dinner with Earl and his mother in the apartment just one night before the supposed murder-suicide:

> "Earl's mom seemed to be in a good mood that night," said Demick. "She made lasagna, then we ate in front of the TV and watched 'Sanford and

> Son.' All of us were laughing and having a great time. I just can't believe they're gone. I don't think Mrs. Sayers could have done what people say she did."

Eli figured if Robert Landau was still alive, he was now eighty-seven. He wondered if Landau or any of his children were still in the Seattle area. He wondered the same thing about Burt Demick.

Eli glanced at his wristwatch: 3:15. "Oh, shit," he muttered. His uncle would kill him.

He deposited a quarter in a coin slot at the side of the scanner and pressed COPY. The machine started to make a humming noise. While Eli waited for the printer to spit out his copy of the article, he glanced up at the library's ceiling and the glass-and-steel angular walls.

A shadow passed over the room as dark clouds filled the sky. It was almost surreal how the sudden weather change outside altered the lighting in this room. It had been so bright in here just a moment ago. Suddenly he noticed the illuminated computer screens at the other desks and the overhead lights. The tall shelves displaying magazines and newspapers seemed darker. Through the open shelving, he could see silhouettes of people on the other side of the periodical racks. Eli's gaze rested on one of them—a man, only a few feet away. Eli could glimpse only the top half of his face through the opening between the shelves.

The man stared back at him with his one good eye.

"Eli McCloud, Eli McCloud, please meet your uncle in front of the beach house!" the lifeguard announced into his bullhorn.

Swimmers were making their way to the shore in droves. Dark gray rain clouds swept over the lake, and the temperature dropped five degrees within minutes.

"Eli?" Kyle called over and over, roaming around the beach's family area as the crowd rapidly thinned out. People were rolling up their blankets and gathering their kids. Some food and candy wrappers fluttered past him as the wind kicked up.

Kyle wandered back to the beach house, but there was still no sign of his nephew. This awful feeling swelled in the pit of his stomach. He kept calling out his name—and even his friend's name—*Earl*. He glanced out at the raft in the distance, rocking back and forth in the choppy waters. There were still about twenty people on it—mostly teenagers who were too stupid to swim in when it was about to downpour.

"Who's Eli? Is he your son?"

Kyle turned and gaped at a handsome man in his late thirties. He was lean and tan, with short black hair that was graying at the temples. He wore blue Hawaiian-print trunks.

"Um, he's my nephew," Kyle said. He looked out at the raft again.

The stranger followed his gaze. "I'll go swim out there and check around. What does Eli look like?"

"He—ah, he's twelve, and thin," Kyle answered. He kept glancing around. "He's got short, light brown hair . . ."

"What color are his swim trunks?" the man asked.

Kyle shrugged. "I'm not sure. He had his shorts on over them when we came here. He went to meet a friend named Earl. He was supposed to check in with me a half hour ago."

"Does he have any tattoos or piercings?"

Kyle squinted at him. "He's *twelve*."

"I'm kidding," the man said. "Be right back."

Kyle watched him run into the water and start swimming out to the raft. The clouds on the horizon grew darker. He heard the distant rumble of thunder. The lifeguard up on his perch put on an orange windbreaker. The beach was emptying out. A few people on the raft were diving off and swimming toward shore. *"Eli! Eli McCloud!"* Kyle tried again.

He saw the man in the blue Hawaiian trunks pull himself up onto the raft. Then he put his hands around his mouth. Kyle could almost hear him calling Eli's name. The handsome stranger wandered around the raft. He stopped to talk to one kid, then another and another. Each time, the kid shook his head at him. Finally, he walked back toward the edge of the raft, waved at Kyle, then shrugged and shook his head.

"Damn," Kyle muttered. He felt some raindrops.

The man in the blue trunks dove back in the water. Some more kids vacated the raft after him. There weren't many people still in the lake. Kyle didn't see Eli among them. He noticed that his Good Samaritan had stopped swimming and now stood in the shallower water. He put his hands around his mouth again and called out for Eli.

Kyle reminded himself that Eli was the son of a cop. He knew better than to get into a car with some stranger. And he was with a friend. Wasn't there safety in numbers? Still, Kyle couldn't help imagining the worst. He could almost hear the TV newscaster tonight: *"The search continues for two missing teenage boys . . ."*

Dripping wet and shivering a bit, the man trotted up to him. "I'm sorry I wasn't any help."

Kyle nodded distractedly. "That's okay. Thank you, thank you very much."

"I'm sure he'll show up," the man said, touching Kyle's arm with his cold, wet hand. "He and his buddy probably just wandered off. There's the playground right up the street, and all the restaurants, and the bakery. I'm sure he's not far."

"What am I going to tell his mom?" Kyle murmured—almost to himself.

"Listen, my name's Dan," the man said. "What's yours?"

Dazed, Kyle blinked at him. "Um, Kyle."

"As soon as I dry off, Kyle, I'm heading down the block.

If I see anyone looking like your nephew, I'll call you. What's your phone number?"

Kyle gave him his cell number.

The man squeezed his shoulder. "I'm sure Eli's all right. I'll call and check in with you, okay?"

"Okay, thanks," Kyle said.

The man hurried over to his blanket on the beach's nearly empty north section. He started to dry himself off, then grabbed his backpack.

Kyle turned toward the other side of the beach. Except for a few stragglers—and some scraps of litter rolling in the wind—the south section was barren. The rain started coming down a little harder.

"What am I going to tell his mother?" Kyle whispered again.

For a moment, Eli couldn't move. He locked eyes with the man on the other side of the periodical stacks. Between the slats in the shelves, he could see the man's dark complexion, and those dark eyes—one clear and the other red from a broken blood vessel or some kind of infection. He was only a few feet away.

There was a flash of lightning, followed by a muted rumble of thunder in the distance. Rain started slashing against the library's windows. But the man kept staring at him—the same way he'd stared on Saturday at the fun fair and yesterday on the bus.

The printer let out a beep to signify that his copy of the newspaper article was ready. Eli grabbed the paper from the printer. His hands shook as he quickly pulled the microfilm spool from the scanner, then he switched off the computer.

Another lightning flash illuminated the whole reference room for a moment, then another crack of thunder—closer this time.

Eli glanced over toward the periodical shelf again. The man wasn't there anymore.

With the microfilm spool and the printed article in his hands, Eli hurried around to the other side of the newspaper and magazine rack. He checked the next row of shelves and the next. All the while, rain beat against the library's windows, and shadows cascaded on the interior walls and floor; it almost seemed to be raining inside as well. Eli kept glancing around for that man with the strange eye and the dark complexion, but he didn't see him anywhere.

Yet he couldn't shake the sensation that the man was still watching him.

Eli hurried to the reference desk and returned the microfilm spool. He missed the pretty librarian from yesterday. This woman was nice enough, but no looker. She was middle-aged, with a long face and mousey brown hair. The lights flickered for a second. The woman glanced up from her work. "My goodness, I hope we don't lose power," she said, taking the microfilm spool from him. "The storm sure came on suddenly. To think, it started out to be a perfect beach day."

Eli suddenly realized his uncle was probably wandering around the beach looking for him in this pouring rain. "Is there a pay phone around here?" he asked, digging into his pocket and feeling for change.

Nodding, the librarian pointed to her right. "There's one by the restrooms. Go down that way and take another right."

"Thank you." As Eli hurried in that direction, he glanced over his shoulder. He didn't see that strange man anywhere. Up ahead was the sign for the washrooms. He turned down the corridor and spotted the pay phone. Grabbing the receiver, he slipped two quarters into the coin slot.

Having stayed with his uncle for nearly three weeks, Eli knew his cell phone number by heart. Uncle Kyle answered after one ring: "Yes, hello?" He sounded panicked.

"Uncle Kyle?"

"Oh, thank God," he said. "Are you all right? Where the hell did you go?"

"Um, Earl wanted to go check out some CDs at Everyday Music, so we grabbed a bus to Capitol Hill," he lied. "We went looking for you to tell you, and even waited around for a while. I thought we'd be back in time—"

"Good God, Eli, I'm about to have an aneurysm here," Kyle said. "I almost got struck by lightning wandering around the beach in this storm looking for your sorry ass."

Eli swallowed hard. "I'm really sorry, Uncle Kyle. I didn't think—um, Earl would take this long." That much was true. He'd counted on finding the article about Earl Sayers in just a few minutes. "Anyway, I'll grab the first bus back to Madison Park."

"No, you'll drown in this rain," his uncle said. "I'll come pick you up. And then I'm going to kill you."

"Is Mom freaking out?" Eli asked, grimacing.

"She doesn't know, and she doesn't have to know. If I tell her I lost you at the beach, she'll go ballistic on the *both* of us. It would be a bloodbath. So—you're at Everyday Music, huh? I'll be there in about ten minutes."

"Um, could you give me a half hour?" Eli asked. "Please, Uncle Kyle?"

"You have twenty minutes, okay?"

"Thanks, Uncle Kyle." He hung up the phone. The buses to Capitol Hill ran pretty frequently. He could make it there in twenty minutes. In fact, he even had time to hit the restroom.

Eli heard another rumble of thunder. He glanced over his shoulder as he headed toward the men's room. No sign of that weird guy.

Somebody was using the only urinal, so Eli ducked into the stall to pee. He heard the other guy flush and then leave. Not a hand-washer. Eli was just finishing up when the lights flickered. For a few seconds the restroom was totally black.

He couldn't see a thing—not even his hand in front of his face. A panic swept through him, and he braced himself against the stall wall for a moment. The lights came back on, and he caught his breath. He flushed the toilet, then turned around and hesitated.

Someone stood on the other side of the stall door. Eli felt as if his heart had stopped beating. He glimpsed the man's beat-up loafers and the cuffs of his jeans through the opening under the door. The man was blocking his way.

Eli backed up, bumping into the toilet. He glanced up toward the ceiling, which was a polished metal and gave a reflection. He could see a dark-haired man waiting outside the stall for him.

The lights flickered again.

He heard the restroom door open, and looked up. The reflection in the metal ceiling showed another man had just entered the restroom. He went to the urinal.

But the dark-haired man didn't budge. He remained just outside the stall—as if standing guard. Eli figured the guy couldn't very well attack him while someone else was in the men's room. He quickly pulled open the stall door.

He almost plowed right into the man—a middle-aged guy with a goatee. It wasn't the creepy man with the bloodshot eye. "Sorry," Eli gasped. Retreating to the sink, he ran his hands under the water and dried them on the front of his shorts.

Then he hurried out of the restroom, without looking back.

When Rikki Cosgrove opened her eyes and gasped, it was as if the last breath had left her body.

She'd scared the hell out of Sydney for a second, and Arlene had even let out a little, abbreviated scream. The old woman was still leaning on her three-pronged cane and clutching her heart as Rikki slipped away moments later.

Sydney watched her eyes roll back and her jaw slacken. The eyes—almost all white—remained open. "She's gone," Sydney whispered, more to herself than to the elderly woman at her side. Along with a crack of thunder outside, she heard a siren getting louder and closer now. But they were too late.

She and Arlene stepped out to the living room while the paramedics tended to Rikki. There were two of them, the shoulders of their blue summer uniforms wet from the rain: a husky, pale woman with brown hair and a good-looking bald black man with a goatee. They'd rolled a collapsible gurney and some resuscitation equipment into Rikki's bedroom. Sydney asked if she could open a window and turn on the fan, and the two paramedics encouraged her to do just that. Some rain blew in, but so did the cool fresh air.

They'd left the apartment door open, and Sydney noticed two more firemen waiting in the hallway. She thought she might be in the way, but the woman paramedic had asked her and Arlene to wait. Sydney heard the two of them in Rikki's bedroom, radioing to the police and announcing a time of death.

Sydney felt horrible for thinking Rikki had exaggerated the severity of her illness. She also felt incredibly disappointed in Aidan for allowing his frail, sickly mother to waste away and die alone in such a filthy apartment.

"Look at this," Arlene said, glancing at the mess on the kitchen counter. "Her poor son, he tried to put her in a nursing home, but Rikki refused to go. He hired a maid and a nurse for her, but she kicked them out. Rikki just wanted him to do, do, and do everything for her—and he did."

Past all of Arlene's chatter, Sydney heard another siren, the piercing wail becoming louder.

"He flew up from San Francisco every weekend for her," Arlene continued. "This was the first weekend he's missed in I don't know how long. I saw this place last Sunday when Aidan was visiting her. It was neat as a pin—if you can believe it . . ."

Sydney glanced over at the easy chair facing the TV. She stared at the indentation still in the seat cushion, and the piles of magazines and trash around it. Beside the chair was a little table, cluttered with junk.

"He asked me to check in on her this week, but Rikki wouldn't let me in," the elderly woman went on. "She kept telling me to go away and mind my own P's and Q's. And the mouth on her, such language. Well, I shouldn't speak ill of the dead. . . ."

Two policemen stepped into the apartment. Sydney backed up and tried to stay out of the way while one of the cops talked to Arlene. The other policeman ducked into the bedroom to consult with the paramedics.

Sydney noticed a cordless phone on the table by Rikki's chair. There was also a used Kleenex, a teacup, and a yellow legal pad. Sydney glanced at the note written on the top page. The print was large, so someone with bad eyesight could read it:

MOM,

—KEEP THE BEEPER WITH YOU AT ALL TIMES IN CASE YOU FALL AGAIN!

—DON'T THROW YOUR DEPENDS IN THE TOILET OR SINK! USE THE DIAPER PAIL IN THE BATHROOM.

—CALL THE SUPER & HE WILL TAKE OUT THE GARBAGE FOR YOU.

—USE THE PLASTIC DAILY PHARMACY THING FOR YOUR MEDICATION. I'VE MEASURED IT

OUT FOR YOU. DON'T TAKE ANY PILLS FROM THE PRESCRIPTION BOTTLES! REMEMBER LAST TIME!

—CALL ARLENE OR ME IF YOU NEED ANYTHING . . .

Below that was a list of important phone numbers—from Aidan's home number in San Francisco to Rikki's doctors to Pagliacci Pizza Home Delivery.

There was another thunder crack. Sydney heard the elevator ring in the outside hallway. A moment later, a tall, tanned handsome man with thick chestnut-brown hair stopped in Rikki's doorway. He had a full hiking pack strapped to his back and wore a white Oxford shirt, khaki cargo shorts, and sandals. There was a policeman behind him. "Oh, God," the young man murmured, visibly dazed. Shucking off the backpack, he let it drop to the floor, and then headed toward Rikki's bedroom.

But the cop stepped in front of him, and shook his head. "If you could just give them a minute, sir," the policeman said.

The handsome man turned to Rikki's neighbor "I saw that ambulance outside, and I was hoping it wasn't . . . Arlene, were you with her? Did somebody call a priest for her? She would have wanted a priest . . ."

Arlene patted his shoulder. "We were with her when she passed away, dear." The elderly woman nodded toward Sydney. "The two of us were at her side. Your mother wasn't alone . . . ."

He gazed at Sydney as if he were just noticing her there for the first time. "Sydney? Sydney Jordan?"

"I'm so sorry. Aidan," she murmured.

Tears welled in his eyes. He walked to her and threw his arms around her. Aidan pressed his face to her shoulder, and began to cry. "I should have stayed with her this weekend," he murmured, his voice choked with emotion. "She thought she was dying, but she's been saying that for years. . . ."

"There now," Sydney whispered, stroking his back. "It's not your fault."

In this strapping, handsome twenty-five-year-old, she could still see the burnt and broken little boy she'd saved from that fire. Sydney still felt a connection to him after all these years. This was the first time she'd actually been able to hug him. "It's okay, Aidan," she said. "It's okay . . ."

Then Sydney started to cry with him.

Beyond the raindrops slashing at the front window of Everyday Music, Eli saw his uncle's Mercedes SUV come up Broadway and pull over to the curb by a life-size statue of Jimi Hendrix playing his guitar. Running out of the CD store, Eli covered his head from the rain with a free music magazine, and then he jumped in the front seat. Uncle Kyle was at the wheel. His eyes narrowed at him. "Where's your friend?" he asked.

"Oh, um, he—he wanted to go to Broadway Video," Eli lied. "He said he'd get home on his own. Thanks a lot for picking me up, Uncle Kyle. I'm really sorry I screwed up. I didn't mean to make you worry."

Pulling into traffic, Kyle studied the road ahead. The windshield wipers squeaked a bit. "I should be seething right now," he said. "Just consider yourself lucky that I met this total hunk on the beach while I was looking for your sorry ass. I was so worried about you, I didn't even pick up that he was interested in me. Anyway, I was just on the phone with him ten minutes ago, and we have a date tonight." At a red light, he glanced at Eli. "Is this too much gay stuff for you?"

"No, it's cool," Eli said. "I'm just glad you're not really, really pissed."

His uncle squinted at him. "Hey, where's your backpack?"

Eli's hand automatically felt along the side of the car seat—even though he knew the backpack wasn't there. He realized now that in his panic, he'd left it in the library. He tried to remember if there was anything valuable in it: his book, a beach towel, and sunscreen.

His uncle pulled forward as the traffic light changed. He was looking ahead once again. "You had a backpack when we went to the beach. What happened? Did you leave it in the store?"

"Um, no, I—I let Earl borrow it," he lied. He figured he'd call the library when they got home. Maybe they had the backpack in their Lost and Found unless that creepy man with the weird eye ended up stealing it.

Eli asked if his mom was home yet. His uncle explained that she was probably still visiting this sick old lady. It was the mother of the kid she'd saved from that fire. "We'll call her when we get home," his uncle said. "I can't stick around too long. I need to get ready for my big date."

Because of the rain, parking spaces had opened up near the beach, so his uncle was able to park right in front of the Tudor Court. They walked through the courtyard together. "Well, it looks like Earl was here before you," his uncle said, as they approached the front door.

For a moment, Eli didn't know what he meant. But then he saw something by the doorstep, and Eli stopped dead.

It was his backpack.

CHAPTER SIXTEEN

A soft breeze drifted through the kitchen window as she washed the dinner dishes. Sydney shook the water off her hands, then turned and grabbed the pot and dish towel from Aidan. "You're a guest here," she said. "And you've been through a hell of a lot today. Let me pamper you, okay?" She pointed to the kitchen table. "Sit."

She'd watched Aidan for nearly two hours this afternoon in his mother's pigsty of an apartment. He seemed shell-shocked as he'd dealt with the police, paramedics, and finally the coroner. Sydney had made her exit when the two men from the funeral home had arrived, but before leaving, she'd invited Aidan to dinner. She'd figured he shouldn't be alone tonight. He'd given her a sad smile and nodded. "Here you are, rescuing me again," he'd said. "Dinner would be great, thanks."

Sydney had returned home to Eli, in her office using her computer, and Kyle, all pumped up about a date tonight with some guy he'd met on the beach. She hadn't heard back from Troy Bischoff, and thought about calling him again. Sydney had wondered if perhaps she'd indeed overreacted about the Heimlich maneuver fax. Maybe Kyle had been right. Yes, the news about Leah and Jared's and Angela's deaths had been a shock, very disturbing and sad. But she'd let her imagination go wild with her theories and paranoia.

Maybe all it took for her to stop obsessing was someone who really needed her right now—someone who wasn't her son.

In fact, she'd even left Eli alone in the apartment for a few minutes while she'd run to the Apple Market to pick up some food for dinner. She hadn't seen any sign of Mr. 59 since Saturday—two days ago. She'd figured Eli would be safe for twenty minutes, and he had been.

While dinner had cooked, she'd jumped into the shower, and then thrown on a pair of white slacks and an orange print top. She'd even put on some makeup. In the middle of getting ready for Aidan, she'd wondered why it was so important that she look pretty tonight.

While polite all through dinner, Eli had seemed uncomfortable around Aidan. Maybe he'd just felt awkward around this stranger whose mother had just died this afternoon. Yet he'd also seemed a bit resentful of the handsome young man at their dinner table, this man who wasn't his father.

Eli was in the living room right now, watching *The Bourne Ultimatum* for the fourth or fifth time.

"That was a terrific dinner," Aidan said, sitting on one of the stools. "I hope you didn't knock yourself out too much."

"Oh, please, a bottle of Newman's Own, some Italian Chicken Sausage, and pasta. I didn't have to do much." In the darkened window above the sink, she could see him sitting at the table behind her.

"Eli's lucky to have a mom who cooks. I grew up on Chef Boyardee and Spaghetti-o's, which I learned to cook for myself when I was eight. Way too often, my mother wasn't around at dinnertime, and I had to fend for myself."

"Well, Eli has had to fend for himself on a few occasions,

too," she said, eyeing his reflection as she scrubbed out the salad bowl.

"It's not the same thing, Sydney," he muttered. "Rikki was a pretty crummy mother. I don't have many good memories of her. Well, you know what she was like. You had to deal with her from time to time. On the way here tonight, I was racking my brain trying to come up with something nice about her that I could hold onto. Right now, I'm just angry with her."

Turning off the water, Sydney dried her hands. She looked at him and shrugged. "Well, maybe anger is what you need right now to get you through this. People grieve in different ways."

Aidan sighed. "Did you see the way everyone was looking at me this afternoon? The cops, the paramedics, the funeral guys—I could tell they thought I was total shit for letting my mother waste away like that." He shook his head. "I can't believe how quickly she slid downhill since I saw her last weekend. I really did as much as I could for her . . ."

"Your mother's neighbor told me how you tried to get her some help," Sydney said, leaning back against the sink. "And you flew up from San Francisco to visit her every weekend. That really adds up—in time and money and patience."

"Well, money hasn't been that much of a problem," he mumbled.

"So—the acting is paying off?" Sydney asked.

"Two commercials for a Honda dealer in Oakland, one for a bank in Sausalito, and eight weeks doing *Barefoot in the Park* for a dinner theater." He gave her a sardonic smile. "My career isn't exactly skyrocketing."

Sydney remembered Aidan's mother saying something about an older woman who was supporting him. She decided not to ask about her.

Aidan glanced toward the wall at her autographed poster of the 1994 Olympic Games in Lillehammer. He pointed to it with his thumb. "I guess if it hadn't been for me, you'd have been on that team, maybe even brought home a medal."

"Oh, I doubt it. There were some incredibly talented skaters that year." Sydney came and sat down at the table with him. "To be honest, I do miss skating sometimes. But I really love what I'm doing now. And that might never have happened if I hadn't . . . been incapacitated for a while. I probably wouldn't have met my husband either. Anyway, I can't complain."

"Speaking of your husband, what's happening with you two?" Aidan leaned forward a little. "Do you mind me asking?"

Sydney hesitated. "We're—separated right now."

Aidan looked into her eyes for a moment, and then he smiled. "Well, he's a damn fool for letting you go. You're so beautiful."

Sydney felt herself blushing. "Thank you," she said. She felt a spark with him. It was strange, like having a little crush on someone she used to babysit. Maybe she was just lonely—or mad at Joe—but she felt a real attraction to Aidan. "As long as we're passing out the compliments—and I'm not just saying this—you certainly turned out to be a very handsome young man."

"For a long time, I wasn't that easy to look at." He tugged down his shirt collar to show his neck. "This was all scarred from the burns," he said. "Well, you remember, you saw what I looked like in the hospital. Anyway, I had extensive plastic surgery two years ago. No more scars. . . ." He unbuttoned his shirt to show her his smooth chest and shoulders. "You'd never know I was that same burnt-up kid. I can go outside with my shirt off now and not scare people."

Sydney stared at his chest and nodded. "Well, they—they did a beautiful job."

He took her hand and guided it to his chest. "Here, feel."

Her fingers glided over the silky skin. She could feel his heartbeat. Sydney nodded again, then gently pulled her hand away.

"They fixed my back, too," Aidan said, buttoning up his shirt. "It was like a miracle—the end to twelve years of agonizing pain." He left the last three buttons undone, and took hold of her hand once more. "Maybe I shouldn't be telling you this, but I feel kind of bad I don't have any more scars. . . ."

"Why in the world would you feel bad about that?" she asked.

"Because I don't have anything left over from that day, but you—you're still limping, Sydney. I did that to you. It's my fault."

She didn't know what to say. She shrugged. "Oh, please, don't worry about it."

He kissed the back of her hand and pressed it against his face.

Sydney gingerly took her hand away, and then patted his shoulder. Even if Aidan was attracted to her, his mother had just died this afternoon. And Eli was in the next room, for God's sake. She could hear Matt Damon on TV, kicking someone's ass. What if Eli had come in there two minutes ago and found her fondling Aidan's bare chest?

She slid off the stool and went back to the sink. Grabbing a towel, she started drying some cooking utensils. "So what are you going to do now?" she asked.

"Well, my mother will be cremated," he said. "I don't think I'm having a service for her or anything. It'll take a few days to clean out her apartment. Right now, I should be looking for a cheap motel. I certainly can't stay at my mother's tonight . . ."

"You're more than welcome to stay here," Sydney offered.

He got to his feet. "No, thanks, I've imposed on you enough. In fact, I should get going. Thanks for a wonderful dinner."

Putting down the dish towel, Sydney walked him toward the front door.

"So long, Eli," he said, passing by the living room. "It was nice meeting you."

Eli put the movie on pause. "Bye. I'm sorry about your mom."

Sydney stepped outside with him. "I hope I'll see you again before you go back to San Francisco."

He nodded and said nothing for a moment. His eyes wrestled with hers. "I—I need to tell you something, Sydney," he whispered at last. "The reason I can afford all these trips back and forth between here and San Francisco is because of this—older woman. Her name's Rita. She's very rich, very high society. She's about sixty-five, and has had about a dozen tummy tucks and face-lifts. It was her surgeon who did the repair job on me. She paid for it. She paid for my back surgery, too. She pays the rent on my one-bedroom apartment. If you ask any maitre d' or salesperson in the finer San Francisco restaurants or department stores, they'll tell you that Rita Bellamy is a raving bitch. But around me, she's very sweet and vulnerable. She saw something in me when I was still hideous-looking. I'm very grateful to her. Anyway, I guess you could say I'm her 'kept man.'"

Sydney stood on the front stoop, her hand still on the outside doorknob. "Why are you telling me this?"

"Because it matters to me what you think," he whispered. "I care about you, Sydney—and not just because you saved my life. I want you to know me. Do you—do you think I'm sleazy for letting this woman take care of me?"

She shrugged. "No, I wouldn't think that of you, Aidan." She couldn't really judge him. Considering how awful his mother had been, and everything life had offered him, he was probably doing the best as he could.

"Thank you," he said. He hugged her. As he pulled away,

his lips brushed against her cheek and touched the corner of her mouth.

"Good night, Aidan," Sydney said, awkwardly pulling back.

"I'll call you, okay?"

Touching her lips, Sydney nodded and watched him walk away.

On the TV, Matt Damon was in PAUSE mode, frozen and suspended in midair as he leapt off a tall bridge. Sitting on the living room floor with the DVD remote in his hand, Eli squinted at her. "What were you guys doing outside for so long?"

His mother shut the front door. "We were just talking, honey."

"Does Dad know that guy?" he asked.

"No, they've never met. The last time I saw Aidan, he was only a year or two older than you are now. I've already explained that to you." She started toward the kitchen. "Anyway, thank you for being nice to him at dinner. He's been through an awful lot today. Poor guy, he's been through an awful lot—period."

Eli followed her into the kitchen. "Does he want to date you or something?"

She started to dry the rest of the cooking utensils. "Eli, I'm fourteen years older than him."

There were several knocks on the front door.

His mouth open, Eli glanced at his mother. She put down the dish towel. "He must have forgotten something . . ."

Eli ran ahead of her and checked the peephole. Aidan stood outside. He looked like he was about to knock again. Eli quickly opened the door.

Aidan seemed out of breath. "I don't mean to scare you,"

he said. "But maybe you should call the police. I was about to leave and glanced back. I saw this creepy-looking guy sneaking around your place. He was peeking into the living room window."

Sydney stared down at the footprints in the muddy garden directly below her living room window. The cop, a slightly beefy, tanned man with a strawberry-blond crew cut, shined his flashlight on the evidence. "Thanks to the rain today, this guy left his calling card," he said.

Sydney shuddered and nervously rubbed her arms. Eli and Aidan stood beside her. Aidan put his hand on her shoulder, but then Sydney caught Eli glaring at them and she delicately pulled away. They followed the cop to the front door. He directed his flashlight beam on the door—around the lock. The wood was chipped in spots near where the catch protruded. Some paint had been scraped away at the corresponding location on the door frame. "Somebody's been trying to force his way in," the stocky policeman said. "And not just tonight; it looks like they've been at it for a while."

Sydney felt stupid for not noticing it earlier. She told the cop about the possible break-in on July Fourth and the dead bird she'd found on her bed on Saturday. "Also on Saturday afternoon," she continued. "I'm pretty sure someone followed me from here all the way out to Auburn. He was in his late twenties, about six feet tall, with black hair and a dark complexion." She turned to Aidan. "You sure you didn't get a good look at the prowler out here just now?"

Frowning, he shook his head. "I just saw him in the shadows. As soon as I got close to the apartment again, he must have seen me coming, because he just shot out of there." Aidan nodded toward the alley on the other side of the courtyard driveway, where the patrol car was parked with its blinkers going. "He disappeared down there. It all happened so fast, I never got a good look at him."

"I think I saw the guy you're talking about at the beach today, Mom," Eli piped up. "He's dark, and one of his eyes is all red and bloodshot, right?"

Sydney stared at him. "Why didn't you tell me?"

Wincing, he shrugged. "I think he was there yesterday, too."

"Good lord, Eli! I asked you about him yesterday, and you said you didn't see anyone like that."

"Did he approach you or threaten you in any way?" the cop asked him.

Eli shook his head. "No, sir. He was just there."

"But he was close enough that you could see his bloodshot eye," Sydney said, edgily.

"Um, the guy wasn't around for very long, Mom, just a few seconds. That's why I didn't remember it until I saw him again today."

The cop said they would step up patrols in the area. He recommended that in the meantime she have a locksmith install metal plate locks on both her front and back doors; and maybe she should install a few more lights outside, too—with motion-detecting sensors. Getting together with the other Tudor Court residents and starting a Neighborhood Watch wasn't a bad idea either.

The cop retreated to his patrol car to call in a report on the police radio. Standing by the front door, Sydney could hear him mumbling and the static-laced muffled responses.

Aidan turned to her. "If that invitation for me to spend the night is still good, I can crash on your couch if you'd like."

"Oh, if you could, that would be great," Sydney said. She worked up a smile for Eli. "I'll feel a lot better with two strong men in the house."

Eli just rolled his eyes at her.

Sydney decided to ignore him. “Could you guys wait here a second?” she asked. “I just remembered something I want to ask the policeman.”

Sydney caught up with the cop before he climbed inside his car. “Excuse me,” she whispered.

A hand on the hood of his patrol car, the cop turned to her.

“I didn’t want to say anything in front of my son.” Sydney spoke in a hushed tone. “But when this character followed me down to Auburn on Saturday, I tried not to push the panic button, because—well, I’m on TV, and if somebody’s following me around, it sometimes comes with the territory. But if he’s preying on my son, that’s a different story altogether. What do you suggest I do about it? And I mean beyond battening down the hatches and creating a Neighborhood Watch.”

The blond cop frowned a bit. “Well, you could get together with a police sketch artist. Or you and your son might come down to the precinct and pore over our files on convicted pedophiles and other sex offenders. You might be able to ID the guy. But unfortunately, unless we catch him trespassing, peeping in your windows, or trying something with your son, we can’t arrest the guy.”

Someone who wasn’t married to a cop might have argued with him, but Sydney understood how restricted they were at times. It was frustrating as hell, but she understood. She thanked the cop and asked for a contact number to set up an appointment with a police sketch artist. She didn’t want Eli looking through those creepy files, but she was prepared to do it.

The young police officer scribbled down a phone number on the back of an unused Seattle’s Best Coffee punch card, and handed it to her. “Call them, and they’ll set it up for you, Ms. Jordan. By the way, I’m a big fan of your work.”

Sydney thanked him again. She had the extra automatic gate-opening device with her, and followed his patrol car halfway down the driveway. Then Sydney pressed the device and watched the gate open for him. The police car pulled out of the driveway and turned down the street. She stood there and watched the gate close again.

She'd considered telling him about the deaths of Angela and Leah and Jared, and how someone had sent flowers in her name to their next of kin. But what could he have done about it? None of the victims had been killed in Seattle or Washington State. And so far, no one had threatened her.

As she started back up the driveway, Sydney warily glanced at the shadowy bushes on either side of her. She shuddered again and nervously rubbed her arms. Sydney spotted Aidan waiting for her by the front stoop. But he was alone.

Then Eli appeared in the doorway. "Hey, Mom, phone's for you!" he called. "Someone named Meredith from New York! She says it's about Troy somebody. . . ."

"How did it happen?" Sydney asked, her hand tightening on the cordless phone. She sat hunched over her office desk. In front of her was the faxed diagram of the Heimlich maneuver. She could hear the TV in the living room. Eli and Aidan were in there, watching the last part of *The Bourne Ultimatum.*

Troy Bischoff's roommate had already explained that she'd returned home from a weekend trip this morning to discover Troy dead in his bedroom. She'd been with the police the entire first half of the day, and making funeral arrangements during the second half. But she'd gotten Sydney's voice mail and wanted to call her back.

"The police are calling it an accident," Meredith told her in a shaky voice. "They say he died from self-strangulation."

Sydney glanced down at the first illustration of the Heimlich maneuver instructions. The outline figure was clutching his own throat.

"What does that mean?" Sydney heard herself ask.

"It's a—a sexual thing," she explained. "Autoerotic asphyxiation, I guess some people are into it. They fix it so they cut off their oxygen supply during sex to heighten the—the intensity of their orgasm. They bite into a lemon or lime to get revived so they don't pass out and accidentally hang themselves."

"And choke to death," Sydney whispered—almost to herself. She rubbed her forehead. "Listen, Meredith, do they know who he was with when this happened?"

"It looks like he was alone, masturbating," Meredith said quietly. "I found him, dangling from this harness he'd made out of his belt. I still don't believe it, even though I saw it with my own eyes. I knew Troy better than anyone, and he wasn't into that kind of kinky stuff. We used to make fun of people who were into really weird scenes like that."

"You said earlier that you talked to the police," Sydney said, reaching for a pen. "Was there one cop in particular, one who was in charge of the investigation?"

"Yeah, I forget his name. He gave me his card. It's in my purse."

"Could you dig it out for me? I'd really like to call this policeman and talk to him."

"Sure, Sydney, hold on."

She stared at the Heimlich maneuver diagram while she waited. Troy Bischoff saved someone from choking to death, and that was how he'd died. Angela Gannon had talked a man from jumping from a fourteenth-floor window; and she'd plunged to her death from that same window. Leah and Jared had foiled two killers who had intended to rob that Thai restaurant and shoot the staff.

Sydney suddenly remembered something from the interview she'd done with Leah and Jared. With the phone still to her ear, she stuck the pen in her mouth, then got up and checked her DVD files. She found Leah and Jared's segment from December and loaded it into her computer's DVD drive.

Meredith got back on the line. "Sydney, are you still there?"

She took the pen out of her mouth, and sat down. "Yes, Meredith."

"The guy's name is Detective Lyle A. Peary," Meredith said. She read off a phone number with a New York area code.

"Thanks, Meredith," she said. "You said you found Troy's body this morning. About what time, do you remember?"

"Around ten."

Sydney stared at the time at the top of the fax sheet: *6:32 A.M.* She knew about Troy's death before anyone else. His killer had told her. And before anyone else, the killer would send Troy's next of kin flowers, and her name would be on the card.

"Sydney?"

"Yes, I'm here. Do you happen to know how I can get hold of Troy's parents? I—um, I want to send them some flowers."

"Well, I wouldn't bother with them. They kicked Troy out of the house when he was seventeen because he told them he was gay. I tracked them down today and called with the news. I just said it was an *accident*. I didn't go into specifics. The mother cried, and then his father got on and said that as far as he was concerned Troy died when he was seventeen. Then he hung up. Sweet, huh?"

"Well, I'd like to talk with them anyway," Sydney said. "Do you have a phone number?"

"It's right here. *Mr. and Mrs. Ronald Bischoff, 501-555-1452.*"

Sydney scribbled it down at the bottom of the fax sheet. "Five-oh-one, where is that, Arkansas?"

"Yeah, some suburb of Little Rock."

"Can I ask you for one more favor, Meredith? If you happen to receive some flowers from me tomorrow, could you get the name and phone number of the florist delivering them?"

"Oh, you don't have to send any flowers, Sydney. Besides, I'm not at the apartment right now. I'm staying with a friend for the next few nights. If you want to do anything for Troy, make a donation to charity in his name."

"I will," she said, scribbling the word *donation* beside Troy's parents' names. "But if the flowers should arrive anyway, could you get the florist's name, please? Call me, and reverse the charges."

"Um, okay," she said, obviously a bit puzzled by the request.

"Thank you, Meredith. I know it doesn't make sense, but it might later."

After Sydney hung up with Meredith, she clicked on the DVD and watched the *Movers & Shakers* segment with Leah and Jared. Her friend Judy had left her the message on the Fourth of July, the night they'd been shot in their apartment. She remembered Judy telling her that the murder scene had looked like a "burglary gone from bad to worse," and one of Leah and Jared's neighbors had found both bodies in the bathroom.

Sydney watched the two of them together in the video short, and her heart broke. They were both so young and cute, such a sweet couple. She thought of Angela, and now, Troy. All of them heroes, and all of them had met such violent, senseless deaths.

But to someone, it made sense.

Sydney watched a visibly shaken Leah in close-up as she talked about the thugs in the Thai restaurant. Leah was crying: *"When I heard they planned to—to take us all into the bathroom and shoot us, I was just so scared. . . ."*

Sydney's finger clicked on the mouse, hitting Pause. She leaned in closer to her computer screen, and played it back again. *"Take us all into the bathroom and shoot us . . ."*

"Oh, God," Sydney whispered, hitting the Pause icon again.

On the computer screen, Leah's face was frozen. Tears were locked in her eyes and her mouth was open. Leah didn't know it at the time, of course. But she was describing exactly how—six months later—she and her fiancé would be killed.

"You've reached the desk of Detective Lyle A. Peary, NYPD," said the man on the recording. Then an automated voice chimed in: *"To page this person, press one now, or leave a message after the beep. If this is an emergency, please hang up and dial 9-1-1."*

Sydney paged him, and left her phone number. Then she called the number again and waited for the beep.

"Hello, this is Sydney Jordan," she said into the recording. She gave him her phone number again. "I've just paged you as well, Detective. I have some important information about the death of Troy Bischoff. I'm a correspondent with *On the Edge*, and I did a story about Troy a few months ago. Someone sent me a fax at 6:32 this morning from Kinko's . . ." She gave him the Seventh Avenue address. "I believe this fax was sent to me by the person who killed Troy. I don't think it was a self-strangulation. I can explain everything to you. Just check with that Kinko's. The manager's name is Paul. This person used a credit card to send this fax, and it's on file there. I'm sorry about the late hour, but I—"

There was a beep. Then the automated voice chimed in again, saying if she was satisfied with her message to press one.

Sydney wasn't satisfied, not yet at least. But she pressed one anyway.

She figured she wouldn't hear back from Detective Peary until tomorrow morning. It was too late—past eleven-thirty in Arkansas—to phone Troy's parents. She'd have to try them first thing in the morning—before the florist delivered the *With Sympathy* floral arrangement from *Sydney Jordan*.

She realized what was happening. The fog of uncertainty had lifted, and it was so terribly clear. Someone was killing the heroes from her *Movers & Shakers* stories. And in a twisted kind of "What goes around comes around" logic, he'd taken the fate from which they'd saved someone and used it to design their murders. He'd furnished her with tokens symbolizing each murdered hero—a broken teapot and some spilled rice, a dead bird, and a diagram on how to save someone from choking. And if she didn't catch on to his cryptic calling cards, there was always a thank-you note from the victim's next of kin for the sympathy bouquets sent in her name. It was as if he wanted her to feel included in each murder.

But who was doing this, and why? This person was making some kind of statement. He obviously had a grudge against her. Maybe it was someone who didn't like one of her *Movers & Shakers* segments about a hero.

Hunched forward in her desk chair, Sydney held a hand over her mouth. She wondered if her stalker was somehow connected to the *Movers & Shakers* killer. Eli had seen him at the beach yesterday and today. So when did this man have time to fly to New York City and kill Troy? Perhaps he was working with the killer, spying on her and Eli, breaking and entering to leave her the occasional cryptic clue.

Sydney was grateful to have Aidan spending the night. She'd left the poor guy parked in front of the TV with Eli for the last forty-five minutes. Getting to her feet, she started toward the living room. She could hear people on TV talking about *The Bourne Ultimatum*, which meant the movie was over, and Eli had moved onto the Special Features.

"You're going to go blind," she said, finding Eli on the floor directly in front of the TV.

He just nodded and kept staring at the screen.

Dead asleep, Aidan was slumped in the corner of the sofa with his head tipped back. He made a faint snoring sound.

"Aidan?" she said. "Aidan, did you want to wash up or anything?"

He didn't move.

"I tried to wake him up earlier," Eli explained. "He didn't budge. He's history. Great bodyguard he's gonna be tonight."

Sydney turned to him. "You have a choice. If you want to share your room, I'll get him upstairs now, and you can stay down here as long as you want. Otherwise, you need to skedaddle so I can make up the couch for him."

Pausing the movie, Eli gave her an apprehensive look. "Would you be ticked if said I don't feel like sharing my room?"

She shook her head, and then sat down on the floor beside him. "No, honey, you hardly know him," she whispered. "And I really don't think it's going to make any difference to Aidan where he sleeps tonight. But I am ticked at you. I can't believe you didn't tell me about that man following you around at the beach yesterday—and today. Why didn't you speak up earlier?"

Eli shrugged uneasily. "I—I didn't want to worry you."

She gave him a wary sidelong glance. "I don't think I'm getting the whole story here, Eli. Something's going on with you that you're not telling me. What is it?"

He let out a nervous laugh. "Nothing, Mom. Nothing's going on."

She stroked his arm. "Sweetheart, this guy following you around could be very dangerous. There have been some strange, disturbing incidents with people I've worked with on my videos. I'm not sure what it's about yet, but I'll tell you once I know more. Anyway, Eli, until further notice, we need to be cautious and on our guard."

He stared at her and blinked. "What kind of *incidents*?"

"Some very serious stuff," she replied. "Like I said, I'll tell you when I know more. But the important thing is, you need to be honest with me. If someone is following you around, or someone is secretly communicating with you, you need to let me know."

Sydney studied him. "Is someone communicating with you, honey?"

He shrugged again. "Just our ghost, nobody else."

Sydney worked up a smile. "Okey-doke," she said, kissing his forehead.

Then she got to her feet and headed upstairs to get some bedding for their overnight guest.

She managed to wake him up and steer him into the downstairs powder room. While Aidan washed his face, Sydney made up the couch with sheets and a pillow. Eli had already retreated to his room.

Aidan was so tired he just nodded groggily and said, "Thanks, Sydney," when she told him that he could help himself to anything in the kitchen and sleep as late as he wanted. Aidan stripped down to his undershorts while she was still explaining that she'd be in her office for a while longer.

"And if the light bothers you, I'll . . ." Sydney didn't quite finish. He had a beautiful, athletic physique, and he seemed so unself-conscious about it. She watched him lie down on the sofa and pull the sheets around him.

"Thanks again, Sydney," he murmured. "Are you—going to kiss me good night?"

She gazed at him. He had a sleepy smile on his handsome face.

"Um, no," she said, crossing her arms. "Sleep well, Aidan."

Sydney retreated to the kitchen. She wasn't sure anymore just how unself-conscious that striptease had been. Maybe he'd been kidding about the good-night kiss. Or maybe he'd just needed someone to be a mother to him and tuck him in for the night. She couldn't really read him. One thing she knew, she didn't want to be like that sixty-five-year-old Rita woman with all the face-lifts in San Francisco.

She poured a glass of the merlot left over from dinner. More than anything right now, she wanted to call Joe and tell him how scared and confused she was. But he was a stranger to her now. He'd become one the minute he'd hit her that afternoon two months ago—maybe even before that.

She almost expected Aidan to show up in the kitchen doorway in just his undershorts, saying he couldn't sleep. But she heard him in the living room, snoring lightly.

Sydney took her wine into her office and called her brother. His machine picked up, and then she remembered his date tonight. She waited for the beep.

"Hi, it's me, and I'm sorry," she said into the machine. "I totally forgot about your hot date tonight until just now. I hope it's going well. As soon as you're free, can you call me? There's a lot going on here, and I really need to talk to you. It's—um, ten-twenty."

Sydney clicked off the phone. Sipping her wine, she stared at the Heimlich maneuver fax again. She wondered how Troy's killer had trapped him. Had Troy picked him up in a bar? Or had the killer set up some kind of *chance meeting*?

Her brother had just met that man on the beach today.

Grabbing the phone, Sydney clicked it on again. She speed-dialed Kyle once more. "It's me again," she said, after the beep. "Listen. Call my cell as soon as you get this. I don't care how late it is. I really need to talk to you, Kyle. I probably won't fall asleep until I hear from you. Anyway, call me right away. Thanks."

Sydney clicked off the line.

It would be a long night ahead.

CHAPTER SEVENTEEN

Evanston, Illinois—Tuesday, 1:54 A.M.

Thirty-one-year-old Chloe Finch hobbled along Evanston Beach, looking for just the right place. She was carrying her shoes, and her feet had gotten used to the cold lake water. It was too muggy and warm for a raincoat tonight, but she wore one. She would need it later. She'd been collecting good-size stones and cramming them into the raincoat's pockets. They would weigh her down when she walked into the lake to drown herself.

The police patrolled the public beach, which was closed. But that didn't stop the occasional skinny-dippers or others who wanted a midnight dip. Chloe had to find an uninhabited stretch of beach. She didn't need anyone trying to be a hero and saving her life.

It meant navigating a break in a fence along one private beach, and then jumping a fence that bordered another. And Chloe wasn't good at jumping fences.

"You're one in a thousand," the doctor had once told her, referring to how many babies were born with clubfoot. She was in good company: Lord Byron; David Lynch; Dallas Cowboy quarterback, Troy Aikman; Damon Wayans; and Dudley Moore. Whenever the topic came up during a date, she always rattled off the list of famous people born with *talipes equinovarus*. She always left Josef Goebbels from that list. Who in their right mind wanted to be grouped with Goebbels? Another one in a thousand—and the one who inspired Chloe the most—was Kristi Yamaguchi, who took home the gold medal in figure skating in the 1992 Winter Olympics.

Chloe became a huge fan of figure skating, but could never do it herself. They'd botched the operation on her foot when she'd been a baby. Three attempts at corrective surgery after that had failed, leaving her left foot slightly deformed. She could walk, but had a prominent limp. On bad days, she needed a cane.

Lately, there had been a lot of bad days, but that had nothing to do with her foot. Then again, maybe if she hadn't tripped over her own damn cane one day last week, she probably wouldn't have met Riley.

Chloe was thin with a long face and a prominent nose that had a little bump in it. This jerky girl in high school used to call her "horse-face," which had hurt her feelings. But oddly, it had also given Chloe a bit of hope about fitting in with everyone; at least the girl hadn't made fun of the way she walked. For the last several years, her short plain brown hair was *Honey Auburn*—that was the color name on the L'Oreal box. She'd never considered herself very pretty, but did the best with what she had.

Yet Riley had made her feel beautiful—for three whole days.

She wasn't killing herself because of Riley. The son of a bitch wasn't worth it. No, Chloe didn't have one big reason for drowning herself in that cool lake. It was a lot of things, piling up.

Piling up, like the stones in her pockets. Chloe was beginning to get tired—walking in the sand with all that extra weight. She stopped at a small, private beach with a narrow strip of sand between Lake Michigan and a hillside of trees and shrubs. The last people she'd passed had been two naked, skinny teenage boys in the water, trying to persuade this girl with them to take off her top—at least. The girl kept shrieking her refusals. Chloe had given them a wide berth. Looking over her shoulder, she could barely see them anymore; they were just specks on the moonlit beach. She couldn't even hear the girl's high-pitched squeals—only the sound of the waves on the shore.

Chloe glanced in the other direction: the beach was empty. There was an old pier with ALDER HILL ROAD—PRIVATE BEACH stenciled in yellow on the side, the letters worn and faded. The pier was made up of three concrete sections that seemed to be crumbling in spots. The slab farthest out was slightly askew and appeared ready to break off from the rest of the pier. Chloe figured she could take a running jump off that last slab, and she'd instantly be in over her head. If the stones in her raincoat didn't drag her down, she'd swim away from the pier and keep swimming until it was too late to turn back. Then she'd give in to the overwhelming fatigue and let the lake swallow her.

She smiled. How satisfying that image was. She'd never felt so in charge of her life until now, just moments before she would end it.

Still smiling, Chloe took one last look around to make sure she was alone. She noticed a strange, bright pinpoint of light in the dense, dark hillside jungle behind her. It seemed to be moving, coming closer to the beach. Chloe heard bushes rustling. She scoured the edge of the thicket and saw a break in the trees and shrubs. There were some stone steps and a crude path that snaked through the hillside woods.

She heard a woman giggling, then a man's whispers. A beam of light illuminated the end of that path. Chloe ducked back into the bushes to avoid being seen.

She watched a dark-haired man holding a lit flashlight to

navigate the end of the trail. He wore a blazer and he'd loosened his tie. He looked handsome in the distance. He had his arm around a blonde in a pretty red cocktail dress. She was still giggling. They looked very much in love.

Assholes, Chloe thought, frowning at them. She'd recently graduated from *lonely romantic* to out-and-out *bitter hag*. That was one more thing she didn't like about herself lately. She had no patience for people in love. They made her step aside on the sidewalk, because God help them if they broke apart for a few seconds. They just had to walk side by side. And they used their "We're a couple" status to check-out-line shop in the store. *Go ahead and get your stupid boyfriend to pick up eleven more last-minute items while you stand in line in front of me, I really don't mind.* And sure enough, she'd find herself bumped in line for some dipshit's boyfriend with a handcart full of crap. "Oh, we're together," the woman would explain when Chloe gave them a filthy look.

And now, here was this beautiful couple out for a stroll on the moonlit beach, and she resented the hell out of them. On top of being in love, they were throwing a cog in her grand exit plan.

"I should be so mad at you," the woman was saying, bumping her hip against his. "Making me get all dressed up so we can go to a drive-thru. . . .

Chloe ducked behind a bush and watched them walking hand in hand toward *her* pier. Maybe they would just keep walking along the shore, and then she'd have this beach to herself again. Was that too much to hope for?

Apparently so, because the twosome turned and walked down to the end of the pier. They embraced and kissed.

Chloe felt tears stinging her eyes. Why couldn't that be her? Just once?

The woman giggled again. Chloe realized her boyfriend had unzipped the back of the red dress. She started to peel down the top part of the dress while he kissed her neck. Chloe could see the woman's breasts in the moonlight. The man's mouth moved down from her neck to one breast. After a moment, he stepped back.

"Good God," Chloe whispered. She realized the man—like her—carried at least one stone in his pocket. Suddenly, he pulled the rock from his blazer pocket and bashed it over the blonde's head. The woman let out a shriek and then a strange warbled groan that was like gibberish. A hand on her forehead, she staggered back from him. Blood was already dripping through her fingers down to her elbow.

With a forceful shove, the man pushed her off the pier. She plunged into the water.

A hand over her heart, Chloe watched them from the edge of the thicket.

The man stood at the end of the pier, gazing down at the lake for only a moment. He threw the stone into the drink. Then he turned and hurried toward the path they'd taken down together.

Chloe recoiled behind the shrubs as he strode past her. She tried to keep perfectly still. He pulled the small flashlight from his other blazer pocket. She could hear him breathing hard, and then his footsteps on the stone path, and bushes rustling.

Chloe's shook horribly as she pulled out her cell phone and dialed 9-1-1. She shucked off the heavy raincoat and started to hobble toward the pier. The operator finally answered.

"Yes, hello," Chloe said, out of breath. "I'm at—at Alder Hill Road Beach. It's a private beach, and I just saw this guy hit a woman over the head and throw her into the lake. I think he might have killed her . . ."

"All right, ma'am," the operator said. "Could you give me your name and the address you're calling from?"

Glancing over her shoulder, Chloe saw the lone pinpoint of light moving back up the dark hillside forest. "My name is Chloe Finch, and I told you, I'm at a private beach on Alder Hill Road. Listen, the guy's getting away. You need to send someone here as soon as possible. This woman's going to need an ambulance . . ."

She raced to the end of the pier, and spotted the woman a few yards away, floating facedown in the silvery water. Her naked back looked so white. The wet red dress—bunched around her waist—seemed to be pulling her down. "Oh, God, I see her," Chloe gasped into the phone. "Please . . . please, hurry!"

Tossing aside the cell phone, she dove off the end of the pier and furiously swam out to the unconscious woman. Flipping her over, Chloe cupped her hand under her chin and started paddling toward shore. She couldn't tell if the woman was still breathing. Her eyes remained closed; her lids didn't even flutter. The lake water splashed away blood from the gash in her forehead—but only temporarily. It didn't look like the bleeding would stop.

Once she reached the shallow water, Chloe grabbed the lifeless woman under the arms and then dragged her to the sandy shore. Her wet, limp body was heavy. Frazzled, Chloe could hardly get a breath.

She rolled the woman onto her stomach, and repeatedly pushed at her lower back. "C'mon, c'mon . . ." Chloe whispered. "Please . . ."

At last, she heard a choking sound, and the woman stirred. She started to cough up water. Chloe was still shaking as she turned the woman over. Her wet blond hair was swept across her face, mingling with sand and blood. She gasped for air and coughed again.

Chloe held her head in her lap. The woman was shivering, and Chloe pulled the top of her dress up to cover her. Then she quickly unbuttoned her own wet short-sleeve shirt. She wrung it out and applied it to the gash on the woman's forehead.

Catching her breath, she could hear a siren in the distance. "It's okay," she said to the woman. "There's an ambulance on the way . . ."

Chloe didn't realize it then, but she'd been right about that man and this woman. Together, they'd thrown a cog in her grand exit plan.

Chapter Eighteen

"I don't get it," Eli said from the backseat of Aidan's rental car. "Why can't I go to Chicago with you?"

Sydney glanced over her shoulder at him from the front passenger seat. "I told you, honey. I'm coming right back tomorrow night. This is not a leisure trip. I did all I could to wiggle out of this, but they need me to cover this story. I'm going directly from the airport to meet with the crew, and tonight, I'm meeting this Chloe person. I won't have time to take you around anyplace."

"This woman must be a real fan of your *Movers and Shakers* stories," Aidan said, his hands on the steering wheel. He smiled at her. "She won't talk to any other reporter but you?"

Sydney nodded. "So they tell me. Only I think she's more a fan from my figure-skating days." She noticed Aidan's smile wane, and realized he indeed still felt responsible for the abrupt end of her career on the ice. She reached over and patted his arm. "You're really sweet to chauffeur us around like this—with all you have going on today. Thanks, Aidan."

"So why can't I stay with Dad while you're working?" Eli piped up.

"Because I have to catch a 10:22 flight, which the network booked for me," she replied. "And your dear mother doesn't have the thousand bucks they'll charge for your last-minute overnight trip to Chicago, sweetie."

It had been a crazy morning with the phone ringing at 6:20. Sydney hadn't caught much sleep at all. She'd had another bout of Internet browsing and going through her *Movers & Shakers* files again. Of the twenty-eight video shorts she'd filmed last year, eight had focused on someone who had saved another person's life. Four of those people had met gruesome deaths within the last two weeks. Of the four others, she could discount her profile on an army private, Justin O'Rourke. He'd already been dead for a week when she'd put together the story about Justin throwing himself on top of a grenade to save his buddies during an insurgent assault in Iraq.

That left three people. Sydney scribbled down a list:

—Eric Ryan, 11, saved friend's younger brother, Eddie Kelly, when he fell down a well.
Clinton, Iowa: Contact: Susan Ryan (mom): 563-555-0505
workingmomsue@brisbee.com.

—Beth Costello, 34, stopped to help stroke victim lying on downtown Chicago sidewalk—moved to Paris for work 2 months ago (& how could you inflict a stroke on someone anyway?).
E-mail just in case: kinsellagal@artistsgallery.com.

—Roseann Fann, 72, returning from swing shift @ rest home @ 4 AM, saw wrecked burning car, called 911, and then pulled man from car, did CPR & saved life.
Milwaukee, WI: Rosie: 414-555-3641
Rosie195@verizoncentral.com.

Sydney e-mailed the three of them individually. She didn't want to frighten them, but she also didn't want to hear tomorrow that Eric broke his neck falling down a well or that

Roseann died in a fiery car crash. She figured Beth was probably safe, since she was out of the country. But why take any chances? *"Recently, I've received some death threats,"* she wrote in her note to each one. *"A few of my* Movers & Shakers *subjects were mentioned by name in these alarming e-mails. Your name wasn't among them. But I just want to alert you about this situation and advise you to be on your guard for the next few days. I hope I'm overreacting here, but I'd rather err on the side of caution . . ."*

While rifling through the scores of *Movers & Shakers* files and pouring over her notes, Sydney resisted the temptation to have another glass of merlot and stuck to sparkling water instead. She also avoided the living room. She could hear Aidan snoring lightly in there.

Every few minutes, she glanced at the clock and thought about Kyle on this date with this guy he barely knew. How well had Troy Bischoff known the man who had strangled him? She left yet another message on her brother's answering machine.

Kyle finally called her at around 3 A.M. He'd had a terrific date with Dan, with whom he'd gotten to second base. Sydney wasn't sure what second base on a gay date was, and she didn't ask. She told her brother about Troy Bischoff's death, and how she'd realized this killer was targeting heroes. Kyle offered to come over, saying she and Eli shouldn't be alone. Then she told him about Aidan spending the night. "I think we're okay for now," she said. "I'm hoping this detective in New York calls me back in the morning. Maybe they'll have a name from the credit card at Kinko's. Then we can let the police solve this. The sooner we can drop this in the lap of the law, the better off I'll feel."

But the phone call at 6:20 in the morning wasn't from Detective Peary. It was from the network news division. A big story was brewing in Chicago. Handsome Derrick De Santo, thirty-three, was the new husband of prominent socialite and heir to meatpacking millions, Abigail Wayland, thirty-eight. Sydney remembered how they were always photographed and written up in the Chicago newspapers and magazines. She remembered the gossip that dashing Derrick was a fortune hunter, and Abigail was a birdbrain for marrying him. There were even rumors Derrick was gay, rumors that would soon be put to rest, because on a seemingly deserted beach in Evanston at approximately 2:15 Central time that Tuesday morning, Derrick slammed a rock against the forehead of his newly pregnant girlfriend, Lenora Swayne, and then threw her into Lake Michigan. Derrick had no idea Chloe Finch, a thirty-one-year-old admissions manager at Northwestern University, was on that same beach watching his every move. She'd saved Lenora from drowning, and her 9-1-1 call had prompted a police dispatch to Alder Hill Road. That was where patrolmen detained Derrick De Santo, leaving the scene in the vintage Porsche Spyder his wife had recently bought for him on their one-year anniversary.

It had all the earmarks of becoming the story of the year, but none of the principal players were talking: not Abigail, not Derrick—not even through his high-priced attorneys—and not Lenora, who was rushed to Northwestern University Hospital for emergency treatment. As for Chloe Finch, she would talk to only one reporter, Sydney Jordan.

"Apparently, she read your autobiography when she was a teenager," the network news executive had explained to Sydney at 6:20 this morning. "She's been a fan ever since your figure-skating days."

"But I'm not a hard-news reporter," Sydney had argued.

"So do it like a *Movers and Shakers* piece, whatever you want. This is great publicity for you, Sydney, and quite frankly, you could use it. Everyone is dying to talk to this woman, and you're the only one she'll see. Now, we've booked you on a 10:22 flight out of SeaTac . . ."

But first she had to drop Eli at her brother's place.

Aidan turned down the hillside dead-end street where Kyle's tall town house loomed over trees and bushes. It was set apart from the other houses. Sydney felt bad foisting her son on Kyle today, when he had a brunch date with this Dan person. She knew Eli wasn't happy with her either.

As they pulled into his driveway, Kyle emerged from the house in a sports shirt and khaki shorts. He had a cup of coffee in his hand. With a crooked smile, he raised his cup as if to toast their arrival and then sipped from it.

Eli thanked Aidan and climbed out of the car first. Sydney heard Kyle tell him that he'd set up a video game on TV for him, and Eli ran inside the house.

"I'm sorry I can't take you to the airport," Aidan told her. "Quarter after nine was the only time this funeral home would see me today, and they're up in Lynnwood."

"Please, don't apologize," Sydney said. "With everything you're going through right now, it's really kind of you to take us here. I hope we can get together again when I'm back in town."

He nodded. "I'd really like that."

She started to open the car door, but he put his hand on her shoulder. "Sydney, before you go, I—I need to apologize for last night. That was really dumb of me when I—you know, when I asked if you'd kiss me good night. I was tired—and maybe a little tipsy from the wine. Anyway, it was inappropriate."

She worked up a smile. "That's okay. I didn't take you too seriously."

He just nodded, then climbed out of the car and retrieved her small suitcase from the trunk. He set it down beside her as she stepped out of the car.

"Thanks, Aidan," she said. "Thanks for everything." She gave him an awkward hug. For a moment, she thought he might try to kiss her. But he didn't.

He gently pulled away and retreated toward the rental car.

At his door, he hesitated. "Sydney? For the record, I was serious last night—inappropriate and clumsy, but very serious."

Before she could say anything, he ducked into the car and closed the door.

"Who's the Greek God, and does he come in Homo?" Kyle asked as Aidan backed the car out of the driveway. "Don't tell me that's little Aidan Cosgrove."

Sydney nodded. *"All growed-up."* She turned to her brother and sighed. "I'm sorry to screw up your brunch plans with this potential new love interest."

"Don't worry about it. I scratched you off my shit list. When I phoned Dan to cancel, he'd just gotten a call himself, a family emergency. He needs to go to Portland. But he's coming over first." Kyle sipped his coffee. "In fact, he should be here any minute. He offered to drive you to the airport."

"Well, that's great, thanks." She peered inside Kyle's open front door. She could hear the video game going at a loud volume upstairs. "Do me a favor and don't let Eli out of your sight. No beach trip today, no matter how much he begs you. It's just too easy for him to get lost in the crowd there."

"Well, if I hadn't lost him for a few minutes there yesterday, I wouldn't have met Dan. But I promise you, I won't take any chances." Kyle put his hand on her back. "How are you holding up?"

"I left another message for that detective in New York. I'm hoping he'll have something for us." With a sigh, she shook her head. "I still can't figure out why this is happening, why he's targeting heroes."

Kyle leaned against the doorway. "After we talked last night, I kept thinking about that weird e-mail you received before all this started."

"*'Bitch-Sydney—you can't save them?'*" she said.

"From *'Second duet'* or something . . ."

Sydney nodded. "*'Second-duet-for-you,'* that was his e-mail address."

"But aside from Leah and Jared, you couldn't find any other *Movers and Shakers* couples who have met an untimely end, right?"

"No, I didn't come up with anyone—thank God."

"When you told me about the hero angle early this morning, it got me thinking." Kyle glanced down into his coffee cup. "A couple of years ago, these two teenage girls from James Madison High School were murdered on the same day—only hours apart. And their bodies were found within a mile or two from each other, too. It happened right here in this neighborhood. Both their throats had been slit."

Sydney just stared at him. She hadn't heard anything about this.

"I don't know if it made the Chicago papers," Kyle explained, "but it was big news around here for a few days. As far as I know, they never found the guy who murdered them. Anyway, the thing of it is, the girls were heroes, Syd. One of their classmates had smuggled a gun into school, and these two girls talked him out of killing an entire class full of kids."

Sydney frowned. "But I didn't do a profile on these girls. I didn't even know them. Are you thinking this was the *'first duet'*?"

"Could be," he said.

"But it doesn't follow the pattern of the other murders. I don't see how it can be related—"

"Well, maybe it was his first time at bat, and he was acting out of blind rage." Kyle shrugged. "Maybe he decided to focus all his attention on you when you moved here. You're a hero yourself, Syd. And you salute heroes in your TV segments. That makes you a prime target for someone with a hero-gripe. All this started a few weeks after you moved here, didn't it?"

Sydney nodded, but didn't say anything. She didn't see a connection between the *Movers & Shakers* murders and these two girls who were killed. The *Movers & Shakers* murderer wouldn't have slit their throats. He would have taken them into an empty classroom and shot them. And then their parents would have received flowers with a card from Sydney Jordan.

Kyle sipped his coffee again. "Maybe I'm talking out of my ass. Anyway, I thought of those dead high school girls after we talked early this morning. And like I say, they never did find who killed them." He glanced up as a red Honda Accord came down the street. "There's Dan now. . . ."

Sydney left her suitcase outside, then ran into the house to say good-bye to Eli. He put his video game on pause while she hugged him. Sydney told him she was sorry he couldn't go to Chicago with her. She also told him she'd be back tomorrow night, and she told him to be careful and mind his uncle.

Sydney had a horrible feeling about this trip.

But she didn't tell him that.

"Goddamn it!"

Dan Spengler shoved his palm onto the steering wheel and the car horn blared. "We're in gridlock. I'm trying not to block the intersection, and this slime-bucket asshole takes a right on red!" He hit the accelerator, and the car sped forward. Sydney's hand automatically went to the dashboard as she braced herself for a potential collision.

"You lowlife weasel!" Dan screamed from his window, almost slamming into the side of the other car. He hit his horn again. "Could you be more of a jerk?" He glanced at Sydney. "What kind of justification does he have for pulling that kind of shit? *'I'm in a hurry?'* or *'I'm just an asshole?'* Wait—wait a minute. Did he just flip me the bird? I can't tell . . ."

The other driver had indeed given him the finger, but Sydney wasn't about to say anything. She didn't want to make

Dan even angrier—if that were possible. He was a handsome man with chiseled features, blue eyes, and short, slightly receding black hair. He was also very scary—at least when he was mad. His face had turned red, and his knuckles were white as he clutched the steering wheel.

"Um, I didn't see him gesturing," Sydney lied, finally letting go of the dashboard and sitting back in the passenger seat.

"I can't get over how some people delude themselves into thinking they're nice, and then they get into traffic and act like total creeps. It just amazes me." Dan took a few deep breaths, and he laughed a little. "Well, great first impression I'm making on you, huh? I'm usually a very pleasant person, honest. But whenever I get on the road, nine times out of ten, there's some jerk driver who makes me lose it. Sorry, Sydney. I didn't scare you, did I?"

"Oh, just a little—for a minute there," she said nervously. Without a doubt, the other driver had been in the wrong, but the way Dan had reacted was unnerving. She wondered if Kyle knew about this guy's angry side.

Her cell phone went off. Sydney grabbed it out of her purse and checked the caller ID: Detective Peary's number in New York. "Do you mind if I take this?" she asked.

"Go for it," Dan said, eyes on the road.

Sydney clicked on the phone. "Hello? Detective Peary?"

"Yes. I got your messages, Ms. Jordan."

"Thank you for calling back. Did you check with the Kinko's on Seventh Avenue?"

"Yes, I followed that up. They let me see the credit card receipt for that fax you were telling me about."

"And?" Sydney said, hanging on his every word.

"Troy Bischoff is the name on the Visa card."

"Shit," Sydney murmured, closing her eyes. What made her think the killer wouldn't cover his tracks?

"I'm closing the book on this one, Ms. Jordan. This guy accidentally killed himself."

"Did you check to see if that Visa card is missing?" Sydney asked. "The killer could have stolen the card."

"Bischoff had a wallet full of credit cards and money in his bedroom, and lots of valuables in his apartment. Why would someone take one card and leave all the rest behind? Anyway, someone at Kinko's found his card yesterday afternoon. Looks like Bischoff forgot it there after he sent you that fax."

"Or maybe the killer left it there," Sydney offered. "Did you consider that as a possibility? Detective, this guy wouldn't have taken Troy's money, because he didn't want anyone to know he was there. He wanted it to look like Troy died alone during this kinky self-strangulation thing."

"Well, if this so-called-killer didn't want anyone to know he was there, why did he send you this fax-clue or whatever it was?" Peary didn't wait for her to answer. "Listen, Ms. Jordan, it's a clear case of death by autoerotic asphyxiation. That's the end of it. That sort of thing happens a lot more than you'd think. These perverts are always doing stuff like this to themselves. They're sick. And then they wonder why some folks can't stand them."

"What?" Sydney said sharply. "Did I just hear you right? You know, I'm a correspondent for a network TV news program—"

"I know who you are, Ms. Jordan," he replied.

"Would you like to repeat what you just said to me for the record?"

"Listen," the detective said. "I'm doing you and your program a huge favor by not dragging this out. I saw the bit you did on this guy a few months back when you made him out to be a big hero. Are you really so eager for your adoring public to know how this deviant died?"

Sydney didn't reply. She pulled the cell phone away from her face and glared at it. "Asshole!" she screamed. Then she clicked off the line. It was all she could do to keep from smashing the phone against the dashboard. "Son of a bitch," she growled, shaking her head.

She sat there silently fuming for another few moments. Then she glanced over at Dan, and he gave her a wary look. "Well, I guess we're even now, huh? I mean, which one of us is crazier?"

She cracked a tiny smile.

"I don't even want to ask what that conversation was about," he said, chuckling.

Sydney managed a weak laugh. "Tell you later when I get to know you better."

Up ahead, she saw the sign for the turn-off to SeaTac Airport. Then she glanced in the rearview mirror and saw his medium-size suitcase on the backseat. He'd put her bag in the trunk. His suitcase was dark blue and had several zippers and compartments. And on the leather handle were two destination tags from his last round trip. In the mirror, she could read the *SEA* on one tag for his return trip to SeaTac. But she couldn't quite make out the airport abbreviation on the other stub.

Sydney casually glanced over her shoulder. Now she saw the old torn tag from his previous trip: *JFK*.

Turning forward, she glimpsed the airport exit as they passed it.

Sydney clutched the cell phone tighter. "Wasn't that the turn-off for the airport back there?" she asked as casually as she could.

He kept his eyes on the road. "My way's faster," he said with a tiny smile.

The seat belt was pinching her, and Sydney nervously tugged at it. She glanced at Dan again—his handsome profile and that little smile. Kyle had just met this man yesterday afternoon. Had Dan Spengler been in New York City the night before? It was awfully strange how he'd just shown up in her brother's life at this particular time.

"Was that phone call about one of your stories for *On the Edge*?" he asked.

"Sort of," she said. "A person from one of those stories was killed." Sydney watched for his reaction. He didn't seem very surprised.

" '*A kinky self-strangulation thing?*' " he asked, quoting from her talk to Detective Peary.

"Yes," Sydney said. She watched him pass another exit off Interstate 5.

"You can tell me to mind my own business if you want," he said.

"It's okay."

"Was he a good friend?"

"Actually, I didn't know him very well," Sydney admitted, squirming in the passenger seat. She looked out her window. At this point, they would have to backtrack to get to the airport.

"What's the name for that—the *self-strangulation* thing?"

"Autoerotic asphyxiation."

"Yeah," he nodded and then switched on his turn signal. "You know, for the longest time, I thought it had to do with phone sex—*audio-erotic affixation*. Shows you how stupid I am."

Sydney didn't respond or even smile. She watched him veer onto the turn-off for 188th and Orilla Road. From the interstate, it looked like the road wound through a forest area. Sydney still clutched the cell phone in her hand. She took a deep breath. "So—was it hot in New York?" she heard herself ask.

He glanced at her and let out a stunned little laugh. "How did you know I was in New York in May?"

"In May?" she repeated.

"Yeah, I was visiting my big brother. He's a widower with two really cute kids. Let me know if you ever want to be fixed up. He's a very well-to-do accountant." He stopped at the light for 188th Street. Sydney saw a small sign with a right arrow that said AIRPORT. "So how did you know I was in New York?" Dan asked. "I don't remember mentioning it to Kyle."

"I noticed the old destination tag on your suitcase," she admitted.

He gave her a baffled grin, then steered the car to the right. "Boy, you don't miss a thing."

"It's a skill every reporter needs," she said. "Is the airport far?"

"About five more minutes if we get a break in the traffic lights." He started to pick up speed.

Sydney told herself she could sit back and breathe easy—at least, for now.

"Mixed Bags," the woman said on the other end of the line. "Can I help you?"

"Yes, hello," Eli whispered into the phone. He was in his uncle's TV room on the second floor, sitting on the sectional sofa that had doubled as his bed for a few weeks a while back. "Is Francesca Landau working there today?"

"Yes, but she's running a little late. She'll be in sometime after 10:15. Can I take a message?"

"No, thanks," Eli said. "But could you, um. . . ." He hesitated. His uncle was down in the kitchen. Eli wasn't sure if he just now heard him coming up the stairs. He'd paused the video game on the big-screen TV. At his side, a large picture window provided a sweeping view of downtown Seattle, Elliott Bay, and the Olympic Mountain range. But his uncle's town house was also close to the interstate, and the sound of traffic was almost like white noise. It drowned out a lot of sounds within the house.

"Yes?" the woman asked.

Eli figured it had been a false alarm. His uncle was still

down in the kitchen. "Um, I need to make sure I have the right Francesca Landau," Eli said. "Is she a lady in her early fifties?"

"Yes, but you better not ask Fran that," the woman said.

"And you guys are in Kirkland, right?"

"Yes, sir, we're here on Lake Washington Boulevard."

"Thank you very much," Eli said. Then he hung up.

When he'd returned home from the library yesterday, Eli had used his mother's computer to check the Internet for information on Robert Landau, the estranged husband of Loretta Sayers and stepfather to Earl and, quite possibly, their killer. All he'd found was an obituary from the *Seattle Times* in 1987. Robert Landau had died from a heart attack at age sixty-six. He'd been survived by two of his children, Mark Landau and Francesca Landau-Foyle, and two grandchildren. There was something in quotes at the bottom of the article: *"He is joined in eternity with his beloved wife, Estelle (1927–1971) and son, Jonathan (1954–1975)."*

Eli wondered why they'd mentioned the first wife, but not Loretta or Earl. And what had happened to the other son, Jonathan, dead at age twenty-one?

He hadn't found anything on line about a Mark Landau in Seattle after 1987. But when he googled *Francesca Landau-Foyle, Seattle*, he came up with an article:

In & Around **Seattle:** Where To Shop
Mixed Bags Boutique . . . The owner of this fun find in downtown Kirkland is **Francesca Landau,** who has created a successful fusion of cosmopolitan and quaint . . .
www.theseattletimes/features/wheretoshop/041605 - 13k

The article, from three years ago, was a dull story about this gift shop Francesca owned, but it listed the address and phone number of the store, and even directions.

Earl's friend, Burt Demick, was now about fifty years old.

Eli had found plenty of articles about him if it was the same Burt Demick. He was a big-shot attorney at a Seattle law firm, Rayburn, Demick, and Gill. Eli had called the law firm yesterday, but some snippy assistant had told him, "Mr. Demick is unavailable right now. May I leave a message?"

"Um, it's kind of personal, but very important," Eli had told her. "When would be the best time to reach him?"

"I'm sorry. Mr. Demick may be tied up indefinitely."

Eli had thanked her and hung up. To his further frustration, he hadn't been able to find a home listing in the phone book for Burt Demick.

Eli had really hoped to talk to Burt, but for now, it didn't look very likely. That left Earl's stepsister.

Eli wasn't certain how much Francesca knew or what she could tell him. He wasn't even sure what he would ask her. But he needed to meet this woman. He needed to find out more about Earl Sayers.

Eli still hadn't made any friends in Seattle. He didn't know anyone close to his own age—except one kid. Eli had never really seen him, but he'd felt the kid's presence in his bedroom for so many otherwise lonely nights this summer. It had taken a while for Eli to accept the fact that he was sharing his bedroom with someone else—someone dead.

He wondered if his mother had noticed he'd stopped loudly banishing their ghost at bedtime not long ago. Somewhere along the line, he'd stopped being scared. And two days ago, he finally learned the identity of his *only* friend, his night visitor: Earl Sayers.

He had to know more.

"What happened?"

Startled, Eli looked up at his uncle, who stood in the TV room entryway.

"Get bored with the video game?" Uncle Kyle asked. "Not enough carnage and mutilation?"

"No, it's okay," Eli grabbed the remote from the sofa and

switched off the game and the TV. "I was just thinking, I need to get my dad a birthday present sometime soon. And I heard there's this really cool store in Kirkland . . ."

"Hello, Mr. Bischoff?"

"Yes. Who is this?"

"I'm Sydney Jordan," she said into her cell phone. On the wall behind her was a huge diagram of an old Boeing 707. Sydney sat at the end of a row of seats in the VIP lounge—as far away as possible from the noisy, crowded bar and a woman with a shrieking toddler. There were a lot of delays this morning, and Sydney's flight was one of them.

"I worked with Troy on a short video for television last October," she went on. "I just wanted to say that I'm terribly sorry for your loss."

On the other end of the line, Troy's father said nothing.

"Um, I sent some flowers," Sydney said. It was a lie, but she needed to find out if they'd gotten any. "I'm wondering if they've arrived yet."

"Yeah, my wife took your flowers down to the church," he said coldly. "I didn't want them in the house. I don't want anything around reminding me of him."

Sydney winced. Troy's roommate had warned her about his parents.

And Troy's killer was repeating his pattern.

"Well, I'm sorry you feel that way, Mr. Bischoff," she said patiently. "If I could please speak to your wife, I just have a question about the florist—"

"No," he cut in. "I don't want you or any of his other friends calling here. Understand?"

He didn't wait for her to respond. Sydney heard a click on the other end of the line.

Sydney stared at her cell and clicked it off. This was the

second homophobic creep she'd dealt with this morning. And meanwhile no one was looking any further into the circumstances of Troy Bischoff's death.

The woman with the loud toddler had decided to move to the same row of seats. She was a pale redhead in a blue summer dress. Sydney wanted to gag the little brat, but she felt sorry for the mother and gave her a sympathetic smile.

The woman nodded tiredly at her. "We're making a lot of friends here in the VIP lounge," she said, over the child's ear-piercing screams.

The kid, a red-haired little boy in shorts and an Izod sport shirt, made a fist and swung at his mom, hitting her in the leg.

"Ouch!" the mother yelped, recoiling. "That hurt!" She grabbed him by the arms and looked him in the eye. "Why did you do that? Why did you hit Mommy?"

Blind rage, Sydney thought.

She remembered her conversation with her brother this morning. Biting her lip, she reached down for her carrying case and pulled out her laptop computer. She hooked it up to the Internet connection on the wall behind her, then went online and pulled up Google. Sydney typed in the keywords: *Madison High School girls murder Seattle*. A bunch of articles came up. She clicked on the most recent one, looking for an update on the case her brother had mentioned. It was from the *Seattle Post-Intelligencer*, dated December 10, 2007:

TWO YEARS LATER

A Mystery Still Unsolved

On December 10, 2005, Molly Gerrard and Erin Travino, Heroes at Their Seattle High School, Were Brutally Murdered; Police Have Yet to Find Their Killer.

Below the headline were photos of Molly and Erin: One was a classically pretty girl with long black hair and glasses, and the other, curly-haired and cute. *"Only a week before they were slain,"* said the caption. *"James Madison High School Juniors, Molly Gerrard (l) and Erin Travino (r) had made headlines when they'd thwarted a fellow student's shooting rampage."*

Sydney anxiously read the article, which featured comments from the victims' parents, expressing their dismay over the lack of progress in the double-murder investigation.

Seattle police were still following several leads, but had yet to arrest any suspects in the case. Warren Tunny, the young man who had smuggled a gun into Molly and Erin's fifth period study hall, was still under psychiatric observation and unavailable for comment.

Sydney wondered: Were Molly and Erin the first *duet*?

The article was over seven months old.

Sydney switched on her cell phone again and dialed directory assistance for Seattle. Fortunately, the screaming child nearby had calmed down, so Sydney didn't have to shout when asking directory assistance for the phone number of Phillip and Hannah Gerrard. But there was no listing. George and Louise Travino's phone number wasn't listed either. And they didn't have a listing for Warren Tunny. Three strikes.

Sydney wasn't really surprised. After two and a half years, they'd probably been hounded and harassed with all sorts of calls about their slain daughters. Sydney wasn't anxious to add to their heartache. But she couldn't let it go either.

She telephoned a friend in the network news office. "Judy Cavalliri," the woman answered.

"Hi, Judy, it's Sydney Jordan," she said, craning her neck to see the monitors. "I'm still in Seattle waiting for my flight, which is delayed. The estimated departure is now

11:15, but I wouldn't bet on it. Anyway, could you notify the film crew for me?"

"Sure, Sydney. You're scheduled to meet with Chloe Finch at six-thirty. Want me to keep that?"

"Yes, thank you," she said. "Judy, do you know someone there in the news office who could dig up a few unlisted phone numbers for me?"

"Yeah, I might."

"Well, I have three names for you, all Seattle residents," Sydney said. "Got a pencil?"

Mixed Bags was in a minimall between a little art gallery and Seattle's Best Coffee. The sun was shining, and it made the waterfront shopping area of Kirkland even more pretty and pristine. From this side, Lake Washington seemed to sparkle. But the congested traffic along the boulevard was a major drawback. "Did everyone and their Aunt Agnes decide to come shopping here today?" Uncle Kyle had groused as they sat idle at one point, bumper to bumper.

Now they stood outside Mixed Bags staring at a window full of purses.

Uncle Kyle adjusted the sunglasses on his nose. "You're buying your dad a purse?" he asked.

"I think they have other stuff," Eli said. "In fact, I may want to get you something, too, Uncle Kyle. So—I'd rather go in there by myself. Could I meet you at one of these other stores in like—ten minutes?"

Kyle shook his head. "I'm not supposed to let you out of my sight, kiddo. Mom's orders. After what you pulled yesterday, I ought to keep you on a leash."

"Oh, c'mon, Uncle Kyle. Please? I want this present to be a surprise for you. C'mon, please?"

"Five minutes," he said, frowning. He pointed to the art gallery next door. "I'll be in there. And if you wander off or disappear again, you might as well go into the witness protection program, because I'll hunt you down and kill you."

Eli nodded eagerly. "Thanks, Uncle Kyle. See you in five minutes." He headed toward the store.

"And don't buy me a stinking purse!" his uncle called.

Eli ducked into the store, which smelled like leather and soap. He'd been right about the place. They had other things besides purses, but mostly for women: travel kits, scarves, soaps and lotions, ornate picture frames, and a few fancy-looking suitcases. Eli focused on the woman behind the counter. She was thin, with frizzy brown hair, and looked around thirty. Francesca Landau was fifty-two, if he'd done his math right. There was a woman with her young daughter checking out purses, and over by the suitcases was a slightly plump woman with brown hair that had a blond streak through it. She wore a black suit with a bright blue scarf tossed over one shoulder. Eli guessed she was about fifty. She was showing this older lady a suitcase with a flower pattern on it.

"Can I help you?"

Eli swiveled around and gaped at the frizzy-haired woman. "Um, hi, yes. I'm looking for Francesca."

She nodded at the woman with the blue scarf. "She's with another customer right now. Can I help you find something?"

"No, thank you. I'll wait for Francesca."

The woman nodded, then went to straighten some candles on a shelf.

Eli turned and looked at Francesca Landau again. She'd been only three years older than Earl when he'd been murdered. It was hard to imagine that woman across the store had been a teenager once. Now that he was here, he had no idca what he was going to ask her. He knew what he wanted to ask: *Did your father kill Loretta and Earl?*

He watched Francesca step behind the counter, scribble

something on a card, and then hand it to the older woman. Eli stepped aside, then held the door open for the lady as she left the store. The old bat didn't bother to say thank you.

He glanced toward Francesca again, and found her standing by the counter, staring back at him.

He stepped toward her. "Are you Francesca Landau?"

She smiled politely and nodded. "Yes. Do we know each other?"

"Um, my Mom said she used to live down the block from you and your family back in the seventies—when she lived in Magnolia." Eli remembered Vera saying that Loretta and her husband had lived in Magnolia before the separation.

Francesca's face lit up. She had a kind smile. "Oh, your mom lived on McGraw?"

Eli nodded.

"What was her name?"

He blanked out for a second. He glanced over at the handbags. "Anne—Anne Burberry."

The smile seemed to freeze on her face and she shook her head. "I'm sorry, I don't remember anyone named Burberry on the block. Was that her maiden name?"

Eli nodded. "Yes, Anne Burberry. She remembers you. She said you had two older brothers and a younger stepbrother. She said all of you were really nice, but your stepbrother and his mom didn't live with you for very long. And they died later or something. Was his name Earl?"

"Yes, that was his name."

"And he died not long after he and his mother moved away?"

She frowned. "Yes, they both died."

"How—did it happen?"

"Who are you?" Francesca whispered. "Did someone send you here?"

Eli shook his head. "No, nobody sent me."

"Well, what do you want?" she asked. "Why are you asking me about these things?"

Eli didn't know what to say. "I'm sorry," he said, backing away from her a bit. "I just—I only wanted to find out about Earl Sayers and his mother. Me and my mom, we recently moved into the town house where they both died—"

Francesca was shaking her head at him. "I don't have to listen to this," she said under her breath. "I had to put up with enough questions and accusations about those two back when I was in high school. It ruined my father, who never hurt a soul. And my brother, he couldn't handle it—all the gossip and suspicion. He hanged himself in his dormitory at school. Did you know that? The police said Loretta murdered Earl in his sleep and then killed herself. Why can't people just leave it at that? Who put you up to this?"

"Nobody, I swear."

She grabbed his arm and led him toward the door. "I don't know who sent you here, but you're leaving—now!" She opened the door and pushed him outside.

Eli almost collided with his uncle, who was heading into the store.

"If you come back here again," Francesca growled. "I'll call the police and have you arrested for trespassing."

"I'm sorry!" Eli called to her. "I didn't mean to—"

But she'd already ducked back into the shop.

"What the hell was that about?" his Uncle Kyle asked.

Eli walked away from the shop's window. He felt awful for making Francesca so angry, and he didn't want her calling the cops because he was hanging around. Up ahead, the door to another clothing store was propped open. Through the glass, Eli spotted a man with a dark complexion, sunglasses, and a green sports shirt. He halted in his tracks.

His uncle hesitated in back of him. "Eli, what's going on?"

Frozen, Eli watched the dark-skinned man step out from behind the glass door. He was talking on a cell phone. It wasn't the man with the weird eye.

Eli let out a sigh, but then glanced around the mini-mall area to make sure the guy wasn't anywhere around. If he was, Eli didn't see him.

"Eli . . ." his uncle said. "For the third and final time, what in God's name is going on?"

Sheepishly he looked back at his uncle, then reached into the pocket of his cargo shorts. "That was Earl's stepsister."

Uncle Kyle squinted at him. "Your friend, Earl, has a stepsister who's that old?"

Biting his lip, Eli pulled out the article he'd copied at the library the day before and showed it to his uncle. "Earl's been dead since 1974. Someone slit his throat—in my bedroom."

Her cell phone rang just as they announced that her flight to Chicago was ready for boarding.

Sydney's friend, Judy, at the news office was calling. She'd only been able to come up with one of the three unlisted Seattle-area numbers: Phillip and Hannah Gerrard. Sydney copied it down, thanked Judy, and told her that she was about to board the plane.

Gathering up her purse and carry-on, Sydney watched several people head for the VIP lounge exit. She stepped back against the wall with the Boeing 707 diagram on it. She switched her cell on again and dialed the Gerrards' number.

A machine answered after two rings. *"Hello, you've reached the Gerrards,"* the woman said in a pleasant voice. *"Please leave us a message. Have a nice day!"*

Beep.

"Hi," Sydney said. "I hope I have the right Hannah and

Phillip Gerrard. My name is Sydney Jordan, and I work for the TV newsmagazine *On the Edge.* I'm interested in doing a story about your daughter, Molly . . ."

That much was true. In that seven-month-old newspaper article, both the Gerrards and the Travinos were still hoping to bring their daughters' killer to justice. It had occurred to Sydney that a segment on the unsolved murders of Molly and Erin was the kind of edgy story the network wanted from her now. Moreover, the national attention might help give police investigators more incentive to solve the case. Finally—and selfishly—it was a story she could cover without having to leave town. So even if this had nothing to do with the *Movers & Shakers* killings, it was still a call worth making.

"I'd only do the story with your permission, of course," she continued. "And your participation, I hope. Let me leave you my phone number and—"

There was a click on the other end of the line. "Hello?" the woman said. "Is this really Sydney Jordan?"

"Yes," she said. "Do I have the right Mrs. Gerrard?"

"Yes, I'm Hannah, Molly's mother," she replied.

"I don't know if you heard any of what I was saying just now—"

"Yes, I did. Listen, my husband and I would be grateful for anything that would light a fire under those police investigators. I'm sure the Travinos feel the same way. Plus I've seen your work, Sydney, and I've always thought you'd handle Molly's and Erin's story in a very dignified, compassionate way."

"Well, thank you very much," Sydney murmured. She was surprised at how quickly Molly's mother seemed to embrace the idea.

"Frankly, I wasn't sure I'd ever hear from you again," Hannah Gerrard continued. "I was going to write to you,

Sydney, but I didn't have your address. It was a bit of a surprise, but I must say, my husband and I were very touched when you sent that beautiful flower arrangement after Molly's death. Thank you, Sydney."

For a moment, she couldn't speak.

"Sydney?"

"You—you're welcome," she murmured, numbly.

She'd found his first duet.

CHAPTER NINETEEN

"I can't believe I let you talk me into this," his Uncle Kyle whispered. "I'm supposed to be keeping you *out* of trouble."

They rode up to the twenty-seventh floor in a shiny-brass-paneled elevator with a trio of men in ties and business suits. Eli's uncle had said earlier that in their casual shirts and shorts, they'd look like a couple of bums wandering into the law offices of Rayburn, Demick, and Gill. But Eli had been in a hurry. And, of course, his uncle had been right.

His uncle had said a lot of things earlier—in the car, as they'd driven back from Kirkland, across the 520 floating bridge. "I can't understand why you didn't share any of this murder-suicide stuff with your mother or me. Sneaking off and lying to the two of us about where you were half the time, it doesn't make sense."

His uncle had been right about that too. Eli had done his best to explain how it had started out with the Ouija board, and then eavesdropping on his mom and their neighbor. After that, it had just snowballed. Besides, his mom had known about the murder-suicide, and had kept it a secret from *him*.

"Oh, God, you two are so much alike, it's scary," his uncle had muttered. "She just didn't want to worry you."

"Well, I didn't want to worry her," Eli replied.

"I just don't get it," his uncle had said. "I don't understand what you hope to accomplish by digging into this old business from thirty-four years ago and bothering these people connected to the case. What did you think the lady back there was going to tell you?"

Eli had to admit he'd screwed that one up. He still felt bad he'd gotten Francesca Landau so upset. At the same time, he'd learned her brother, Jonathan, had hung himself a year after the deaths of Loretta and Earl. Francesca's father hadn't been the only suspect in the case; clouds of suspicion had hovered over her college-age brother as well.

Eli felt he could learn more from Earl's friend, Burt Demick. In the article Eli had copied, Burt had said: *"I don't think Mrs. Sayers could have done what people said she did."* If he didn't believe the official findings back then, Mr. Demick must have developed his own ideas about who had killed Earl and Loretta. Eli wanted to hear them.

"So—have you thought about what you're going to ask him?" Kyle said—once the trio of businessmen stepped off on the twenty-first floor.

Glancing up at the lighted numbers above the elevator doors, Eli shrugged. He felt a little nervous. He didn't want this unscheduled visit with Mr. Demick to end in a big blowup like the one with Francesca. "I guess I'm gonna ask him what he thinks really happened that night," Eli replied.

The elevator doors opened and a *ding* sounded. They stepped off on the twenty-seventh floor. To their right was a pair of glass doors; one of them had the suite number stenciled on it: 2701. It was a fancy reception area, with mauve carpeting and pale sofas and cushioned chairs. Some square pedestals held different vases and sculptures under protective display cases, and Jackson Pollock-like art hung on the walls. Behind the big mahogany desk sat a beautiful brunette, impeccably dressed in a red suit. And behind her, on the wall, pewter letters spelled out: RAYBURN, DEMICK, & GILL.

The receptionist looked up at them coolly. "May I help you?"

Eli noticed a silver dish full of Andes mints. "Are these free?" he asked.

The woman nodded.

"Just one," Uncle Kyle muttered. He scratched his temple with one finger and smiled at the receptionist. "Hi. I'm an attorney with Trotter, Gregg, and Associates, and I met Mr. Demick a few weeks back at this luncheon at one of the downtown hotels here. I keep thinking it was at the Westin . . ."

She tilted her head and stared at him. "Mr. Demick was a guest speaker for the Washington State Lawyers Club at a luncheon in June at the Hilton. Could that be where you saw him?"

Uncle Kyle snapped his fingers. "That's it, thank you. We talked for a bit after his speech, and Burt—I mean, Mr. Demick—he said to stop by the offices and pay him a visit if I was ever in the neighborhood. Anyway, here I am—with my nephew, and without an appointment. Is there any chance we can stick our heads in and say hello?"

She nodded at the sea foam green sofa. "If you'll have a seat, I'll see if Mr. Demick is available." She reached for the phone.

Popping the Andes mint in his mouth, Eli retreated toward the sofa with his uncle. "Who are Trotter, Gregg, and Associates?" he whispered.

"Greg Trotter was this guy I had a crush on in high school," his uncle replied under his breath.

Just as they sat down on the sofa, Eli saw two men emerge from the hallway at their left. They passed through the reception area. "I'm going to get even with you out on that golf course next week, Burt," said the stocky, balding one in the gray suit. "You can bank on that."

Dressed in a dark blue suit, a tall, thin, handsome man with wavy gray hair winked at his golf buddy and shook his hand. "Well, we'll just see about that, Bob," he laughed. Then he opened the glass door for him.

Uncle Kyle nudged Eli and they both got to their feet. "Mr. Demick—Burt?" his uncle said, approaching him with his hand extended. "Hi, I'm Kyle Jordan. We met at the Lawyers Club lunch last month at the Hilton."

With a slightly baffled smile, Burt Demick shook his hand. His eyes darted back and forth from Kyle to Eli. "Well, good to see you again."

Kyle nodded at Eli. "This fine-looking lad here is my nephew, Eli. He's doing a report for summer school that might interest you."

Mr. Demick shook his hand. He had a firm grip. "It's nice to meet you, Eli."

Eli just nodded nervously.

"I'm a little pressed for time right now," Demick said, glancing at his wristwatch. "I was about to head out. But if you'll make an appointment with the receptionist—"

"Oh, we were just taking a shot and hoping you'd be in," Kyle said. "I know you're busy. How about if we rode down in the elevator with you?"

"Sure, that's fine," Demick replied, seeming a bit distracted. "Excuse me." He went over to the receptionist and said something to her.

For a moment, Eli thought a pair of security guards would suddenly show up to toss them out. But instead, Demick turned, smiled at them, and waved for them to join him as he strode toward the glass doors. He held one open for them.

"Thank you," Eli said, and the man patted him on the shoulder.

"So—what's your report about?" he asked, walking to the elevators with them.

"Um, it—it's for a history class," Eli lied. "We had to pick something out of an old newspaper and report about it. I found an article from the seventies, and they—they mentioned you."

"When Eli showed me the article," Kyle added. "I told him, 'I know this gentleman.'"

"Well, you've got me intrigued," Demick said, pushing the button for the elevator. "An article from the seventies, you say?"

"Yes," Eli nodded. "It's about these people you knew back when you were sixteen—Loretta and Earl Sayers."

Demick just stared at him for a moment. Then he rubbed his chin.

"Um, in the article," Eli continued, trying not to stammer. "You said Mrs. Sayers couldn't have killed Earl and herself. I—I was wondering what you think actually happened that night. I figure it would be good to get your respective."

"Perspective," his uncle corrected him.

Demick let out a long sigh. "Well, that was over thirty years ago—quite a tragedy, very sad. I really didn't know them that well . . ."

Eli remembered Vera talking about Burt's car blocking hers in the driveway. She'd made it sound as if it had happened several times.

The elevator chimed, and then the doors whooshed open.

"I talked to one of their old neighbors," Eli said, stepping into the empty elevator with his uncle. "According to her, a lot of people thought Earl's stepfather might have killed them."

Demick followed them into the elevator, then he pressed the lobby button. "I'll tell you, Eli, I used to think the same thing. Then people started saying Earl's stepbrother might have been the guilty party. And that poor young man took his own life." He patted Eli's shoulder. "It took me a while to accept the official explanation. But I agree with it now. Ms. Sayers killed her son and then shot herself. She was a very emotional, high-strung woman. Like I said, it was a real tragedy."

Eli frowned. He'd thought there would have been a lot more to it than that, and yet all three people he'd spoken with—Vera, Francesca, and now Earl's pal, Burt—accepted the murder-suicide explanation.

"What was Earl like?" he asked.

Demick smiled sadly. "Oh, he had a great laugh, and he was kind of a goofball. But he was smart and polite, too." Demick nudged him. "You remind me a little of him, Eli."

After a moment, Uncle Kyle nudged him on the other side. "So—do you think you have enough for your report?" he asked, a bit of irony in his tone. "Does that finish it up?"

Eli just nodded.

The elevator chimed, and then the doors whooshed open again. "Thanks so much," his uncle said, shaking Demick's hand as they stepped out to the lobby. "We're grateful for your time—and your candor."

"Yes, thank you, sir," Eli piped up.

Demick shook his hand and winked at him. "I hope you get an A."

"Let's do lunch some time," Uncle Kyle said.

Demick pulled a business card from the pocket of his suit coat, then handed it to him. "Give my assistant a call," he said. "Bye, now."

Then the thin, distinguished man strode through the lobby and out the revolving door.

"We need to get you and your mom out of that apartment lease," his uncle said. "It's a wonder you've slept a wink in there the last few nights." He handed Eli the business card. "Here, a souvenir."

With a sigh, Eli glanced at the card.

"I can't believe he didn't throw us out on our asses,"

Uncle Kyle said. "So—does that seal the deal? Does that answer all your questions about what happened way back when?"

Sam frowned. "I guess so."

His uncle put a hand on his shoulder as they moved toward the revolving door. "And you're satisfied?"

"No, I'm not," Eli admitted, gazing down at the floor. "Not really."

She had an exclusive scoop on the so-called "Story of the Year," and yet Sydney couldn't stay focused on it. In front of her, she had all the information they'd faxed her this morning about Chloe Finch and what had happened on that Evanston beach about thirteen hours ago.

But Sydney couldn't stop thinking about this twisted killer's *first duet*.

The deaths of those two teenage girls had been a Seattle murder case; so now she could go to the Seattle police about the hero-killings. But even with Mr. and Mrs. Gerrard to back her up about the flowers, it would take a lot of explaining—and more information about the other deaths—in New York, Portland, and Chicago. She kept thinking about a Chicago cop who might be able to help her if only she had it in her to call Joe and admit she needed him.

On the plane, Sydney forced herself to read more about Chloe Finch, who was thirty-one, single, and lived alone. According to the reports, she'd been walking along the beach for about an hour when she caught Derrick De Santo trying to murder his pregnant girlfriend.

Police had recovered Chloe's raincoat and shoes at the scene, and they'd found a few stones in the pockets of the raincoat. Chloe had said she was collecting them for the garden at her apartment building.

Sydney wondered if the police really believed her.

* * *

The production assistant sat with Chloe Finch on a park bench along the beach off Lake Shore Drive. It was approaching "magic hour"—about 6:45—with the sun just starting its slow descent. It was the best light for taping. The shimmering lake and the golden-hued Chicago skyline made for a perfect background.

As Sydney and her crew made their way toward the bench, she saw Chloe get to her feet and limp toward them. Sydney had seen her photo, and found Chloe prettier in person. She hadn't known about Chloe's foot problem until now.

She gave Sydney a wry smile, and then shook her hand. "No, I don't have a pebble in my shoe," she said. "It's one reason I'm a fan of yours. I don't walk so well either. Plus I'm a huge figure-skating fan. I read your autobiography twice, and have seen *Making Miracles: The Sydney Jordan Story* at least five times—even though Amanda Beck is horrible in it. The girl couldn't act her way out of a wet paper bag."

Sydney laughed. "So—is that how come I got this exclusive?"

"Oh, totally, your reporting doesn't have a damn thing to do with it."

Sydney chuckled again. Usually she spent a lot of time trying to put her subjects at ease, and here was the subject helping her to relax. She quickly introduced Chloe to her crew—two cameramen and a soundman. Chloe had already met the production assistant. While the shot was being set up, Sydney and Chloe sat down on the park bench where she would interview her. Chloe quietly explained that she admired Sydney's *Movers & Shakers* pieces. "I knew you'd treat me with respect," she said.

Sydney nodded. "I will, but you'll need to be honest with

me, Chloe. I read the reports. Those stones in the pockets of your raincoat reminded me of how Virginia Woolf went about drowning herself."

"Clever lady," Chloe murmured, with an ironic smile. "I got the idea from *The Hours*."

Sydney put her hand on Chloe's arm. "You went down to that secluded beach at two o'clock in the morning to kill yourself, but you ended up saving someone's life. That's the story I want to do here, Chloe."

Chloe glanced out at the lake and sighed. "I don't know how it'll go over with the university if they find out one of their executive employees was contemplating suicide last night."

Sydney shrugged. "Maybe they'll pay for some therapy sessions. I wouldn't mind that. Do you want to talk about it?"

Chloe balked. "Now—or later in front of the camera?"

"Well, you'll probably hold back a bit while we're taping," Sydney whispered. "And it'll take another ten minutes to set up. So you might as well give me the uncensored version now."

"So—why did I want to off myself?" Chloe said, pushing back her auburn hair and looking out at the water again. "It's a bunch of things, really. I've had this cat, Hutch, ever since college and he went and died on me three weeks ago. Cat cancer. Suddenly I realized how lonely I was. I've never had a boyfriend. My friends call me the *one-date-wonder*. I don't know if it's my foot problem or the fact that I don't have the kind of looks most guys go for. I just haven't been lucky in the love department. I didn't realize it, but I was becoming this awful, bitter person. But then, two weeks ago, I met a guy." She laughed a little. "It was kind of embarrassing, actually. I'd just tripped over my cane on the stairs of the Administration Building, and he came to my rescue. His name was Riley, and he said he was a graduate student. I really liked his looks—cute and stocky, like a football player, and his eyes were to die for. That night, we went out for dinner and ended up necking like crazy outside the front door of my apartment building. He wanted to come up, but I wouldn't let him."

She gave Sydney a melancholy smile and shrugged. "I held out for twenty-four whole hours. It was pretty wonderful making love with him. I was crazy for the guy. I know it sounds corny, but Riley made me feel beautiful. God, I'm such a sap . . ."

Tears filled her eyes as she gazed out at the lake again. "Our third date was supposed to be dinner at the Ambassador East, but first he wanted me to meet some friends of his at this slightly seedy bar downtown. Riley led me in there, and he seemed so proud of me when he introduced me to his friends. There were six of them, and they had dates, too. I kept thinking, 'Riley has to be older than these guys. They all seem so young.' And then I got a look at their dates. I'm sorry, but it was like a freak show—all these sad, clueless characters. All of them were so much older—or heavier—or uglier than the young men who had brought them to the bar. That's when I realized Riley had taken me to a *'dogfight.'*" She wiped a tear away and glanced at Sydney. "Do you know what that is?"

Sydney put her hand over Chloe's. "I think I know what you're talking about," she murmured. "Oh, Jesus, Chloe, I'm sorry."

She'd heard stories about frat brothers or army buddies who made bets on who could scrape up the ugliest date. They called them *dogfights*. And the women they'd chosen to bring to these competitions weren't supposed to have feelings.

"I overheard Riley tell his friends that he qualified for

twenty bonus points, because he'd fucked me," Chloe muttered. She rubbed her eyes, and then let out a sad, little laugh. "Whew! When I heard that, I just started crying and got out of there as quickly as I could. I don't know whether or not Riley won the dogfight. But you want to hear the totally crazy part? I kept waiting for the son of a bitch to call me and apologize. I'm such an idiot—I thought he might have really felt something for me—despite everything. How stupid can you get? I waited five nights for that *kid* to call me. Then last night, I went to the beach. I'd decided that was where I'd kill myself. And I was suddenly content, at peace. I haven't been that happy in a long, long time. I finally figured out a way to stop feeling so miserable. Anyway, I thought I'd found the perfect spot until Derrick and his girlfriend showed up."

Sydney handed her a Kleenex.

Chloe wiped her eyes and blew her nose. "So—is that what you want me to say for the folks watching at home?" she asked.

Sydney nodded. "We'll probably edit some of it," she said delicately. "I'll ask you about what you witnessed down on the beach, and rescuing Lenora, of course. I might also ask about your foot problem. Would that be okay?"

"Hey, I just told you about the most humiliating experience of my life," Chloe said. "I think I can talk about my foot problem. By the way, you'll love this, too. When I first spotted Derrick and Lenora on the beach, they looked so pretty together and so much in love. I thought, *'I wish I could be her.'* Hah, I can sure pick them, can't I? Three minutes later, he was bashing her brains in."

Sydney asked the production assistant to fetch a mirror. She said nothing, and just gently patted Chloe on the back until the assistant returned with a hand mirror from the SUV.

"Go ahead, and fix your face so you look pretty," Sydney told Chloe, setting the mirror on her lap.

"Huh, we don't have that much time," Chloe said, opening her purse.

"Oh, shut up," Sydney smiled.

Chloe pulled some lipstick from her purse. "I just knew you'd be nice," she murmured.

"Do you think it would be too trite if I worked in a clip from *It's a Wonderful Life*?" Sydney asked. "I'm thinking of that scene when James Stewart is about to commit suicide by jumping off the bridge, but he ends up saving Clarence instead."

It was 8:20, and they'd just finished taping with Chloe. Sydney had hugged her good-bye, and they'd talked about getting together the next day so Chloe could see the edited piece before it was aired as a feature story on the network's nightly news.

Sydney sat in the backseat of the SUV with her soundman, Matt, who had on his earphones and listened to what they'd just recorded. Up front were her cameramen, Brendan and Jamie. Brendan was driving. She'd worked with these guys on most of her Chicago-based *Movers & Shakers* stories for several years. It felt good to be on an assignment with them again. She always used to bounce ideas off them.

"Yeah, I like that *Wonderful Life* angle, but keep it brief," Brendan warned. "You've got a lot of stuff here."

"You don't think it might trivialize what Chloe was going through?" Sydney asked. She really liked Chloe Finch, and wanted her to be happy with this segment—almost as much as she wanted the network to be happy with it.

"The viewers will eat it up," Jamie said from the passenger seat in front. "Hey, you know, the Cook County Recovery Shelter is just a few blocks from here. Want to pay a visit to Ned? He'll be pissed if he finds out you were in town and didn't see him, Syd."

She'd done the *Movers & Shakers* segment on Ned Haggerty over two years ago, and he'd kept in touch with her ever since. Homeless and alcoholic, he'd been living in and out of traveling boxcars for a few years, when he saved the life of a Burlington Northern yardman, who had tripped and fallen on the rails. The unconscious man would have been run over by a train if not for Ned. The *Movers & Shakers* piece had made Ned a local celebrity. He went into rehab, then ended up living and working at the Cook County Recovery Shelter, a dormitory for homeless men just out of rehab.

"I really don't think I have time to drop in on old Ned," Sydney said. She still had to check into her hotel and figure out how to edit Chloe's piece down to four and a half minutes. "I'll drop him a postcard when I get back to Seattle."

Matt took off his earphones. "Were you guys just talking about Ned Haggerty? It's a real shame what happened, isn't it?"

Sydney stared at him. "What do you mean?"

"Yeah, what are you talking about?" Jamie chimed in.

"You guys didn't know?" Matt asked. He turned to her. "Jesus, I'm sorry. Somebody should have told you, Syd. Ned was killed last week. He went on a bender and passed out in a railroad yard—right on the tracks. A train ran over him."

Overhead, a swirling fan stirred up the stuffy air in the tiled lobby of the Cook County Recovery Shelter. Matt and Brendan had stayed outside in the SUV, but Jamie sat waiting for her on one of the lobby's two avocado-green Naugahyde-covered sofas. There was a big bulletin board on the wall; it was full of job listings and fliers. Seated behind the Formica-top counter was Gary, a balding man in his midforties with a gray mustache and a short-sleeve checked shirt. Sydney had met him once before when Ned had proudly given her a tour of the facility.

"As you can see," Gary said. "We got your flowers. Somebody saved one."

At the far end of the counter, someone had set up a little tribute to Ned Haggerty. It was a framed photo of Ned, who had gray hair and a wizened face. In the picture, he was grinning as if someone had just told a joke. Sydney's heart broke as she gazed at it. A pressed dried flower had been placed at one side of the photograph under the glass. Tucked in the frame was a card saying *With Sympathy* in silver preprinted script, and then a note typed by a computer printer: *We'll all miss you, Ned—Sydney Jordan*.

Matt had said that Ned had been killed last Monday night. About twenty-four hours later, in another part of town, Angela Gannon had fallen to her death. At first, Sydney had wondered why she hadn't received a cryptic little souvenir of Ned's demise, but then she remembered the Monopoly train token that had been left on Eli's desk. Eli had found it just minutes before she'd discovered the dead robin on her pillow.

"Do they know any more about how it happened?" she asked Gary.

Leaning on the counter, he shook his head. "Nope. Ned was last seen in this crummy bar near the railroad yard. He was getting drunk with this younger guy who looked homeless. They left the bar together around one in the morning. At four-thirty, one of the Burlington Northern switchmen heard a scream, and found Ned on the tracks. A freight train had run over him, cut him in half."

Sydney winced. "Did they ever find the younger, homeless man?" she asked.

"Nope," Gary said, frowning. "And I tell ya, I'd like to

hunt down the son of a bitch myself. Ned hadn't touched a drop in over two years—until this fella came along."

Sydney glanced at the photo of Ned. She fingered the sympathy card stuck between the glass and the edge of the frame. She pulled it out and saw the imprint on the bottom of the card:

Uptown Flowers—12291 Uptown—Chicago
773-555-9254

Chapter Twenty

"Hi, you've reached the McClouds . . ." Sydney listened to her own greeting, which Joe obviously hadn't changed yet. She couldn't help taking that as a good sign. Despite the woman answering their phone at six yesterday morning, perhaps he wasn't really ready to move on. Sydney kept asking herself, *Why should you care?* But she did.

She waited for the recording to finish up, and then the beep sounded. "Hi, Joe, it's me," she said nervously. "I'm in town here at the Red Lion Airporter Inn. I'm just in for the night. I know you don't want to see me. But there's something going on here that's pretty scary. I need your help, Joe. Could you call me back here?" She gave him the hotel's phone number and reminded him of her cell number in case he'd forgotten. "It doesn't matter how late you call back. Please, just give me a shout, okay? I—" Sydney hesitated. She was about to say *I love you*. It came so naturally to her. It was how she'd always said good-bye to him on the phone when calling from a lonely hotel room on the road.

"I'd really appreciate it, Joe," she said instead, and then she hung up.

Usually the network sprung for nicer hotels, but this was all they could get at the last minute. It was a rambling, three-story structure with several wings. Sydney had a second-floor room with outside access so people were walking back and forth outside her window every few minutes. Forsaking her view of the parking lot and a Shell station, Sydney had closed the sheer drapes for a little privacy, but she still saw images and shadows passing outside that window from time to time. The room was decorated in jade, taupe, and salmon. Thank God it had an honor bar. She'd already drunk a single-serving bottle of chardonnay to the tune of nine dollars. She'd barely touched her room-service French dip, and the tray was still over by the TV.

Her first call hadn't been to Joe. Uptown Flowers had closed for the night, and she'd gotten a recorded message about their hours of business. She'd also checked her e-mail, and there was a note from Angela's sister:

Dear Sydney,

Sorry it s taken me a while to get back to you. The flowers you ordered came from Botanicals at the Glenn in Glenview. Their phone number is 847-555-5249. I hope that s some help!

Your flowers and the thoughtful notes were greatly appreciated, Sydney. We re just taking it one day at a time here. Thank you again.

Sincerely,
Elizabeth Gannon Grogen

She'd tried calling Botanicals at the Glen, but they were closed.

Sydney had also phoned her brother again and told him all the latest developments. She'd asked him to double-lock everything before going to bed tonight and to keep close tabs on Eli.

"We'll be okay," he'd replied. "You look after yourself. I

don't like the idea of you alone there in some hotel. Did the desk clerk look like Tony Perkins?"

"More like Toni Tennille," she'd told him. "It was a woman. I'll be fine. I'm staying in with the door triple-locked. Is Eli close by?"

"Yes, and he's got an interesting story for you. But I think we'll wait until tomorrow to tell it."

"What are you talking about?"

"Here's Eli."

Her son had gotten on the line. "Hi, Mom . . ."

"Hi, honey. What's this *interesting story*?"

"It's about our ghost, but Uncle Kyle says you don't need to hear it now. Are you seeing Dad?"

Sydney had told him it was highly doubtful. But that had been over an hour ago, and now that she'd phoned Joe, she realized how much she wanted to see him again.

It was hard to focus on Chloe's segment, though Sydney had already taken three pages of notes on editing and scoring it. There was another single-serving chardonnay bottle in the honor bar. She made a deal with herself that she could open it as long as she watered down the wine with some ice.

The digital clock on her night table read 10:09. Sydney was wearing a red striped T-shirt, jeans, and sandals. She grabbed the ice bucket and her room key, then unlocked all the locks and stepped outside. A blast of warm summer air hit her. From the railed walkway, she glanced down at the gas station and the parking lot—not much activity. She noticed some fireflies in the bushes bordering the lot. Sydney turned and made sure her door was locked before she moved on.

About ten doors up ahead was a lighted sign for the stairway. She figured the ice machine—or at least a sign for it—had to be in the general vicinity. She strode past several windows to the other rooms off the walkway; all of the curtains were closed—except one. Right before the door to the stairs, a man sat alone at a desk by his window. He was about thirty, thin, and extremely pale with short black hair. He wore a dirty white T-shirt. It looked like he was repairing a small radio or something. He had a screwdriver in his hand. As Sydney passed his window, he just glared at her. Trying not to stare back, she kept walking. But out of the corner of her eye, Sydney saw him quickly stand up.

Opening the stairwell door, she balked as the inside overhead light sputtered. She listened for footsteps or the sound of a door opening behind her, but she could only hear traffic noise. That odd-looking man must have stayed in his room.

To Sydney's right were the stairs. She noticed an ICE & VENDING MACHINES placard on the wall had an arrow indicating they were straight ahead. Ice bucket in hand, Sydney started down the corridor. Recessed lights illuminated an isolated portion of the empty, dark hallway. Perhaps this was supposed to create a serene effect, but Sydney just found it creepy.

She came to an intersecting corridor, where another placard showed the ice and vending machines were to her left. As Sydney turned the corner, she heard a click. It sounded like a door opening. She paused and looked over her shoulder, but the corridor was vacant. To her left, she passed a door marked STAFF ONLY that was open a crack. The room beyond it was shrouded in darkness.

At last, she spotted a small annex where they kept the ice machine and two vending machines for soft drinks and snacks. Sydney filled up the bucket. The clanking noise seemed loud in the quiet hallway.

As she headed back down the hall, she saw the STAFF ONLY door. It was wide open now. Sydney felt the hair bristle on the back of her neck. She crept past the room—giving it a wide berth. It was just a small closet with rolls of toilet paper and cleansers on the shelves. Clutching the ice bucket to her stomach, she continued down the corridor. As she turned the corner, Sydney glanced over her shoulder. She saw a dark figure dart across the hall into a shadowy doorway. He'd moved so fast, she couldn't see what he'd looked like, but it was a man about six feet tall.

Sydney turned and started running. Ice cubes spilled out of the bucket as she raced down the hall. At the door to the outside walkway, she hesitated and looked back again: no one. Catching her breath, she waited a moment to make sure she was alone. The light above her flickered again.

She stepped out to the walkway. Her hand was shaking as she reached for her keys. She passed that window again, where that strange man had been glaring at her, but his drapes were shut now. Sydney hurried to her door. She was still trying to get her breath as she staggered into the room. Then she quickly triple-locked the door.

"All for a lousy watered-down glass of chardonnay," she muttered, setting down the ice bucket and the room key.

The hotel room telephone rang, startling her.

Sydney immediately thought of Joe. She snatched up the receiver during the second ring. "Yes, hello?"

Silence.

"Hello?" she repeated.

Then there was a click, and the connection went dead.

He stood under the sputtering light by the walkway door, a cell phone in his hand. With his other hand, he ran an ice cube over his forehead. It had dropped out of Sydney's ice bucket as she'd scurried down the shadowy corridor minutes before. It was funny to watch her run with that slight limp of hers. He was still grinning as he thought of it.

Now she knew about him, but no more than he wanted her to know. He controlled the flow of information. She knew his pattern by now. So many of her *heroes* were dying, but she probably didn't understand why yet.

Molly and Erin had been the work of an amateur. But he'd

honed his killing skills since then. He'd become an expert at planning everything in advance and anticipating Sydney's next move.

At one time, Sydney might have felt close to the *Movers & Shakers* heroes he'd killed. She'd certainly gotten to know them while filming their segments for that TV show. But she might not have even known they'd died if he hadn't left her little clues. And if he wasn't sending flowers in her name to the deceased's next of kin, would she have sent them herself?

She might have felt bad about those people dying. But she hadn't felt really devastated yet.

That would soon change—when the next one died.

"Hi, this Sydney Jordan in room 2129," she said to the hotel operator. She was sitting on the edge of the bed—with its salmon-jade-taupe bedspread. "I've just had two hang-ups in a row. I was wondering if those calls came from outside or from the lobby."

"One minute, please, Ms. Jordan."

Sydney sipped her chardonnay on the rocks. Even if that man skulking around the hallway earlier hadn't been after her, she still didn't feel safe. And the second hang-up had just about put her over the edge.

"Ms. Jordan?" the operator came back on the line. "Those calls were coming from outside."

"Well, I'm—I'm thinking of changing rooms if I get another hang-up like that. It's kind of disturbing."

"If you'd like, I can forward all your incoming calls to voice mail, Ms. Jordan."

She thought of Joe. "Um, no, thank you. Don't do that yet. I'll let you know if I get another one. Thank you."

Just as she hung up with the hotel operator, her cell phone rang. Getting to her feet, Sydney snatched it up from the desk and checked the caller ID. She recognized Joe's cell number. She clicked it on. "Joe?" she said.

"Yeah, hi."

"Did you just try to call me on the hotel phone?"

"No. Why? What's going on?"

She stepped back, then sank down on the edge of the bed. "I think I'm going a little crazy here," she admitted, her voice cracking.

"What's your room number?" he asked. "I'm here in the lobby."

She heard him knocking on the door.

Sydney had quickly changed into a black sleeveless top, brushed her hair, and applied some lipstick and mascara. The whole time she wondered why she was making such an effort for someone who had seen her first thing in the morning for the last fourteen years. This was the same man who had gotten involved—however inadvertently—in a drug heist that resulted in the deaths of three people, including Arthur Pollard. He'd taken that blood money, and when she'd confronted him about it, he'd hit her. Then he'd ordered her and their son out of the house.

Now, here she was, trying to look pretty for him. How screwed up was that?

By the time she looked through the hotel door peephole at Joe, she was angry at him—and herself. Still, Joe looked handsome with his blond hair slicked back, that summer tan, and the white and blue pinstripe shirt she'd bought him years ago. It had always been her favorite on him, and Joe knew it. She realized Joe—in his own way—must have made an effort for her, too.

Sydney unlocked the door and opened it. For a moment, they just stared at each other across the threshold. "You look really good, honey," Joe whispered finally.

"You . . ." Sydney didn't finish. She threw her arms around him and buried her face in his shoulder. She hadn't held him in over two months. His arms enveloped her. She kissed his neck, relishing the smell of him again.

"God, I've missed you," she heard him whisper.

He kissed her deeply. Then he pulled her away for a moment to gaze at her. She could see tears in his eyes. He started to kiss her again.

That was when Sydney forced herself to break away. She shook her head. "This isn't why I wanted to see you, Joe," she managed to say. She glanced back at her hotel room—and the bed. "I need your help for something. Could we talk down in the bar?"

As they strolled through the hotel's maze of shadowy corridors together, Joe started to put his arm around her, but she gently pulled away. She told him everything that had been happening—starting with the murder of Leah and Jared nearly two weeks ago. Joe had heard about Angela Gannon's death, but not about the others. Sydney needed him to use his connections to find out more about Angela's *suicide* and Ned's *accident.* She now had the names of the Chicago-area florists who had delivered flowers in her name to Angela's sister and the Cook County Recovery Shelter. Working backward, she hoped to track down who had originally placed the orders.

"Give me those names, and I can check them out for you tomorrow," Joe said, sipping his beer.

They'd sat down at a table in the corner of the small, dimly lit lounge. A big tropical fish tank behind the bar provided the strongest source of light and the most color. All the furniture was chrome and glass—or chrome with black leather upholstery.

Sydney had ordered a club soda. She didn't need any more alcohol tonight. She had to keep a clear head. She wrote down the florists' names on a cocktail napkin and handed it to him. "Thank you, Joe," she said.

"And you don't have any clue as to who's behind all these hero-killings?" he asked.

She shook her head. "Do you?"

"What do you mean?"

"I keep wondering if the guys who were involved in that drug heist might have something to do with it."

Hunched over his beer, Joe frowned. "I doubt it. They wouldn't do something so—elaborate. Besides, once you stopped snooping around, you stopped being a concern to them. With you and Eli in Seattle, I don't think they'd go after you, not anymore."

She stared at him. "What do you mean *not anymore*? Were they planning to kill us?"

He shrugged. "I'm not sure, but I couldn't take any chances. Polly was a loose end, and look what they did to him."

Sydney studied her husband's face for a moment. "Oh, my God, I'm so stupid," she whispered finally. "That's why you hit me. That's why you literally kicked me out of the house that day and sent Eli packing, too. You needed to get us out of there. You were afraid they'd come after us."

Tears welled in Joe's eyes again, and he nodded. "I'm sorry, honey," he murmured. "I didn't think it was safe for either of you to stay there. I couldn't think of any other way . . ."

She remembered Joe in his parked car, keeping guard outside the Holiday Inn that night he'd thrown her out. And then he'd had his sister look after her and Eli.

"I can't believe I didn't figure out what you were doing," she said, touching his cheek. "That letter you sent last week, you said you didn't want to see Eli or me for a while—"

"I still don't want to take any chances," he explained. "I'm trying to figure out who I can trust and how to resolve this. You asked me a while back why I didn't go to Len. But

I think he's involved. He's the one who sent me on the raid that night with all these guys I didn't know very well."

"What about Andy McKenna? You can trust him, can't you?"

"Yeah, but I don't want to endanger him or his family. So for a while there, I pushed him away." He let out a long sigh. "Sydney, you need to believe me, I had to take that money. There was no other way. They set me up."

"But how?" she asked.

"These two cops, Jim Mankoff and Kurt Rifkin, were in one patrol car, and I was with this guy Gerry Crowley in the other." He sipped his beer. "When we got near the pier area, Mankoff and Rifkin went in first—on foot. Gerry and I were in the car covering the exit. After a while, I started to think something was wrong and wanted to call for backup. But Crowley kept telling me to stay put and wait just a little longer."

Joe rubbed his forehead. "Well, by that time Mankoff and Rifkin had already captured these two small-timers—Ahmed Turner and Somebody Laskey, I forget his first name. They'd knocked them both unconscious and dragged them into the front seat of the minivan. They'd already unloaded most of the cocaine, and stashed it on a boat. All they had to do was shoot the guys, fire off a few rounds, and crash the minivan into some drums of creosote. They knew I'd be the first one on the scene, and I'd be stupid enough to believe the whole setup." He let out a sad laugh. "You know me, always wanting to believe in the good in people."

He shrugged. "And with my reputation on the force, I would have been a pretty solid, irreproachable witness. But I got antsy, waiting there. I kept thinking my guys were in trouble. Gerry Crowley said we should wait it out, but I went down to the warehouse area."

Joe took another hit of his beer. "I caught them still setting it up. I saw Mankoff with a silencer, shooting Ahmed

Turner in the throat. I guess they'd already broken Laskey's neck. Meanwhile, this Rifkin clown was hauling the last load of cocaine from the back of the minivan. That's when I knew I was screwed. In the minivan window, I could see Gerry Crowley standing right behind me with a gun drawn. It wasn't his police gun. I knew he was going to kill me and they'd plant the gun on one of the dead suspects. An *officer down*, that would have given even more credence to their story that the suspects had resisted. I was as good as dead. I didn't have any choice, so I just smiled a little and said to them, *'I don't know how you guys plan to pull this off, but I'm going to say my fellow officers acted professionally and responsibly. So what's my cut?'*

"As soon as I told them that, I saw Gerry Crowley behind me, lowering his gun. And the other two guys chuckled. I knew if I hadn't said that, I would have been dead."

Sydney remembered the *Tribune* article quoting Joe about the raid-gone-awry. His *"my fellow officers acted professionally and responsibly"* line had been exactly what he'd said.

"I volunteered to stand guard at the other end of the pier, but they sent Crowley with me. I think they were afraid I'd radio in what they were doing. And of course, that's just what I would have done. Anyway, the other two guys rigged the minivan to crash into the drums and then set fire to it. The boat took off with the cocaine—which meant they had a fourth guy working with them. They shot off a few rounds and Crowley called in for backup during the ruckus."

Joe swallowed down some more beer, draining his glass. "We were writing reports the rest of the night, and there wasn't ever a minute when one of those guys left my side. I couldn't shake them. Crowley and Mankoff walked me out to the car when we finished up at eight-thirty that morning. And on the floor in the front seat was a bag with thirty-two thousand dollars in it. Don't ask me how they got it at such short notice, but they did. And it's still up there in that toolbox on the garage shelf."

"Oh, Jesus, Joe," she whispered, squeezing his hand. "What are you going to do?"

"I'm still not sure yet," he sighed. "But I think you and Eli are better off in Seattle until this thing gets resolved."

"Why didn't you tell me all this two months ago?" she asked. "I would have stayed, Joe. I would have stuck by you."

He nodded. "I know you would have. That's why I didn't tell you. That's why I hit you and kicked you out. I needed you and Eli far away so you wouldn't be in any danger."

Sydney sighed. She was thinking how pointless Joe's sacrifice had been. She and Eli were still in danger. Joe's corrupt cohorts may have given up once she'd taken Eli and moved to Seattle. But this madman who had made a game out of murdering heroes was relentless. He'd gone to Portland, New York, and Chicago to kill in her name.

And Sydney had every reason to believe he was here now—maybe even in the hotel.

She squeezed Joe's hand again. "Could you stay with me—at least, until I've changed rooms?"

Joe called the front desk to arrange the room switch while she packed. He stayed with her until she was settled in a new room on the third floor. It looked exactly like the other room—with the same color scheme—only there was no outside access, and no strangers walking past her window. She actually did feel a little safer.

"I'll call you in the morning," Joe told her, before opening the door to leave.

"Thanks, Joe," she said.

He gently kissed her on the cheek. Sydney touched his face for a moment.

"Aren't you going to ask me about the other morning?" he said.

"You mean when I called you and some woman picked up the phone?"

He nodded. "Yeah, I was in the shower. When I came out of the bathroom, she said I'd had a hang-up. So I star-sixty-nined it. Remember Carla?"

Sydney remembered her. She was a fellow cop who had a crush on Joe. He appreciated the attention, but had made it clear to Carla that he was happily married. "So—that was Carla yesterday morning?" Sydney asked.

He nodded again.

"That's why I didn't want to ask you about it," she said in a shaky voice. "I was afraid your answer would be something like this."

He sighed. "Ever since word got around that you'd left me and moved to Seattle, Carla's been—*campaigning*. I was lonely night before last, and got myself drunk, and got up the nerve to take her home."

Sydney bit her lip. "And to our bedroom . . ."

"I couldn't go through with it, honey," he said. "Carla was so hurt—and upset. And I felt like a shit. I spent the night *cuddling* with her, and didn't sleep a wink. I was disgusted with myself the whole time. It was the longest, most excruciating night of my life." He shrugged. "It was the price I paid for this stupid, feeble attempt to forget you."

His eyes searched hers. "But I couldn't forget you, honey. I'm more in love with you now than I ever have been. I don't expect you to forgive me now, but well. . . ." He quickly kissed her on the mouth. "Sleep on it, okay?"

Touching her lips, Sydney just stared at him and nodded.

Then Joe ducked outside, and she triple-locked the door after him.

CHAPTER TWENTY-ONE

For a moment—as the clock radio went off, blasting her favorite Windy City oldies station—Sydney thought she was home on Spaulding Avenue again. She still smelled Joe on her skin. His face and the sound of his voice were recharged in her memory. Sydney almost expected Joe to roll over, kiss her shoulder, and murmur, "Morning, babe." But she was alone in bed in her jade, taupe, and salmon room at this Red Lion by the airport.

Carly Simon's "Anticipation" serenaded her as she staggered out of bed. She wore an oversized T-shirt. On her way to the bathroom, something caught her eye. An envelope had been shoved under her door. It was probably just the hotel bill, but Sydney retrieved it anyway. The legal-size envelope had been lying on the carpet with the flap side up. Wiping the sleep from her eyes, she turned it over—and all of a sudden, she was wide awake. It was as if someone had punched her in the stomach.

Scrawled across the front of the envelope were the words: *BITCH SYDNEY*.

Her hands trembling, she tore open the envelope. It seemed empty at first. But then she shook out a small piece of paper about the size of a credit card. It fluttered toward the floor, but Sydney grabbed the paper in midair. It was a pass ticket for the Chicago El.

Pushing the hair back from her face, Sydney studied the ticket. It took her a few moments to understand. Joe rode the El to work every morning. And years ago, Joe had become a hero when he'd saved all those people from a deranged gunman on the El train.

All of the murdered *Movers & Shakers* heroes had met the same type of death from which they'd rescued other people. Joe had been one of her first subjects, and he was about to be gunned down on the El—unless it had already happened.

Frantic, Sydney checked the digital clock radio on her night-table: 7:32. Joe caught the Brown Line at 7:35 every weekday morning.

Sydney grabbed the phone and called his cell. It rang twice, and then a recording clicked on: *"Hi, it's Joe. You've reached my cell. Leave a message. Thanks."* But this was followed by a prerecorded voice reciting different options for leaving a message: *"To page this person, press one. To leave a message for this person . . ."*

Sydney anxiously paced around the hotel room, waiting for the beep. Finally, it sounded: "Hello, Joe?" she practically screamed into the phone. "Listen, this hero-killer, I think he's after you, Joe. He's going to shoot you on the El. Whatever you do, don't get on the El train this morning! I'm at the hotel. Call me when you get this."

She clicked off the line, certain that Joe wouldn't understand what she was talking about. She called him again to try the paging option. But Joe picked up this time. "Honey, did you just call me?" She could hear traffic noise in the background.

"Yes," she said. "Did you get my message? Are you on the El?"

"Not yet," Joe replied. "I'm standing here on the platform. I can see the train coming—"

"Oh, God, don't get on it, Joe!" she cried. "This hero-killer left a message under my door. He's going to shoot you on the El—"

"Sydney? Sydney, you're breaking up. I can't—"

For a moment, the line seemed to go dead, but then he came back on. "You still there? I can't hear you. The train's coming . . ." The roar of the El train began to drown him out.

"Don't get on that train!" she screamed again. "Joe, listen to me . . ."

"You're still breaking up. I'll call you back."

"No!"

Then she heard the shot.

Joe almost dropped the phone.

The second shot hit a streetlight directly above him. There was an explosion of glass, and one piece grazed his cheek. Past the sound of the train wheels churning and clanking, he heard a third shot.

About a dozen people were standing on the platform, glancing around for the source of the loud pops.

"Everyone, take cover!" Joe yelled, scurrying behind a trash can. "Get down!"

Suddenly, they scattered around the train platform—ducking behind billboards and streetlight poles. A few women were screaming. One woman hovered over her young daughter, shielding her. Two older teenagers, who looked like gang members, had almost tripped over their low-riding jeans as they scurried for cover behind a brick partition.

Three more shots rang out. One bullet just missed Joe. He heard it hiss past his right ear.

He realized the gunman must have made himself a sniper's nest in a nearby building.

Its engine roaring, the train rolled into the station. Then the brakes let out a loud, surrendering squeal. The doors whooshed open. "Don't move!" Joe yelled. "Don't get out! There's a sniper shooting at us!"

Some of the passengers must have already caught on to what was happening. Joe saw them trying to duck below the train's windows or hovering at the edge of the doorways.

"But this is my stop!" one woman-passenger was saying.

Joe glanced at the train, where one car down a thin, blond woman in her mid-forties was emerging through the doorway. She had a cell phone to her ear and was oblivious to everything that was going on around her.

"Get back!" Joe yelled at her.

She just gaped at him.

Suddenly, two more shots were fired, the second one hitting the concrete platform, causing a little explosion just inches from the blond woman's feet. Shrieking, she dropped the phone. But she just stood there, waving her hands around her head. Another blast resounded, just missing the woman again. With a spark, the bullet ricocheted off the train wheel.

"Shit," Joe muttered, slipping his cell phone into his pocket. He jumped out from behind the trash can and hurried toward the woman. All at once, several blasts rang out and a hail of bullets soared past him. He grabbed the woman, who struggled and screamed as he dragged her toward the brick partition. A few other people were huddled there, including the two guys who looked like gang members.

Joe heard more shots—until they finally dove for cover behind the partition.

Then nothing.

The El doors shut, and with a groan, the train started to pull out of the station.

Joe kept waiting for the next shots. He wondered if the sniper was reloading. People stayed frozen in their hiding places. A few women were crying.

Joe realized the sniper had been aiming at him specifically. He'd been shooting at the blond woman just to draw him out. It was as if the gunman knew he'd feel compelled to save her.

He took the cell phone out of his pocket. "Sydney? Are you still there?"

"Joe? Are you all right?" Her voice was still breaking in and out.

"Yeah," he said, catching his breath. He touched his cheek and saw blood on his fingertips. "I don't think anyone's hurt. You better get off the line. I need to call for backup."

"But Dad's okay?" Eli said into the phone.

He sat at his uncle's green-tiled kitchen counter with the cordless in his hand. His uncle had coffee brewing, and the aroma filled the house. Kyle set a box of Rice Krispies and a cereal bowl in front of Eli.

"Yes, Eli, he's fine, thank God," his mother assured him on the other end of the line. "He just got a scratch on his cheek. He'll probably call you tonight."

"But they didn't catch the guy—this sniper?"

"No, unfortunately they didn't," his mother replied. "They're saying it was a gang-related shooting. A couple of gang members were on the platform with Dad."

"Did you get a chance to see him?" Eli asked anxiously.

"Not this morning, but we saw each other last night."

"Are you guys getting back together? Are we moving back home?"

"We'll talk about it when I see you tonight, okay?"

"Can't you at least give me an idea what's gonna happen?" he pleaded. "Please?"

"Well, if we do move back, it wouldn't be for a few more weeks," she said. "Now, that's all I'm going to say. I have to finish up editing here, honey. I love you, and I'll see you tonight. Could you put Uncle Kyle on the line?"

"Love you too, Mom," he muttered. Then he handed the cordless phone to his uncle.

"Thanks, sport," he said. "There's Hawaiian Punch in the refrigerator, and bananas in the bowl over there. Knock yourself out." With the phone to his ear, he wandered out of the kitchen. "Hey again, Syd . . ."

Eli grabbed the milk and the punch out of the refrigerator, then sat down and started eating his Rice Krispies. He wasn't happy with the news that it might be a few more weeks before he could have his old life back. And there was no guarantee it would even happen. His dad was getting shot at, and here he was, thousands of miles away. He couldn't really be sure his mom was telling him the whole story either.

His uncle had gone upstairs with the cordless phone. Eli could barely hear him now. He realized his uncle was whispering.

Putting down his spoon, Eli left his cereal half-eaten and slipped off the counter stool. He crept to the bottom of the stairs and listened. "No, Dan didn't call me," his uncle was saying. "But maybe he's just playing it cool. . . . What do you mean?" There was a long pause. "So basically you're saying Dan is this psycho killer. Well, then you're insinuating it. He took off when you did, because he had a family emergency—in Portland. He isn't in Chicago, Syd. Y'know, this really pisses me off. This is the first nice guy to show some interest in me in like a year, and you're making him out to be a psycho."

Biting his lip, Eli kept perfectly still at the foot of the stairs.

"You're a fine one to make character assessments," his uncle was saying. "Shit, after what Joe did to you, you should be consulting a divorce attorney instead of still pining after him. What about *Joe* for a suspect, huh? Don't forget, two of those people were killed in Chicago."

Eli couldn't believe what he was hearing.

"Well, you started it with all these questions about Dan," his uncle was whispering. "And I really like this guy. I swear—it's as if I'm not allowed to have a personal life while you're here. I didn't mind putting you guys up for a few weeks. And I don't mind looking after Eli. He's a great kid. But I'm kind of tired of being a babysitter here. I mean, when you called me yesterday morning, you practically acted like it didn't matter that I had a brunch date. I was supposed to drop everything and look after your son so you could cover your news story . . ."

Eli winced. His uncle's words stung. He'd had no idea he was such an imposition. His mom had dumped him on his uncle, who didn't want him here. He glanced over at his half-finished bowl of cereal—and then at the front door.

"Forget it," his uncle was saying. "I'm sorry, Syd. Here I am, worried about you and I'm screaming at you. I'm just edgy and pissed off, probably because Dan didn't call. My luck, you're right. He probably is a psycho . . ."

Eli felt inside the pockets of his cargo shorts for money and his house keys. He could no longer hear his uncle's voice as he crept to the door. Slipping outside, he quietly closed the door behind him and started up the street.

Eli wasn't exactly sure where he was going, but he didn't want to stay where he wasn't wanted.

The phone was ringing when he stepped inside the apartment. Eli let the machine pick it up. As he looked around the living room, he could hear the recording start on the machine in the kitchen. *"Eli, are you there?"* It was his Uncle Kyle. He sounded upset. *"If you're there, please, pick up . . ."*

Eli had taken the Number 11 bus back here. He'd been so depressed and disillusioned that he hadn't thought to look around at the other passengers for the man with the weird eye. He'd only remembered at the last minute before getting off at his stop. Eli hadn't seen him on the bus, and he hadn't seen him near the apartment complex either. It was odd, but Eli wasn't scared of him anymore. *Go ahead and kill me*, he imagined telling the man, *nobody gives a shit about me anyway.*

He wondered what awful thing had happened between his mom and dad. The way his uncle had been talking, it had sounded as if his dad was a murder suspect or something. It didn't make any sense.

"Listen, Eli, if you get this message, please call me back right away," his uncle was saying on the machine. His voice even cracked a little. *"I'm going nuts here. I can't believe the way you just disappeared like that. Call me, okay, kiddo?"*

"Kiddo," Eli muttered, sneering. "Jerk, acting like you care."

He tried to call his dad's cell, but it was busy. Taking a fruit roll-up out of the cabinet, he wandered into the dining room. He glanced over at the built-in breakfront, and his eyes strayed down to that bottom drawer. On Saturday, his mom had hidden his dad's letter in that drawer. Eli wondered if it was still there.

He quickly stuffed the roll-up in his mouth and opened the breakfront's bottom drawer. He rifled through old bills, receipts, instructions, and warranties. "C'mon, where is it?" he said, his mouth still full. There was something in that letter his mom didn't want him to see.

"Goddamn it!" he yelled. In his frustration, he yanked the whole drawer out and dumped its contents on the floor. He shuffled through all the papers, but still didn't see that envelope with his dad's handwriting on it. Had his mom thrown it out?

He noticed an envelope that had fallen in the gap beneath the drawer, and he reached into the opening and took it out. It was an old bill from a place called the Bon Marché. It even smelled old. The envelope was addressed to Dr. John

Simms at this address. The postmark in the corner was dated May 2, '89.

Eli peeked into the empty drawer sleeve and noticed more envelopes trapped against the breakfront's backing. He reached into the opening again and felt something sharp stab his finger. "Shit!" he muttered, pulling his hand out. He checked his index finger and saw a small splinter at the tip. He managed to squeeze it out, then he reached inside the drawer again until his whole arm was in there. He felt three envelopes and one piece of loose paper. But as he took them out of the drawer, he could tell none of them had been the letter from his dad. All of them were old, stained, and musty-smelling. There was another bill to Dr. Simms, and a loose receipt from Bailey/Coy Books from 1987. The second envelope was addressed to Ms. Loretta Sayers-Landau here at the Tudor Court Apartments.

"Oh, my God," Eli whispered.

The return address on back showed the note was from R. Landau on McGraw Street in Seattle. Eli pulled a birthday card from the envelope. The cover showed an old black-and-white photo of a little girl in a party hat. She was about to blow out the candles on her birthday cake. The preprinted inside message read: *ANOTHER YEAR YOUNGER!* Below that was a note:

Dear Loretta,

I know you don't want to hear from me. But this is your birthday, and I need you to know that I'm thinking of you & wishing you well. Happy Birthday.

Always, Robert

Eli looked at the fourth envelope—addressed in sloppy script to Loretta Sayers here at the Tudor Court, again. There was no return address, just *Hallmark* on the back flap. The postmark read: NOV 6, '74. Only a few days later, Loretta and her son would be dead.

Eli reached into the envelope. It was another card—a cheesy photograph of a couple embracing on a bluff in front of an orange sunset. They wore really ugly polyester-looking clothes from the seventies. *"Someone Special Like You . . ."* was preprinted in swirling script at the bottom of the card. Inside, in the same script: *". . . Makes My Day Complete."*

Above and below this sappy sentiment was a note in the same sloppy script:

Dear Loretta,

You can't just stop seeing me. It isn't fair & I won't stand for it. Maybe you think you can treat your husband that way, but I'm not him. We love each other & you know it. If you don't see me again, you'll be sorry. Only a whore would act this way. Do you know how much you've hurt me? I deserve better. I've been very good to you. I'm so angry at you & yet despite everything I still love you. Please let me be with you at least one more time. Despite everything I still love you.

Chris

Eli didn't know who Chris was. In everything he'd read about Loretta Sayers, he hadn't run across that name. But obviously, Chris was some lover Loretta had scorned. And he was so mad and so much in love with her, he'd practically threatened her if she didn't see him again. *"Despite everything I still love you,"* he'd said that twice.

The old Hallmark card had been stuck in the back of the breakfront all these years. Obviously, the police hadn't seen it; otherwise, this Chris person would have been a suspect in the deaths of Loretta and Earl.

Eli wondered why Loretta would save a correspondence like this unless it somehow amused her that she could drive a lover crazy. Or perhaps Earl had walked in on his mother reading it, and she'd stashed Chris's card in the drawer. The same thing had happened just a few days ago when he'd walked in on his mom reading that letter from his dad.

Eli raced up to his room, and found the number for Evergreen Point Manor. He called them from the phone in his mother's room. When the operator answered, he asked to talk to Vera Cormier. "She might be out in the garden if she's not in her room," Eli said. "It's really important that I talk to her."

While he waited, Eli heard a beep on the line—another call, probably his uncle again. Part of him really wanted to tell Uncle Kyle what he'd just discovered. But he was still angry and hurt. The beep sounded again, but Eli ignored it.

Finally, he heard a click, then ring tones. After the second one, somebody picked up. "Hello?"

He recognized Vera's voice. "Hi, this is Eli," he said. "We talked the other day—you know, about Loretta and Earl Sayers . . ."

"Well, hello again, Eli. How are you?"

"Fine, thanks. I'm sorry to bother you, but I'm wondering if Mrs. Sayers ever mentioned someone named Chris. Like a boyfriend, maybe? Do you remember that name?"

"No, dear, I'm sorry . . ."

"Maybe Chris was one of the other neighbors," he suggested.

"No, that doesn't ring a bell," she replied.

"Are you sure?"

"Yes, I'm sure, dear. I don't remember anyone named Chris."

He sighed. "Okay, well, thank you, Mrs. Cormier. Have a nice day."

"You, too, bye now." Then he heard a click.

Undaunted, Eli dug into the pockets of his cargo pants until he found a business card. Then he dialed the office number for Burton C. Demick.

"Rayburn, Demick, and Gill," the woman answered. "Mr. Demick's office, this is Cheryl. How can I help you?"

"Yes, is Mr. Demick in, please?"

"Who's calling?"

"Um, my name's Eli, and I met him yesterday. I was there with my uncle."

"One minute, please."

While he waited, Eli sat down on the edge of his mother's bed. It wasn't long before the woman came back on the line. "I'm sorry. Mr. Demick is in a meeting. Would you like to leave your number?"

"Um, that's okay. Thank you." Then Eli hung up.

He was better off talking with Mr. Demick in person. There was a good chance he knew this Chris person—or at least he might have heard Earl talk about him. In fact, maybe *Chris* was short for Christine. Chris could have been a girl. That would explain why the marriage to Mr. Landau didn't work out. Maybe Loretta had been a lesbian.

He remembered his uncle saying yesterday that they should have changed their clothes before visiting the law firm. So Eli retreated to his room and put on a clean white short-sleeve shirt, long navy blue pants, and a striped tie. His good shoes were horribly uncomfortable, so he just put on some black Converse All-Stars. He got some more change for the bus, and just in case, he dug out that twenty-dollar bill with the missing corners the psychic lady had torn off.

With Chris's Hallmark card in his hand, he hurried downstairs.

The telephone rang again. Eli hesitated, waiting for the machine to come on. He glanced down at the envelope. *This could be evidence,* he thought. He shouldn't just be carrying it around. Ducking into his mother's office, he found a big manila envelope, and slipped Chris's correspondence inside it.

Meanwhile, the machine let out a beep, and he heard his uncle again: *"Eli, it's Uncle Kyle giving it another shot here. Please, pick up. Please? Okay, I'm convinced something is seriously wrong here. I'm calling the police. If you're there, please pick up. If you get this message—"*

Eli snatched up the cordless. "Hi, Uncle Kyle."

"Oh, thank God!" his uncle cried. "I was convinced you'd been abducted! Why did you just disappear like that?"

"I heard you talking to Mom upstairs," Eli muttered.

There was dead silence on the other end of the line.

"I'm sorry that you got stuck with me," Eli added.

"Oh, Eli, I'm such an ass," his uncle said woefully. "Please, don't say that. It's not true. I was just mad at your mom. Listen, stay put, and I'll come pick you up. We'll go do something fun. Let me make it up to you . . ."

"No, thanks," Eli said. He was still mad. "I'm going out. Don't worry about me. I'll call you later."

"Eli, please—"

"Bye," he said. Then he hung up. A minute later, Eli was out the door and double locking it. He could hear the phone ringing again on the other side.

With the manila envelope tucked under his arm, Eli turned and walked away.

The Number 11 bus pulled up toward his stop. Already Eli was sweating through his white shirt. It had gotten muggy out. And on top of that, he perspired when he got nervous. He felt so close to solving this thirty-four-year-old double murder.

He glanced up at the rain clouds darkening the sky. He hadn't thought to bring an umbrella.

Obviously, he hadn't been thinking at all; otherwise he would have noticed the man across the street earlier. Eli caught a glimpse of him climbing into a white Taurus. The dark-skinned man wore sunglasses and a red shirt, but there was no mistaking who he was. Eli wondered how long he'd been there, watching him.

The bus suddenly pulled up, blocking his view.

Eli stepped aboard, paid his fare, and quickly took a seat on the left side so he could look out the window at the man. As the bus lurched forward, he saw the white Taurus pulling out of its parking spot. "Shit," he muttered under his breath. He turned forward and saw two punk, teenage girls staring at him from across the aisle.

"You look like a Jehovah's Witness," one of them said. Her friend giggled.

Eli didn't say anything, but he felt this awful pang in his stomach. He turned away and gazed out the window again. He couldn't see the white car. But he knew it was following him.

"I'm sorry, Mr. Demick left for the day," the receptionist told him. It wasn't the pretty brunette from yesterday. This one had very short platinum-blond hair and dark red lipstick. She nodded at the manila envelope in Eli's hand. "Is that for him?"

"Um, yes," Eli said. "I—ah, I need him to sign for it. Could you tell me where he went? It's urgent he get this."

She held out her hand. "If you leave it with me, I'll see his assistant gets it."

Eli shook his head. "No, I'm sorry. I really need to hand it to him in person and get his signature."

With a tiny frown, the receptionist reached for her phone. "One minute, please," she said. She punched a few numbers, and then her voice dropped to a whisper as she talked to someone on the line. Eli couldn't hear her. He wondered if she was calling security on him.

He was amazed he'd made it this far. Getting off the bus earlier, he'd kept a lookout for that creepy man, but he hadn't seen him or the white Taurus. It had just started to rain as he'd hurried into the lobby of Mr. Demick's building. While waiting for the elevator, Eli had thought he'd spotted the man again by the revolving doors. But it had been another guy in a red shirt.

The blonde hung up the phone and smiled at him. "Are you from Coupland and Douglas?" she asked.

Eli didn't know if that was good or bad, but he took a chance and nodded.

She pulled up something on her computer, then scribbled on a notepad. "Mr. Demick went home for the day. This is his address." She handed him a piece of paper. "Are you on a bike or did you walk over?"

"Um, I walked."

"Well, he's in West Seattle. You'll need a cab. I'll call one for you." She reached for the phone again. "And I'll call Mr. Demick and tell him you're on your way." She nodded at the envelope again. "You know, you're late. We were expecting that at nine o'clock."

"Yes," Eli said. "I know. They got held up in the—the copy room. Thank you for your help."

"It'll be a yellow cab out front," she said.

Eli nodded politely, then turned and quickly headed for the double glass doors. Just as he stepped out to the foyer, one of the elevators let out a ding and the third door down opened. The swarthy man in the red shirt seemed out of place amid the businesspeople riding the elevator with him. He still had his sunglasses on.

Swiveling around, Eli ran down the hallway and ducked into the first door with an Exit sign over it.

"Wait!" he heard the man shout behind him.

He staggered into an ugly stairwell with white walls and grey steps. Racing down the first flight of stairs, Eli tried the door to the twenty-sixth floor, but it was locked. "Shit!" he hissed.

Above him, he heard the door open.

He scurried down the next flight of stairs and tried the door on twenty-five, but it was locked as well. He ran as fast as he could down to the next floor. The footsteps above him echoed in the stark stairwell. The man seemed to be gaining on him. "Eli?" the man called. "Eli, stop!"

But he kept running. How did that guy know his name? What was going on? Eli tried the door on the twenty-third floor. He even banged on it repeatedly.

"Goddamn it, Eli!" the man yelled. "Stop! I'm a friend of your father's!"

The voice was right above him now.

Eli didn't believe him. How often did child killers use that "I'm a friend of your dad's" line?

He turned and raced down another flight, where he saw a fire extinguisher bracketed to the wall. Eli grabbed it. The man's footsteps got louder and closer. "Eli, wait up!" he called. Eli saw his hand moving down the railing just half a flight up. His shadow began to sweep over the landing.

Just then, Eli threw the fire extinguisher at his feet. The tinny, clanking sound reverberated through the stairwell. So did the man's sharp cry as he tripped over the extinguisher and fell. "Goddamn it!" he bellowed.

Eli didn't wait to see how far the creepy guy had fallen or how badly he was hurt. He'd already turned around and bolted down the next group of steps. Eli tried the door on the twentieth floor, and to his utter relief, it was open.

"Eli, wait!" the man called. "I know your dad . . ."

Eli shut the stairwell door, and it cut off the sound of the stranger's voice.

He took the elevator from the twentieth floor down to the lobby, where he saw the yellow cab waiting in front of the building. Eli was still catching his breath as he headed out the revolving door. He had the manila envelope tucked under his arm, but stopped in the rain for a moment to check his pockets for the piece of paper with Mr. Demick's address on it. "Oh, no," he murmured. "Oh, no, please, God . . ."

Just when he'd thought he was getting the hell out of there, he would have to go back. Dejectedly, he wandered over to the cab and opened the front passenger door. "I'm doing a delivery for a law firm," he said to the driver—a middle-aged, thin black man with gray hair. "Are you waiting for me?"

The taxi driver nodded.

"I'm sorry, but I have to go back and—"

The driver was still nodding. "Going to West Seattle, right? 1939 Henley Court?"

Eli broke into a grateful smile. "Yes, sir. You bet. Thank you."

He quickly climbed in back. As the cab pulled into traffic, Eli felt such overwhelming relief. It lasted about thirty seconds. That was how long it took for him to realize where he must have dropped that piece of paper with Demick's address on it.

In the stairwell, of course.

"Well, Sydney, it's about time you called me. I only gave you my cell phone number—like last week!"

The pretty, twenty-two-year-old brunette salesgirl behind the counter at Beautiful Blooms had been chewed out on several occasions for chatting on her cell phone while at work. But Jill was the only one in the flower shop at the moment. There weren't any customers, and Glenn, the gruff fifty-something owner was out making a delivery.

Jill had developed an instant crush on Sydney Jordan when

he'd first walked into Beautiful Blooms about two weeks ago. She thought it was cool how he spelled his name that different way. For someone so cute and funny, he had kind of a sad job. He'd explained to her that he helped people with the estates of their recently deceased relatives. He worked all over the country: Portland, New York, Chicago. He was always sending his new customers flowers with sympathy cards. It was a pretty sweet gesture. Jill had waited on him a few times now, and always flirted up a storm. She couldn't believe he'd finally called her on her cell, and he was asking if she'd like to go out with him.

"You mean, like a date?" she teased.

"You bet, like a date," he said. "I want to take you out to breakfast tomorrow around 9:30."

"Oh, I'd love to, but I have to work," she said, crestfallen. "Can't we make it another time?"

"Well, can't you call in sick?" he countered. "I'd really like to see you, Jill. And if we meet for breakfast, we'll have the rest of the day together—if we want. I know it's what I'd like."

Jill let out an exasperated, giddy, little laugh. "I'm tempted . . ."

"C'mon, let's do it," he urged her.

"I guess I could call in tomorrow with some excuse," she said, leaning on the counter.

"That's my girl," he said on the other end of the line.

Jill felt absolutely light-headed while he explained that he'd pick her up in front of Seattle's Asian Art Museum in Volunteer Park. It wasn't too far from her apartment. And they could walk or drive to the Coastal Kitchen for brunch—depending on their mood. And then they'd see where the day took them.

"Sydney, that sounds awesome," she said into the cell phone. A customer walked into the flower shop, but Jill turned her back to her.

"Then it's a date," he said on the other end of the line. "Listen, I need to cancel that order from yesterday, the one to Mrs. Joseph McCloud at number nine, Tudor Court in Seattle. It didn't work out with the client the way I planned. Did that order go out yet?"

"Not yet," she replied. "We'll just credit it back to your account. You still have a lot of money left over from that cash deposit you made."

"I may have a couple of more orders for delivery tomorrow," he said. "One will be to a Seattle address and another to someone with the last name Finch in Evanston. I'll phone them in later today. But if we don't connect, we're still on for brunch tomorrow morning, aren't we?"

"We sure are," Jill replied. "It's a date, Sydney."

The overly tanned, forty-something blond woman answering Mr. Demick's front door was wearing a tennis outfit. A pair of sunglasses were perched on top of her head. "Yes?" she said, with a slightly icy look.

Standing on the front stoop in his tie and short sleeve shirt, Eli wondered if she, too, thought he was a Jehovah's Witness. He showed her the manila envelope. "I have something here that requires a signature from Mr. Burton C. Demick."

She nodded. "Oh, well, come on in." She called over her shoulder. "Honey, you need to sign for this! Burt?" There was no answer. With a big sigh, she rolled her eyes. "Wait here just a minute," she muttered, heading off to a room on her right. "Burt? Burt, for Christ's sake, I'm going to be late for my tennis lesson. You've got to sign for this . . ."

Her voice faded. Eli waited in the front hallway, a very pale green foyer with a marble floor and a sparkling crystal chandelier overhead. Demick's house was one of those newly built "McMansions"—set back from the street on an isolated piece of property with a lot of trees.

During the cab ride here, Eli kept thinking about that man. *I'm a friend of your dad's*, the guy had said. If he was really a buddy of his father's, why was he sneaking around like that? How come his mom hadn't recognized him when she'd first spotted him in their driveway?

The taxi here had cost twenty-two bucks, which had practically cleaned him out. Eli had paid the driver, and sent him away. Now he wasn't sure how he'd get home.

Eli heard footsteps, and he glanced up to see Mr. Demick coming down the hallway. He wore a turquoise golf shirt, white shorts, and sandals. His legs and arms were tanned and hairless. Demick's eyes locked onto his, and he seemed to balk at the sight of him.

Eli nervously cleared his throat. "Hi, Mr. Demick. My name is Eli. I don't know if you remember me from yesterday—"

"Yes, I remember you," he said. He had a strange half-smile on his face that didn't quite conceal his irritation. "My wife thought you were a messenger boy. What are you doing here?"

"Um, I just had one more question for you, sir," Eli said. "I was wondering if Earl or Mrs. Sayers ever mentioned someone named Chris."

"*Chris*," he repeated.

Eli nodded. "It might even be short for Christine. I'm not sure if it's a man or a woman." He reached inside the manila envelope and pulled out the old Hallmark card. "Y'see, the reason I got interested in Earl and his mother was because I live in their old place by the beach at Lake Washington. And I found this card today."

Demick frowned. "I don't have my glasses. Come on into my study."

Eli followed him down the hall and into a room with a big, mahogany desk. A state-of-the-art computer monitor sat on top of it, along with a large antique lamp that had a bronze golfer figurine as its base and a golf-ball design on the shade. On one wall there were old framed prints of people golfing and some framed diplomas. Behind the desk was a floor-to-ceiling picture window with individual little panes; a few of them had stained-glass designs. But it didn't obscure the view to the large, well-manicured backyard. There was a patio just outside that window with some wrought-iron furniture.

"I don't remember Earl or his mother ever talking about someone named Chris," Demick said, retrieving his glasses from a pile of paperwork on his desk. He slipped them on, then reached for the Hallmark card. "Let's have a look at that . . ."

Eli handed it to him. "You know how you said you weren't sure at first if Mrs. Sayers killed Earl and herself. Well, this Chris person could have done it. I mean, he's really mad in that letter. And the postmark is just a few days before Mrs. Sayers and Earl were killed."

Demick opened the card and read it. A sour look passed over his face, and he heaved a sigh as he closed the card and handed it back to him. "You're right, Eli," he said finally. "I think we should show this to the police. Have you contacted them?"

Shrugging, Eli shook his head. "I haven't even told my uncle about this yet. In fact, would it be okay if I called and told him where I am? I just want to let him know I'm okay."

"Certainly," Demick said, nodding at the phone on his desk. "Help yourself. Sit down. I can leave if you want some privacy."

"No, this is fine," Eli said, walking around to his side of the desk. He reached for the phone. "Thanks very much."

Demick opened the top side drawer. "I have this police lieutenant's business card in here . . ."

Eli was about to dial his uncle's number when he noticed a yellow legal pad on Mr. Demick's desk. He'd scribbled some notes, and at the bottom of that top page, Eli read: *"Despite everything, I recommend that all parties concerned . . ."* It was the exact same sloppy script that had scrawled those words, *"Despite everything, I still love you . . ."*

Eli glanced at the antique brass name plate on the fancy pen holder: *Burton Christopher Demick.*

He turned toward Mr. Demick, and froze.

Loretta and Earl's killer had a gun in his hand.

"It was you," Eli murmured. The receiver fell out of his hand. "But you—you were Earl's *friend* . . ."

With an icy stare, Demick nodded. "And the poor sap had no idea I was fucking his bitch mother for over a year."

All at once, he reeled back, then brought the butt end of the gun down on Eli's head. "Snoopy little bastard," he growled.

It was the last thing Eli heard before he collapsed to the floor.

Chapter Twenty-two

Sydney gazed at Joe's handsome profile and the Band-Aid covering the cut from the piece of glass that had hit him on the train platform. She sat in the front with him in his Honda Civic as they drove along Mannheim to O'Hare. Joe's eyes were riveted to the road ahead.

He'd spent most of the day answering questions and trying to convince his fellow cops that this morning's sniper incident might not have been gang-related. He hadn't won any converts with his theory of a hero-killer. He hadn't mentioned anything about the hero-killings to the press. "There just isn't enough evidence to go public with it yet," he'd explained to Sydney. "Besides, you're the one who should tell the story, not me."

Both she and Joe would be on the news tonight.

Sydney had done her best to stay focused on the Chloe Finch story. She'd managed to finish editing and scoring the segment by 3:25—with only minutes to spare before its deadline. The segment would run on tonight's national news. She wasn't too crazy about the piece and thought her *It's a Wonderful Life* angle might have been too corny. But she'd shown it to Chloe, who had loved it.

Within a few hours, Chloe Finch would be another one of

her *heroes*. And while Sydney didn't want to frighten her too much, she'd warned Chloe to be on her guard for nutcases and stalkers. "Now that you're going to be famous, you need to be extra cautious, okay?"

She was hoping after tonight, Chloe wouldn't have to be looking over her shoulder. They were a lot closer to tracking down this maniac. Joe had managed to make some calls and traced the flower delivery orders. Both had originated from a florist in Seattle called Beautiful Blooms. Sydney knew the place. It wasn't far from Kyle's house.

"I hate sending you back to Seattle alone," Joe said, following the airport signs for Departures. "If I can get out from under this El-shooting business, I'll catch an early morning flight there tomorrow." He took his eyes off the road for a moment and glanced at her. "Would that be okay with you?"

Sydney smiled at him and nodded. "That would be more than okay. It would be terrific."

He once again focused on the traffic ahead, but reached over and took hold of her hand. "Listen, I hope you're not too angry about this, but I asked a buddy to watch over you and Eli."

"For tonight?" she asked.

"For the last couple of months," he admitted. "Luis has been checking in on you from time to time ever since you moved to Seattle."

"What?" Sydney murmured.

"I just wanted to be positive that Crowley, Mankoff, and Rifkin hadn't sent some hood to Seattle to tie up loose ends."

"Luis," she said. "Is he a Latino guy with an eye infection of some kind?"

Joe nodded. "Yeah, he was complaining to me the other night that he wasn't getting any sleep. He said he must have broken a blood vessel or something."

"How come I don't know this guy?"

"Well, if you knew him, he wouldn't have been able to follow you around. Luis is a good guy. He used to be a street kid, and I plucked him out of this gang when he was about sixteen. Now he wants to be a cop."

Sydney rubbed her forehead. "Good Lord, I thought he was a stalker—or possibly this hero-killer. Was it really necessary for him to follow us around everywhere?"

"Actually, he started out checking on you just occasionally. But about three weeks ago, he noticed someone sneaking around outside your apartment. So Luis increased his surveillance. He isn't sure if this guy's an obsessed fan or what, but he's been very elusive. Luis still hasn't gotten a good look at him yet." Joe sighed. "When you told me last night about this guy fixated on you and killing heroes, I figured that's the creep Luis has seen."

Sydney just nodded.

Now it made sense why Luis—Number 59—had sneered at her when she'd first glimpsed him. If the guy was a friend of Joe's, he probably thought she was a mega-bitch for leaving her wonderful hero-husband. It was a bit unsettling, but at the same time, she took solace in knowing this Luis person was keeping his one good eye on Eli right now.

Joe pulled the car over to the curb in front of the terminal entrance. Shifting into Park, he turned to her and smiled sheepishly. "So are you mad at me for getting you a bodyguard without asking you?"

Sydney shook her head. "No, it's very reassuring. I'll sleep better tonight."

He climbed out of the car and helped her with her luggage. They embraced, and Sydney kissed him on the lips.

"I'll see you tomorrow—in Seattle," he whispered.

"I hope so," she said, grabbing her bags.

"Kiss Eli for me," he said.

Nodding, Sydney gave him one last smile, and then headed inside the terminal.

* * *

Eli's head throbbed so badly, he thought he might throw up.

But he couldn't. There was a gag in his mouth. It took Eli a few moments after regaining consciousness to realize why he couldn't move or feel his arms. Hog-tied behind him, they'd fallen asleep. He lay facedown on the Oriental rug in Demick's study, feeling sick and utterly helpless. Blurry-eyed, he tried to focus on Demick, who stood over him. But Eli was in so much pain, he couldn't lift his head to see Demick's face.

A weird, high-pitched ringing filled his ears. He didn't quite hear everything Demick was saying. He'd mentioned something about his wife not being back for another two hours, and by then, they'll have taken a little drive to Snohomish National Forest.

"It might be months before anyone finds your body there," Demick said.

That part Eli heard—very clearly.

Demick explained how—thirty-five years ago—he'd started having sex with Loretta Sayers while she was still married to Mr. Landau. Their affair had become even more intense after she'd left Landau and moved to Number 9 at Tudor Court. Earl had never caught on to what was happening between his sixteen-year-old buddy and his mother. "I'd come over there and hang out with him. She'd cook us dinner," Demick explained. "Then I'd leave—and a few hours later, usually around one in the morning, she'd meet me at a motel—or sometimes the beach—and we'd fuck our brains out. It was the best, hottest sex I've ever had. We had a damn good thing going. Nobody knew. The closest we came to getting caught was when she occasionally slipped and called me Chris in front of her kid. That was Loretta's pet name for me. She used to call me that in bed."

His face pressed against the carpet, Eli only had a view of

Demick's feet and his tan, hairless legs as he paced in front of him. Beyond that, Eli saw raindrops slashing at the big window. The awful ringing sound kept coming in and out while Demick went on about how Loretta had unceremoniously dumped him.

From what Eli could understand, Demick had gone over there to see Earl on a Saturday night. It had been after he'd sent Loretta that card. Every moment he'd caught Loretta alone, he'd begged her to meet him later, but she'd refused. So on Sunday night, he'd broken into the Sayers' town house apartment. He'd known where they'd hidden their extra key outside. And he'd known where Loretta had kept her gun. But he didn't use it on Earl.

"I slit his throat while he was sleeping," Demick said. He stopped pacing. With his foot, he nudged Eli and turned him onto his back. "You wanted to find out what happened, so I'm telling you. Eli." Demick stared down at him. Eli saw that he had a big sofa pillow in one hand and his gun in the other. "There was a lot of blood, and it got awfully messy. Fortunately, I was wearing her dishwashing gloves. If I had to do it over again, I would have smothered Earl with his pillow. It's much neater. He didn't die right away. He struggled for a few moments. But I kept a hand over his mouth. He wasn't able to make a sound. We didn't wake up Loretta down the hall. She was still sleeping when I crept into her room."

A tiny smile flickered on his face. "I woke her with a kiss on the cheek. Then I put my hand over her mouth and led her into the bathroom. She saw I had the gun. She didn't struggle or try anything. I made her strip and get in the tub. Then I shot her in the head."

Horror-struck, Eli listened to him. He kept wondering what Demick planned to do with that pillow.

"You know, Eli, I'm not proud of what I did. I was sixteen years old, and just went crazy that night." He shook his head.

"I can't believe Loretta held on to that letter. For the first few weeks afterward, I kept thinking the cops would find it. Finally, I was able to convince myself it was okay. I haven't had to think about Loretta and Earl for a long time—not until you and your uncle walked into my office yesterday." He sighed, and put the gun down on the edge of the desk. Demick's back was to the window as he stared down at him. "It's funny, but you remind me a bit of Earl. And like I say, if I had to do it over again, I would do it the neat way . . ."

Demick crouched down close to him. "It'll be easier if you don't struggle."

Just over Demick's shoulder, Eli glimpsed something past the rain-beaded window.

The dark-haired man in the red shirt crept toward the house. Eli watched him grab a wrought-iron patio chair.

Then all at once, Eli couldn't see anything. Demick pushed the pillow down on his face. Eli tried to turn his head away, but he couldn't. It felt as if the man was smashing his nose in. Eli couldn't breathe. He thought he might swallow the gag. There wasn't any air coming into his lungs at all.

Suddenly, he heard a deafening crash. The pillow slipped away in time for Eli to see the patio chair toppling inside the room amid an explosion of glass.

Demick got to his feet, swiveled around, and grabbed his gun from the edge of the desk. To Eli's utter horror, he turned toward him and fired. A shot rang out.

Panic-stricken, Eli tried to roll to one side, but it was too late. He felt a sharp pain searing through his arm.

The dark-skinned man, his dad's buddy—Eli now realized that was true—picked up the patio chair again.

Demick spun around and shot the man. But the bullet didn't slow him down. The dark-haired stranger smashed the chair over his head.

Loretta and Earl's killer fell onto the floor, just missing Eli.

Gasping for air, Eli watched his dad's friend clutching at his side as he reached for the phone. Blood seeped between his fingers. "Operator, I need an ambulance right away," he said, catching his breath. He worked up a smile for Eli and nodded to him.

"You'll be okay, kid. Hang in there . . ."

"Hey, Chloe, I saw you on the news tonight."

Chuck, her neighbor from downstairs, was coming up from the basement with a load of laundry. Chloe had just stepped into the lobby of her apartment building. It was a three-story, old-world charmer with thirty units. Most of the neighbors knew each other.

And now most of her neighbors—along with the rest of the nation—knew that she'd been on a beach contemplating suicide night before last. Everyone also knew about her unwitting participation in a fraternity dogfight. For the interview, she hadn't said anything about having had sex with Riley, but she'd admitted that she'd been interested in the son of a bitch. Compared to Derrick De Santo's pregnant girlfriend and his rich, airhead wife, Chloe came out as the one least-duped. The way Sydney Jordan had put the segment together, Chloe felt she'd emerged as a hero, and the *It's a Wonderful Life* spin on her story gave her a newfound optimism.

Still, Chloe knew there would be some backlash—mainly people treating her like a mental outpatient. But she'd gotten past the worst of it. She'd warned her mother yesterday about what she'd revealed in the interview. Her mom had called about a half-hour ago, right after the broadcast. "I guess it wasn't so bad," she'd finally concluded. "But you'll start seeing a therapist soon, won't you, honey?"

Chloe had watched the news in a bar, and had been both

happy and oddly disappointed that nobody in the place recognized her as the woman up on the TV. She'd had a Cosmopolitan by herself and toasted herself.

It sure beat being dead.

She worked up a smile for Chuck, a sweet, slightly nerdy guy with glasses and receding brown hair. For a while, Chloe had entertained the notion he might like her, but there was no spark.

"So—did I come across as a pathetic loser or a major psycho?" she asked, leaning against the mailboxes.

"None of the above," Chuck replied. "I really like the way you were so honest. And c'mon, you're a hero. I think you did great."

"Well, thank you," she grinned. She got her mail out of the mailbox—mostly bills. "I hope you'll tell everyone else in the building the same thing when they're talking about that nutcase, Chloe, in 307."

She started up the stairs.

Lugging his laundry basket, Chuck followed her. "I think they're just happy all those reporters stopped hanging around outside the building this morning," he said. "Then again, maybe they *all* haven't gone. I saw some guy lingering around earlier tonight. Hey, by the way, I Tivo'd the broadcast. Want me to save it for you?"

Chloe paused on the second-floor landing. "Well, thanks, Chuck," she smiled. "But Sydney Jordan gave me my own DVD copy."

"I'm saving it anyway," he said. Then he started down the hallway. "Take care, Chloe!"

"You, too!" she called to him. Then she continued up to the third floor.

Stepping into her apartment, she flicked the hallway light switch. But nothing happened. In the darkness, Chloe hesitated before moving into the living room and switching on the lamp. She saw her computer monitor's fish-tank screen saver was on. She almost always turned off the monitor before stepping out. Something wasn't right.

Chloe wondered about that man Chuck had seen lingering outside the building. And she remembered Sydney's warning about stalkers.

Warily, she checked the kitchen and tried the back door. It wasn't locked. She'd locked up before leaving earlier—she was almost certain. Yet it didn't look as if the lock had been tampered with. Chloe opened the door and glanced out at the back stairs: no one. Leaving the door open a crack, she went to investigate the rest of the apartment. She peeked into the hall closet, then headed toward her darkened bedroom.

She stopped dead. Chloe thought she saw something move in there. Maybe it was just her own approaching shadow. She hesitated for a moment, and thought about running downstairs and getting Chuck.

All at once, a figure emerged from the darkness in her bedroom. Chloe saw the outline of a man.

She started to scream.

The man lunged at her, pinned her against the wall, and covered her mouth with his gloved hand. "Don't let out another sound or I'll fucking kill you," he growled.

Trembling, Chloe eyed the gun in his other hand.

He pressed his face against hers. He was wearing a ski mask, but she still felt his warm breath swirling in her ear.

"Strip for me," he whispered.

Sydney's flight was delayed. She waited in the boarding area with her laptop plugged in. She was checking the various news coverage of this morning's sniper attack at the El station. Everyone was still calling it a gang-related incident.

She thought about the *Bitch-Sydney* envelope with the El

pass inside it. The killer had broken his pattern this time. He'd given her his clue *before* going after his prey. She wondered why he'd done that.

They finally announced that boarding would soon begin.

Sydney was about to switch off her computer when she noticed a new e-mail from chloefinch@northwesternu.edu. The subject heading was "Good-bye."

She clicked on the e-mail, and the standard caution came up about not opening the e-mail if she didn't know the sender. Sydney figured she knew Chloe pretty well now, so she opened it. A cartoon figure popped up on the screen. It was a little girl looking like a Kewpie Doll. She sported a red bikini and stood knee-deep in wavy water. A cartoon sun was smiling down on her. Then the waves started to rise until only the Kewpie Doll's eyes and the top of her head were above the water. Sydney gazed at the e-mail subject again: *Good-bye.*

"Oh, my God," she whispered. "Chloe's next. He's going to drown her . . ."

"Please . . . please . . . just take whatever you want and leave me alone," Chloe whispered.

Trembling, she stood naked in the empty tub. She tried to cover herself. He kept looking at her, up and down. And all she could see of him were his eyes through the two holes in his ski mask.

In his gloved hand, he held a gun to her head. "Get down on your knees," he growled.

Chloe obeyed him.

"Turn on the water," he said, crouching down so they stayed at eye level. "You're going to fill up the tub. Make it a comfortable temperature, Chloe. No need for it to be as cold as that lake water the other night."

Kneeling in the tub, she stopped covering her breasts for

a moment so she could turn on the water. She heard him chuckle behind the mask. He gently grazed one of her nipples with the tip of his gun.

"Cut that out, asshole!" she growled, tears in her eyes. She covered her breasts again.

She heard him snicker, "Huh, feisty." He stood up straight. Keeping the gun trained on her, the man backed away to the toilet, then lowered the lid and sat down. "Do you know six hundred and ninety-one people drowned in bathtubs last year?" he asked. "Of course, a lot of them were infants and toddlers. But adults drown in bathtubs, too."

The lukewarm water was now up past the backs of Chloe's legs.

"Sometimes people slip, hit their head, and drown—in only two feet of water," he continued. "It's a lot like that woman on the beach. She got hit on the head and nearly drowned in Lake Michigan. But you rescued her. You know, if you hadn't saved her, I wouldn't be here with you right now. Are you still glad you played hero, Chloe?"

Past the sound of the tub filling, Chloe heard the phone ring in the living room. The man obviously heard it, too.

"That—that's probably my neighbor downstairs," she said. "He knows I'm up here. If I don't answer, he'll figure out something's wrong. He'll be knocking on the door next."

"Shut the fuck up," he hissed. "Turn off the water."

The pipes let out a squeak as she turned off the water. She could hear the answering machine click on: *"Hello, this isn't really Chloe, but an amazingly lifelike recording of my voice. Leave a message and the real me will call you back."*

The beep sounded. *"Chloe? Chloe, it's Sydney, are you there? Please, pick up. It's urgent. I'm going to keep talking until you pick up. I just tried your cell, and there wasn't an answer there either. Listen, I think you're in danger. I'm calling the police next. Someone just sent me an e-mail on your account. It—it's thirty-five minutes old. I think he might have broken into your apartment and sent it from there . . .*" She hesitated, and then the tone of her voice suddenly changed. *"I . . . I'm now talking to the man who sent me that e-mail. Are you still there? I want to talk to you. Do you have the guts to talk to me? Why—"*

The beep sounded again, cutting her off. *"End of message,"* announced a recorded voice.

Wide-eyed, Chloe stared at the man in the ski mask. She continued to cover herself. "Who are you?" she asked.

"Turn the water back on," he said.

But Chloe didn't move.

Finally, he stood up and turned on the water. All of a sudden, his hand shot out at her and he grabbed Chloe by the hair, almost snapping her head back. He brought his covered face close to hers. "I can smell the alcohol on your breath. They'll say you were drunk . . ."

"No, wait!" she shrieked. "Please, no!" Her screams echoed off the tiled walls.

Still holding onto her scalp, he slammed her head against the faucet.

Dazed, Chloe slumped into the water. It started to turn pink from the gaping wound on her forehead. He continued to hold her by the hair, and pushed her down toward the water.

The dunking revived her. Chloe struggled, clawing at his face, trying to scratch at his eyes. She pulled his mask halfway off, blinding him.

Then she heard Chuck's voice calling out: *"Chloe? Your back door's open! I heard a scream. Chloe, are you okay?"*

The man in the ski mask hesitated, pulled his mask up over his eyes, and glanced toward the front hall. He let go of Chloe's wet hair, shoved her against the tiled wall, and then scrambled to his feet.

Chloe heard her neighbor running down the corridor. "Chuck!" she screamed. "Watch out, he's got a gun!"

Still trying to adjust his mask, the stranger barreled down the hallway.

"Hold it!" she heard Chuck yell.

There was a clamor, and then footsteps—racing toward the back door.

"This is the final boarding call for Flight 59 to Seattle," they announced over the speaker.

"Are you sure she's okay, honey?" Sydney asked. Clutching the phone to her ear, Sydney glanced over toward the boarding gate, where a few stragglers were still checking in.

"I just got off the phone with a cop who was at the scene," Joe told her. "They took Chloe to the hospital in an ambulance. It looks like she'll need some stitches in her forehead. Otherwise, she'll be okay, they assured me of that. The good news is that both Chloe and her neighbor got a halfway decent look at the guy. That's a start." Joe paused. "Did they just announce the last call a minute ago?"

"Yes," Sydney said.

"Then you better skedaddle," he said. "I'll try to find out more—and get a description of the guy. See you tomorrow in Seattle. Take care, sweetheart."

The man in seat 17A was one of very few people still awake on the darkened plane. But he kept his overhead light off. He liked sitting there in the shadows, planning.

His flight was scheduled to arrive at SeaTac at 11:50 P.M., three hours after Sydney's flight was due. She and Eli would probably spend the night at her brother's place.

He liked anticipating her every move. He wondered how far she'd gotten tracking him down through the florists.

He'd made it more challenging for himself today by providing Sydney with his clues *before* going to kill the last two heroes. It was a necessary step. He was conditioning her, pulling the strings and making her dance.

This morning, while looking through the scope of his sniper's rifle, he'd watched Joe McCloud answer his cell phone on that El platform. He'd known it had been Sydney calling him. She'd also phoned Chloe, trying to warn her as well. But both warnings had come too late. Sydney hadn't really saved either of them. His lousy marksmanship had saved Joe, and his lousy luck—with that downstairs neighbor—had saved Chloe. He might have failed twice today, but so had Sydney.

He thought about Chloe's neighbor. Had that guy gotten a good look at his face? Probably not. He was too busy being a hero.

Even if the guy could ID him, it didn't really matter. Let the police hunt begin. He didn't need much more time.

Sydney had failed twice today. And now he was getting ready for her final test.

It was just hours away.

CHAPTER TWENTY-THREE

At 3: 40 A.M., when Sydney finally crawled into her brother's guest room bed, she listened to the traffic white noise from Interstate 5, and thought about her night. She hadn't expected to spend three hours at the hospital when she returned to Seattle this evening.

Kyle had met her at the airport, and told her about what he'd dubbed *Eli's Big Adventure*. Having suffered a bullet wound in the shoulder and a slight concussion, Eli was in satisfactory condition at Swedish Hospital. And Sydney, upon learning this, was a basket case—until she'd gotten to see her son.

He was in great spirits. Even as a little boy, Eli had been a very good patient. He was delighted with the fact that all three family members had been on the news tonight.

Burton Christopher Demick wasn't doing quite as well as Eli was—with nineteen stitches in his head and murder charges for the 1974 deaths of Loretta and Earl Sayers. On one of the evening news channels, Francesca Sayers, whose late father and brother had once been suspects in those murders, called Eli McCloud a hero.

Sydney refused to leave Eli's side. He was one hero this monster wouldn't get. Kyle and the hospital administration finally got her out of there by posting a security guard outside Eli's room.

Down the hall from Eli, Luis Fernandez was listed in stable condition after taking a bullet in the abdomen. Sydney needed to thank him in person for saving her son's life. "I know you probably think I'm a bitch because I left Joe," Sydney told him. "But I had my reasons at the time. Anyway, this bitch is very grateful for what you did earlier today and for what Joe says you've been doing for two months now. Thank you for being our guardian angel, Luis."

From his hospital bed, the swarthy man with the bloodshot eye cracked a smile. "You make it hard to hate you, lady. You're very welcome."

Joe called her later—at 2:30 A.M. Chicago time. The police claimed to have caught the man who had attacked Chloe. They'd nabbed him trying to break into an apartment seven blocks from Chloe's place. He fit the vague description Chloe had given police: Caucasian, about thirty, no facial hair or scars, approximately six feet tall, about one hundred and eighty pounds. The suspect also had a rap sheet that included indecent exposure, assault, and armed robbery. Chloe and her neighbor would be identifying him at 11:30 in the morning.

"He's not the guy," Sydney insisted.

"Well, they won't find that out until 11:30," Joe said.

Lying in Kyle's guest room bed, Sydney tossed and turned. Even though Eli was safe, and probably in his best mood since their move to Seattle, she couldn't stop worrying about him and thinking how close she'd come to losing him today. She thought of Joe, and how she'd almost lost him as well.

Aidan had left a message on her answering machine at home: *"I hope your trip to Chicago was successful. If you're coming back tonight, I'd love to take you to lunch tomorrow. I owe you a meal. You can reach me tomorrow at my mother's place. I'll be cleaning there all day. Take care."* The time on his call had been 5:40, so he couldn't have seen Eli's story on the news yet.

Sydney barely slept at all, she was so wired—and so aware of every creaking floorboard, every branch that scraped against a window, every sound that rose above the white noise. She didn't want to go through this again tomorrow night. She prayed by then, they would have found this killer, whoever he was.

"Oh, you were probably right yesterday, suspecting Dan," Kyle said, four hours later. He set a plate of French toast in front of her. "He was just too good to be true. And the way he just showed up out of the blue the other day is really fishy. Plus as soon as I told him yesterday that you needed me to look after Eli because you were going out of town, suddenly *he* had to go out of town, too." Kyle shook his head and frowned. "I'll bet he's your psycho killer. I tell you, my taste in men. My very first crush was Rolf in *The Sound of Music.* Look what a son of a bitch he turned out to be."

"Did Dan ever call from Portland?" Sydney asked, sitting at the kitchen counter with a coffee cup in her hand. She stared down at her breakfast.

"No," Kyle sighed. He glanced at his wristwatch. "I better get ready for work. I hate these first days back after I take an extended weekend." He pointed to the uneaten French toast he'd set in front of her. "You haven't touched your breakfast. Don't you want it?"

Glancing up at him, she shook her head. "I'm sorry, I'm just too nervous to eat."

He took her plate away. "I'll just freeze this." He pulled some sandwich bags from the kitchen drawer. "You know, as long as we're considering people who suddenly just dropped into our lives, have you thought about Aidan? After all these years, he conveniently turns up. And he had a crazy, over-bearing mother—that's classic serial killer stuff."

Sydney was too tired to argue with him. But Aidan had

come back into her life by accident, because his mother had died. And Mrs. Cosgrove had been the one to reestablish contact, after seeing her on the local news. The murders had started about a week before Mrs. Cosgrove passed away, so no one could say her death suddenly triggered this killing spree.

"Oh, I'm probably talking out of my ass again," Kyle said, sticking the plastic bags of French toast in his freezer. "If Aidan was the killer, he could have easily bumped you off when he slept over at your place night before last. And he didn't. So I guess that lets him off the hook."

Sydney couldn't quite agree with her brother's logic. Of course, Aidan was no murderer. She'd saved his life. Why in God's name would he have turned against her?

If anything, Aidan's presence in the house had more than likely kept them alive the night before last.

Then again, over the last two weeks, this killer had probably had several opportunities to murder both her and Eli. But it was all a game for him. With the tokens of his murders, and the flowers for his victims' next of kin, he was enjoying this. He wouldn't have wanted her dead yet. That would have put an end to the game.

Still, Sydney had to wonder if—after the two failed murders yesterday—he was growing tired of this game. He had to know she was on to him. He couldn't prolong it any longer. He was running out of time.

And so was she.

When Sydney first spotted the mess on her dining room floor, her heart stopped. She thought it was some kind of message about another killing. But then Kyle reminded her that Eli had discovered the old Hallmark card after dumping out the contents of that breakfront drawer.

Kyle had driven her back to the apartment so they could

pick up a change of clothes for Eli to wear when he left the hospital this afternoon.

Sydney checked her messages. There was a new one—made only twenty minutes ago: *"Hi, Sydney, it's Aidan again. I read about Eli in the morning papers. You must be really shaken up, but it sounds like he's okay. If there's anything I could do for you guys, don't hesitate to ask. I understand if you're too busy to call back. But if you want to touch base, I'll be at my mother's apartment all day. Take care, and say hi to Eli for me."*

She retreated upstairs to Eli's room. Stepping through his doorway, she saw something on his pillow and stopped in her tracks. At first, Sydney thought it was another dead bird. But then she came closer and saw it was a china figurine of an angelic little boy. His shoulder and arm were blackened. Someone must have held the figurine over a flame. Sydney immediately thought of Eli, her latest hero, her little boy, lying in his hospital bed with a shoulder wound.

Breathless, she ran into her bedroom and called the hospital. "Eli McCloud's room, please," she said, once the operator answered. "He's in 204."

It rang once. "Hello?" Eli answered.

"Hi, honey, how are you?" she asked anxiously.

There was silence for a moment.

"Eli? Are you all right?"

"Not really, Mom," he whispered. "There's this guy here in my room . . ."

"What?" she asked, a panic sweeping through her.

"Want to talk to him?" Eli said in a normal tone.

Sydney was baffled for a moment until she heard the voice on the other end of the line: "Hi, sweetie."

"Joe?" She put a hand over her heart and let out a little laugh. "When did you get in? Why didn't you call me? I would have picked you up."

"I touched down about thirty minutes ago and came directly here. Where are you? How soon can you make it over?"

"I'm here with Kyle at the apartment," she replied, plopping down on her bed. "I'm hitting the florist after this, and then I'll be right there. But listen, I just got another calling card—a china figure of a little boy, only the arm and shoulder are all mangled and burned up. He left it on Eli's bed."

"Oh, Jesus," Joe murmured.

"The last two times he's gone after a hero, he gave me a souvenir *before* he actually went in for the kill. The tokens have become warnings now, Joe. I think he's going after Eli next. Please, honey, don't leave his side—not even for a second . . ."

The clerk behind the counter at Beautiful Blooms was an Armenian man who reminded her a bit of Danny DeVito. He was checking his computer records and card files.

Sydney anxiously drummed her fingers on the countertop. Between the plants in baskets hanging overhead and the buckets of flowers scattered throughout the store, there wasn't much room to move around.

She'd driven to the florist—with Kyle following in his car. He'd waited until she'd stepped inside Beautiful Blooms, then he'd waved good-bye and driven off.

"Yeah, we've had several orders here for Sydney Jordan recently, most of them out-of-state deliveries," the florist said. "What do you need exactly?"

"I'd like to see the credit card that was used to pay for these orders," Sydney said.

"Oh, that I can't do," the florist replied, shaking his head. "Besides, Mr. Jordan always pays in cash."

"*Mister* Jordan?" she said.

The florist nodded. "He's one of our best customers. Why are you asking about him anyway?"

"Because I'm Sydney Jordan." She fished her wallet from her purse and showed the man her driver's license.

In turn, the florist dug out a sales slip for her. Sydney studied it. It was a July 9 order for a $49.90 sympathy bouquet, delivered to the Cook County Recovery Shelter in Chicago. The sender's address and phone number were hers. The spelling of her first name was identical.

"Have you ever seen this Mr. Jordan?" Sydney asked.

"No, my salesgirl, Jill, has always waited on him. In fact, I think she has a yen for him."

"Is she here?"

"Nope, called in sick this morning."

"Well, may I have her phone number?" Sydney asked. "It's very important that I speak to her."

The short man let out a sigh, and scribbled the phone number on the back of a small sympathy card. "I doubt you'll get ahold of her. I just tried calling her a half hour ago, but she wasn't picking up."

"Could I see the other sales slips you have for his orders?" Sydney asked.

With another sigh, the florist dug out several sales slips and shoved them across the counter at her. Sydney examined them. All the next of kin to her slain heroes were there—along with special instructions about the sentiments on the sympathy cards from *Sydney Jordan*. Two of the slips had the word CANCEL scrawled across them. One was for delivery to a Mrs. Stephanie Finch in Evanston, and the other to Mrs. Joseph McCloud at Number 9 Tudor Court in Seattle. She wondered how come they hadn't noticed that it was the same address *Mister* Sydney Jordan had been calling his own.

"One more order is being delivered tomorrow morning,"

the man said. "It's local, a Seattle address." He showed her the sales slip.

Sydney glanced at the name of the recipient: *Ms. Rikki Cosgrove*. She read the instructions for what was to be written on the card: *"I'm so sorry for your loss. Aidan was a wonderful young man. I'll miss him. Sydney Jordan."*

"Oh, no," Sydney whispered.

How could she be so stupid? The burnt little boy figurine was Aidan.

Obviously, the killer didn't know Aidan's mother was dead.

Grabbing her address book out of her purse, she looked up Rikki's phone number and dialed it. There was no answer. Yet Aidan had phoned from there an hour ago, saying he'd be there all day. *God, please, don't let him be dead already,* Sydney thought.

"Listen, thank you," she said to the florist.

As she hurried out of the store, Sydney phoned the hospital again and asked for Eli's room. Joe answered this time.

"I was wrong about the figurine," she explained edgily. "It isn't Eli. He's going after Aidan Cosgrove. I'll explain it to you later. Aidan's at his mother's place . . ." She gave Joe Rikki's address. "Could you come meet me at Rikki's place? Oh, but wait. I don't want you to leave Eli alone . . ."

"Don't worry, I'll get Luis to keep him company," Joe said. "And don't go in that building by yourself. Wait outside for me."

"Thank you, honey." Sydney clicked off the line.

Then she jumped in her car, started up the engine, and pulled out of her parking space. Another car nearly plowed into her. Sydney heard the tires screeching and then a blast from the horn.

"Damn it, Sydney," she muttered to herself. "Stupid." Tears in her eyes, she glanced up at the rearview mirror. The other car was still sitting there.

Sydney pressed harder on the accelerator. The last time she'd gone to Rikki Cosgrove's apartment, she'd been too late.

She didn't want that to happen again.

The morning sky had turned overcast as Sydney climbed out of her car and hurried toward the ugly, nine-story building's front entrance. She pressed 808 several times, but there was no answer. Then Sydney glanced at the door and cringed. The lock was broken.

She didn't see any cars coming up the street in either direction. Sydney remembered Joe telling her not to go in there alone. She tried waiting for a few moments, but became impatient and ducked inside. She rang for the elevator, and then searched inside her purse for the cheap little canister of pepper spray she'd been carrying around for ages. She found the canister and shook it.

Jabbing the elevator button again, she finally gave up and headed for the stairs. The stairwell was gloomy, gray cinderblock and smelled musty, but at least, she had somewhere to run if attacked. Between the stress and all those stairs, her leg was starting to give out. Winded and clutching the banister, Sydney hobbled up the last two flights.

She was still gasping for air as she staggered out of the stairwell toward Rikki's unit. But when Sydney saw the door to 808, she stopped dead. The door was slightly ajar.

With the pepper spray in her grasp, she rang the bell, and then knocked.

No answer.

"Aidan?" she called tentatively. Sydney stepped inside and got a waft of ammonia smell. He'd said he'd been cleaning. Stuffed garbage bags and stacks of boxes had been shoved against one wall. Piles of folded linen and blankets occupied the tattered sofa. On the coffee table were a bunch of envelopes and photos.

"Aidan?" she called out again. Peering into the bedroom—with its stripped bed and stained mattress—she saw no one. Off the bedroom, the door to Rikki's bathroom was open a crack, and beyond that, darkness.

Sydney wandered back to the living room. There was no evidence of a struggle anywhere. She picked up a photo album from the coffee table and glanced at the family photographs: Rikki, Aidan, and whoever happened to be Rikki's boyfriend at the time the photo had been taken. In the pictures, Rikki and her suitors looked like lowlifes; Aidan was beautiful and somber. There was an envelope full of Aidan's modeling shots when he'd been a child—national ads. Sydney recalled her ghostwriter friend, Andrea Shorey, mentioning that Aidan was the breadwinner in the family.

Amid these professional modeling shots, Sydney discovered a group of Polaroids, all of them of that same handsome boy—only shirtless. The snapshots focused on bruise marks and cuts on his thin body. There was even a close-up of a spot on his arm where someone must have burned him with a cigarette. "My God," Sydney whispered, grimacing at the photos. Her heart broke for him.

She set them down again on the coffee table. Why in the world would Rikki keep these horrible, incriminating pictures?

The window curtains fluttered, and Sydney noticed a small piece of yellow paper drift past her feet, then a piece of turquoise paper. It was Monopoly money. She glanced over toward the corner of the living room and saw more loose Monopoly currency scattered there. The board was set up on the floor—like someone was about to play a game.

Sydney shuddered. She took a few steps closer to the board

game on the floor. The thimble and top hat tokens were on the board. Nearby was the Monopoly box, old and faded, with layers of withered tape holding together the corners. Sydney remembered Eli trying to tell her about the little train token. *"Well, it was on my desk,"* he'd said. *"And I didn't put it there. Do you think your stalker guy broke in and set this on there?"*

More brightly colored, fake bills drifted past her as she moved the old Monopoly box to the sofa and opened it. She examined the other tokens.

"Are you looking for the train?"

She swiveled around and gaped at Aidan in the doorway. He closed the door behind him. "You have the train token, Sydney. I gave it to you."

Joe had gotten Eli into a wheelchair and rolled him down the hall to Luis's room so they could keep each other company for a while. After what they'd been through together, they were like old army buddies. Joe had caught a taxi outside the hospital, and was now on his way to Rikki Cosgrove's address. But there were traffic problems, and Sydney wasn't answering her cell.

As he sat in bumper-to-bumper traffic in the back of that smelly cab, Joe began to wonder about that burnt little boy china figurine Sydney had found on Eli's bed. He began to wonder—if heroes were being murdered—whose life had Aidan Cosgrove ever saved?

"I wanted you to see those photos, Sydney," Aidan said. "I wanted you to see the extent of my mother's abuse." He stood between her and the doorway, his hands in the pockets of his jeans. He wore a white button-down shirt, untucked.

His stance wasn't threatening, and yet Sydney knew he wouldn't let her leave.

Aidan had been manipulating her all this time. He'd played her perfectly. And just in case she still hadn't realized how he'd trapped her, he'd left her one final clue—the Monopoly game. Every time there was a slight breeze, more loose bills drifted across the carpeted floor.

Aidan's eyes stayed riveted on her. "I supported my mother—and her various scumbag boyfriends—with my modeling," he explained. "But I was still their punching bag. My mother said I deserved what I got, because I was a smart ass." He chuckled cynically. "She blamed me for the fact that she could never keep a man."

He nodded toward the coffee table. "One of the modeling people discovered what was being done to me, and she took those Polaroids for child protective services. They couldn't make the charges stick against Rikki and her current flame at the time, but it sure as shit ended my legitimate modeling career. Oh, I still got some assignments from time to time, but it was never the same.

"Then there was the fire, and that finished my modeling days for good. But you have to hand it to Rikki. She still used me to raise money—parading around her broken, scarred, burn-victim poster child. And you helped her. I was a cash cow for my worthless mother—and for you, too, Sydney. It's because of me you went into the *hero* business."

"I was trying to help you, Aidan," she murmured.

"Well, you didn't," he said evenly. "My life just got shittier. After the fire, I was still getting the crap kicked out of me by Rikki and her boyfriends, only it was worse. I was in constant pain from my back injury. And my dear, sweet mother was taking—or selling—all my pain medications."

Sydney was devastated by these revelations. She felt so sorry for him, but that didn't make her any less afraid and revolted. "I haven't talked with your mother in years, have I?" she asked. "It was you who called me this weekend, wasn't it?"

"Oh, yes, Sydney," Aidan said—in his mother's weak, whiny voice. He smiled a little.

Sydney remembered finding Rikki Cosgrove rotting away in her deathbed. The dying woman could barely talk. And yet, an hour before she'd been strong enough to call and ask her to come over. Why hadn't she realized it then?

"That story I told you about the woman in San Francisco is true," Aidan said, stepping closer to her—backing her toward the window. "Thanks to this rich bitch, I used to fly up here and look after my mother on weekends. Once she became immobile and helpless, I stayed on full time. I did a good enough job imitating my mother on the phone and through the door so no one knew how ill she really was. And I let her rot. I starved her. She was in a lot of pain, but I didn't give her any medication. I pretended to come and go on weekends, but for the last few weeks I've been here the whole time, watching her die—and thinking of you, Sydney."

"But why go after me—and all these people who never did you any harm at all?" Sydney asked. "For God's sake, *I saved your life*, Aidan."

"I didn't want to be *saved*, Sydney," he growled. "I wanted to die. I started the fire that day—on purpose. I was going to kill my mother. I planned to watch her burn, and then I was going to jump out the window—*to my own death.* But you had to play the hero. So what happened? I was left scarred, and in constant pain. And my mother just kept making money off me and letting her boyfriends slap me around. It was worse than being dead, Sydney. I would have been better off if you hadn't interfered. You're responsible for all those years I suffered after the fire. But you made out all right, didn't you? Hell, you made more money off me than my mother did."

Stunned, Sydney kept staring at him. She had tears in her eyes. She remembered calling to young Aidan as he'd stood out on the ledge of that burning building. She'd asked if anyone else was in the apartment with him, and the frightened child had shaken his head. And at that press conference—her first time meeting and talking with him—that burnt, broken little boy had whispered to her: *"I really, really tried not to land on you. I didn't expect you to catch me."*

Part of her wanted to reach out to him—and reason with him. But she didn't dare. She stole a glance out the window, hoping to see Joe down there. But there was no sign of him. She looked at Aidan again. "Please, Aidan, there's already been too much killing and suffering. I know you've had a raw deal, but that's no reason . . ." She could see he wasn't listening. He was looking past her—at the window.

Sydney quickly glanced over her shoulder; still no sign of Joe.

"Listen to me," she said. "If you turn yourself in and tell your story to the police, they'll probably be more lenient with you, maybe even get you some help . . . ."

"Did you call Joe?" he asked. "Is that why you keep looking out the window? Are you waiting for him to show up?"

Sydney sighed. She locked eyes with him and nodded. "Yes. And he'll probably have the police with him—"

"No, not your Joe. He'll come alone, because he needs to play the hero." Aidan reached back and pulled a gun out from under his shirttail. "I'm afraid Joe won't be able to save you, Sydney. But I am giving *you* a chance to be a hero today . . ."

Backing up, Aidan kept the gun trained on her as he took a can of charcoal-starter out of the front closet. He handed the can to her. "Squirt some of this on the carpet and around the bedroom doorway," he said.

Sydney didn't move. She realized what he'd planned for her. She'd saved him from burning to death; so now she would die in a fire.

"Do it," he growled, eyes narrowed at her. "Or do I have to? You know, I might just spray you with this stuff, Sydney. Strike a match, and do you know how fast you'd be engulfed in flames? Would you like that?"

She reluctantly complied and squeezed the tin can. A braided line of charcoal starter shot from the spout, soaking the ugly beige carpet and dripping down the doorway frame to Rikki's bedroom.

"Squirt some over there," Aidan said, pointing to the bedroom's carpeted floor. He led her into the bedroom. "And get the mattress, too. You know, I've always been fascinated with fire. Kind of funny, coming from a burn victim, isn't it? But I think that just made me respect fire even more. Hit the wall around the bathroom door. That's it, get it real good . . ."

The sharp smell of charcoal starter began to overwhelm her. But Sydney followed his orders, and prayed Joe might get here on time—with backup. With her free hand, she furtively felt the outline of the pepper-spray canister in her pocket.

Keeping the gun at her head, Aidan opened the bathroom door and switched on the light.

Sydney gasped.

Lying unconscious in the tub was a half-naked young brunette. Her lip was bleeding, and her hands and feet had been bound with a black cord. Around her in the tub were wads of rolled-up newspaper. "Sydney, meet Jill," Aidan said. "She works at the flower shop. She's a very sweet girl, twenty-two years old. She wants to be a teacher, because she's crazy for kids. We had a date this morning, and she told me all about herself. Squirt some of that stuff on Jill, and make sure you soak the paper around her."

"No," Sydney said. "That's enough, Aidan. It's over . . ."

"Don't pull that strong-lady shit on me," he hissed, directing the gun at Jill. "Do what I tell you or I swear to God, I'll shoot her right now."

Tears in her eyes, Sydney swallowed hard and finally

obeyed him. Her hand shook horribly as she squirted the flammable liquid around the helpless young woman. She kept trying to think of a way to distract him so she could reach for her pepper spray.

"Jill and I are offering you the opportunity to be a hero again, Sydney," he said. "You don't have a very good chance of getting out of here alive once I start the fire. Your leg is a bit of a hindrance, too. And if you do live, no doubt you'll get burned—badly. There will be scars and pain. Maybe you'll finally have an idea of what I endured for years and years. But I know you, Sydney. You'll want to rescue Jill, which will delay your escape, and then—well, if the two of you don't die in this fire, you'll both wish you had."

Horrified, Sydney glanced at the unconscious woman in the tub. Aidan was right, because all she could think about was rescuing her. Maybe if she turned on the shower and doused the young woman with water, she could get her through the blaze with only a few minor burns.

But then Sydney saw that he'd pried off the hot and cold water knobs, and her heart sank.

"C'mon, there's more to do," Aidan said, nodding toward the bathroom door.

Biting her lip, Sydney gave one last look at the young woman in the tub. As Aidan led her back toward the living room, she felt the soaked carpet squishing beneath her feet. Her hand strayed toward her pocket.

He stopped in front of the coffee table, where he'd set out the family album for her to find—along with those awful Polaroids and his old modeling shots and contact sheets.

"Did you like my pictures, Sydney?" he asked. "Wasn't I a beautiful kid?"

Nodding, she inched her fingers into her pocket. "Of course you were, Aidan."

"Take some of those eight by tens and the contact sheets and roll them up for me, real tight—so it's like a baton."

Reluctantly, Sydney took her hand out of her pocket. She put down the can of charcoal starter and did what he'd told her to do. She realized she was making a torch for him.

"All right, now, soak one end of it in the charcoal starter," he said. "I never did like any of those pictures. They just reminded me of how she used me."

Sydney squirted more of the flammable liquid on the rolled-up photos. The smell of it was starting to make her ill. All the while, she heard a sound from down the corridor: the elevator humming. Maybe Joe was on his way.

Aidan watched her every move. "Okay, now, put down the charcoal starter and hand me the baton you just made."

Trembling, Sydney complied. In the distance, she could hear the elevator doors whoosh open, and then a faint *ping*.

Aidan grinned. "Well, I think that might be your Joe to the rescue . . ."

"Joe, watch out!" she screamed. "It's a trap! He's got a gun—"

Before she could get another word out, Aidan slammed the butt of his revolver against the side of her head.

Stunned, Sydney fell to the floor. It took a moment for her to focus again. She blinked and saw Aidan hovering by the half-open door, the homemade baton in one hand and his gun poised in the other.

"Joe, look out!" she yelled.

Just then, he came to the doorway.

Aidan fired the gun twice. The loud shots reverberated in the near-empty living room. Joe darted back toward the corridor—out of sight. There was a heavy thumping from footsteps.

Sydney couldn't tell whether or not he'd been hit. Struggling to her feet, she reached for the pepper spray in her pocket. She still wasn't sure what had happened to Joe. But Aidan had tucked the gun under his arm and now set a lighter to the makeshift torch.

Lunging toward him, Sydney doused him with the pepper spray.

The torch-baton exploded and flames crawled up Aidan's arm. Shrieking in terror, he dropped the gun and the makeshift torch. The photos used to assemble it separated and fluttered around the room. Sections of carpet soaked with the charcoal starter now ignited, and the flames licked up at the walls. Screaming, Aidan hit his arm again and again to extinguish the fire eating away at his flesh. He weaved over toward the window and tried to smother the flames with the curtains.

Sydney spotted the revolver on the floor, and she dove for it.

The room filled with smoke, and a fire detector let out a shrill monotonous beep. The Monopoly money drifted around her—some of the bills were on fire.

Pulling herself up, Sydney glanced over toward the door. She still didn't know whether Joe was alive, dead, or wounded. She heard someone coughing, but it sounded like the woman in the bathroom. The smoke and flames in the next room had become so thick Sydney could barely see anything past the bedroom doorway. In all the confusion, she'd lost sight of Aidan.

Then she spotted him again—by the open window. His arm was charred and bloody. But he was staring at her, half-smiling.

Sydney aimed the gun at him, but she knew as well as he must have, she couldn't pull the trigger.

He just nodded at her, and then started out to the window ledge.

"No!" she screamed.

"You can't save me this time, Sydney," he said. "You can't even save yourself."

Aidan climbed out the eighth-story window, then pushed himself off the ledge.

For a few moments after that, everything was a blur. Someone set off the building's fire alarm. The shrill beeps and the constant ringing assaulted her ears. Black smoke swelled from the blaze in the bedroom, and yet Sydney blindly made her way in there—and then to the bathroom. Somehow, the flames hadn't moved across the tiled bathroom floor, but the room was swelteringly hot and red ashes darted around her like incendiary moths.

The young woman in the tub had managed to untie the black cord around her ankles, and now she struggled to her feet. But she was disoriented, and coughing from all the smoke.

Grabbing a robe off the hook on the bathroom door, Sydney plunged it in the toilet and then quickly wrapped it around the young woman.

Sydney felt a blast of heat as she led the girl out of the bathroom. Her hair was singed. Flames began to lash at her legs and arms. She could barely see anything in all the thick black smoke. She tried not to breathe it into her lungs. It felt as if she were being strangled.

Suddenly, someone covered her and the young woman with a blanket and guided them out of the bedroom's inferno. She knew it was Joe. Past the murky blackness and the shrill, deafening alarms, she sensed it was him. Joe led them toward the door. As they fled the smoke-filled apartment, the blanket slipped and she finally glimpsed him. His face was scorched red in spots, and burn marks covered his arms.

Sydney clung to him as they hurried toward the stairwell with the young woman. The stairs were crammed with people making their escape. Coughing and gagging, Sydney couldn't quite get a breath. "Just another couple of flights, honey!" she heard Joe scream. But she could barely hear him over the alarm—and now, sirens. They finally made their way outside, where fire engines sped up the street.

Sydney coughed and coughed until she spit up a black bilelike substance. Everything hurt. Her eyes had dried up, and she kept blinking so she could focus on what was happening around her. She saw the dazed young woman plop down on the little stretch of lawn in front of Rikki's building.

A bit farther down, she noticed Aidan's broken body sprawled on the sidewalk. Sydney winced. The poor, abused, little boy who had wanted to die fourteen years ago had finally realized his ambition.

"You okay, honey?" she heard Joe ask.

Nodding, Sydney at last caught her breath. She wiped some soot away from her face and worked up a smile for him.

It looked as if Joe was trying to smile back at her. But he started to cough. Blood spilled over his lips.

Panic-stricken, Sydney stared at him, and for the first time she noticed the bloodstain on his shirt—along with a small hole, where the bullet had ripped through to his stomach. He staggered forward, and she caught him in her arms.

"I—I'm sorry," he gasped.

Under his weight, Sydney collapsed to the ground, but she managed to sit up and cradle him in her arms. "Oh, no, no, no," she cried, rocking him.

"Tell Eli I'm sorry, too," he whispered.

Sydney kissed his forehead and touched his cheek. She helplessly watched him slip away. She couldn't save him.

All she could do was hold on to Joe's hand as he took his last breath.

Epilogue

His room in the Spaulding Avenue house just didn't seem the same. Dressed in his khakis, white short-sleeve shirt, and a tie, Eli sat at the end of his old bed. His navy blue blazer was draped over the back of his desk chair. Though he'd only taken a few items to Seattle, the room seemed so empty now—and so quiet.

Yet he could still hear the bagpipes playing "Amazing Grace." They'd given his dad a policeman's funeral. At least a hundred patrolmen on motorcycles and another fifty patrol cars had escorted them from the church to All Saints' Cemetery. Their lights flashed and sirens wailed. Eli guessed there were a hundred more cops—all in blue shirts and ties—saluting his dad's casket at the gravesite. There were dozens of reporters and TV vans, too.

He and his mom managed to keep up a stoic front, but when those bagpipes began playing "Amazing Grace," Eli could see her starting to tear up and tremble. He took hold of her hand.

His other hand was out of commission, still in an arm sling from the bullet wound in his shoulder.

His dad's friend, Luis, had gotten out of the hospital and flown back to Chicago in time for the service. Uncle Kyle was there, of course, and so were Aunt Helen and Eli's twin cousins. His buddies, Brad and Tim, were there, too. They'd even hung out with him for a little while yesterday, but it had been kind of a strained reunion. They'd seemed a bit nervous around him—like they'd expected him to burst out crying at any minute. He couldn't really blame them, because he'd been worried about that himself. For now, Eli had managed to have his sudden crying jags when no one else was around. His buddies had wanted to hear all about Earl and Loretta Sayers and what it had been like getting shot. But Eli didn't want to talk about it.

The only one he really wanted to talk to about it was his dad. And he was gone.

A weird thing had happened at the funeral. He and his mom must have shaken about four hundred people's hands. But when his dad's friend and superior officer, Uncle Len, came up to shake his mother's hand, she glanced down at the ground and stepped back. Uncle Len looked a bit peeved for a moment, but then he'd moved on.

Eli had asked his mother about it in the limousine on their way home. "I'll tell you after the brunch," she'd said, patting his hand, "if I don't lapse into a coma before then. I'm exhausted. Still, I'm glad they did this for your dad."

About eighty people came over for the brunch. Uncle Len wasn't one of them.

Aunt Helen had helped his mom with the dishes, and had just left. He and his Uncle Kyle had helped clean up, too, dismantling and stacking a bunch of folding tables and chairs they'd rented. Now he could hear Uncle Kyle in the guest room down the hall, talking to his new boyfriend, Dan, on his cell phone.

Eli was tired—but too wound up to take a nap. He sat there in a daze.

There was a knock on his door.

"Come in," he called.

In her stocking feet, his mother stepped into the room. She carried her black high heels. With a sigh, she sat down on his bed. "You were terrific today, honey," she said, putting her arm around his good shoulder. "Your dad would have been really proud."

"Thanks," he said. "You did pretty well, too, Mom."

"Listen, Eli, I think it's time you finally knew why your dad and I split up for a while," she said.

"You don't have to tell me if you don't want," he muttered.

"Well, I do want," she replied. "And it's still not quite resolved yet."

He squinted at her. "What do you mean?"

She let out another long sigh. "It all started back in March, when your Uncle Len sent your father on a special assignment with some officers your father didn't know very well. . . ."

Eli listened to his mother, and kept shaking his head over and over. Suddenly it made sense why she'd packed up their stuff and moved to Seattle. He couldn't believe his dad had taken that drug money—and let those corrupt cops get away with murder for over three months. Eli wasn't sure what he'd expected his father to have done, but he felt so disappointed in him, especially now, after his policeman-hero's funeral.

"Somehow he should have stood up to those guys," Eli murmured to his mother.

"Your dad thought it might endanger us if he did," his mother explained. "So now it's up to us to stand up to them, Eli. If we don't, we'll be looking over our shoulders for the rest of our lives, and the people who made your father's life so miserable will get away with it." She stroked his head. "But this means going public about your dad's involvement in this sordid business. Even though he was an unwilling participant, he still took money from them. And a lot of people will think that's no way for a hero to act. I know, I thought so myself."

"What do you think *now*?" Eli asked.

She patted his back. "I think your dad was a good man and a good cop. He earned the funeral he got today. And we owe it to him to make sure these creeps pay for what they did."

Eli nodded, and then he hugged her. When his mother hugged him back, he could tell she was careful not to press against his wound.

She said she had to make some calls, and left him alone.

Eli curled up on the bed. He found himself missing Seattle, and wondered if they'd be better off living there. It would give them a chance to start over again—without this drug heist business hanging over their heads. Besides, Chicago just didn't seem like home anymore without his dad.

Eli closed his eyes to sleep, and a tear slid down the side of his face.

In his head, he could still hear the bagpipes playing for his father.

From their garage, Sydney retrieved a toolbox containing exactly thirty-two thousand dollars. She called her news contacts at the network and the chief of police, who had been at Joe's funeral that morning.

Within forty-eight hours, the Chicago police arrested four officers for their involvement in the Fort Jackson Point Pier drug heist. Len Sparks, Jim Mankoff, Kurt Rifkin, and Gerry Crowley were charged with—among other things—murder, conspiracy to commit murder, drug trafficking, extortion, and fraud. In an effort to make deals with the prosecution, they all turned on each other. They were all so dirty and corrupt; Joe was the only one to emerge from the group semivindicated.

The media attention showered on Sydney didn't tarnish her career any. The network wanted to take full advantage of her current high profile, and for them she shot a tribute segment to Jared and Leah, Angela Gannon, and Ned Haggerty. It was featured on the national *Nightly News*.

She didn't include Erin Travino or Molly Gerrard in the tribute. Now that the girls' murders had been solved, their parents were no longer interested in having their tragedy rehashed on network TV. Sydney respected that—much to the network's story editor's chagrin.

They kept shoving these tawdry and sensational assignments at her, but Sydney refused. She wanted to cover stories about people who did good and made a difference. She still believed in heroes even when they were slightly flawed.

Sydney heard from one of her hero-subjects the first week in August, when she and Eli returned to Seattle. She got an e-mail from chloefinch@northwesternu.edu, with the subject heading: *Top Dog*. The e-mail came with the standard caution not to open it unless she knew the sender. When Sydney clicked on it, a photo began to emerge in sections. It was of Chloe Finch beside a pleasant-looking man with glasses and receding brown hair in front of the Buckingham Fountain. Chloe had a small mark on her forehead from when Aidan had bashed her head against the bathtub faucet. Otherwise, she looked rather pretty—and very happy. *"Dear Sydney,"* she'd written. *"My 2nd week in therapy & my 3rd week with Chuck. I think I'm in love. Thinking of you & wishing you the best. Take care, Chloe."*

Chloe wasn't the only one in love. Kyle was still seeing Dan. "Except for his road rage issues and the pinky ring, he's really pretty wonderful," Kyle told her. "And I think he's going to give up the pinky ring."

They fixed her up with Dan's widower-brother, Brian, while he was in town, visiting from New York. He was very tall and handsome—with salt-and-pepper hair. He took her out to dinner at the Dahlia Lounge, and Sydney had felt a little spark of interest. But it was too soon for her to think about dating again. Besides, he was in New York. Nevertheless, they were e-mailing back and forth, and it felt nice to know someone was interested.

She and Eli had consulted his Ouija board, and when he asked, "Will Mom have a boyfriend next year?" it answered, *"Yes."*

For now, she was alone—and she didn't mind it.

She didn't even mind that Eli refused to sit with her on that sunny Friday afternoon. What twelve-year-old boy in his right mind would want to be seen with his mother at the beach? So she had her blanket in the middle section—and he had his way over on the south lawn, where all the families were. Sydney looked a bit pale in her red one-piece swimsuit. She was all slick with sunscreen and wore a straw hat.

The beach wasn't too crowded, and she could easily pick out Eli in his green Hawaiian-print trunks as he jumped off the raft's high dive, swam back to the raft, and did it again—and again—and again. Eventually, this other boy—tan, but painfully skinny in baggy blue trunks—started talking with him in line for the diving board. The other boy was putting his hands above his head and miming a dive. Eli was nodding.

Within a half-hour, he and his new friend were taking turns diving off the low board.

Once Eli and the other boy swam to shore, he came to her blanket. "Mom, this is Chad," Eli said, dripping wet and out of breath.

She shook Chad's cold, damp hand.

"Chad wants to know if I can come over to his house for dinner tonight."

Once she got confirmation with Chad's mother, Sydney settled in for a night alone. She ate a grilled-cheese sandwich and tomato soup while watching an old Doris Day movie on cable—on the big-screen HD TV Joe had bought months ago. Then she e-mailed Brian in New York.

When Eli came home at 10:30, she asked him how his dinner at Chad's house had gone. He made a face. "They have one of those pug dogs who wouldn't stop panting and drooling. I kept thinking he was going to keel over or something. I don't think this dog liked me. And Chad's mother made me eat brussels sprouts—and then I started to gag, so she backed off. You're a better cook, Mom. Can we get a dog?"

"We'll see." She smiled. "So—do you think you made a new friend?"

He shrugged. "I don't know. He's okay. We'll see. I'm still hungry." He ducked into the kitchen and made himself a sandwich.

They'd stayed on at Number 9 Tudor Court. Since Burton Christopher Demick's arrest for the 1974 murders of Loretta and Earl Sayers, Eli had stopped hearing voices in his bedroom. Sydney had hung the Georgia O'Keefe print on the bathroom wall again. That had been two weeks ago, and it hadn't fallen yet. She took that as a good sign. They no longer witnessed any creepy, unexplainable occurrences in the apartment. It was as if the dead were finally at peace there—and so were the living.

But when she went to bed that night, Sydney was reminded once again that she and Eli weren't completely alone. Laying there in the darkness, she sensed someone else was in the bedroom with her. She heard a sigh, and a shadow passed over her. Something brushed against the side of her face—by her ear. It felt like a kiss.

She knew it wasn't just a ghost. It was Joe.

She would let go of him soon enough, Sydney realized that. Until then, she knew he'd watch over them.